W9-BKW-705

PRAISE FOR LAURIE ALICE EAKES

REGARDING *A LADY'S HONOR*

"Beautiful nineteenth-century Cornwall offers a contemplative setting for this dramatic romance that involves murder, suspense, and a surprise villain."

—*Romantic Times*, ****¹

"Eakes delivers beautifully written romantic suspense set in Cornwall during the Regency era."

—*Publishers Weekly*

REGARDING *A NECESSARY DECEPTION*

"Laurie Alice Eakes is one of the best storytellers the world has today."
—Delle Jacobs, award-winning author of *His Majesty, the Prince of Toads*

"Eakes weaves the fine silk threads of historical richness, dangerous intrigue, and forbidden romance into a flawless literary tapestry . . . that will leave readers breathless."
—Louise M. Gouge, award-winning author of *Then Came Faith*

"A page-turning story with an in-depth knowledge of the period, an eye for detail, and an escalating mystery that will keep readers guessing till the end."
—Ruth Axtell Morren, author of *Wild Rose* and *The Rogue's Redemption*

WITHDRAWN

Regarding *Lady in the Mist*

"Readers will not be able to put this gem of a novel down."
—Romantic Times

"Secrets, suspense, and a sweetly told love story make this a highly rewarding read."
—Cheryl Bolen, Holt Medallion–winning author of
One Golden Ring

WITHDRAWN

TRUE AS FATE

ALSO BY LAURIE ALICE EAKES

TRUE AS FATE

The Ashford Chronicles:

Book 2

LAURIE ALICE EAKES

Waterfall
PRESS

This is a work of fiction. Names, characters, organizations, places, events, and incidents are either products of the author's imagination or are used fictitiously.

Text copyright © 2017 by Laurie Alice Eakes
All rights reserved.

No part of this book may be reproduced, or stored in a retrieval system, or transmitted in any form or by any means, electronic, mechanical, photocopying, recording, or otherwise, without express written permission of the publisher.

Published by Waterfall Press

www.brilliancepublishing.com

Amazon, the Amazon logo, and Waterfall Press are trademarks of Amazon.com, Inc., or its affiliates.

ISBN-13: 9781503942899
ISBN-10: 1503942899

Cover design by Mike Heath | Magnus Creative

Printed in the United States of America

To my classmates at the Seton Hill University master's program in Writing Popular Fiction; the faculty, especially Lee McLaine for suggesting I apply to the program; and Victoria Thompson and Barbara J. Miller, who advised me on this novel every step of the way.

This principle is old, but true as fate, Kings may love treason, but the traitor hate.

—Thomas Dekker, Elizabethan dramatist
and pamphleteer

PROLOGUE

Devonshire, England
Sunday, 4 June 1813
8:00 p.m.

*S*eventeen miles of barren moorland lay between Ross Trenerry and freedom. Less than a mile lay between him and Dartmoor Prison, and the alarm bell was beginning to ring, warning the Somerset militia guarding the American and French prisoners of war that eleven of those men had escaped.

"Too soon." Ross glanced over his shoulder, already feeling iron shackles holding him down again, as they had too often since the American merchantman on which he served as first mate had been captured by a British privateer. Or maybe this second capture would simply get him hanged.

"Faster, lads. We've got to move faster if we want to stay out of the *cacheau*." Ross tried to project encouragement into his voice, though he shuddered at the memory of the cold, dark structure built for recalcitrant prisoners.

All knowing how many times Ross had been isolated in the *cacheau* during the past seven months, the ragged line of men glanced at him, then tried to obey. Ross saw the effort in their gaunt faces running with sweat despite the chilly evening, the straining of limbs robbed of once formidable muscles from hauling lines, climbing rigging, and lifting cargo aboard the merchantman *Maid of Alexandria*. But the uneven stone path and eight months of near starvation had weakened all of them, especially Wat, already an old man before the English had captured their schooner and they'd all ended up in Dartmoor as prisoners of England.

"It will go badly with you if you are caught." The echo of Ross's admonition came from Kieran Ashford, the privateer owner, who was helping them escape for the sake of his wife, Deirdre, daughter of the *Maid*'s deceased captain. At least that's what he claimed. With the alarm bell clanging its warning that prisoners had escaped, Ross suspected a trap, a betrayal.

He flashed a glance at Ashford. "Who knew besides you, Deirdre, and your sister that we planned this?"

Ashford either did not hear or chose to ignore Ross. Lady Chloe, the sister who had brought him food and blankets and promises to keep him going through the months at Dartmoor, glared at him, but said nothing except "Faster."

"Faster." Ross repeated the admonition above the persistent clang, clang, clang. "Come on." He slipped a hand beneath Old Wat's elbow.

Wat shook his head and slumped against a boulder beside the narrow track cutting through the gorge. "Can't. Go on without me."

"A little farther is all," Lady Chloe spoke, lagging behind for a moment. "We have traps set and ponies waiting."

The drum of running, booted feet joined the rhythm of the bell.

Ross froze, refused to look, to watch the enemy bear down upon them. He knew what would happen if the soldiers caught them—worse confinement in the *cacheau*. Darkness. Fetid air.

"Run," Ashford called. "A hundred yards and we can trap them."

The men picked up their pace to a trot. Bare feet slapped and rattled against the rocky path. Their breaths wheezed. Ross's breath chilled in his lungs. None of the men could move any faster, and pursuit sounded louder, closer. Too close. The soldiers couldn't achieve more than a trot on the stony, uneven ground, but they surely moved swiftly enough to overtake the Americans within minutes. Despite himself, Ross glanced back. He counted eight men with musket barrels raised and ready to fire.

"Go. Go. Go." His voice was hoarse.

He halted. Old Wat wasn't with them. Turning, Ross caught sight of the man still slumped against the rock, his face gray beneath the layer of dirt they all wore.

And the soldiers drew closer, close enough for Ross to see faces. Five minutes' grace was all Ross figured he had to get free with the others.

Wat pressed one hand to his chest and waved Ross on with the other. "Leave me."

Ross glanced at the approaching soldiers, then down the hillside toward the crew and freedom. Wat was his mentor, a surrogate father.

Ross sprinted back to the old man. "Come on. Ashford set a trap down a bit." Or so he claimed.

"No, lad—"

"Don't argue." Ross lifted the old man over his shoulder and headed downhill. His legs felt like year-old carrots. Wat sagged against him, dead weight. No, not dead. Not—

Muskets cracked above the drum of footfalls, drum of heartbeats. Ross tasted tin, the bile of fear. Soldiers were still too far away to fire with accuracy. But soon, too soon, a minute or two, he'd be in range.

Run faster!

He staggered under the old man's weight, slight though it was.

More muskets resounded. Wat jerked, and Ross smelled the metallic stench of blood.

3

"Please, no!" He forced himself into a run. Fire blazed in his lungs. More gunfire rattled, and pain slugged into his shoulder. He stumbled over an outcropping of granite, then landed on his knees. Sharp pebbles cut through the frayed cloth of his woolen breeches, and Wat slid onto the ground, dead. No one survived a wound like the one gaping on the old man's back.

Ross closed his eyes, willed his body to find the strength to rise, keep going. The soldiers grew louder, nearer. Another minute, another shot. Ahead, nothing of the others echoed down the gorge. Good, they were away . . .

Running footfalls pounded on the path, quicker, lighter than those of the soldiers.

Those footfalls thudded toward him. He lifted his head, stared. He wasn't mistaken. Someone ran toward him, Lady Chloe, who had corresponded with him against even Deirdre's will, who, disguised, had visited him in the prison, who had given him hope that all the English weren't scoundrels, that the war would not last forever. As in a dream, she swept toward him, leaping over the rocks with the long-legged grace of the deer back home in Carolina.

"Sir." Her face still obscured beneath the floppy brim of a hat, she dropped into a crouch before him. "Let me help you." Her voice was soft, melodious.

"No." Ross shook his head. "I'm hit—"

"I can get you up." She held out narrow, long-fingered hands. On one finger, a ring glowed like a slice of moonlight with sparks of blue and green. "I am stronger than I look."

"But you're a woman." And what those approaching soldiers would do with a female, he didn't want to consider.

She laughed. "And I will not leave Deirdre's best friend to my countrymen." She moved closer, close enough to slip her hands beneath his elbows, close enough for him to smell lily of the valley and violets above his prison stench.

4

The sweetness of the lady swirled through his head, springtime incarnate, dizzying. No, blood soaking down his arm made him dizzy. His head throbbed like boot heels on stone. Soldiers nearer. Musket blasts.

He grasped her ladyship's arms and lurched to his feet. "Wat?"

"I am sorry." She slipped her arm around his waist. "We have to leave him."

"I tried—" His throat tightened.

"Save your breath." She propelled him forward.

The ground rocked beneath his feet like an earthquake. The sides of the hill seemed to draw nearer, sway, dim. He reached for something steady and found his arm going around her ladyship's waist. She was warm, slender but sturdy. His other arm wouldn't work. He was cold on that side. Numb. Lady Chloe warmed his other side, kept him going. Faster. Faster. The ground slipped beneath his feet. Thumping reverberated through his body from the wound, through his ears from the soldiers' feet. He glanced back and saw the soldiers' faces, their mouths stretched in grins, so sure were they of victory.

"Not yet." He thought he shouted, but feared he only whispered.

"This way." Beside him, Lady Chloe rounded an outcropping of blackish granite, and the grinning faces vanished from sight. "We have got to climb."

Ross stared at the steep bluff, lower than the gorge sides where the soldiers still marched, yet formidable to a weakened man. He noted the broken scrub pine, earth scored where rocks had lain. "The others went this way?"

"Yes, we have sturdy moorland ponies on the other side of that ridge."

"But the soldiers will catch us."

"Not if we create a little diversion." She grinned. "Deirdre planned a trap. It is up to us to carry it through." She spun away from him to lean against a boulder. "Help me push this if you can."

"Of course I can." With one hand he could. He'd do anything to remain near her warmth, her courage.

They shoved the rock. Pain sliced through his shoulder. The rock remained immobile, and the soldiers sprinted forward. Half a minute would bring them abreast. They'd capture Lady Chloe and Ross.

Ross pushed on the rock again. Lady Chloe joined him. The boulder moved perhaps a handspan.

A volley of musket fire sent splinters of granite spiraling into the air. Ross thrust both hands against the rock. Blood gushed down his arm. No pain. Cold seized his body. Darkness clouded his sight. His ears roared. Taking a deep breath to gather more strength, he found dust and gunpowder filling his nostrils. But the next thrust worked. The boulder tilted, swayed, rolled. Cries of alarm rose from the soldiers.

As the hillside began to collapse, barring the soldiers' way, a cry of triumph rose from her ladyship. "That will stop them long enough." She grabbed Ross's hand and started climbing. Rock fragments, earth, and heather showered them, stung Ross's wound. He bit down on heather blossoms, tasted bittersweetness.

No more gunfire roared behind them. The soldiers were eerily quiet. As one, Ross and her ladyship paused halfway up the side of the gorge to glance back. The redcoats swarmed around the far side of the boulder, pushing, shoving, and making no forward progress. Two men tried to climb the steep sides of the gorge.

"We did it." Lady Chloe's voice was soft but so full of triumph she might have shouted.

Ross couldn't stop a grin from curving his lips. Nor could he stop himself from succumbing to the temptation of her ladyship's smiling mouth. Briefly, for no more than a heartbeat or ten, he kissed her, reveling in the human contact, the softness of her lips, the sweetness of her mouth.

Then a shout drew his attention away from the lady kissing him back with abandoned fervor.

Ashford grasped his good arm. "Get moving. That landslide will not hold the soldiers forever."

Ross nodded and headed across the moor where a straggly line of ponies headed toward the sea. Her ladyship started to join him, but her brother caught hold of her arm and swung her away.

"Go home."

"I cannot. You need my help."

Ashford's mouth pursed, but he gave a brusque nod of acknowledgment and stalked away.

"Come along, Mr. Trenerry." Lady Chloe grasped his arm. "I will see you get to freedom."

She helped him and the others get off the moor and into a rabbit warren of caves, and after that, Ross's memories grew dim, as loss of blood and wound fever took over his existence. When he regained his senses, the rest of his crew was gone. Nor was Lady Chloe anywhere in sight. Instead, her beautiful younger sister, Lady Juliet, sat holding his hand, while she read to him from Shakespeare's sonnets.

"You are awake," she cried. "This must be the happiest day of my life."

In that moment, as weak as a kitten and with no idea how long he had lain senseless, Ross believed that moment might be his happiest as well.

Chapter 1

Devonshire, England
Wednesday, 25 October 1815
11:15 a.m.

I have made plans to elope with a traitor." Lady Juliet Ashford flung herself across her sister's bed and buried her face in the counterpane.

Chloe Ashford set another stitch in her embroidery, and suppressed a sigh over Juliet's histrionics. "I can imagine no man less likely of being a traitor than Mr. Vernell."

"Not Mr. Vernell," Juliet said into the mattress.

Chloe set another stitch, gold thread against lavender silk, a ball gown meant for the spring and one more useless London Season. "Was not Mr. Vernell supposed to propose to you today?"

"Yes, but I have changed my mind and sent word to Ross that I am ready to elope with him instead."

Chloe jabbed the needle through the silk ball gown and her pink muslin skirt and into her thigh. She gasped, when she wanted to cry out with a pain that ran deeper than the puncture in her leg.

"You have made plans to run off with Ross Trenerry?" She kept her tone neutral, as though the notion did not fill her with irritation toward a sister who had come too close to endangering the entire family during the war, and contempt toward the man who preferred a flibbertigibbet like Juliet to the lady who had saved his life. "Again?"

"Of course again." Juliet rolled onto her back, hopelessly twisting her skirts beneath her, and gazed at the bed canopy as though reading the pages of one of her romantic novels on the silk hangings. "But this time it is all right because the war has been over for months and months." Juliet flung an arm across her face. "At least I thought it was all right this time until Deirdre arrived and told us the Americans want to hang him."

"Deirdre is here?" Chloe cast aside her embroidery and shot to her feet. "And Kieran? Why did you not tell me? Did they bring the children?"

"I just told you, and they brought the worst news." Juliet's response ended on a wail. "I so thought we could be happy now the war is over."

"As I told you last year, Juliet, you and Ross did not know one another well enough to know whether or not you would be happy together."

A year and a half earlier, Chloe had tried to comfort a broken-hearted Juliet thwarted in her plans to elope to Guernsey and meet Ross for a clandestine marriage that would have ruined the entire Ashford family if Chloe had not stopped it.

"Our hearts knew one another." Juliet sat up and covered her face with her hands. "At least I thought they did."

"How many times do I have to tell you that such an understanding happens only in novels?"

"You also said men are only heroes in novels, but Kieran was a hero for Deirdre, and then Ross was so brave during the war . . ."

"Ross was the enemy during the war." Chloe took a deep breath to clear the anger from her voice, if not her heart. "His only heroic actions were against Englishmen."

"That is not true and you know it." Juliet pummeled her fists on the bed.

Chloe winced as though those small hands beat on her chest. "All right, not always, but every other action he took during the war speaks against him, especially contacting you."

"He was answering the call of his heart."

Chloe snorted.

"Do not be such a killjoy." Juliet glared at Chloe through the tumbled tresses of her hair. "Just because you have never been in love does not mean you can dismiss the tender feelings of my heart."

"Of course not." Chloe turned away so her face betrayed nothing to her younger sister.

Juliet was wrong. Chloe had been in love. At the least, she thought she was. But when the object of one's affection proved so vastly unworthy, the ache of unrequited emotions turned to anger mixed with disdain and now not a little guilt.

"I am only twenty-three." Chloe hid her feelings behind the mundane. "That gives me plenty of time to fall in love."

"You will be twenty-four in three days. That is positively on the shelf, and I have no intention of joining you there." More tears spilled down Juliet's face. "I hoped not to, anyhow."

"You are to receive a formal proposal from Mr. Vernell today." Chloe leaned against one of the tall, carved bedposts. "He is handsome and wealthy and soon to become a member of Parliament."

And a dead bore. But he was the steady sort Juliet needed to counter her notions of heroism gleaned from the novels she read incessantly.

"So why the waterworks?"

"Because—" Juliet broke off to heave a sigh screaming of exasperation. "I have finally heard from Ross and wrote back that I will meet him, even elope with him if that is his wish."

Chloe's body tensed, ready to stop the man in his tracks at a moment's notice. "Is it his wish?"

"He did not say so specifically, but I am certain this is his wish. Or was certain until Deirdre and Kieran arrived with the news." Juliet gulped. "Deirdre said the Americans have declared Ross Trenerry a traitor."

"Nonsense." The word snapped from Chloe's lips. "America never knew a more loyal subject or citizen or whatever they call themselves."

"That is what I thought." Juliet sobbed hard enough to make the bed ropes creak. "But Deirdre—Deirdre just s-said the Americans claim he is."

Chloe swallowed against dryness in her throat and smoothed Juliet's tumbled black hair away from her face. "Calm yourself, then tell me what Deirdre said."

"I do not know. I ran away as soon as I overheard Deirdre telling the others that Ross has been declared a traitor to his country."

Chloe shook her sister's shoulder. "Talk sense. Deirdre would never say that of Ross Trenerry. They were friends for years before the war."

"But she did say it." Juliet raised her head to show red-rimmed blue eyes. "I was coming in from a walk. I did not sleep well last night because I knew Mr. Vernell was to propose to me today, and I was never quite certain I wanted to wed him, and especially not after Ross got a message to me saying he has come back. You know I have looked for a message every day since the war ended, and, at last, he got a letter to me through our secret postbox . . ."

Chloe closed her eyes. She should have repaired the mortar on that loose stone in the wall.

She should have paid better attention to Juliet's comings and goings of late, but when Ross had not contacted Juliet at the end of the war nearly a year ago, Chloe believed he had decided to stay away from England and Juliet.

"Exchanging letters in that havey-cavey fashion is no way to court a young lady." To Chloe's own ears, she sounded like a stiff-necked spinster. "Continue with your tale. What did this missive from Ross say?"

Juliet's eyes brightened. "It said that he wanted to see me."

"Nothing more?"

"He did not need to say more. I know what he meant—marriage at last."

"He would not—" Chloe stopped herself from claiming Ross possessed more sensibilities than to offer marriage, especially a clandestine one, to a young woman he scarcely knew.

Perhaps he would do something so ungentlemanly now that he was in some kind of trouble and needed an alliance to a powerful family. Chloe scarcely knew him—but she knew him better than Juliet had. Juliet knew him from two nights of nursing him through wound fever after she caught Chloe sneaking out in the middle of the night to tend to the injured escaped prisoner of war hidden in the caves below Bishops Cove, the Ashford estate. Chloe had known him through her visits to Dartmoor Prison during the seven months prior to the escape, disguised in her brother Kieran's old clothes, taking blankets and food and what coin she could spare from her pin money to ease the plight of the captured Americans. A few comforts in their imprisonment was the least she could do for the Americans captured by Kieran in his brief stint as a privateer. Chloe knew Ross from his fevered ravings for the weeks before Juliet caught her slipping down to tend to him. Chloe knew him from the harrowing escape from Dartmoor and that moment when he kissed her—a moment she should forget.

"So he contacted you after knowing he is in some sort of difficulty." Chloe glowered at a painting of the sunset burning through clouds above a roiling sea as though it were a portrait of Ross Trenerry she could shrivel with the power of her glare. "I thought even he would have more honor than that. But then, if he has done something to get himself accused of treason, he must have changed."

"He must have, and my heart is shattered." Juliet sniffed and mopped at her eyes with the backs of her hands. "But I do not wish for him to be captured either if he comes here to see me."

"Then simply do not respond to his message."

"But I told you I already did. I told him to meet me in the park at midnight."

"Of course you did." Chloe's nose wrinkled. "And no gentleman would comply with such a suggestion, but then, Ross Trenerry is no gentleman."

"He is. He—"

Chloe cut Juliet's protest off with a slash of her hand. "We do not need to argue with the merits of Ross Trenerry's progenitors. You were foolish to respond to his message with such a suggestion, and whether or not he will meet you at midnight or come to the front door as is right, you say he is now accused of a crime, and therefore you cannot meet him at all."

"You sound like my old governess."

"I sound like your sensible big sister who does not read silly novels. Now you must deliver a new message to your postbox and tell him you have changed your mind and do not wish to see him."

"But I do if he is innocent."

"You cannot until we know he is."

"I know." Juliet bowed her head, but no more tears fell. "The difficulty is, I cannot leave the house. I told Mama I am not feeling well so Mr. Vernell could not propose to me this afternoon, as I was sure I could have persuaded Ross to elope to Guernsey with me tonight."

Chloe crossed her arms beneath her considerable bosom. "You were going to attempt another dash for Guernsey tonight and had not told me?"

"I would have left a note."

"Of course you would have." Chloe wanted to bang her head against the wall. "Write another message for Ross instead, and I can simply exchange one message from you with another."

Juliet bounced off the bed. "Will you do this for me?"

"I will do anything to stop Ross Trenerry from harming my family."

She had already attempted that, not that anyone knew just how far she was willing to go to protect her family and how much it had cost her heart, her soul, to do so.

Juliet hesitated. "You must make certain no one sees you. If the letterbox ceases to be secret—"

"Juliet." Chloe spoke over her sister's admonitions. "When will you cease believing life is to mimic one of your novels?"

"When I cease being the only member of this family who has never had an adventure."

"I would say trying to escape to a Channel island to meet up with an enemy privateer is quite enough adventure for any lady."

"But I never got so far as the boat that was to take me across, thanks to you. You had the true adventure with how you got him out of prison and all."

"He still preferred you." Chloe tasted the disappointment, the hurt, and, yes, the hint of envy-born anger, and turned away. "Write your note for him."

"What shall I say?" Juliet settled herself at Chloe's desk. "I will seem like the most horrible of jilts."

"Not to a man who had no business paying his addresses to you." Chloe strode to the door. "I am going to find Deirdre and learn what is at the bottom of these accusations."

"Do you think this could be some kind of mistake?" Juliet glanced up, her eyes, dark blue rather than golden brown like Chloe's, widened with an expression of hope.

"I will know more after talking to Deirdre." It was the best answer Chloe would give her sister.

But Juliet returned the lid to the inkwell. "If you think I might be able to elope with him after all . . ."

"Regardless of the outcome, you cannot elope with Ross Trenerry or any other man who will not court you right and proper."

"I suppose you are correct." With a sigh, Juliet removed the lid to the inkwell and dipped in the quill. "I will tell him we must wait. That is not jilting him."

"Juliet, you cannot—" Chloe pressed her lips together.

The truth was, now that the war was over, Juliet could marry Ross Trenerry whether or not he was a fugitive. Juliet was of age.

Regardless of how Chloe's disdain for him had grown over the past two and a half years, she struggled to believe Ross was a traitor to America. She needed to know what news her brother and his wife, Chloe's good friend Deirdre, had brought. Not the sketchy details Juliet provided with her histrionics.

She slipped out of her bedchamber, leaving Juliet brushing the quill back and forth across her chin as she stared at a blank sheet of foolscap. Voices led Chloe to the morning room, cheerful with yellow chrysanthemums on the Chinese wallpaper and the yellow striped cushions despite a cloudy October day outside.

The gentlemen stood at her entrance. With a nod to her father and Mr. Vernell, Chloe crossed the room to kiss her brother on the cheek and embrace his wife.

"What a surprise to see you both. Did you bring the children?"

"They are in the nursery sleeping at last." Deirdre smiled.

"And that is a miracle." Kieran rubbed red-rimmed eyes. "I do not know where those two get so much energy."

"From me." Deirdre patted his arm. "You poor old thing."

Not for the first time since Deirdre came into her brother's life and heart, Chloe experienced a twinge of envy over the hollowness of something missing in her own life. She doubted she would ever meet a man who would love her as much as Kieran adored Deirdre, nor one she could let herself love with the devotion Deirdre showed toward Kieran. She had thought so once, but that had been when she was nearly as young and foolish as Juliet.

Shaking off the momentary sadness, she asked, "To what do we owe the pleasure of your company? I did not think we would see you until Christmas."

"Sad news." Deirdre shot a glance toward Mr. Vernell.

He looked downcast. Chloe supposed Mama had informed him that Juliet would not be receiving callers that day. She was a silly chit to risk forfeiting a proposal from a man with Vernell's patrician good looks, impeccable manners, and excellent prospects.

"But I don't wish to bore your guest with the tale," Deirdre added.

"Would you like some coffee?" Mama asked. "I can send for fresh."

"No, thank you." Chloe perched on the edge of a chair. "I should have some tea sent up to Juliet."

"I am sorry she is feeling out of curl," Vernell said in his rich baritone. "I would hope—" He shrugged and rose. "But I should leave you all to this reunion."

Papa and Mama made token protestations that he was welcome to stay, but with Juliet refusing to see him that day, his presence was de trop and awkward.

With him gone, Chloe turned to Deirdre. "Juliet was babbling some nonsense about Ross Trenerry being accused of treason against his country?"

"It is apparently true." Kieran's voice held more satisfaction than it should have.

Surely he had stopped being jealous of Deirdre's old friend after three years of marriage.

"What did he do?" Chloe asked.

"I learned this from a peculiar source," Kieran continued in a more sober fashion, "so details are always suspect. But apparently his privateer was captured near our coast one night. His men were tossed into Dartmoor and he vanished for the duration of the war."

Chloe tried to mask her shock with a show of confusion. "Surely that alone cannot make him a traitor. I mean, would he not merely have been sent to another prison, or perhaps paroled as a captain should be? To call a man traitor for that seems . . . unfair . . . or . . ." She trailed off under the scrutiny of her family.

"There's no record of him being imprisoned or paroled," Deirdre said.

"And his crew said he came ashore shortly before the capture," Kieran added.

Of course he had. He had come ashore to leave a note for Juliet, the contents of which had sealed his fate—sealed it more disastrously than Chloe had imagined possible.

"That seems like little enough to go on to call a man traitor." Chloe's tone was sharper than she intended, reflecting the piercing blow to her conscience.

"It is enough to make him stand trial for treason." Papa cradled his Sevres cup in both hands and studied Chloe over the rim. "If he was not up to no good, some kind of record of his imprisonment or parole would appear. The navy is meticulous about records."

Chloe shook her head. "I do not see how this is possible. He wanted nothing more than to fight for America."

"He is a Trenerry," Kieran said. "From the ones in Cornwall to the ones in America, they are all lawless."

"Considering that my own children helped him go off to fight against England," Papa said in a dry voice, "you should not be casting stones at the Trenerrys."

"I find this difficult to accept as well." Deirdre tugged on a strand of her loose coppery hair. "He was always a loyal and faithful friend aboard my father's ship."

"War changes men," Papa said.

Chloe looked at her parents. Neither of them knew Ross, but they knew war, had suffered themselves in the last conflict between England and America.

"Does war change a man so much he would turn traitor toward his own country?" Chloe posed the question for form's sake alone.

She knew the query was moot. Ross had not betrayed his ship and crew and gone free himself. He had been in a prison hulk. She knew that for certain because she was responsible for him being there, however unintentionally.

"A man desperate for money might turn traitor." Papa reached for a handbell and gave it a sharp ping to call in a footman. "Or if someone in his country did something for which he wanted revenge, a man might turn traitor."

"It made my father greedy and violent," Mama said, "during the last war between our countries. He was never loving, but he had not been mean before the war came."

While a footman took away the clutter of coffee service and congealing cream, Chloe studied Deirdre's face. She looked as fatigued as her husband. From worry or from two days of travel from Hampshire to Devon with two children under three years of age?

"There is never," Papa said once the footman departed, "good cause for a captain to betray his men."

He'd been in His Majesty's Navy for fifteen years, long before his children were born, and understood the laws of the sea and loyalty to ship and crew. But Deirdre had been aboard her father's merchant ship with Ross for six years and surely knew him better than anyone. If she believed these stories, Ross was in deep trouble.

"So," Chloe asked a little too brightly, "how did you all learn this news before we heard anything?"

"That's the peculiar part." Deirdre tucked a strand of hair behind one ear. "I was shopping in Portsmouth and was approached by Freddie Rutledge, who gleefully informed me of the fate of my former shipmate."

Chloe stared, her mouth agape. "Freddie Rutledge? But he does not speak to Ashfords."

"Unless he is imparting bad news for one of us." Kieran's hands fisted on his buckskin-clad knees. "Not that just him speaking to one of us is not bad news in itself."

"We should warn your parents they will be hearing from him as well," Deirdre said.

Mama stiffened on her chair. "Why would that man wish to speak to us?"

"Something about turning over a new leaf." Deirdre curled her upper lip.

She and Kieran, indeed all the Ashfords, had reason to sneer at thoughts of Frederick Rutledge. If that heir to a barony had changed his ways any more than leopards changed their spots, all the Ashfords would be shocked. He had lied and cheated in an attempt to protect his sister's reputation at Kieran's expense, hurting him and all the Ashfords.

"He could be lying." Chloe spoke aloud before she realized she intended to do so.

"I wish he were." For the first time since Chloe entered the parlor, Deirdre's composure broke and her lower lip quivered. "But he has, apparently, made friends with the American attaché in the past few years and learned the news from him."

Chloe willed herself to be calm.

"So tragic—about Mr. Trenerry, that is, not Mr. Rutledge. He can return to America with his attaché friend for all I care." Afraid she was going to be sick, Chloe rose. She needed air. She needed a few uninterrupted moments to think.

She started for the door, but hesitated in the center of the Wilton carpet. "What will happen to Mr. Trenerry if he is caught?"

"If he is here in England," Papa said, "he will be turned over to Mr. Beasley, the American attaché in Plymouth, then transported back to America for trial."

"If he is in England," Kieran said, "he will be caught."

Especially if he responded to Juliet's message and arrived at Bishops Cove at midnight.

Hoping he had not yet retrieved Juliet's note, Chloe excused herself with the explanation she should send tea up to Juliet, then slipped into the estate office to write her own note. *Stay away or you will be captured.*

Warning him was the least she could do for the mistake she had made that got him imprisoned in one of the derelict ships the English called prison hulks, and now, possibly, condemned as a traitor.

Warning note in hand, she headed across the parkland. Outside a pedestrian gate in the wall, she rounded the corner and walked along the stone edifice until she reached the overhanging tree. Beneath branches good for climbing should one not be able to leave by the gate, Chloe found the loose stone the three Ashford ladies had used over the past three years.

"Please still be there. Please still be there." As she worked the rock free, Chloe found herself begging for Juliet's note telling Ross to meet her at midnight to still be in place.

But the hollow behind the stone was empty.

Chapter 2

Devonshire, England
Wednesday, 25 October 1815
11:30 p.m.

*R*oss had never before set foot on the land oddly named Bishops Cove. The estate was the favored home of the Earl of Tyne, not a bishop, and the cove was a mere indent in the cliffs a hundred feet below a walled house, gardens, and regimented parkland of trees surrounded on three sides by farms and pastures of sheep. Beyond, the vast wasteland of Dartmoor with its prison and great walls.

The memory of that prison and those walls gave Ross pause as he approached the stone wall of Bishops Cove. Climbing it was easy for a man who had spent eight of the past ten years at sea climbing rigging in calm and storm. Reaching the ground on the other side would be no hardship either. Plenty of trees offered access to branches like a grand staircase to a sailor. But walls and locked iron gates held a man inside.

A shiver raced up Ross's spine and down his arms, a residual of the cold that never left him these days no matter what the outside temperature. Charleston, South Carolina, in August hadn't warmed him.

Devonshire, England, in October and its walls chilled him to the bone. Yet Lady Juliet Ashford awaited him beyond that wall, and that was enough lure to overcome the worst apprehensions of imprisonment.

The all-too-real possibility of imprisonment pricked at his conscience. With the shadow of a hangman's noose dangling over his head, he had no right to meet with Juliet. He had told her he couldn't see her until he cleared his name. But her note pleaded with him to come for five minutes. He would be safe from capture inside the parkland.

Allow me just this once to touch your hand. Until I have that tangible proof of fingers entwined with fingers, I will forever doubt that you are aught but a dream.

Those sweet words enticed him to throw caution to the wind for just these few moments. If Juliet felt safe, then surely he would as well. She would not lead him into danger, into entrapment within the walls of her father's estate. She didn't wish for him to be shipped back to America as a prisoner to face trial and a noose if he was found guilty of a crime he had not committed.

To convince her of his innocence, if she needed any convincing, was nearly as much a lure as her plea. He needed her to believe in him. Everything for which he fought during the war, had dreamed of during his second imprisonment, had planned on since the war ended, depended on Lady Juliet still wanting his attentions.

With the assurance he would lose himself in the anonymity of Plymouth once he gave Juliet her wish for the entwining of fingers, Ross leaped, grasped the top of the wall, and found toeholds between the stones. In seconds, he was up and over the wall. The young oak whose branches pointed to the makeshift letterbox also made for an easy descent. The mere whisper of branches against fabric broke the quiet of the night as he lowered himself to the ground.

Follow the wall until you reach the path. At the end of her missive, Juliet had dispensed with the poetic plea and turned to the practical. *Follow the path to a clearing with a fountain and benches, but have a care for the watchmen.*

Ross had a care for the watchmen. He kept his footfalls light and ducked into the shadow of the trees each time he heard a sound he didn't recognize as being a part of the night.

A lessening of the darkness beneath the canopy of tree branches told him he approached a clearing. Ross passed two of these before he reached the one Juliet described, with its fountain and ornamental benches. The fountain was silent for the winter, but the marble statue of swans on a lake gleamed like a beacon.

Ross paused just inside the tree line. A swish, no more than a whisper of fabric against fabric, sighed from the other side of the clearing. Either a shadow moved or a gust of wind swayed one of the young pine trees toward the clearing.

Except he neither heard nor felt a breeze beneath the taller deciduous trees.

Still within the shelter of the woods, he reached his foot out as far from his body as he could manage and tromped on a pile of dry leaves. Their crackle sounded like a blazing fire in the stillness.

The shadow detached itself from the trees and moved farther into the clearing. "Mr. Trenerry?" Her voice was a vibrant murmur.

A thrill of anticipation ran along Ross's spine. He shook it off and stepped into the meadow. "Juliet?"

"Juliet is not here."

He clasped the lady's hands. "Who are you?"

The woman flinched, as though he held her hands too tightly. "I am Lady Chloe."

"Of course." He released her. "Where is Lady Juliet?"

"She is not coming. She——"

"Then why did she send word to meet her here if she isn't coming?" Anger roughened his voice.

"You told her to meet you."

"I did no such—"

Tree branches snapped from behind Lady Chloe. Shadows detached from the trunks and sprinted across the clearing. Starlight limned the silhouettes of upraised cudgels in the running men's hands.

"Run." Lady Chloe shouted the admonition and tried to grab Ross's hand.

He spun away from her instead, facing the assailants. One man swung a cudgel toward his head. He ducked and parried the blow with an upflung arm. Chloe launched herself at the second man. He knocked her aside as though she weighed no more than a pillow and dashed his cudgel at Ross's head. Ross caught his arm and kicked. Both men went down. A punch to the attacker's middle. His cudgel against Ross's ribs. He grunted with the pain, but managed a punch against the assailant's nose. Blood spurted dark in the moonlight. Howling, the man rolled away.

Ross sat up in time to see Lady Chloe raise her skirt high enough to kick the wounded man in his ribs, and then his companion dove toward Ross. The cudgel swept down. Before Ross raised his arm high enough to deflect the blow, hard wood met his skull and the world went black.

"Mr. Trenerry!" Chloe tossed back her cloak with one hand so she could grasp her pistol.

Steel flashed in the moonlight. Chloe flung up her other arm to ward off a blow as Ross had deflected the cudgel. But this was a knife. The razor edge bit into her arm. She screamed in shock and pain and brought up her knee, sending the knife-wielding man staggering away. Free for the moment, she raised her pistol and fired into the air.

Muttering epithets against unnatural females and worse, the two assailants broke away, one running for the trees, the other stumbling behind. They left Ross in their wake, a crumpled, solid mass on the dead grass.

"Mr. Trenerry?" Weak-kneed, Chloe knelt by Ross, praying he wasn't dead.

He lay so still she feared at first he had succumbed to some wound, a terrible blow on his head or perhaps a stab wound.

She ran her hand across his face, felt the flutter of a pulse in his neck, then the moist warmth of breath from between his lips. He was still alive, but while he remained unconscious, how badly hurt he might be she didn't know how to assess in the dark without touching him all over. She could perform such an intrusive act if necessary, yet she doubted they had time before men from Bishops Cove descended upon them.

"Ross." She spoke his name in an undertone, though she doubted anyone for half a mile around had missed the crack of her pistol fired to scare away the assailants, especially not the Ashford outdoor servants. "Mr. Trenerry, can you hear me?"

He might have groaned, but she could not be sure she heard above the rush of blood in her ears.

"We need to get you out of here."

If Ross were caught, he would be condemned to another prison.

"Ross, get up." She ghosted her fingertips across his face.

He remained motionless.

Footfalls crunched along the path and through the trees. "Who is there?" asked an Ashford gamekeeper.

Chloe struggled to lift Ross. Perhaps if she could drag him beneath the lip of the fountain, she could claim she had frightened off men from the clearing and was there alone. Yet Ross would likely die in the cold if left there all night, and she did not believe she would be allowed to sneak out again before morning.

The footfalls drew closer. Men called to one another about the direction from which they had heard the gunshot. They would reach the clearing in moments.

"Ross, wake up." She grasped him beneath the arms and tried to pull.

She knew her strength was not insignificant. She could pull herself up into a tree by a low-hanging branch. But Ross Trenerry was a big man, tall and muscled, and her left arm had begun to throb. A gush of warmth warned her she was bleeding. With every inch she managed to drag Ross across the ground, more blood flowed down her arm.

And the closer the footfalls drew.

She paused to shove her handkerchief up her sleeve and reached for Ross's shoulders once more.

"What the deuce do you think you are doing?" One man in the lead, several Bishops Cove servants burst into the clearing.

Chloe kneeled on the grass, breathing hard. She had failed to save Ross from capture yet again. She owed him his freedom, and she had given him another imprisonment. And three and twenty or not, she was going to be in deep trouble with her father for this night's escapade. All she could do was brazen it out, get Ross the medical attention he needed, then help him to freedom.

Chloe glanced up at her father's head gamekeeper. "We have to get this man into the house."

"Lady Chloe?" The gamekeeper flung up one arm to halt the other men. "What are you doing here?"

"Never you mind that." Chloe stood, sick and dizzy. "We need to get an apothecary for this man."

"Call the constable, more like," the watchman said from beside the gamekeeper. "Did he hurt you, milady?"

"No, no, he is a friend."

That white lie served her purpose for the moment.

"Hurry. It is cold out here."

"Then a young lady oughtn't to be meetin'—"

"You may express your opinions to my father," Chloe interrupted the gamekeeper. "At present, I insist you take this man into the house."

Into the first stage of a new imprisonment.

"He is a friend of Lady Ripon." She used the title Deirdre despised but had to accept as the wife of a viscount.

The servants understood the authority of that title. The watchman stooped and slipped one hand beneath Ross's head. Chloe realized the man only had one hand, and the gamekeeper couldn't stoop at all; his right knee didn't bend. The other two men appeared just as infirm in one way or another. They were men only her father, who sympathized with the plight of military men no longer physically fit to serve England, would hire as gamekeeper and watchmen. They could patrol the grounds, but they could not lift a man Ross's size.

Chloe stooped with care, her left arm throbbing. "I will get his feet."

"Lady Chloe," the gamekeeper said, "That isn't proper."

"Neither is leaving him here helpless in the cold." She caught hold of Ross's ankles, sheathed in the sturdy leather boots of a seaman. "You can help carry him once we have him up. Ready?" she addressed the one-handed watchman.

"Yes, milady."

They lifted. Pain ripped through her arm, and she felt the warm trickle of blood slide down the inside of her sleeve. Just a trickle, not a gush this time. Not a deep wound—she hoped.

Once they had Ross at waist level, the gamekeeper insisted that he take hold of Ross's legs instead. Dizziness sending the starlight spiraling above her, Chloe let him. Tucking her cloak around her against the chill of the night, she followed the men toward the house, hoping Ross would be all right. Except how could he be, when he was now as good as captured? Because of her failure to keep him safe—again. She couldn't dwell on one more mistake where Ross was concerned. She had to think of how to explain to her father what she was doing in the park with Ross Trenerry. Papa was not going to be pleased. But no good excuses came to her mind by the time they reached the house.

Addison, the peg-legged butler, stood in the entryway with a branch of candles. "Lady Chloe, what is this about?"

"We need an apothecary for Mr. Trenerry, and"—she sighed—"you had best rouse my father."

Addison turned toward the library. "Lord Tyne is—"

"Right here." Papa stepped into the library doorway, his deep blue eyes stern. "Who is this man?"

"It is Ross Trenerry." Chloe made herself walk up to her father. "I went to warn him that he was in danger, but there was an attack . . ." She glanced at the gaping servants and their burden. Ross's face was ashen, and blood trickled into his dark hair. "He needs care, Papa."

Her father nodded to the men. "Take him to the white bedchamber and send for the apothecary. Do not forget to bind him to the bed." He touched her shoulder. "Are you all right, daughter?"

"Yes." She couldn't look at him as she lied. Her arm pulsed with pain, and she thought it was still bleeding. But her cloak covered the wound.

"Do you know who attacked you?" Papa demanded. "Should I send for the constable?"

"The men will be long gone by now. And the scandal!" Chloe watched the servants carrying Ross up the stairs. "It is bad enough he's now in our house, is it not?"

"It may be."

He stepped back, gesturing for her to precede him into the library. "Come inside here and tell me what you were doing with a man I would rather you did not know."

She entered the lofty chamber on unsteady legs. She welcomed the nearness of the chair beside Papa's desk. It wasn't comfortable; those directed to sit there weren't supposed to be at ease. The soft chairs stood near the fire. But it was a sturdy chair with a high back that held her upright when she wanted to fold like a fan.

Then Papa walked around the desk and dropped onto the edge of his own chair, and she wished her seat had arms she could grip for further support. "What were you doing in the parkland at midnight, Chloe?" His voice and eyes were no longer stern; they were sad, tired. He wasn't angry with her. He was disappointed in her, and that was worse.

He was going to be more disappointed in her when she finished spinning her web of lies; if he ever found out she had deceived him yet again.

No, not if—when. Papa always found out the truth in one way or another. Chloe feared the consequences of that day, guessing she would be sent to her widowed aunt in Northumberland, or worse, her great-aunt the duchess in the Lake District, or, worst of all, presented with a potential husband she would not be able to refuse. And then she would have to plan her own escape.

She needed to simply speak the truth, yet she could not drag Juliet into this fiasco. Papa loved and wanted the best for all of his children, but Juliet, the youngest, the liveliest, the prettiest, was certainly his favorite. He knew the role Kieran and Chloe had played in the escape from Dartmoor that included Ross Trenerry. He did not know Juliet had insinuated herself into nursing Ross in the cave, nor how Ross had fallen for Juliet. Chloe would keep him from learning the truth of Juliet's poor judgment as long as possible.

"I am waiting," Papa said.

"I know." Chloe knew she was taking too long to speak. Unable to look Papa in the eye, she bowed her head. "I wanted to elope with him. But I changed my mind after learning he had a price on his head, so I went to the rendezvous in order to warn him away from here."

"You thought you might elope with him?" A rough edge to Papa's voice warned Chloe he was angry after all. "How could you know this man, this enemy, well enough for such a dire step as marriage?"

"We exchanged letters before the escape, and then I nursed him for a gunshot wound before he got away to France . . ." She allowed her voice to trail off.

"Of course you did." Papa sighed. "So I can presume you have corresponded since the war. Perhaps some notion of star-crossed lovers finally being able to live out their destiny?"

"Yes, sir."

Papa remained silent for several moments. Too many moments. Then he slapped his palm against the oak of his desk. "Balderdash."

Chloe jumped. Her head shot up.

Papa caught her gaze and nodded. "Yes, you are Chloe, not Juliet, so let us start this Banbury tale again. Why were you in the parkland at midnight?"

"To warn Ross Trenerry to run."

"Why?"

Chloe hesitated.

"Do not tell me you intended to elope with him. That is Juliet's sort of non—" He stopped. His eyes narrowed.

Chloe's breath snagged in her throat. *Do not ask. Do not ask. Do not ask.*

"Juliet was the one who intended to elope with this American traitor, was she not?" Papa asked despite Chloe's silent pleas.

Chloe did not answer. Not doing so was her only defense, and a poor one at that.

"How did she meet him?" Papa asked.

Chloe sought for moisture in her mouth, while blood oozed down her arm.

"I thought you and Deirdre were the only Ashford ladies who risked life and limb and the reputation of this family, not to mention our freedom, to succor the enemy."

"We were." Chloe could answer this with confidence. "We visited Deirdre's crew in Dartmoor, and you know about getting them away."

"I could scarcely not know." Papa's tone was dry, his mouth tight. "But Juliet was with me in Plymouth."

Chloe started to cross her arms beneath her bust, but the wound on her arm pulled. Her face twisted in pain, and she dropped her hands to her lap. "She followed me to the caves one night and slipped in after I'd gone. He was just beginning to recover from wound fever and thought she was some sort of angel or princess or simply our lovable Juliet."

She couldn't go on. This part hurt too much, despite the number of times she told herself it should not, the truth that Ross preferred Juliet to her.

"And you expect me to believe that brief acquaintance convinced her to wait for him these past two and a half years?" Scorn dripped from Papa's tone.

Chloe shook her head, then blinked against the spots dancing before her eyes. "He apparently said some lovely things to her, and for a lady addicted to novels as is our Juliet, that was enough. And I believe they managed some correspondence during the war."

"Of course they did." Papa sighed. "How I, a former officer in the British Navy, could end up with such treasonous children I do not know."

"Our American mama?" Chloe attempted a smile.

"Do not blame your mother." For a moment, his face was fierce, then it softened. "Unless it is to remind me that she raised you all to be compassionate and generous to those less fortunate. Apparently we forgot to tell you that giving aid to the enemy is not what we meant."

Nor would they talk about how Mama had not always been a loyal English wife, but a spy in Papa's very household during the American Rebellion.

"If Juliet spent so little time with this man," Papa said, "then how can she have wanted to elope with him?"

"She says their hearts knew one another."

"Oh, Juliet." Papa swiped a hand across his eyes, looking fatigued all of a sudden. "She is, of course, safely tucked up in her bed?"

"She is."

"While you carry out the role of protecting everyone around you from everyone else." He gazed at her with such love Chloe's eyes misted with tears.

"I simply wanted to warn him away and not to wait for Juliet." She blinked the moisture from her eyes. "But I failed and now I suppose you will have to turn him over to the Americans for trial."

"To preserve diplomatic peace," Papa said, "I cannot see any other way at present."

"But what if he is innocent of treason?"

"We do not know that, Chloe, so it is not for us to decide. It is up to the American courts to judge him innocent or guilty."

"They seem to have already judged him guilty." Chloe could not withhold the bitterness from her voice.

"My dear, you cannot protect him from his own actions."

"But what if they are the actions of someone else?"

"You cannot protect him from those either." Papa rose, rounded the desk, and held out his hand to her. "I will see to it he is well taken care of and sent to the Americans with some comforts. It is the least I can do for my daughter-in-law and the friend he was to her in the past. Now it is off to your room for you."

Sadly admitting that Papa was right and she could do nothing for Ross at the present, Chloe allowed her father to raise her from her chair. Then she headed up the stairs. She had to grip the railing to keep herself from toppling backward. She didn't feel more blood dripping, and no one seemed to have noticed her wound. Each step feeling as though lead weights filled her boots, she reached the top of the stairs and headed down the corridor to her bedchamber. She paused at her door, knowing she should go inside as Papa instructed. But Juliet should know about Ross's capture.

At that moment, the short trek to Juliet's room seemed like a hundred miles, and she leaned against her door, her conscience hurting more than her wounded arm.

She was almost positive Ross was innocent. She knew he had been in a prison hulk after his privateer was captured. She also knew how his brig had been caught.

She had betrayed him. Despite the warning Chloe had delivered when he fled England the first time, then after Juliet's thwarted elopement, Ross had come ashore to deliver a message to Juliet. This time, the note had said nothing about him leaving captured British sailors in the caves. He had left Juliet a note saying he had made all the money he intended to privateering and told her how she could get to Guernsey to meet him without risking her safety as she had the time she had tried to go on her own.

Whether or not Ross had decided to quit privateering, he was still the enemy. Juliet going to meet with him would have made her a traitor to England. With too many in the Admiralty still knowing of Mama's activities in the previous war with America, the taint would have spread to the entire family. Everyone from Papa down to the children would have lost everything, perhaps even their lives, if the Crown decided to make examples of the Ashfords and seen they were hanged for treason.

Ross and Juliet knew nothing of Mama's escapades during the last war and likely did not realize the danger of an elopement. But Chloe did, and, to protect her family, she had watched and waited and sent one of the tenants loyal to her—since she paid his rent when he fell on hard times—to inform the coast guard of an enemy privateer in the region of Bishops Cove. Once Ross was captured, Chloe had reasoned, she could help him escape with the understanding he would stay away from Juliet until the war was good and over.

Through more tenants she had aided over the years, she had helped Ross's crew escape from Dartmoor. But Ross had not been sent there.

Nor had he been paroled as she thought he would be as a ship's captain. He had been sent to a prison hulk in the Nore. She had bribed an official at the Admiralty to look up the records.

And if she could bribe an official to seek out the records of Ross's imprisonment, someone else could as easily bribe a similar—or the same—clerk to destroy those records.

"But why?" She beat her fist on the doorframe as she posed the query she had asked too often since Ross's capture.

Why had he not been given parole? Why had he been sent to a hulk instead of Dartmoor? Why could she not have found a better way to be rid of Ross Trenerry?

Chloe tried to assuage her conscience with reminders that she had only intended to protect her family and the hundreds of people whose livelihoods depended on the Ashfords maintaining their current privilege of life and property. Too often, especially now, those reminders were not enough to stop the guilt. But helping Ross and Juliet discover if they did indeed love one another would help.

The instant she informed Juliet that Ross was captured and in one of the house's dozens of bedchambers, Juliet would fly to his side. The image of Ross once more waking to find his lady at his side made Chloe feel just a little unwell, but bringing together a couple she had torn apart was the least she could do to make up for her mistake with Ross.

With a sigh, she pushed herself away from her door and continued down the corridor. She pushed open Juliet's door. The room was dark and quiet. Too quiet. Chloe hesitated on the threshold, listening for breathing, the rustle of bedclothes. She heard neither.

"Juliet?" She spoke in a whisper.

No response came. She stepped into the chamber and closed the door.

"Juliet?" she said aloud.

Silence.

Surely Juliet would not have rushed to Ross's bedside, even if she'd learned already what had happened. Papa wouldn't let her stay. But Juliet might once again wish to play the role of the ministering angel heroine.

Annoyed that Juliet could again be the one present when Ross regained consciousness, Chloe stomped to the bed in search of a candle and strike-a-light. She found both amid a collection of novels and hair ribbons scattered across the bedside table, and set spark to the wick of a candle. Light flared, danced across the bed. The empty bed. No, not quite empty. A note lay on the pillow, where Juliet's head should have rested.

Chapter 3

Devonshire, England
Thursday, 26 October 1815
6:30 a.m.

*R*oss woke to candlelight that lanced across his eyes like noonday sunshine. He tried flinging up one arm as a shield, but his hand was trapped, tangled in—a rope.

He tried lifting the other hand to investigate. It also remained all but immobile. He flexed his legs, straining to raise them. In the stillness of his surroundings, the surface beneath him wavered with a creaking as loud as a ship's timbers. But he couldn't make his legs move.

Breath snagged in his lungs. He squeezed his eyelids together and concentrated on breathing, long, slow breaths that assured him no weight lay on his chest. No iron band was crushing his skull. Only his hands and legs were secured to—what? A bed, of course. Softness beneath him. A coverlet over him. *No need to feel cold.*

A shiver passed through him. He fought the urge to struggle against his bonds. Every motion hurt his head, and he needed that for thinking, for remembering just how he'd gotten caught. By whom this time?

Too many people wanted him—anyone who knew of the price on his head, or the man Ross needed to catch to prove his innocence. He was certain no one had followed him to the Ashford estate, and his rendezvous with—

"Juliet!" Her name emerged as little more than a croak from his dry throat.

Memory returned with a jolt. He had, at last, gotten a message to her and told her he would see her when he was free. But she had responded with a letter begging him to come to the park and see her just once more. Afraid she would attempt the same escapade of running to him, as she had during the war, Ross had gone to dissuade her from trying to join him in his exile, temporary though he intended it to be.

For all that, she had not come to meet him. Her sister had—and moments later, he was attacked. They were both assaulted. She hadn't been helping the men battering him—she had been helping him fight them off.

Good heavens, was she all right? He remembered nothing after the cudgel crashed against his skull.

He made himself open his eyes. The movement pulled against the band around his head. A bandage, of course. He'd been hit hard. But he wasn't concussed. His surroundings didn't blur or multiply.

Not that he could make out much of those surroundings beyond the candle's radius. A swath of darkness covered half of one wall. Another oblong shade cloaked most of another wall. Bed curtains obscured the rest of the chamber. But he saw enough to know that he was in a bedchamber, not a prison cell. He was tied to the bed frame, it not a narrow, hard cot, or worse, lashed to a ship's mast in the dank cold of an English autumn.

Suddenly, the light didn't hurt quite so much, and the coverlet warmed him. He could escape from a bedchamber in a house. He could work free of ropes given time. Servants could be bribed, persuaded, or overwhelmed. Houses offered numerous avenues of escape. Once free, he could learn how Lady Chloe Ashford fared, and assure Juliet he would return once he was free to call on her openly, begin their courtship in a proper manner. They could discover if the tug toward one another commenced in a dark, dank cave was a true meeting of hearts or born of the intensity of a danger passed and uncertain future ahead.

He believed he knew the answer. How could any man not want a lady as beautiful, as kind and full of life as Lady Juliet? In the past two and a half years, she was not absent from one vision of the future he worked toward—a home, a family, a wife, and children capable of charming his family into accepting him back into their fold. With a wife like Juliet, they would see he was no longer the reckless, selfish youth they had sent packing.

All his plans, all his dreams were for nothing if he couldn't prove his innocence.

He half opened his eyes this time and saw a line of light along the swath of darkness across from him. It was cold, gray light. Dawn light. As far north as England in the autumn, that must be between six and seven o'clock. Surely the house would stir soon.

As though his thought conjured it, a rattle of china on silver sounded beyond his chamber door. Then he heard the rasp of a key turning in a little-used lock, and the rattling grew louder.

"Do you be awake?" The voice was pure Devonshire and female. A moment later, a cherubic face with red-rimmed eyes beneath a starched white cap peeked around the edge of the bed curtains. The aroma of coffee and fresh bread wafted across the bed, and his mouth watered. "Aye, I see that you be alive still. I'll be fetching his lordship then."

His lordship!

Ross's blood ran cold. The smell of coffee and bread now made him feel ill. "Wait. Which lordship?"

The maid whisked from sight.

His lordship!

Ross balled his hands into fists. The ropes cut into his arms. He tugged against the restraints, twisted, strained. Pain made him grit his teeth. He ignored it and strained harder.

Pull. Stretch. Distant voices gave him the impetus to channel all his strength into freeing his hands. *Jerk. Twist.*

A trickle of warmth over one hand told him he'd made himself bleed. *Good.* The blood would lubricate the ropes. He would get himself free despite "his lordship" coming. His nameless, faceless lordship.

No, not nameless. Ross knew who would walk through that door.

He yanked on the ropes with renewed vigor. His wrists bled more, but the ropes remained fast. Someone knew how to tie knots. Of course he did. Garrett Ashford, now Lord Tyne, had run off to the British Navy as a youth. He collected former sailors for his servants.

Ross was a sailor, too, and had had more than his fair share of experience with ropes.

As the chamber door opened again, Ross twisted his left hand free of its bond. He kept it secured beneath the coverlet, a weapon in reserve should he need it against Juliet's father, not that Tyne would assault a wounded man tied to a bedstead. The assault in the park was far different a matter, however.

Yet Lady Chloe wouldn't fight her own father's men.

Momentarily distracted by this inconsistency, Ross lost track of the earl's progress until he whipped open the window curtains. Light, more pearl than gray now, delineated a tall, well-built man with a profile as classic and flawless as any artist could have created. Strong blood, that of the Ashfords, for the Earl of Tyne to pass the good looks even to the daughters and remain in the man's late middle age. Except Juliet had always smiled in those last meetings in the cave before Ross's men came to spirit him out of England. Garrett Ashford didn't smile. When he faced Ross, his mouth looked like nothing more than a fissure in a granite wall.

Ross raised himself as far as he could without revealing one hand was free. "Lady Chloe? She's all right?"

"She is, no thanks to you." Tyne's voice was cold and dry. "But you have her to thank for your life."

Ross couldn't suppress the sigh of relief, nor his next question. "And you to thank for me being tied?"

"Can you expect anything less?" Tyne asked. "You are accused of being an enemy to your countrymen, and, apparently, you are also an enemy to my family."

"I'm neither—"

"You arranged to meet my daughter Juliet last night." Tyne took a pace toward the bed. "Now she is missing."

"Missing?" Ross stared at him. "But you said she—"

"Juliet is missing."

His heart skipping too many beats, Ross jerked against his bonds. "How? She requested to meet me, but her sister showed instead."

If possible, Tyne's face grew harder. "She was taken from her bed-chamber sometime last night."

Ross closed his eyes and tried to breathe. "Who would do such a thing to her?"

"That is what I want you to tell me."

Ross looked Tyne in the eyes. "I can't tell you."

Tyne took another pace toward the bed. "Cannot? Or will not?"

"I can't." Beneath the shelter of the bedclothes, Ross began to work his other hand free. Now, for Juliet's sake as well as his own, he needed to escape, needed to catch the only likely person who would try to capture him and would know enough about him to take Juliet, too. But he couldn't tell Tyne who that was, not when it was probably a member of his own family. From what he knew of Ashfords, they would see Ross burn in hell before they let him speak against one of their own.

"I doubt very much that an attack on you and my daughter disappearing at the same time are a coincidence."

Ross shook his head, and the room spun around him. "But I thought she was safe on your lands."

"Or you would be safe once wed to an Ashford." Tyne held his gaze with a look as sharp as marlinespikes.

"I had no intention of marrying her while I have this cloud hovering over my life. She begged me to see her and I—" Ross stopped.

He didn't help his case by sounding like a recalcitrant schoolboy denying he had set the woodshed on fire while playing with gunpowder. Intending to meet Juliet, even for a brief good-bye, had been a mistake. He had simply ached for a new memory to replenish those he had revisited in his mind again and again to get him through the dark days on the prison hulk and his recovery after his release.

Ross knew how a rendezvous with Juliet appeared to Tyne. Capture the daughter and the Ashfords would become his ally in proving his innocence—or gaining him asylum in Britain.

He changed tack from denial to enquiry. "Could she have left on her own?"

"Since you are here, I think that unlikely." Tyne's voice alone should have sent icicles into the air.

"Did whoever took her leave a note?"

"Not a line." Tyne bit out each word as though he found them distasteful.

Ross found the answer intolerable. Unreasonable. Demands for a ransom accompanied an abduction. The Ashfords were wealthy. But this man wanted to hurt Ross, not the Ashfords. More reason for him to get free.

He strained harder against his ropes. "We've got to search for her then."

"We have been . . . since midnight." Tyne's Adam's apple bobbed above his stock, and he turned his back on Ross.

Inside the chamber, the only sound Ross heard was his own heart beating. Outside the room, more dishes rattled. Female voices hummed in unintelligible exchange. Then someone knocked on the door. "Papa, may I come in?"

Ross's heart stopped beating. The speaker sounded so much like Juliet!

Tyne scowled. "I would rather you did not."

The door clicked open. "Rather or not, you know you need me here." Carrying another tray of coffee and bread, she glided into the room on a froth of blue muslin skirts and an ivory silk shawl. Her face was nearly as pale as her wrap, and as grim as Tyne's. "Has he told you anything yet?"

"I have nothing to tell him," Ross said.

"But you have to know who has taken my sister, Mr. Trenerry."

Ross shook his head, gritting his teeth against a fresh onslaught of pain in his skull. "I don't know."

Tyne faced him again, his stony mask back in place. "I think you know and are simply not saying."

"Sir, I—" Lady Chloe shot Ross a warning glance, and he closed his mouth, more in surprise than obedience.

"Papa, the man has been injured," her ladyship said. "Let him have some breakfast. He might be more inclined to talk if we make him comfortable."

Tyne took the tray from her and set it on a low table beside the bed. "You have a kind heart, Chloe, but I would rather you leave us and allow me to deal with him. I have dealt with prisoners before."

Ross glared at him. "I'm not one of your naval prizes."

"You would be better off if you were." Tyne glowered right back. "I would not consider you a trait—"

"Papa," Lady Chloe said. "Mama is so distraught she is crying."

Tyne's face softened for an instant, then he returned a cold glare to Ross. "For that alone, making my wife cry, I will see you regret your involvement with my family." He grasped her ladyship's elbow.

Her face tightened with either pain or anger. Whatever caused the spasm to twist her lovely features, her body remained immobile. "I will stay to see he eats, Papa."

"Not without me here. We shall send in a footman or two to see to his breakfast. The man is too much of a menace to my children for me to want you near him." Tyne propelled her toward the door, where he paused to glance back. "I shall return."

Thinking that sounded like a threat, Ross waited only long enough for the door to close behind them before he began working loose the knot of the rope on his right wrist. The blood had made the knot stiff. But he had to get away, find Juliet, his lady, his love, catch those who dared to so much as frighten her. He could get loose for her sake. He hadn't been idle during the past six months of freedom and had regained much of the strength he'd lost during his second term as a British prisoner of war. Between the dexterity of his left hand and the strength of his right arm, he freed his right wrist.

The quilted satin coverlet slid off the bed. Then the rope fell away the same instant the door opened and Chloe Ashford strode into the room. She glanced from his face to his hands, pursed her lips, and left the chamber.

Ross began working on his feet. If the lady had gone for assistance or more rope, he intended to be loose, free to fight. The silver tray and coffeepot would make handy weapons. Or the chamber pot?

The ropes on his ankles proved easy to untie with both hands free. But when he tried to stand, his head felt as though it were spinning on his neck like a loose bung in a keg, and the bandage over his wound felt like it was all that held his brains inside his skull. He dropped onto the stool beside the bed, his head in his hands. *Get moving. Someone will be back.*

He grasped the bedpost and willed strength into his legs, willed away the sickness, the dizziness. He had to get around the bed. The serving tray sat on the opposite side. If someone came, he wouldn't have a weapon.

The door opened. Realizing he sat on a far better weapon than the tray, he grabbed up the stool. Lady Chloe marched in alone.

"You can brain me with that." She gestured at the stool with a bundle she carried. "But from the look of you, you will not get far without assistance."

"You might be right at that." Ross set down the stool. He could never strike a woman, not even for freedom. "But you shouldn't be here against your father's wishes. I'm a menace, remember?"

One corner of her mouth twitched upward. "Sit down before you fall down, Mr. Trenerry. I am going to bandage your wrists."

Glad to do so, he sat on the edge of the bed, a high bed that kept him nearly at her eye level. "I'd appreciate that." He gazed into her golden-brown eyes.

They didn't sparkle as Juliet's had by lantern light in the caves, but they were rather remarkable behind short but thick black lashes.

"And after you bandage me up," he continued, "I'll do whatever I must to discover why Juliet disappeared."

"I think you must already know." She set her bundle on the stool he had abandoned. "Since you are the ransom the abductors require."

Chapter 4

Devonshire, England
Thursday, 26 October 1815
6:50 a.m.

*R*ansom?" Ross arched his eyebrows toward a hairline that bore too many threads of silver for a man of no more than twenty-six or -seven years. "What's your game, Lady Chloe? Your father said there is no ransom request."

"No game, I am afraid."

Chloe looked at Ross and wished no one were playing games. In the increasing light, he didn't appear strong enough to fight anyone's battles, least of all his own. His complexion was pale, and his skin was taut across his prominent cheekbones. His eyes, those dark eyes that had haunted Chloe's dreams for three years, had left her wakeful and guilt-ridden for the past year, lacked the intensity she remembered from their first meeting; they looked suspicious, wary. She didn't blame him, not after what he had suffered at the hands of the Ashfords.

"There is a ransom." Chloe crossed her arms over her chest, wincing at the tug on her injured arm. "I, um, took it."

"What did you take?" Light flashed in Ross's eyes, and she realized they were a deep blue-gray, not black as she'd always thought.

"When I went into Juliet's room last night to tell her what happened with you, there was a ransom note on her pillow." She stared at the wardrobe on the other side of the bed, at the window across from the foot of the bed, at the table with the coffee service beside the bed—anywhere but at Ross. "I took it."

"Why." The single word emerged from Ross in a menacing growl.

Aware of his size and how alone they were, Chloe snatched up her bundle as though a bottle of witch hazel and soft cloth could protect her. "Because . . . because you are the ransom."

Ross paled. "Explain."

"Whoever took Juliet will give her back in exchange for you."

Ross said something a gentleman should not speak in front of a lady, muttered an apology, and pressed his palms to his temples as though fearing his brains would explode from his skull. "Whoever attacked me in your woods last night must have taken Juliet when they failed with me."

Chloe nodded, unable to speak for the lump in her throat.

"So why didn't you tell your father?"

"If Papa knows what the ransom is, he will have to choose between turning you over to the Americans or getting his daughter back safe." Chloe gripped her elbows. "If he does not turn you over to the American attaché, he will raise suspicions about our family abiding by the law. Yet if he does not deliver you as the ransom, we may never see Juliet again, at least not alive and well."

Ross's eyes flashed. "But if you had told him last night, he might have been able to catch up with the abductors."

"By the time Papa rallied men for a search, whoever took Juliet would have long since had her at sea."

"How do you know they took that route?"

"Because the note says you are supposed to show up on Guernsey by October 31."

"I should have guessed." This time, Ross did not apologize for his expletives. He struck the mattress so hard feathers poked through ticking and sheet.

Chloe stood motionless, waiting for him to calm, feeling vindicated for her decision not to tell Papa about the ransom note. She had been right in thinking Ross knew exactly who had kidnapped Juliet.

On his feet now, Ross prowled around the room, grasping the armoire door handle without opening the door, gripping the window frame without shoving up the sash, returning to brace one hand against a bedpost.

"Choosing between keeping his duty to his country by turning me over to the authorities and choosing to get his daughter back is a deuced awkward choice for a father." Ross gave Chloe a narrow-eyed glare. "Or a sister—if the decision was difficult."

"I beg your pardon?" Chloe took a step backward. "Are you accusing me of something?"

"Should I be?"

"No, never." Chloe met his gaze full-on. "I adore my sister. I have spent a lifetime keeping her safe from danger and folly and—"

"Me."

"I beg your pardon?" Chloe flung up her hands.

He caught hold of them and stood close enough for her to smell the sea on his clothes along with a hint of something sharp and pleasant, the tang of lime. His hands were warm and callused, warm and strong enough to hold her in place without applying painful force.

The last time she had been this close to him, he had kissed her. The memory of those moments on a bleak hillside, of the danger they had weathered, coupled with his current nearness left her knees weak and her mouth too dry for speech.

"Something about this entire situation is foul." Apparently nothing stopped his ability to speak. "You meet me instead of Juliet. I'm attacked, and Juliet disappears with a note for a ransom only you see. Can you explain that to me?"

"I can." The two words emerged as a croak. She swallowed to produce some moisture and tried again with better results. "I can. I have the ransom note with me."

She yanked her hands free and plucked the note from her pocket.

Ross snatched it from her fingers and stared at it, his face whitening before his long fingers crushed the foolscap into a walnut-sized ball. He then smoothed it out, folded it with care, and tucked it into the pocket of his breeches.

"I'm sorry, Lady Chloe. I'm a little out of my head at the moment." He took several deep breaths before he continued. "But this note's existence doesn't explain why you met me instead of Juliet."

Still reeling from his apology, Chloe thought of no subterfuge and blurted out the truth. "She did not wish to meet you once she learned you had a price on your head."

Ross barked out a mirthless laugh. "Surely you can do better than that, my lady. She had to have already known my difficulties with the law before she wrote begging me to meet her."

"We learned from Deirdre and Kieran, not you."

"I wrote her two days ago saying we would have to postpone our meeting."

"She received no such message. The one she received—"

"She must have. I posted it myself. I didn't trust it to anyone—" He broke off and shoved his hands into his breeches' pockets, glaring at Chloe. "Before that, I had posted another message in the hole-in-the-wall letterbox. I never told her I wanted to meet with her in the middle of the night. I said I wanted to call on her, if she thought I would be received. She was supposed to respond whether I should come to the front door like a proper gentleman worthy of her, or if I should be on my way."

"She never received such a message from you." Chloe's head spun as though she had taken a blow to her skull.

Perhaps that was what the note Juliet mentioned had said. She might not have reported it thus because she wanted to make her insisting he meet her in the woodland seem reasonable in response.

"At least she did not say the note mentioned courting her properly." The admission nearly strangled Chloe.

"I sent that message asking Juliet to wait for me six months ago, long before I knew I'd be accused of treason."

"Indeed?" Needing something to do other than glare at Ross, Chloe pulled a bottle from the bundle of soft cloth for bandages, and yanked out the stopper. The astringent odor of witch hazel released between them like an invisible cloud. "I am supposed to believe you after Juliet told me she didn't receive any messages from you until yesterday morning? That just happened to be the day after Deirdre learned of your . . . treason."

Ross stared at her, a look of bewilderment on his face. "I sent the first message a month after I was released from prison."

"An entire month?" Chloe heard the sarcasm in her voice, but, afraid she was going to believe every word he said to her when she wasn't certain she should, she could not stop herself. "Why an entire month?"

"I needed money and a plan for the future and—" Ross bent his head. His dark hair, rough-cut and too long, fell forward, but not far enough to conceal the hint of a flush along his cheekbones. "Did you see any of the men after they were released from the hulks?"

Chloe's stomach churned. She had seen a line of prisoners headed for a transport vessel back to America. The men had been little more than skin and bone, much of the former exposed through the holes in their clothing. They had sported beards and long greasy hair.

Guilt nearly doubling her over with a pain in her middle, she stared at the toes of her walking boots peeking from beneath the hem of her skirt. "I saw some men one day while sailing on the Thames."

"Then you understand why I would stay away at first." Ross pressed his fingers to the bandage around his brow. "We weren't pretty. I couldn't let her see me like that. So I went to France to collect the money I had squirreled away there, and spent some time in the South. Sunshine. I wanted to come for her birthday." He looked at her with eyes black with grief.

"Why did you not do so?" Chloe asked with difficulty.

"France was in turmoil, and getting to my money wasn't all that easy." He tugged at the head bandage as though it were too tight. "I wasn't coming here as a pauper. But I thought it was all right. She knew I was coming." He dropped his hand to his thigh and looked at Chloe, his eyes clouded. "How could she say she only received my message yesterday?"

"I have no idea. Perhaps—"

Footfalls sounded in the corridor. Ross glanced at the door and Chloe tensed, wondering if it was her father. He'd likely lock her in her room for being there with Ross against his orders, but not even that likelihood could drag her away. She needed his help too much if she wanted to get her sister home safe and sound.

The footfalls passed, and Ross stood, swayed for a moment, then leaned against a bedpost, arms crossed over a chest that was no longer mere skin and bone. "I got to Le Havre shortly after word of Waterloo reached there. I learned there that a Charleston ship captain was leaving word in all the major French ports that I was needed at home, that my mother was ill. I . . . hadn't heard from my family in nearly a decade, so I had to go. I sent the message to Juliet via a smuggler and said I would call on her on the twenty-fifth of October. I figured that gave me enough time to cross the Atlantic and stay a bit, then come back here.

But finding a ship taking passengers was right difficult." He twisted his lips into the mockery of a smile at the understatement of his words.

"So you looked for a response on the twenty-fourth?"

He turned his head and stared at the lightening sky and autumn-fallow fields beyond the window. "I went to leave her another message saying I would return when I cleared my name. But her response was already there, begging me to meet her." He scrubbed his hands over his face, and his voice emerged muffled from behind his palms. "I know I shouldn't have gone, not with a price on my head, but I didn't want her to think I had abandoned her."

"No, of course not." He seemed so distraught, Chloe's heart softened just a bit—though not enough to stop her from asking the next question. "Were you planning to elope with her?"

His hands dropped to his sides. "No, ma'am, I most assuredly was not. What kind of loose screw do you take me for?"

"You contacted her during the war."

"Not for my own sake until that last time."

Chloe curled her upper lip. "I am quite certain you did not wish to see her at all when she came to play ministering angel to your wounded men."

"They weren't my men. They were yours."

"They were your prisoners you brought here deliberately to contact or impress Juliet with your altruism."

They had been wounded English sailors Ross had pulled from the sea and delivered to the cave where he had made his own recovery rather than take them prisoner. It was an admirable act of philanthropy and dangerous bravery, and Chloe could not stop herself from admiring him for it. Yet her suspicions of why he performed those acts of courage and kindness had stamped down the calf-love she had thought she felt toward him during her visits and correspondences with him while he languished in Dartmoor. He did it to contact Juliet, and that contact with Juliet endangered the Ashford family. They needed no more scandal attached to their name. The Ashfords already walked a fine line with the Crown after Kieran married an American noncombatant prisoner of war during the latest conflict with Deirdre's country. Added to that, Kieran's old nemesis, Freddie Rutledge, did his best to raise suspicions that the Ashfords had helped prisoners escape from Dartmoor Prison. And of course, the Crown knew of Mama spying for the colonies in their revolt against Great Britain thirty-five years earlier.

Papa was right—compared to the Ashfords, the Cornwall Trenerrys' smuggling was nothing. But that did not stop Chloe from wanting to protect her family. On the contrary, she needed to protect them even more, and Ross had endangered all of them when he sent for Juliet.

"You should not have involved Juliet." Remembering she still held the bottle of witch hazel, Chloe soaked a cloth with the pungent tincture and grasped one of his hands. "You know you hoped for a tête-à-tête or more with an impressionable girl." She slapped the wet cloth onto one of his abraded wrists.

He sucked his breath in through his teeth. "Of course I hoped to see her. Her laughter and bright spirit, her warmth kept me sane when the fighting grew intense."

Chloe fixed him with a hard look. "You are aware that if Juliet had been caught committing treason by corresponding with you, you would have gotten your revenge on the Ashfords for putting you into Dartmoor."

"Why would I want revenge on the Ashfords?" He knit his brows in seemingly genuine bewilderment. "You all got us out of prison."

"After you suffered for seven months and one of your crewmates died." Chloe laid the witch hazel on the bed and began to wind a soft, clean cloth around Ross's wounded wrist.

He closed his eyes and joined the tincture on the edge of the bed. Color rose up his neck and he stared at a point beyond Chloe's shoulder. "I was careful I never met Juliet so she couldn't be accused of consorting with the enemy, as long as I was a privateer captain, but I did want to make a good impression. I wanted her to remember me with the same regard with which I remembered her."

"She remembered you with too much regard." Chloe again picked up the bottle of witch hazel. "This will sting."

"I found that out the first time." He held up his bandaged left wrist.

"It works well for cleaning a wound." She dabbed at his right wrist with more care. "We can argue about the foolishness of you corresponding with my sister, but that is not bringing Juliet home."

"No, ma'am." His mouth formed a tight, thin line.

"Then let us discuss what will bring her home." Chloe wrapped a cloth around his wrist and held it in place rather than tie it into a bandage. "So tell me why someone wants you as a ransom. How large is the price on your head?"

"I don't know for sure." He gazed past her shoulder. "Great enough someone is going to a lot of trouble to catch me and see me hanged."

"Including kidnapping my sister."

"That shows a measure of desperation." He drew his hand free, rose, and turned his back on her. "It's not the first time they have tried to see me captured. They left all those messages around France how I was needed at home, but when I got to South Carolina, I learned Momma wasn't in the least ill, and I was not welcome. Worse than not welcome."

Chloe studied Ross's rigid back, his shoulders held too straight, his head lifted too high—the posture of a man in firm control of his emotions.

"But you got away."

"I got away. My family helped me escape—to spare them the scandal, of course."

"And you came running straight for Juliet." Chloe felt as unyielding as Ross appeared.

"I came to England for other reasons, but I delivered a new message because of having sent the previous one."

"Ah, yes, the disappearing message." Chloe began to tidy up tincture and cloths and the fallen coverlet. "Why would Juliet claim she did not receive the second message and only found the first one yesterday?"

"Because someone," Ross said in a tight voice, "has kept that message until he could be fairly certain that I'd arrived in England."

"Someone?" Chloe set bandages and tincture on the bedside table. "Who knows you well enough to know of your connection to Juliet?"

"I don't know." His voice was soft, rough.

Hers was rough, but not soft. "Oh yes, you do. You came straight to England after learning you had been accused of treason."

"I said I don't know." He gripped the bedpost, and his knuckles gleamed white.

"Look me in the eye and tell me that, Ross Trenerry."

He looked at the rug beneath his feet—feet in fine woolen stockings. The servants had removed his boots, not just from his feet, but from the chamber, a problem she would have to rectify—after she remedied all the rest of the difficulties of getting Ross away from Bishops Cove.

She stalked around to face him and poked a finger into his chest. "Why will you not tell me who you believe has Juliet?"

Ross raised his head and his eyes were hard. "I've been accused of a crime I didn't commit. So I'm not about to toss out names without proof."

"But you have a good notion who it is."

"I have only suspicions."

"How?"

"He was my British informant, the true traitor in this game."

"A British traitor?" Chloe nearly choked on the words.

Ross inclined his head. "He kept me informed of merchant convoys heading out of the Channel."

Chloe felt sick. "How did he inform you?"

"We met on Guernsey at regular intervals."

"Guernsey, of course."

Chloe wanted to snatch hold of Ross's hand and race off to the Channel island at once. "Guernsey," Ross repeated the name. "That's why I think my accomplice took Juliet."

"But why?"

"He needs to get rid of me before I can reveal his identity."

"But you said you do not know his identity."

"I don't for sure. He always wore a disguise, a different one each time. And we met in a dim place so I could never see him clearly. His voice never changed, though. It was likely a pretense as well, but it never changed. More cockney than society, and high-pitched . . . I don't know how to explain it, but I do know I would recognize it anywhere." In contrast to her, Ross seemed perfectly calm as he rounded the bed to pick up the silver coffeepot, touch the side as though testing its temperature, which could be no more than barely warm by now, then shooting a jet of dark liquid into the earthenware mug provided on the tray—servant's dishes for the prisoner.

That Ross was still a prisoner calmed Chloe, reminding her of what they needed to do despite broad daylight.

"How can you find a man whose name you do not know and whose face you have never seen clearly?" She managed to pose the question in a reasonable tone.

"I managed to learn a few things about him over the year and a half we worked together. And he will be on Guernsey, we now know."

"We now hope." Chloe began to pace around the room grinding her toes into the center of the flowers on the carpet. "Without a name, without a clear description, you may never find him."

"And he may not be the one who laid the information against me." Ross gripped the coffee mug with both hands. "But I can begin by getting Juliet home without getting me captured."

"Yes, finding Juliet is our first priority." Chloe silently blessed him for his ability to think when her thoughts ran in a dozen different directions. "We can concentrate on why you were accused of treason later. First we need to get you away before my father turns you over to your countrymen."

"We?" Ross raised one eyebrow. "Who is we?"

"Us. You and me." Chloe took a deep breath, then plunged. "I am going with you."

~~~

After urging Ross to eat some of the bread and butter and then rest, Chloe descended the stairs and entered the winter parlor, where her mother and Deirdre sat beside a crackling fire. Mama had embroidery in her lap she wasn't stitching, and Deirdre stared into the flames rather than at the book in her lap. Steam puffed from the spout of a silver teapot, filling the room with the scent of jasmine, Juliet's favorite tea, Juliet's scent. Mama would want to surround herself with Juliet's favorite things. No doubt the book in Deirdre's lap was one of the novels Juliet read incessantly.

Chloe wanted to assure them that Juliet was probably all right. Surely the kidnappers would not harm her if they expected to exchange her for Ross in a week. But that might be a naïve presumption on Chloe's part. From what she had learned during the war of how prisoners were treated, she knew men who had been reasonable one day could turn vicious the next when granted enough power over another being. But her reasons for keeping quiet about the ransom note remained.

Not sure she could be in the same room with Mama and Deirdre and not blurt out the truth, Chloe hesitated too long on the threshold.

Mama glanced up and waved her forward. "Do not stand in the doorway and let all the cold air in. Come join us for some tea while we wait for word."

Chloe closed the door, then crossed the blue-and-gold Wilton carpet to drop to her knees beside her mother's chair. "This is all my fault,

Mama." She laid her head against Mama's arm. "I should have told you Juliet met Mr. Trenerry and developed a *tendre* for him."

"Yes, you should have." Phoebe stroked Chloe's hair. "It's not your responsibility to persuade her not to get into scrapes nor to go along with her. Nor, I should add, to protect us. We are not old and frail yet."

"I thought I could stop her from corresponding with that man . . ." Chloe sighed. "I told her it was treason. But she had spent enough time with him to think she was in love and . . . I failed."

She'd done a great deal of that in the past year—made plans that seemed sensible when she created them, then went awry when she executed them.

"A good thing Kieran's out searching for Juliet," Deirdre said from the other side of the hearth. "I'd hate to think what he might do to Ross with him helpless." She shook her head. "Why Kieran despises Ross so much, I can't comprehend."

"He never forgot that you were willing to risk your life and the life of your baby to get Ross out of prison."

"But he got him out himself," Deirdre said.

Chloe lifted her head. "Because he needed to show you he loved you."

"You'd think he could have found something less drastic." Deirdre smiled, her strong features going soft.

Chloe's heart ached. If only she could find someone who loved her like Kieran loved Deirdre—or someone she herself could love with such devotion.

An image of Ross flashed through her mind. She shoved it away. Ross wanted Juliet, not her, and Chloe would help him get her back for him to court, as she had helped Kieran and Deirdre realize they loved one another. Sometimes Chloe feared the man she was supposed to love had died at Waterloo or Trafalgar, or on a convict ship bound for Australia.

Her lips twisted into a self-deprecating sneer, and she bowed her head. "This is all my fault. I told her about how Ro—how Mr. Trenerry ran back to save his crewmate who had fallen behind during the escape. With all the novels she reads, she thought that wonderfully heroic and brave." She caught a tear on her fingertip and flicked it away, as she had tried to flick away her own opinion of Ross's actions. "And I did not notice her following me into the cave. I should have noticed." Her sleepless night of wrestling with whether or not to tell Papa about the ransom note catching up with her, Chloe struggled not to turn into a watering pot.

Mama rested her hand on Chloe's head. "I can't say I approve of you helping Mr. Trenerry on your own as you did, but you couldn't leave him there to languish."

"Kieran helped some." Chloe got hold of her emotions and smiled at Deirdre. "Though he was rather preoccupied with his wife."

"Not to mention how the military was watching him." Deirdre ruffled the pages of the book in her lap. "Sometimes one gets away with far more as a woman than one can as a man."

"You all get away with far more than you should." The sweetness of Mama's voice, her slurred American accent so like Ross's, was forever incapable of sounding harsh. "I don't know why our children—and that includes you, Deirdre—think they have to sneak about like criminals. Do you all not trust us? Did we expect too much of you that you must rebel?"

"Mama Phoebe," Deirdre protested.

"Perhaps you have not expected enough." Chloe rubbed her aching eyes. "You always treated us so much like we were perfect children, we were afraid to tell you we are no such thing."

"Neither Phoebe nor Garrett are fools," Deirdre said. "You'd think they'd know what rapscallions you are."

Chloe made herself smile. "No sense making them think the worst of us either."

Mama touched Chloe's cheek. "We could never do that. If Juliet was unhappy about marrying Mr. Vernell, she didn't need to elope."

"She would have happily wed Mr. Vernell," Chloe said, "if Mr. Trenerry had not returned."

"And he's a fool for being so besotted with a female he would risk coming here to see her," Deirdre said. "Now he'll end up in the hands of a Charleston jury, and it'll go badly for him. They don't much like him in South Carolina."

"What a sad man to have so many enemies," Mama said.

"He seems to have made enemies for a good reason back home." The instant Mama and Deirdre stared at her with upraised eyebrows, Chloe realized she should not have defended Ross, but she brazened out the moment. "Regardless of what he may or may not have done during the war, he did free those slaves, and who can but think that is something good in the man?"

At sixteen, Ross and a cousin had taken upon themselves the mission of freeing a number of slaves from a South Carolina plantation. Due to the loss of "property," the plantation owner had been unable to sell some of the men and women to pay several debts and had gone bankrupt. Ross's father had disowned him. Ross had sought refuge on a merchantman with Daniel MacKenzie, the captain and Deirdre's father.

"Of course there is good in the man." Deirdre slammed the book onto a side table. "He sacrificed a great deal for my sake, even for Kieran's sake, when we were on Bermuda. But he also holds a great deal of resentment about how South Carolinians treated him."

"Then why would he fight for America?" The question burst from Chloe before she thought she might sound as though she were defending him.

The consequence was raised eyebrows from Mama and Deirdre.

"In the last war," Mama said, "most men became privateers to make money from taking British merchants, not necessarily patriotism."

"But Mr. Trenerry—" Chloe snapped her teeth together.

She could not defend him on that score. He had told Juliet he was quitting the dangerous game of privateering because he had made enough money and therefore was no longer her country's enemy. She was glad she had destroyed the missive. Its contents were more likely to condemn him than defend him if it landed in the wrong hands.

"He never said anything good about England either," Chloe concluded.

"But if they paid him enough to help root out privateers," Deirdre said, "he might have . . ." She brushed her hand across her eyes. "I don't know. None of this seems right for the man I called friend."

"So terribly sad." Mama reached for her teacup and cradled it in both hands. "He was a good friend to you, Deirdre."

"I always said he was trustworthy." Deirdre shot to her feet. "But now I learn how he endangered all of us by coming ashore during the war." She stalked across the parlor to one of the long windows overlooking the gardens. "Now I learn he intended to elope with Juliet, when he surely knew he had a price on his head."

Chloe hesitated only a moment before coming to a decision and to blazes with the consequences of Mama and Deirdre learning she had talked with Ross at length. "He had no intention of eloping with Juliet before or after he had a price on his head."

"And how would you know this?" Mama and Deirdre asked together.

Chloe shifted on a chair that had suddenly become as uncomfortable as one carved of stone. "I talked to him this morning. He only came to meet her last night because she begged him to, and he could not resist seeing her again." She swallowed against a tightness in her chest. "I believe he truly cares for her."

Deirdre spun to face her, and Mama's eyes widened.

Chloe's cheeks heated. "Both of you know that love makes one do foolish things."

Mama and Deirdre both smiled.

Deirdre's faded at once. "It doesn't justify bringing danger to her, dash it all!" She slammed her fist into the window frame. "I should be out there searching."

"It wouldn't be right," Mama said. "For the men to be walking around with guns this time of year is understandable. If you put on breeches and did so, the neighbors would wonder."

To the best of their ability, they were keeping Juliet's abduction a secret. If the countryside found out, her reputation would be ruined. Family friend or not, Vernell wouldn't be able to marry her and still maintain respect from his fellow members of the House of Commons. A man in government seeking a knighthood needed to maintain his reputation, and that meant having a wife above reproach.

But would he want Juliet now? Doubtful, since she'd made her preferences clear.

"Can we trust the servants not to talk?" Chloe asked.

"When they owe their lives, let alone their livelihoods, to Papa Garrett?" Deirdre responded.

"Of course we can trust—" Mama broke off at a tap on the door. "Yes?"

Addison opened the door. "I'm sorry to disturb you, milady, but there's an American and some other gentleman here to see his lordship."

Chloe bolted to her feet. "Who?"

Addison looked at Mama, then Deirdre. "A Mr. Beasley."

"Beasley himself?" Chloe pressed her hands to her middle. "The attaché?"

"For prisoners," Deirdre said.

"I've sent someone to find Lord Tyne," Addison said, "but Mr. Beasley seems . . . agitated, so I thought he shouldn't be kept waiting alone."

"Then I must see him." Mama rose with the slow stiffness of a woman ten years her senior. "Make him comfortable in the estate office. Take him coffee and assure him someone will be with him shortly."

Addison bowed acknowledgment, then limped out.

Mama smoothed the sleeves of her jade-striped spencer. "I'm not certain he'll find me an acceptable substitute, since I'm an expatriate American."

"I'll go with you," Deirdre said, "though the man doesn't like me much after all those letters I sent him about the terrible conditions at Dartmoor."

"What will you tell him?" Chloe swallowed a sourness in her throat. "I mean, Mr. Beasley cannot take Mr. Trenerry with him. The man was injured last night."

On their way to the door, Mama and Deirdre paused.

"If he wants to take Mr. Trenerry away," Mama said, "we have no choice but to let him. A peer of the realm can't harbor an American criminal."

Deirdre crumpled her gray merino gown in her hands. "I may ask Mr. Beasley to allow Ross to recover here for a day or two, but I doubt he will listen to me either. After all, I married an Englishman during the war."

"As though he has proven to be so—what is the word you used, Mama?—patriotic toward America." Chloe curled her upper lip with contempt for the man who was supposed to see to the welfare of American prisoners of war. Through his mismanagement, many of the prisoners had died in a prison riot months after the peace treaty was signed.

"No need for you to come, too," Mama said to Chloe.

Chloe counted on that. She needed to get to Ross. If he was going to escape, the time was now.

She waited until Deirdre and Mama started down the main staircase, then slipped into the corridor. She had one foot on the step when she heard a familiar voice in the entry hall, a familiar, English voice.

She spun on her heel and rushed to the balustrade. She was not mistaken. Freddie Rutledge stood beside a stranger in top hat and caped greatcoat.

Her nails dug into the carved railing with such force she feared she might wrench it from the floor, as she stared at the man who had caused so much trouble for Kieran, the man who had come too close to killing her brother in a poorly executed duel. How dare he stand there all elegant blond good looks, bowing to Mama and Deirdre as though he were acceptable *ton*!

How did not matter. She needed to get to Ross. Yet she could not turn away from the tableau in the entryway.

"My lady Tyne, you are gracious to allow me into your lovely home." Rutledge's voice dripped practiced charm.

As if Mama had any choice.

Rutledge oozed on. "It is a terrible time, I know, and I have taken advantage of Mr. Beasley coming to see this prisoner to insinuate myself into your presence."

"My daughter-in-law said you might arrive." Forever gracious, Mama inclined her head.

Deirdre crossed her arms over her middle. "This is not a good time for personal discussions."

"I am aware of such, Lady Ripon, but I feared rejection." Rutledge bowed his head in a humility Chloe doubted sincere, for all he sounded and looked contrite at that moment.

"We can discuss the strife between our families later, Mr. Rutledge." Mama turned toward the other man, who yanked his hat from his head to reveal a flush creeping up his face. "Mr. Beasley? Please come into the estate office and have some refreshment while we await Lord Tyne's return. You, too, Mr. Rutledge."

"Thank you, ma'am," the American said.

"Thank you, my lady." Rutledge glanced from Mama, to Deirdre, then tilted his head back just enough to flash a grin at Chloe.

Mortified he had caught her spying on them, she swung away from the balustrade, gathered up her skirt, and bolted up the steps. She must get to Ross's room at once, but first she detoured to her own chamber to collect her pistol.

∽

"You expect me to escape in broad daylight?" The scorn in Ross's voice suggested he believed she had gone mad.

"I have to." Chloe handed Ross his coat and a pair of Kieran's old boots. "Beasley is below."

"Devil take it!" Ross swung his legs off the bed. When he stood, he wavered, and his face paled.

Chloe caught his arm. It felt firm beneath her hand, the muscles strong, supple, but he had been struck on the head. "We'll never escape like this. I will have to hide you in my room."

"Then your daddy can geld me for going near you, too," Ross muttered. "Thank you, my lady, but I'll take my chances with a Charleston court."

"If no one kills you before you get that far." Chloe headed for the door, still clutching his arm, compelling him to accompany her. "My room is safe. If they search the house, they will find me there alone and not look further."

"With no other choice but to go to prison again, I suppose I must admit it's worth the attempt." He freed his arm from her hold and clasped her shoulder.

Chloe thought he needed to do so for support. Yet the sensation staggered her. She thought she had broad shoulders for a woman. The size of his hand made her feel delicate.

She opened the door. Someone was coming. More than one person. She heard the murmur of voices and the tramp of many feet on the uncarpeted stairs. Papa or Kieran must have returned already and was bringing the American up to Ross.

"Quick." She darted across the corridor and flung open another bedchamber door. "In here."

Ross followed her into the chamber. Cold and dark with the draperies drawn, the room reeked of too much lavender sprinkled over the shrouded furniture to keep the moths away.

Chloe's nose twitched and began to tickle. She held her breath, willing back the sneeze as she closed the door a heartbeat before the footfalls and voices rounded the corner.

"A neat trap," Ross said. "Do I hold you hostage now?"

"No, but—" Chloe gave him an uncertain glance. "I hope your head for heights is up to climbing across the roof to get to my room."

"I'm a sailor. I'm used to heights."

"That is to our benefit." Chloe dashed to the window and released the catch.

Cold damp air swirled through the opening. She hoped no one in the hall felt the draft beneath the door. She hoped Ross wouldn't fall on his poor head and save the Americans the cost of a rope. She didn't have time for hope.

With only an instant's thought to modesty, she kilted up her skirts and stepped onto the low windowsill. "Follow me. And do not look down."

The latter was an admonition to herself as much as to Ross, for thirty feet below the window lay the flagstone terrace. Less than thirty inches to the right, however, ivy grew thick and strong around a downspout, coiling like a spiral ladder to the ground and to the roof. Chloe grasped the vine with her right hand and swung herself against the ivy-covered spout. With her knees, she gripped the makeshift ladder until her feet, agile in kid slippers, found toeholds. The lead pipe creaked against its moorings, but it would hold.

Her hand threatened not to hold her. When she grasped an upper limb, her wound opened. Blood soaked through the bandage and her sleeve like water through gauze. Dizziness threatened to weaken her, made her nauseated. Her fingers wanted to let go, ease the pain.

Below her, she heard Ross Trenerry's muttered curse, then the click of the window latch. She didn't need to look down to know that he was balanced on the two-foot-wide window ledge with little to hold onto, unable to go farther if she remained where she was.

She shoved her right hand under the coiled branch, then reached up with her left hand for another hold. Her feet followed. Right foot. Left foot. Her pistol banged against the pipe like an alarm.

Now her hand was below the wound. Blood ran down her forearm onto her fingers, onto the pipe. The cold lead grew slippery. She lost her grip. For a breath, she hung unbalanced, her left arm hung limp at her side.

"Will that spout hold us both?" Ross asked in a conversational tone.

"It should." Despite the pain, Chloe forced her arm upward.

The wound isn't that bad. Not that bad at all.

It felt as though the knife had severed half her upper arm, though she knew it hurt and bled worse than it was. She managed to catch a handhold and not cry out.

Below her, the pipe shifted, groaned.

She moved faster. The blood flowed faster. Two pipes wavered before her eyes, and she had to swallow down bile.

Another six feet to go. It looked like a dozen. Somewhere a man shouted, and another man answered from farther away inside the house. Chloe gritted her teeth and kept going. She needed two hands to grasp the gutter and haul herself over the coaming and onto the slates of the roof. A sob escaped her lips as she used her forearms to support her weight. She needed to reach across the gutter and grasp the edge of the stone coping that stopped the slates from sliding off. Her right arm obeyed her command to reach. Her left arm did not. It lay in the gutter as sticky and useless as last season's leaves.

"Lady Chloe?" Ross Trenerry was close beneath her. "You're bleeding."

"I will be all right in a moment. I need a moment—"

They didn't have a moment. She had to move. Now. Before someone saw them clinging to the wall like the ivy.

With a groan, she flung her right arm toward the next handhold. The momentum dragged her into the gutter as far as her waist. Her feet lost their purchase on the ivy, and she hung by fingers and breasts with her feet swinging free, useless.

Then Ross had one hand on her ankle. He set her foot on something sturdy—his shoulder. He set her other foot on his shoulder and raised himself higher, lifting her up and over the stone coaming and onto the slanting but sturdy foundation of the roof. He lifted himself up beside her, and she set out again, climbing the slates to the roof peak, then dipped where one wing met the other.

On the far side of the crown, Chloe sprawled on her belly. Ross subsided next to her. Pain pulsed through her arm. The roar of blood through her ears was all she could hear.

Then Ross leaned over and spoke into her ear. "If you truly intend to get me away, we can't stay up here. Someone's bound to come up here searching."

"Yes, but I think they will come here last." Chloe pushed herself to a sitting position. "They will come through the attics, and that is difficult since all our servants are lame in some way and my father is not a young man."

But she had to consider Vernell and Kieran. Deirdre, too, for that matter. But Kieran and Vernell were out looking for Juliet, and Deirdre might stay with Mama.

"There are two ways to get onto the roof from the attics," Chloe continued. "They should come out both windows at the same time to prevent escape, so we have to—"

Voices rose from below, surely too near to rise from the ground floor. Then Papa's voice rang out from farther away, but with his words as distinct as they must have been when he'd issued orders from his quarterdeck thirty years earlier. "I want a man at every door and low window. Kieran and Vernell will flush him out from inside the house."

Chloe moaned. "They all should not have gotten back to the house so soon."

"Apparently they have." Ross looked as tense as Chloe felt. "I suggest you get back into the house as fast as you can and pretend . . . pretend I abducted you, but you got away. That will preserve your reputation or any talk you helped me."

"But they will catch you."

"I can hide in a house this size."

"I am not going to abandon you yet." Chloe pushed herself to her knees. "We have to get into the attics before they do. There are four rooms and so many places I know of for you to hide, they could search for us for hours."

Ross stood and rested one hand on Chloe's shoulder. "You should abandon me here. If you're caught with me, you'll get into trouble you don't deserve."

"You're in trouble you do not deserve."

"I was the fool who came to see Juliet, though I knew better." For a moment, he looked so sad, so lost, Chloe wanted to wrap her arms around him and reassure him all would be well.

But things were far from well, and she stiffened her spine. "I am doing this so we can all see Juliet again."

"But, my lady—"

"We do not have time to argue." Chloe made her tone brisk. "The stairs down to the house are closest to the north window, so we will head that way."

Chloe turned north across the flat, central roof, walking as though she were full of confidence. She slipped her hand into her pocket to feel the assuring hardness of her pistol.

She halted at the screech of hinges ahead of them.

"Back." She spun toward the south.

Ross was already turning, leading the way back. "Where?" He flung the word over his shoulder. "I don't see—"

Chloe glanced back to see what had stopped Ross and swayed against him so he had to wrap one arm around her.

"Hiding behind a woman, Trenerry?" Henry Vernell asked, as he stepped out of an attic doorway and onto the roof.

Chapter 5

Devonshire, England
Thursday, 26 October 1815
8:35 a.m.

*R*oss stared at the man in front of them through narrowed eyes. "If it's the only way to make you English listen—"

Chloe shoved her elbow into his solar plexus.

He jerked back, slipped on wet leaves, and had to throw out his arm to catch his balance, the arm he'd wrapped around Chloe's waist. He caught hold of her arm. But she jerked away, leaving him with his hand outstretched and his palm sticky with her blood. She'd been wounded, probably because of him.

He felt sick with guilt, but in a flash knew how he could help her, how he could ensure no one blamed her for his escape from the bedchamber, to the roof.

He held up his hand so the frosty Englishman could see the blood, and he made himself smile. "I made her come with me."

The man's upper lip drew back. "Why, you barbaric—" He leveled his pistol at Ross's head.

Ross locked both arms around Chloe so she couldn't jab him again. "That horse pistol isn't very accurate, mister. Dare you risk her ladyship's head?"

"He will not," a voice said from behind, "but I have your whole back for a target."

Ross sighed as he imagined iron bands already clamping around his wrists and ankles. Or maybe just a rope around his neck. He might have been able to bluff his way past this wiry stranger, but not the man behind him. The man behind him was no stranger.

"Let go of my sister, Mr. Trenerry," Kieran Ashford said, "or I will cripple you at the least."

"Just release my right arm." Chloe spoke so softly Ross wasn't sure he heard her.

"Trenerry." Kieran's pronunciation of the name emerged like a pistol shot.

"I'd rather you shoot to kill," Ross said. "Better than pris—"

"My arm," Chloe screamed. Then she raised her knee, visible with her skirt kilted up, and kicked.

Her heel caught Ross high on the inside of his thigh. His leg buckled and he went down, dragging Chloe with him. She was free in an instant and scrambling to her feet with a pistol in her hand. Her right hand. The one she'd wanted him to free. Ross wanted to hold his head in his hands and laugh like a Bedlamite. Or maybe he should just turn himself over to Kieran Ashford. He'd be safer with the brother than he was with the sister.

Who the deuce was he to think she needed his help in any way? She held a ladylike pistol pointed at his head, too. Unlike Vernell and Kieran, Chloe's pistol was at close enough range to be very accurate.

"He is *my* prisoner," Chloe said.

Ross glanced from Vernell to Kieran and clenched his fists against a shiver that ran up his arms.

"Not now that we are here." Vernell cast Ross a glance sharp enough to cut an anchor cable. "We will take him down to your father and Mr. Beasley."

"I do not think we will." Kieran's speculative tone drew Ross's full attention.

The corners of Kieran's mouth were tight, but he held his head cocked to one side, and his eyes were dancing.

Suddenly weary from three years of fighting, running, and hiding, Ross wondered if surrender might not be a welcome rest now. If only a noose didn't lie at the end of that rest.

He could overpower Lady Chloe in a heartbeat, but the other two would gun him down even faster. Time to wait his chance and then run—again—leaving Lady Chloe and her misguided notions of helping him behind.

Time to watch Kieran Ashford, Viscount Ripon, and see what game he was playing.

"Since he seems to have coerced her into something," Kieran was saying, "I think perhaps we should allow my sister the privilege of delivering the prisoner to his countrymen."

"But she is a helpless female."

Helpless? With a pistol inches from his nose? Ross nearly laughed aloud.

"I am scarcely helpless, Mr. Vernell." Chloe moved the pistol even closer to Ross's nose.

Ross met her gaze. Her lids at half-mast, she appeared intense. The hands holding the pistol were steady. Lady Chloe Ashford was anything but helpless.

"Jezebel," he mouthed.

She smiled and grazed the pistol muzzle against Ross's nose and glanced toward the stranger. "Get out of our way, Mr. Vernell."

"Lady Chloe—" Vernell scowled. "If he overpowered you once, with you having a pistol, how can you manage to get this man all the way below stairs?"

"I will accompany her, of course," Kieran said.

Deciding that getting away was best for all the Ashfords, Ross surged to his full height, batting the pistol out of the way. Chloe staggered back. Ross didn't wait to see if she fell. With the hope that she did not, he sprang for the sloped side of the roof. A shot rang out. He went down. No jolt. No pain. No wound. Broken slate a foot from his head. Reflex from battle had served him well. If armed, he'd have rolled and shot back. He rolled, but only to see who had fired.

The too-self-possessed Englishman. Smoke nearly the same sooty gray as the sky drifted from the muzzle of his pistol. Chloe and Kieran stared at him as though he were the criminal.

"You nearly got him, Mr. Vernell." Chloe sounded more accusatory than admiring. "You will bring everyone running up—"

"Chloe." Kieran cut her off.

Vernell gave her a bewildered look. "Trenerry is an escaping prisoner."

No, he wasn't escaping. He was lying there like a sailor caught in the rigging, not trying to get away at all. He needed to move while Chloe argued with Vernell. Vernell didn't have another shot, and Chloe seemed intent on helping the escape no matter how Ross tried to get her out of it. But Ross didn't know about Kieran and others, who would surely come if they'd heard the blast.

Ross began climbing again.

"Do not," Kieran called to him.

Ross swung over the peak of the roof.

"Stop him." Vernell's voice rose three notes. "Ripon, the man knows who's taken your sister."

"And shooting him will get me answers?" Kieran's voice dripped with sarcasm. "Trenerry, you are not going to get free going down the ivy. We have men stationed along the terrace."

Ross reached the gutter and looked down. The height was no difficulty for him, but the size of the blunderbuss cradled in the hands of a man on the flagstones below brought back his headache. He'd faced smaller cannons in battle.

Behind him, footfalls scraped against the slates. Ross glanced back to see Kieran poised on the roof peak. No pistol pointed at him, just an expression guaranteed to freeze molten iron. The slates beneath Ross felt like that frozen iron.

"You have a better chance with Chloe and me than him." Kieran spoke so softly Ross barely heard him. "Come back."

"Between Scylla and Charybdis," Ross muttered.

Kieran grinned and tilted his head to one side, the side, Ross knew, where he'd lost part of one ear in a duel and now wore his hair long to hide the scar. "I told you two years ago to leave my family alone. But now you are involved with my sisters."

"And you want my nutmegs for breakfast."

"Only if I want my wife to take mine."

Ross stared at Kieran. "Deirdre—"

Kieran made a silencing gesture with his left hand. With his right, he raised his pistol to aim at Ross. Speaking loud enough for anyone within a quarter mile to hear, he said, "You are safe with the Ashfords, Mr. Trenerry."

Ross snorted. "When you have to turn me over to my so-loving countrymen? How much of a fool do you think I am?"

"One who allowed a female to get you into this fix in the first place."

"A female who needs my knowledge to get her free."

Telling his nemesis that much was a risk, but Ross needed to take it, needed the advantage of surprise.

Unfortunately, Kieran showed no surprise. "We guessed as much. The circumstances of Juliet's disappearance were too coincidental not to involve you."

"And you think I will give you useful information for finding her if you turn me over for hanging?"

"For trial."

Ross emitted a bark of mirthless laughter. "I've been back to Charleston. I have already been condemned there without a trial. And even if they will show justice to me, I can scarcely assist you from across the ocean."

"Which is why my father is negotiating with Beasley at this very moment, trying to persuade him you are too injured to be moved."

"Considering I managed to climb onto your roof, Mr. Beasley isn't about to believe your father."

A pounding in his head made him doubt the wisdom of the climb—or any other actions he had taken in the past two days.

He pressed his fingers against his temples. Tied or not, that bed he had awakened upon suddenly seemed like a blessed haven.

"Beasley will listen to my father." Pure Ashford arrogance dripped from the son and heir to the earldom.

Ross choked on a sudden urge to laugh. If only he thought Kieran Ashford was joking, he might have laughed out loud. Ross had been raised in privilege, but nothing like these Englishmen.

"I can't take the risk he won't listen," he said.

"And we cannot take the risk someone will think we helped you escape." Kieran held out his hand as though offering friendship. "Come peacefully. My father has intimidated greater men than the American attaché into bowing to his will."

Ross nodded, fully ready to play the acquiescent prisoner. He had learned to do that in the hulks, as he had not learned it at Dartmoor. One received fewer blows if one pretended to be cowed.

Cautiously, he headed back up the roof. When he was far enough to see over the peak, he caught a glimpse of Vernell clutching his pistol like a club, wearing an expression of white-lipped fury. Chloe's face was so void of expression she was probably hiding a number of schemes behind her pretty face. With her skirt still tucked into her sash, she exposed some assets no man not her husband should be privileged to view.

On their climb to the roof, he'd been too occupied with the spots of blood she left behind on the ivy to notice more than the fact that she wore shoes of a leather so thin they were little more than gloves for the feet. Now he had a moment to take in the sight of her knees glowing a pale ivory above white stockings smoothed over nicely curved calves leading to dainty ankles.

Ross smiled at the sight. He knew he risked getting shoved off the roof for what he was about to say, but considering how he was trapped, he figured it was a risk worth taking to get away from all Ashfords in Devonshire, to get to the one he wanted to find on Guernsey. "If I had a sister with legs like that, I'd lock her up."

"The deuce!" Kieran swung toward his sister.

Ross slammed his shoulder into the other man. Then he bolted, sliding down the slates, landing hard on the flat central roof. His leg, bruised where Chloe had kicked him, spasmed. His head throbbed. But he ran away from the two Englishmen and one Englishwoman and toward the open attic window. Shouts rose behind him. Three voices at once. Maybe a fourth? A thud sounded loud enough it should have shaken the roof. Someone cried out. A feminine cry. Chloe hurt? He hoped not. He didn't look back to see. She had her brother to protect her. Ross needed to protect himself.

The instant he spun toward the window, a shot blasted between the roof peaks. Ross dove through the window. He landed in a chamber packed with enough chests and trunks to make a merchantman's hold look sparsely laden. Narrow passageways wound between the bounty. Too narrow. Too many passages for him to move with any haste. Someone—several someones—were surely right behind him. They could each pick a route and corner him like a smuggler's cutter in a cove, trap him as those two English schooners had trapped him a year earlier.

Footfalls pounded toward the open window. He needed to move, pick a route and commit himself to that direction. They could play hide-and-seek until he found the exit and maybe a path down to freedom.

He headed down one of the warrens between stacked trunks and cumbersome furniture. Surely one of these pieces offered a hiding place, a way to deter pursuit.

The footfalls drew nearer, quick and light. Chloe with her lovely long legs—legs as long as those tall Juliet would also have. Chloe might still be bent on helping him.

He couldn't take the risk his nearest pursuer wasn't Chloe. The man Kieran had called Vernell was tall and wiry. And he had been quick to shoot. If he'd taken the time to reload, he might try that again, despite the Ashfords' protestations.

Ross increased his pace. Darkness closed around him. The odors of dust, mice, and oiled wood clogged the air, his nose, his mouth. He had to move slowly, grope his way between boxes as small as jewel cases and as large as coffins. His hunters would also have to go slowly. On second thought, not Chloe. Not Kieran. They would know the attic.

A thud landed on the floor behind Ross. He quickened his pace. His shin connected with a steel-banded trunk. Teeth gritted, he slowed again.

The footfalls behind him did not. No, they were no longer behind him. Their owner had taken a different passage through the maze of household castoffs. Now more footfalls rang on the floorboards, the heavy tread of men's boots. Voices rumbled from behind him, from ahead of him. Others had arrived, no doubt brought up to the attic by Vernell's shot or the man who had seen Ross from the terrace.

A chill racing to his marrow, he leaned against a cupboard, his teeth gritted to stop them from chattering. The tramp of feet on wooden planks at both ends of his passageway sounded like those of the guards tramping the upper deck of the prison hulk. The smooth wood beneath his hands turned into the cold, slimy beam they'd chained him to in the lowest portion of the hold.

His gut told him to run. His good sense reminded him he had nowhere to run. Regardless of Chloe's, and maybe even Kieran's, good intentions to help him, they couldn't protect him from capture now that others had arrived.

He needed to hide. Hiding might trap him. On the other hand, the action might give him the time he needed to elude them enough to slip past pursuit.

Another thud closer at hand, this one followed by a feminine cry of distress, vibrated the floor beneath him, as though someone had knocked over a heavy chest. Men called to her.

"Are you all right, Lady Chloe?"

"Yes, just clumsy. It is dark in here."

She sounded almost atop him.

Ross slid his hand along the cupboard door until he found the handle. It was more a hasp that fitted over a ring. A lock hung from the ring, but it wasn't closed, so he could get inside, provided the cupboard was empty. But so could anyone else.

He opened it anyway. He had no time to find someplace better. The hinges made no noise. Dry air smelling of cedar and lavender wafted over him, then engulfed him as he pushed inside amid billowing folds of silk and velvet that sighed as if in protest to his intrusion.

His hand shook on the edge of the door. Not far off, someone sneezed—hard. Footfalls drew nearer, and he couldn't get the door shut.

With it open, he could breathe and find a hint of lesser darkness. With it closed, he was a little safer from capture.

The light footfalls drew nearer. Too near. If he moved the door, the shift would draw attention to the armoire. He may have heard the clothes rustle. She sneezed again, lightly, delicately, directly on the other side of the door.

"Chloe, where are you?" The rich tones of the Earl of Tyne rang through the attic.

Ross held his breath.

"Over here, Papa." Chloe sneezed again.

Ross began to push at the door. He could take her hostage, use her for certain to gain his freedom.

The idea that doing so made him a felon indeed made him hesitate. In that half beat of time, Chloe shoved on the door, forcing Ross to press his back against the rear wall of the cupboard. "No one is here." She pushed the door shut.

Silk swathed around him like a shroud as the hasp snicked over its ring, locking him inside.

Chloe leaned against the armoire, wishing she hadn't discarded her shawl so she could hide her wound. She wanted no one to see it and believe Ross had truly been the one who injured her. He should not have lied about it on the roof, though she understood why he had—he was protecting her from consequences of helping him escape from the bedchamber, wanted her family to believe he had coerced her into helping him. If no one saw her wound, she could say he lied and the blood was his own. Ross did not need stabbing her to be added to his list of crimes.

"Are you all right, Chloe?"

She looked at her father striding toward her along the passage, a lantern in one upraised hand, and wondered how she could tell him one more lie. She should announce that Ross was in the cupboard behind her, that she'd closed the hasp to keep him there, and that they could get Juliet back if they turned Ross over to the kidnapper. And she would have betrayed Ross yet again. She could have his death on her conscience forever.

Chloe took a deep breath of the lavender still lingering in the air so she would sneeze again and could retreat behind her handkerchief. "Other than the way lavender always makes me sneeze, Papa."

"He did not hurt you?" Garrett's hand tightened with a gentle squeeze. "Vernell said—"

"Vernell says too much," Chloe muttered. "Mr. Trenerry lied about hurting me."

"But you have blood on you."

"His blood." Chloe stared at the spots of blood and grime on the skirts Kieran had made her loosen from her sash so that the fabric fell to her shoes. "His blood."

"Hmm. The ropes, I suppose." Garrett turned as Kieran came around the end of a row of boxes. "No one?"

"I was certain he came into the attic," Kieran said, "but he may have kept going and gone down the side of the house. There are the balconies on this side. With everyone coming up, he might have done it undetected."

"Be damned." Garrett scowled. "You and Vernell take the men back downstairs. Chloe, go to your room and take time to change your dress. Half of an hour."

"Yes, sir." Chloe edged past him, keeping her injured left arm away from his line of sight.

She had half of an hour to clean and redress her wound, change her gown, and prepare herself to meet her father. Heaven only knew when she would be able to release Ross from the cupboard.

Did he have enough air in there?

Chloe glanced back, hoping to catch Kieran's eye. He was not looking her way.

Her father was. For a heartbeat, he held her gaze with a tender, loving expression that made her heart squeeze until it felt as tight in her chest as a walnut in its shell.

He was not angry with her.

With the knowledge that he had every reason to be furious, had enough reason to lock her in her bedchamber for a year of solitary confinement, she turned and fled down the stairs to her room.

No one waited for her there. Relieved, she poured water from the pitcher into the basin. The water was cold now, but it would do. She removed her ruined gown and petticoat, and began washing dirt and blood from her skin.

She'd torn her stockings. A long, red scrape showed through a rent in the silk. It looked dreadful to her, yet Ross had told Kieran he should make her keep her legs covered. He'd said it as though he admired the way they looked. He liked the way something about her looked.

She caught herself staring at the textured silk of the wallpaper as though it were a face and gave herself a rough shake. She had no right to think of Ross Trenerry that way. He belonged to Juliet.

Suddenly, her shoulders slumped. Her hair, tumbling around her face like Juliet's, felt as heavy as a drenched cloak. Albeit unwittingly, she had sent him to what was little better than a floating coffin, and today he had pretended he had abducted her, forced her to help him, saving her from nothing more serious than her father's displeasure and possible disgrace in the neighborhood.

She could weather Papa's displeasure. She had been doing so since she could walk. He had never done anything to hurt her. Mostly he simply curtailed her freedom, which was awful, but she could work around restrictions on her movements. As for disgrace in the neighborhood, she did not much mind that, for her own sake. She preferred her excursions to the tenant farms more than tea parties with the gentry. She loved watching the children while weary mothers got some much-needed rest or household chores finished. She enjoyed assisting those women with preserving the garden produce. Those were not pursuits a lady was supposed to enjoy, but Chloe chose the sweet air of a meadow over the stifling atmosphere of a drawing room every chance that came her way. She appreciated the loyalty she received from the tenants far more than the sly innuendo of parlor gossip she expected from her peers.

Yet she hated oversetting her parents, especially Mama, who wanted her daughters as happily married and settled as she had been for the past thirty-five years. Mama and Papa gave Chloe so much— more freedom than most single ladies enjoyed, a great deal of pin money, and love. Harsh or not at times, Papa loved her, and every action he took stemmed from concern and love for her, for his family. Chloe understood that. She was the same. Above all else, the family must be protected.

And in preserving the family, Chloe must get Ross safely away so she could return Juliet. For Juliet, Chloe must somehow help Ross prove his innocence. She had robbed Juliet and Ross of their happiness together, or at the least, a chance to discover if they could have happiness together, and must rectify her error.

But not by telling Ross what she had done to him. She would then be obligated to go to America and testify on his behalf, if a woman was even allowed to do such a thing in America. She was not sure even the Ashfords could weather that kind of scandal. Perhaps even worse, he would never wish to ally himself with a family, two of whose members had sent him to an English prison. That would hurt Juliet far too much.

Chloe knew her younger sister. Juliet was not above deciding she could never love anyone else, whether or not she knew Ross well enough to know if she loved him. Look how she had already been on the verge of throwing over Henry Vernell for Ross Trenerry. And if Juliet was unhappy, Mama and Papa would be unhappy.

Chloe slapped herself on the side of the head. "Why did I not simply leave well enough alone?"

The answer was simple and clear—Juliet had nearly gotten herself killed trying to go to Ross. Chloe had taken the only route she knew to get him out of Juliet's orbit.

Knowing the reasons did not mitigate her guilt, especially not now that Ross was a man on the run and Juliet was in danger.

She must get him free as soon as possible. He might not have enough air in that armoire. He might go mad in the coffin-sized enclosure. But she was uncertain how far they could get away from the house without help.

As she washed her wound and wrapped fresh linen strips around her arm, she wondered whom she could trust. No one in the household. Kieran had been fair to Ross on the roof, but he believed Papa could delay the American attaché. Chloe did not wish to depend on that belief, and any delay was merely temporary anyhow.

A number of tenants owed Chloe favors. Some had helped her in the past. They would likely help her again if she could get word to the right ones.

Hastily, Chloe snatched another petticoat and gown from the clothes press and tugged them over her head. She had to ring for a maid to do up the hooks in back, but the soft blue merino, with the addition of a shawl over her shoulders, would hide the fact that her left arm was a little thicker than the right. While waiting for the maid to arrive, she exchanged her torn stockings for fresh ones, and donned half boots.

Plyton, the maid she and Juliet shared, responded to her call, and without needing instruction, began fastening the row of hooks up the back of Chloe's petticoat and gown.

"Do you want I should do your hair, milady?" Plyton asked.

Chloe glanced in the mirror at her tangled mane, then at the clock ticking on the mantel. "No time. You may go about whatever else is needed."

Plyton's eyes teared. "There's naught with Lady Juliet missing. And to think I oft complained about having to pin up her hair a dozen times a day."

Chloe touched the middle-aged woman's arm. "Why do you not go home for a day or two? Your sister can use help with the little ones."

"Aye, milady, but if you're needing me . . ."

"I will manage."

A knock on the door prevented any further protests to which Chloe might have to respond. Plyton opened the portal to admit Papa. She dropped into a curtsy, then rose and slipped past him to disappear down the corridor.

Papa closed the door and faced Chloe. "You look considerably better, child. But are you quite sure he did not hurt you?"

"Quite sure." Chloe picked up a hairbrush and began working the snarls from her hair by feel. "He barely even touched me."

"Hmm." He gave her a narrow-eyed look. "Then perhaps you had best tell me what did happen after you returned to see him against my orders."

Chloe bowed her head to watch the toe of one boot grind the center of a flower patterned into the carpet. "He was bleeding from freeing himself from the ropes, Papa." Even to her own ears her voice sounded far younger than her twenty-three years. "I had to help him. I got some witch hazel and bandages—"

"You should have sent for the apothecary. Tending a male guest, let alone a male prisoner, is not your responsibility."

"I wanted to talk to him about Juliet."

Papa crossed his arms over his chest. "What about her?"

"What he might know about why someone would try to take him and then take Juliet instead."

Papa continued to look at her, mouth set in a grim line.

Chloe swallowed. "You know most men will talk to a lady more freely than a man at times. That is why Mama was such an effective spy in the last war with America."

"Do not invoke your mother's past actions to get yourself out of trouble." His tone was stern, but his mouth had softened, and a spark of humor lit his eyes. He uncrossed his arms and shoved his hands into the pockets of his coat. "So while he was talking to you, did he reveal anything useful?"

Not that she was going to divulge.

"Such as where we might find Juliet?" Papa persisted.

Chloe shook her head. That, at least, was not a lie.

Papa grunted. "If I believed in such things, I would say that man must be a will-o'-the-wisp to have escaped. But he will not for long, not after he has hurt both of my daughters."

"He did not hurt me. You do not understand."

"He used force to abduct you. That is unforgivable."

"But—"

Papa stepped forward and rested his hands on her shoulders. "You know how much this family needs to have a care regarding our loyalty to the Crown. Although we always are honest subjects, we have taken actions that others would be happy to use against us."

"Like the Rutledges."

Papa nodded. "Like the Rutledges, whatever Freddie Rutledge claims about burying the past."

"You think that poppycock, too?"

"Joanna—Mrs. Brown she is now—returned from Greece with her husband and baby last week, an occasion that makes me more inclined to believe Mr. Rutledge would rather see us to perdition than bosom beaux."

"But he has nothing to stir up. He knows nothing of Mr. Trenerry or the Dartmoor escape." Chloe's voice rose with an edge of panic sharpening in her chest.

"Except he has befriended Mr. Beasley, and who knows what Beasley has learned of how Americans escape from Dartmoor."

"Papa." Chloe could not breathe.

"This is one of many reasons why I wish to separate Trenerry from our family as quickly as possible and bring Juliet home." He tucked one finger beneath Chloe's chin. "If you know any reason why Juliet would have a connection to Trenerry, you will tell me, will you not?"

"It is truly nothing, Papa. She had a *tendre* for a man she thinks is some kind of hero from a novel. You know how she is."

She suspected that was all Juliet felt for Ross. His affections seemed to be somewhat stronger. Either way, the two of them deserved a chance to find out how deeply ran their feelings—did they not?

"I know Juliet has odd notions about what her husband should be like." Papa sighed. "That is why I hoped for a match between her and Henry Vernell. He is so sensible."

"He was not sensible with Mr. Trenerry today," Chloe said.

"You cannot blame the man." Papa's mouth tightened again. "Trenerry was trying to take away his lady. Then he tried to take you. But he will not get far. Henry Vernell is going along the coast to ensure none of the fisherfolk carry Trenerry out of the country. And Kieran has a group of men seeking him inland. I expect he will head for Cornwall and his Trenerry connections there. We will catch him before he reaches the north coast."

"And then?" Chloe's voice was a croak.

Papa drew his thick, graying brows together. "I will see he is tried here in England for daring to touch my daughters before I let the Americans have him to hang."

"And . . . Juliet?"

"We will find her." Papa stroked her cheek. "I am going out to help Vernell."

Chloe twisted her hands together. "Shall I go to see Mama?"

"She is in her studio painting. You know she prefers to be alone there. I want you to stay here."

"Here?" Chloe took a step backward. "In my room? Imprisoned?"

Like Ross.

Papa gave her a long, inscrutable look before nodding. "Yes, here. It is for your own good. Confinement until we catch this man and see him locked up where he cannot escape."

But Ross had already been in a place like that because of the Ashfords. He did not deserve another round of imprisonment.

Heart a leaden weight, Chloe stood motionless as Papa left and turned the key in the lock behind him. Then she paced the perimeter of her bedchamber carpet with enough vigor to send her heavy skirt swirling around the ankles of her sturdy boots. Each flower the Axminster artisans had woven into the carpet became a target for her heels to strike, grind, crush as though they were her ideas, her actions. Those actions that brought harm, not good. Those actions that never turned out as she intended.

She had to make her next plans turn out. Now, more than ever, she had a responsibility to help Ross escape. She could not be responsible for sending him to yet another prison. She could not remain in her bedchamber, a submissive, dutiful daughter with no concern but that of her own safety. Remaining there might bring her parents peace of mind for a while. But matters would be far, far worse if Ross broke his silence and talked about Juliet's actions during the war.

Chloe paused at one of the two long, narrow windows that graced one wall of her bedchamber. As was the situation with all the family's rooms, these windows gave onto a balcony. She suspected her father had placed a guard on the terrace below the balcony so that she couldn't climb down. But Chloe intended to go up. If she waited for night, no one would be able to see her. The worst danger lay in the possibility that her mother would be in her studio in the other attic and hear Chloe open the casement only yards away from Phoebe's aureole window. But Ross would suffocate in that cupboard. At the least, she had to let him out as soon as full darkness fell. Yes, she could bring him down to her chamber, and they could wait until midnight to leave.

Throughout the afternoon, she made plans, rested, and searched her drawers, her jewel case, and each reticule she possessed to scavenge every last farthing they might yield. The result wasn't as much as she would have liked. She'd spent too much of her pin money on the tenants. But the four pounds, three shillings, and sixpence she did locate would buy passage across the Channel and provisions for a few days.

At six o'clock, Plyton brought her a light supper and asked if she should return to help Chloe undress.

"Unfasten my hooks now," Chloe said. "If I am stranded here, I may as well be warm in bed with a good book. Perhaps that will take my thoughts off my sister."

"Yes, milady." Plyton's dark eyes filled with tears. "And I've permission from your lady mother to leave in the morning."

Chloe hoped the maid would be gone before the family discovered her other lady had vanished, too.

"Have a safe journey," Chloe said.

She turned her back to the maid to have the hooks undone. She was tempted to offer a bribe to Plyton to leave the door unlocked, then decided that would raise suspicions. So she slipped into a night rail, bade goodnight to the maid, and set fresh tapers in the candelabra. They would have to burn late into the night so no one would realize she wasn't in her room. Then she gathered up her bundle of provisions, wrapped her fur-lined cloak around her, and went to the window. Her hands shaking, Chloe opened the casement. Cold, damp air slapped her in the face. Her cloak and night rail kilted at her waist, she stepped onto the balcony, closed the window, and walked to the side, where a wooden latticework, up which wisteria grew in the summer, formed a barricade between her section of the gallery and Juliet's and formed a convenient ladder. Hauling herself up pulled at her wounded arm, making it bleed again. She felt the blood seep through her sleeve. Cleansing. She bit her lip against the pain. Punctures needed to bleed.

Hers should have been stitched. It hadn't been long or deep until she had demanded too much of her injured arm. Repairs would have to wait, though. Once she had Ross safe . . .

Thoughts of Ross locked in a cupboard for hours spurred her into climbing faster up and over the edge of the roof. Through the blackness of a cloudy night, she caught a glimpse of light. Her mother's studio. She had to keep going, risk being heard. Perhaps anyone who might hear her would think the wind had lashed flying branches against the roof. Perhaps she would be well away before anyone investigated in the other attic or her bedchamber.

As quietly as possible, she climbed over the roof, then sprinted across the center of the house. No light shone from the south end, so she entered the other attic from that side. All was quiet and dark. The air felt close, as though no one had had the windows open that afternoon. Her nostrils flared. She did not even smell lavender. She detected something else familiar, yet indefinable. Afraid she would sneeze, she did not sniff too hard. The scent could be anything in a place where she had played as a child and used for hiding things as an adult.

One thing hidden in a trunk was her breeches. She found them by memory and feel and exchanged them, as well as a shirt and jacket, for her nightgown. Dressed in Kieran's boyhood clothes, complete with top boots, Chloe stored her night rail in the trunk, closed and locked it, then turned to the row of clothes presses. Her outstretched hands encountered the armoire. Smooth, cool wood. Cold, hard metal. Her breath held so she wouldn't sneeze, she flipped the hasp off the ring and opened the door. Warm air puffed lavender sachet from the opening. She sneezed as a satin gown slithered off its hook to land at her feet. Nothing else moved.

Other than old clothing, the cupboard was empty.

Chapter 6

Devonshire Coastline
Friday, 27 October 1815
Midnight

*R*oss sat with his back against the cave's granite wall and tucked his hands inside his coat to stave off the bite of damp sea air. He wanted a fire. He possessed a single candle lantern glowing in a corner of the chamber that was no longer as comfortable as it had been in June of 1813, when he'd awakened from fever dreams to the warmth of Juliet's sweet smile. Now the light showed him Deirdre's strong, full-lipped mouth drooping with sadness, and her leaf-green eyes shadowed from more than the flickering flame.

"Why won't you tell us where Juliet is?" Deirdre posed the question in a weary voice.

The moment she freed him from the armoire, she had asked him to tell her what he knew of Juliet's disappearance. He told her he couldn't do so. She hadn't spoken to him all the way from the attics, through a silent house, and along a circuitous route to the caves. Now that they were hidden deep underground, the querying began again.

"I need to find her myself." It was the best answer he could give her.

"It won't give her to you, you know. The Ashfords will never allow a union between you and their precious daughter."

"Even if I'm a free man?"

"Maybe then." Deirdre settled against the wall beside him as though ready to sit out the night.

Maybe she was. Maybe she was prepared to remain there until he talked or he tried to slip away to find Juliet. She hadn't explained her reasoning for freeing him, but he guessed her intent was to ensure he didn't get turned over to his countrymen before the Ashfords found Juliet and his connection to her abduction. Yet if they found her, his quarry could escape.

"Do you think you love her so much you are willing to risk angering the Ashfords like this?" Deirdre asked.

"I think I do, but then, I haven't seen her in two and a half years."

"And precious little then."

"We spent several hours here." He clutched his aching head. "It was enough to give me hope. She was like sunshine in this cave, in my life. And she cared what happened to me. Do you know—"

No, he could not say something that sentimental aloud—how, other than Deirdre helping him get out of Dartmoor in the first place, no one had truly cared about him and what happened to him for over a decade. If he opened his mouth to speak, he feared he would blurt out something nonsensical, maybe even childish like, "I just want to be loved. I want a family."

He said what would not mortify him if Deirdre scoffed at him. "I'm tired of being a fugitive."

"Then tell us where Juliet is, and the Ashfords will help you."

"Help me?" Ross emitted a bark of mirthless laughter. "Help me onto a ship bound for Charleston."

"Chloe, Kieran, and I have been trying to get you out of that. Our price is Juliet's whereabouts."

"I don't know her whereabouts."

He didn't—at that moment.

"I don't know who has taken her."

He just had suspicions.

"I can't tell you more than I already have."

"Can't, or won't?"

"It boils down to the same thing, doesn't it?"

Deirdre sighed and rose. "I'll bring you some food and blankets in a bit. Maybe then you'll be willing to tell us what you know."

"What's to stop me from simply walking out of here?" Ross stood as well, his gaze going past her to the black maw of the cave.

"Do you think you can find your way? You are welcome to try, but I don't recommend it." Her teeth gleamed in a wolfish smile.

She was right. He didn't know the twists and turns that had brought him to this inner chamber. He might find his way by logic, and then again, he might take one wrong turn that would lose his way forever until some smuggler discovered his dried bones.

"So I'm still a prisoner." Suddenly, Ross needed to fight the urge to surrender. He was weary of running. He was weary of being at the mercy of others. He was weary of losing everyone who once cared about him. He wanted to be free to run toward someone and something that mattered—love, laughter, a home that didn't smell of mildew and bilgewater.

If he told Deirdre where to find Juliet and when, the Ashfords just might help him escape his countrymen's determination to see him punished for a crime he hadn't committed. But the Ashfords would not know to protect his informant. They might even kill him in the rescue of Juliet. He was likely to hang for his abduction, and then Ross could not prove his innocence.

If he could even prove it with his informant, a dubious prospect at best.

No, somehow, he must get free of the cave and go on his own.

Except Lady Chloe knew the truth. Earlier, she had seemed determined to help him for her own reasons. Yet Deirdre had freed him rather than Chloe. From that action, Ross could only conclude Chloe had changed her mind.

He couldn't blame her for that. She would be ruined for helping him. He had done his best to make the others believe he had forced her to help him to protect her reputation. If she helped him further, though, he could do nothing to spare her reputation beyond refusing her help.

"Keep a close watch on Lady Chloe," Ross told Deirdre.

"Believe me, we shall. She is too strong-willed for her own good."

"Sounds like a female crewmate I used to have." Ross smiled.

Deirdre laughed and touched his shoulder. "Oh, Ross, you were such a good friend once. What happened to you that you would turn traitor?"

"I didn't." He ground the words between his teeth, as his body tensed, fists clenching. "How can you believe it of me?"

"You were angry about how your family disowned you."

"That's my family, not an entire country." He turned his back on her and stalked across the cave. "And they helped me get away this last summer. They don't seem to be so angry with me anymore, nor I them. But I have no hope of mending fences there if even you believe me capable of betrayal of my country." Anger draining from him, he rested his battered head against the cold, damp stone of the cave wall. "Go away, Deirdre, if all you are going to do is make accusations against me."

Deirdre made no sound for several moments, then her boot heel scraped on the floor as though she turned. "I'll return. Please reconsider telling us what you can about why Juliet was taken."

Ross didn't respond. He remained with his back to the cave opening until her footfalls died around a curve. She had left the lantern, which meant the opening to the underground tunnels was either close or she knew them well enough to find her way in the dark.

He didn't think the opening was all that close. If it had been, he would have heard the sea. The only water his ears detected was a steady drip, drip, drip somewhere beyond the cave's opening.

He slid to the floor again, so cold and tired he feared he would tell the Ashfords whatever they liked the next time one appeared. Then again, Chloe might tell them herself. She owed him nothing. She only wanted her sister back, and if she had her brother and sister-in-law working with her, she didn't need him.

He needed to wait until morning when light from the exit would help to guide him, provided it wasn't around too many twists and turns. Yet escaping in daylight was tricky at best and impossible at worst. If he found the opening from the light, he could hide again until dark. That still gave him plenty of time to reach Guernsey.

Acquiring a boat to cross the Channel was easy. He could sail any one-masted vessel alone. If he knew nothing else, he knew how to handle anything that floated.

Because of his experience, he had ended up captain of an American privateer plying the Channel. At first, the convoys were difficult to attack. They were well-guarded by naval vessels. But then a man contacted him and offered an arrangement to benefit them both. Ross had taken it. He wanted to deal as many blows to England as he could after they had imprisoned him and his crew and one of them had died senselessly. He had been invincible for a year.

During that year, several British merchantmen fell into his hands. He would not imprison their crews. He set the men free on one of the Channel islands or even along the southern coast of their country. Twice he had been close enough to Devonshire to leave some wounded men in the same cave in which he had recovered. He then notified Juliet of their presence so she could get them help. It would not harm her to help her own countrymen.

"There is a secret letterbox I can leave you messages in," she had told him right before he left the caves in June of 1813. "And if you are able to come ashore long enough to fetch them, you may leave one in return."

He had found several messages from her. They were as light and chatty as she had been in the cave. He savored every word like a ship-wrecked man consumes water when rescued.

He had written back to her, amusing anecdotes about life at sea, and nothing about the horrors of fighting. He made no promises. He took care not to make direct contact with her, except for that one time when she had been beyond imprudent and tried to elope to meet him on Guernsey. If anything had happened to her then, he would never have forgiven himself.

He was having a difficult enough time forgiving himself now.

"If only I hadn't tried to meet her in the park." Groaning, he dropped his face into his hands.

She had said for him to do so would be all right, but he knew better than to trust the assurances of a lady who thought she wanted to live the life of a heroine in a novel. She was warm and kind and amusing, and he was quite sure he adored her, but prudent she was not.

And neither, apparently, was he, or he wouldn't be hunkered down in a freezing, damp cave, another sort of prison, with only poor ideas of how he would escape to rescue Juliet and capture his informant.

Feeling as though he were suffering through a Halifax winter instead of an English autumn, Ross stood, then began pacing the rocky chamber. Ten paces across, like the quarterdeck of the vessel on which he'd first privateered. Six paces the other way, the amount of space he'd had to stride in his cabin during the year he'd been a privateer captain.

He had to get free again, prove that he was worthy to have Juliet. He needed her with her sparkle, her warmth . . . He changed direction in his steps. His boot heels rasped on the cave's gritty floor. The tide was ebbing; it sounded no louder than his own breathing. If Deirdre didn't arrive soon, he would have to wait at least eight hours to cross the Channel. Daylight would be upon them by then. He would have to wait until the next ebb tide. He'd be underground an entire day like a body in a tomb.

Shivering, he paused near the opening to the chamber. Silence descended like a fog. He could have been deafened, except he heard the scrape of a shoe on stone.

"Deirdre?"

Ross received no response save for another scrape, a closer grating hiss of leather on sand-glazed stone.

Ross stepped back from the doorway and reached for his knife. It wasn't there. An Ashford had taken it away from him, and now he was weaponless in a cave with someone stalking toward him in silence.

A bulky figure hurtled through the doorway and straight at him. Ross dropped and rolled, kicked out at the lantern. The glass shattered. The candle died. Acrid smoke and darkness filled the chamber. Dust from the floor filled Ross's mouth, his lungs. He swallowed, holding down a cough.

The other man's harsh breathing seemed to echo off the walls. That made finding his direction difficult. Ross hoped his attacker would have the same difficulty locating him.

Careful to make as little noise as possible, he sat up and reached for a shard of glass. It was hot, searing his fingers. *Probably slicing them, too.* But it was a weapon that would as easily slash the stranger's skin.

If it was a stranger.

Ross curled his free hand into a fist.

A whoosh of air warned Ross to move. He feinted to one side, then dove the other way. Mistake. His foot kicked glass. It sounded as loud as the Dartmoor alarm bell the night soldiers learned of their escape far too quickly.

Ross moved. Not fast enough. The man was on him, knocking him back. Ross's spine struck the wall. He lashed out with the glass, connected.

The man cried out, jerked away. Ross moved again, slid sideways, banged another wall.

The wrong way, you fool!

He was in a corner. He was cornered. The stranger was upon him again with a knee in Ross's groin and the cold, smooth steel of a blade at his throat.

The tinkle of breaking glass brought Chloe to a halt outside the cave where they had hidden Ross after Dartmoor. She doubted he could find his way there, and knew of nowhere else to look after discovering the armoire empty. If Kieran or Deirdre had freed him, surely they would secure him in this most secure of places.

Someone was in the cave, but she had no way of knowing if it was Ross. Smugglers used the rock tunnels as well. Not about to come face-to-face with one of the free traders, she snuffed her candle and pinched off the hot wax so she could slip the taper into her pocket. She could not leave until she knew whether or not Ross was indeed in the cave. If he was not . . .

She pressed her back against the wall of the tunnel. Scarcely daring to breathe, she strained her ears for a clue to the cave's occupant. Occupants. Thuds, a grunt, boot heels scraping on the floor. At least, persons struggled in the cavern. A strange fight. They brawled without words, without the epithets hurled at one another like fisticuffs she had witnessed in town. If Ross were in there, he might need help. If strangers fought—

She would worry about that later.

Chloe set her bundle on the floor beside a stalactite, then glided forward. The toe of her boot struck a loose stone. It rattled no more than a second, moved no more than an inch or two, but in the narrow rock passage, the noise sounded as though she had fired her pistol. She froze. Every hair on her body seemed to stand on end. Then she sensed more than heard a rush of movement toward her. She leaped aside. Not fast enough. The body struck her shoulder, knocked her back against the cave wall. She slumped, gasping for air, inhaling that familiar scent she'd caught in the attic.

The man who'd struck her kept moving, running, sure-footed even in the blackness. The other man approached her with stealthy, sliding steps. He moved close enough for her to inhale the freshness of salt air too common on the coast to be reassuring.

She drew her pistol from the inside of her cloak. "Mr. Trenerry?"

"Were you expecting to find someone else down here?"

"A body cannot be too safe about whom one meets down here." She touched his sleeve, ran her hand up the smooth wool. "But I am so glad."

"Since you just scared off a would-be killer, I'm right glad to see you, too."

"Who? A smuggler?"

Ross gave out a harsh bark of laughter. "I imagine he's done his share of smuggling. And now I'd like to get as far away from here as possible as fast as possible."

A tingle of memory raced through Chloe, the echo of Ross saying that over two years earlier as his fever dreams fretted about the whereabouts of the other crew members who'd escaped, and the risk the Ashfords were taking to help him.

"How did you get here?" Chloe asked.

"Deirdre. She intended to keep me here until I tell her where to find Juliet." Bitterness dripped from his tone like water from a cave roof. "I didn't know she intended for me to die for not telling her straight away."

"Mr. Trenerry, you know Deirdre, of all people, would never hurt you."

"I plan to make sure neither she nor anyone else does." He covered her hand with his. "But I can say that I find it dashed peculiar that she brings me here, and not half an hour later someone tries to slit my throat. Seems logical to me to believe it's an Ashford."

"It is not logical at all." She struggled to keep her voice low, but it vibrated with her rising fury. "Kieran and I saved your life on the roof, and you said yourself Deirdre brought you down here, and she brought you here instead of turning you back over to my father."

"Forgive me if I'm not comforted by your words." Ross's tone was dry.

Chloe hugged her arms. "No one in my family wants you dead or you would be dead."

Ross stepped toward her and lowered his voice. "Maybe they are afraid I will be caught and reveal too much to the authorities."

Chloe gritted her teeth. She was going to scream. She was going to bash Ross over the head with her pistol butt. Part of her wanted to leave him in the cave, let him find his own way out of England. Most of her knew she could not, especially not now.

"You are determined to believe Kieran still holds ill will toward you because of Deirdre sneaking about and going to Dartmoor to see you."

"No, not that—the information I hold about his activities during the war."

"You mean the escape? I doubt you would reveal that and harm Juliet's reputation." Chloe set one hand on her hip. "Truly, Mr. Trenerry, we know better than—" Understanding hit her like a palm across her lips, and she caught her breath. "You think Kieran was your informant."

"The circumstances fit."

"They most certainly do not." Chloe struggled to keep her voice quiet and calm, but the quiet drip of water from the roof sounded like a squall. She spoke even more softly. "Kieran would not kidnap Juliet."

"He would to lure me to a rendezvous, since he knows how to keep her safe."

"He would never distress our parents in such a way."

"Men who commit treason will do anything to protect themselves."

Chloe ground her teeth to hold back hurtful words she knew were untrue.

"I know. I should know, right?" Ross voiced her unbroken taunt aloud.

"Wrong." The fight ebbed from Chloe. "We will discuss this later. Right now, I need to get you out of here. Obviously you are not safe down here."

"I have no intention of going anywhere with you, Lady Chloe Ashford." He emphasized her surname.

She sighed in exasperation. "But you need my help."

"I've had quite enough help from Ashfords this day, thank you kindly."

"And who will help you get to Guernsey?"

"I have myself."

"And you have done such a fine job of keeping yourself safe these past three years, have you not?" The instant she snapped out the retort, Chloe wanted to kick herself, as if that would be enough to obliterate the sting of guilt.

If she had not sent him to prison, he would have done just fine for himself, even if he had destroyed her family. Now she felt obligated, responsible to help him reach Juliet and his informant unscathed and free.

"I can lead you out of the cave and keep you safe until you can get a boat to Guernsey." She made the bold promise believing every word.

"I will appreciate guidance out of this maze, but I will manage the rest on my own."

"How?"

"I don't know until I get outside."

"I do and plan to stay with you." Chloe changed tack. "Do you not think Juliet will be better off having her sister there when you find her? And what if she is in distress? How can you manage her histrionics and capture your informant?"

"I can save Juliet's reputation by marrying her. I will not be responsible for ruining yours."

Chloe started to argue, but knew he was right in that. She had taken far too many risks with her reputation already. One more slip and she would end up in Northumberland or worse, married off to someone suitable, to her parents and society, but objectionable to her. And yet, she owed this man his life. What was her reputation worth if he were caught and hanged?

"You cannot stop me from going with you," she declared.

"I could tie you to a stalactite?" Ross touched the back of her neck, then stroked his fingers down her braided hair and slid them across her shoulder, where he rested it with a pressure no heavier than a feather boa.

It was not a caress. He was probably trying not to strangle her. Nonetheless, her body quivered with pleasure in his touch.

"You would not dare tie me to anything." Her voice emerged as a croak.

"Oh, yes, ma'am, I would to avoid going anywhere with another Ashford. But I'd send a message as to your whereabouts."

"All right then." She pretended to agree with him. "I will get you out of here and to a place you can hide."

"Thank you for seeing sense. Now how do we get out of here? I broke the lantern. Can you find your way in the dark like Deirdre did?"

"No, but I have a candle." Chloe retrieved her bundle, took out her strike-a-light, and tried to light her candle. When she failed to fire the gun-like flint-and-steel mechanism, she realized her hands were shaking. She forced everything from her mind but the task at hand. The third time she fired the strike-a-light, sparks shot from the steel, bright as fireworks in the blackness, and the candlewick caught fire. She blinked and looked up to find Ross standing beside her, watching her with laughter dancing in his eyes.

"Is there anything you can't do, my lady?"

She dropped her gaze. "Too many things. Let us be going." She hefted her bundle over her shoulder and turned toward one of the tunnels off the main chamber.

"That's not the way we came in," Ross said.

"It is a better way out. Less likely to be used by smugglers."

"Or your family?"

"Ross—" She started walking, leading the way through a maze of stalactites and outcroppings creating a natural labyrinth. It was narrower and lower, and not even she and Kieran used it often for that reason. But it was prudent tonight—she hoped.

Ross followed her on quiet feet, followed her closely enough that they could have talked. They both remained silent. She suspected that he listened as she did, kept his ears alert for a sound that might indicate pursuit.

Or help. She mustn't forget that Deirdre had said she would return with supplies for Ross.

Ahead, gravel crunched.

Ross's hand covered her lips. "Don't make a sound."

"The light." With one hand still across Chloe's mouth, Ross reached forward with the other and snuffed the candle. Then he drew her backward along the passageway. He half expected her to kick him, but she went with him willingly. Later he would worry about why she wasn't fighting him. For now, he concentrated on finding a place to hide from the owner of the footfalls striding toward them. The tunnel was narrow. He drew her back until he felt the walls open around him. Not much. The break was no more than a fissure wide enough for a body. For two bodies. They would be out of the main passageway. With luck, whoever approached them down the tunnel would pass without noticing their hiding place.

"Go in ahead of me," Ross said.

She hesitated.

He caught the flicker of torchlight up the tunnel. Chloe stiffened beneath his hand, and again, he prepared to stop her from crying out. But she turned away from him and shouldered her way into the narrow crevice. He slipped in behind her. The confines brought him up right against Chloe's side. She stood perfectly still, absolutely silent, a soft, warm statue in the blackness. He had to squeeze close to her to keep from protruding into the passageway, and she drew in her breath. For a beat, he thought she intended to scream after all. Then he remembered her wounded arm, and tried to move away from her to keep from injuring her further. Movement away proved impossible. Surely coffins had more room.

Surely the owner of the footfalls could hear the pounding of his heart. It felt as though it beat loudly enough to echo off the tunnel walls. Ross had to hold his breath to ensure he didn't gasp like a man being crushed.

The rock was solid. It wasn't the partition boards the guards could use to make a man's space so small he couldn't raise his arms to shoo away the rats. He couldn't raise his arms, but he could get out of this prison once the other person passed.

That other person drew nearer. Ross smelled burning pitch, and the light grew brighter, bright enough to show a cranny in the wall if anyone looked.

Ross squeezed farther into the crevice, closer to Chloe's softness. He heard her swallow, and with a silent groan he realized he wasn't pressing against her arm; his own arm rested firmly against one of her breasts.

He closed his eyes and drew forth the memory of Juliet smiling down at him when he regained his right senses. It was an image he had used in the hulk to banish the nightmares. She had kissed him on the brow when his eyes opened. For a moment, her softness pressed against him . . .

He laid his brow against the rock wall, for once welcoming the cold dampness. No matter how much he needed distraction from internment and an approaching intruder, he couldn't think of Juliet that way, disrespecting her and distracting his mind and hindering his body if he needed to fight.

The light bearer drew nearer. Ross bunched his fingers into fists, the only weapon he possessed.

The footfalls drew level. Torchlight flared. He tensed, but the footfalls continued, as measured as those of the guards pacing the deck of the prison hulk. Only these diminished, faded, disappeared.

With a silent sigh of relief, Ross wedged his way back into the passage. Darkness greeted him as complete as the silence. Suddenly, he could breathe as freely as he had on the open sea. For the moment, he was still free.

He turned back toward the fissure. "Can you get us out without a candle?"

"Yes." Chloe's voice was hoarse but steady. "But if that was Deirdre—"

"Deuce take Deirdre."

And, for her sake, he would find a way to get rid of Chloe sooner than later.

With a sigh like a gust of sea breeze, she turned her back on him. "Hold my shoulder, and raise your other hand up to protect your head. The tunnel gets low near the seaward entrance."

She didn't exaggerate. In a few steps, the passageway grew wider, but the roof dropped so low he had to walk hunched over as he had moved below decks on the hulk.

It was no different on any ship. He thought about his own schooner in full sail over crystal blue water. The image was so clear he could hear the roar of wind over waves, smell the sea, feel the kiss of briny air on his cheek.

He did smell salt and fish. Icy wind eddied around him. The roar was a lashing, angry surf pounding against jagged rocks. They rounded a curve in the passageway, and wind struck them with the force of a titan's trident. Chloe staggered back against him. He wrapped his arms around her, holding her upright, holding her close with the exhilaration of wild wind and freedom.

For an instant, she rested her head against his shoulder. He continued to hold her, needing the warmth that filled him where she touched him.

Then she jerked upright and pulled away from him. "We have to go somewhere else." The gale snatched her words and flung them at him like darts. "The tide reaches this far up."

"Where?" Though a jagged rectangle ahead proclaimed outside was lighter than the cave, the night was still too dark for navigation in unfamiliar territory.

He felt rather than saw Chloe shrug. "Up."

"That sounds right better than down," Ross muttered.

Chloe grabbed his hand. "Come."

He followed her into the open. Icy air lashed mist against his face. He welcomed it like a caress. He might be stranded on a deuced island, but he was still free, climbing up a hillside that more rightly should be called a cliff, following this Ashford lady. The familiarity of the act comforted him, exhilarated him, even if it wasn't the Ashford lady who had later stolen his heart. Soon, Juliet would be with him, safe. Then he'd free himself from the price on his head.

Chloe paused near the crest of the hill and glanced back. Ross followed her gaze. Nothing below but the phosphorescent spume from the sea shooting into the night like escaping birds. No sign of pursuit lay behind them—yet.

"We will get across the road," Chloe said. "Mrs. Alday's cottage is only two fields over."

Only. Suddenly, the idea of walking across the road seemed too fatiguing to accomplish. The kind of sleep he'd gotten after a bump on his head didn't prepare him for hours in a cupboard and the cave.

Stopping means death. If Old Wat hadn't stopped . . . He drank in bracing sea air and trudged the last steep yards. They crested the hill, and the coastal road stretched in long curves to either side. A ditch lay before them, deep and noisome, and across from them, a line of hedgerow was darker blackness against the sky.

"Through the field," Chloe said. "We will have to crawl under the hedgerow, but that is not so difficult."

Fatigue or not, he had to go on as though nothing were difficult. He leaped the ditch, then turned back to offer Chloe his hands. She laid her hands in his and leaped the ditch with the grace of a deer. Immediately, she released his hands and darted across the road. He followed her to the line of dense conifers.

"Only crawl through the hedgerow," Ross muttered as he struggled to follow her through a gap beneath the prickly branches. "I'm going to look like a porcupine."

"A what?"

"A small animal that hides quills in its coat and stabs you with them if you try to touch him." Ross pushed his way through the shrubbery and started to stand. Then he heard the sound, the crunch like a boot heel on shale.

Chapter 7

Devonshire Coastline
Friday, 27 October 1815
Midnight

*C*hloe lay her hand on Ross's head to keep it below the hedge line. Another rattle of stone sounded from across the road. The person from the cave? Kieran or Deirdre? Whoever it was had extinguished his torch, so she couldn't peer through the bushes and see his face. He had stopped moving, too. Listening as she and Ross were? None of them could stand motionless for long, shivering in the autumn wind off the sea.

Ross touched her cheek, then leaned toward her and murmured into her ear. "Can you run bent over?"

She nodded.

"Then let's be on our way."

She turned her head so she could speak against his ear, and she smelled salt spray in his hair, felt the softness of the heavy strands. "He will hear us."

But the footfalls were moving away, quietly tramping along the road.

With a sigh of relief, she took Ross's hand in hers and headed across the field at a lope. In the spring, sheep would fill that meadow. Now, in mid-autumn, the sheep were kept closer to the home farm, inland from the sea and more protected. Only hay ricks raised obstacles they needed to skirt. The grass was short and made little sound beneath their feet.

Then they reached another hedgerow, one planted thickly to keep the sheep in separate fields when necessary, and neither of them could crawl beneath it. Nor could they climb over. The bushes were too high, the limbs too fragile.

"I did not realize—" Winded, Chloe leaned against a hay mound and scanned the field they'd just crossed. She saw nothing. "We will have to go around."

"Is that so bad?"

"It adds a mile."

"Hmm." Ross leaned on the hay rick beside her. "Safety?"

"I am mostly certain." No one in her family should discover her absence until morning. "If you lift me up, I can jump down the other side."

She crossed the two yards of shorn grass that separated the hay mounds from the hedgerow. Ross followed. She heard the brush of his footfalls like the whisper of hands on silk. When those hands touched her, lifted her up—

She concentrated on the shrubbery. She must not catch her clothes in the branches and tear them. She must not land like a sack of feed on a barn floor. She must not care that Ross's hands were large enough to make her feel as tiny as her mother.

Ross turned his back to the hedge so that he faced Chloe, and crouched. He studied her for a moment, then he touched the collar of her cloak. "Easier if you take this off."

"Yes, of course." She unclasped the gold frogs that held the mantle together and let it slide to the ground. If he deserted her, she hoped he would take it with him. It was a female's garment, but the fur would keep him warm.

"You'll be cold now," he said.

"I am all right."

He cupped his hand against one of his knees. "Step from here to my shoulder. Can you grab the branches without hurting yourself?"

"The needles are soft. But you—Mr. Trenerry, if I step onto your shoulders . . . I think we should move a hay rick."

"You're far lighter than a hay rick, my lady." His voice held a note of laughter.

"Well, yes, but . . ."

He looked up at her, and by what feeble light the night offered, she caught his smile. "Only a weak man couldn't lift you, my lady, and I'm not there yet."

Oh, lud, no wonder Juliet had fallen for him. No wonder *Juliet*? Who was she trying to fool? She had once succumbed to his moments of charm. Those tender emotions lay behind her. She needed to keep them that way because he belonged to Juliet. When she got over that hedge, she should start running and keep on running until Ross Trenerry was a vague memory along with her fantasies that were worthy of no one older than a schoolroom miss. Except she had to help Ross get to her sister and his informant.

Chloe swallowed. "All right." She placed one foot in his cupped hands and reached past him to grasp the nearest branch. The needles weren't soft, but she welcomed the sting against her palms; they kept her from feeling too much for Ross—until she had her other foot on his shoulder and her thigh brushed his cheek. She heard the rasp of his whiskers against her woolen breeches. She jumped and nearly lost her balance.

"Easy does it, my lady."

There, he had distanced them with that formal address.

Steadier, Chloe reached for a higher branch so she could step onto his other shoulder. Her ankles and calves bracketed his head.

Then his hands curved around her calves, and a shudder ran all the way up her legs.

"Do you need me to stand?" he asked.

Chloe wished she could dive right over the hedge as she stood. Perhaps if she landed on her head, she would gain some sense.

"If you can stand," she managed to answer him.

"Thank you, ma'am, for your confidence in my manhood."

Oh, she didn't doubt his manhood. That was her problem.

"Hang on tight." He stood, rising slowly so she could grab higher and higher branches and keep her balance on the way.

Then he had her high enough so that she had to bend to keep her grip. "I am going to let go now."

"You can jump this?" His voice held little of the strain she would have expected of a man holding her over his head.

She swallowed. "Yes. Let go."

He released her, and she jumped. She landed more like a three-legged feline than a graceful kitten. The impact knocked half the wind from her lungs, but she was up and running at once, not slowing until she neared the far side of the field. She could not approach the house panting like a Newcomen mine engine. She'd scare the widow.

Chloe paused at the edge of Mrs. Alday's land. A light shone in a cottage window. Not a good sign at an hour past midnight. But no one would look for Ross there. No man on the run would risk going to a cottage that close to the estate. Perhaps Mrs. Alday was ill.

Chloe took a step toward the house, then saw someone pass that window, someone far too tall for the petite, middle-aged seamstress. Holding her breath, Chloe approached the hedge on the cottage side of the field. A kitchen garden, no more than churned earth now, separated hedgerow from house. Chloe wished the widow didn't use her land so efficiently and had planted some flowering shrubs instead, something that would allow her to creep closer to the house and listen while remaining concealed. She could see little and hear less from her position thirty feet from the house, but she remained there, waiting, as still as the walls of the cottage.

The cottage door creaked. Voices suddenly drifted toward her on the wind, a man's and a woman's. He was leaving by the kitchen door around the corner of the house. She could not see him, but when he stepped into the yard between kitchen door and chicken coop, the male voice was far too clear.

"I apologize again for disturbing you, Mrs. Alday." The man was, as Chloe feared, her brother.

"I have not seen her or any strangers." Mrs. Alday sounded shaken. "Nor heard anything odd either."

"I'll stay with her all night." Chloe tensed at the sound of Deirdre's voice—and her words. "She'll need someone to send a message if Chloe comes here for help."

Kieran cleared his throat. "I will be riding west. With no sign of Juliet's whereabouts." The kitchen door closed, and a moment later, Chloe heard hoofbeats on turf.

Feeling as though she dragged a ship's anchor behind her, she turned from the hedge and slogged back across the field with her eyes straining for a flash of movement, and her ears alert for the sound of a horse coming her way, a warning that Kieran had decided to investigate the empty fields for signs of Ross and her. Kieran, who should not have known she was gone. Someone must have looked in her room.

The horse moved toward the lane on the other side of Mrs. Alday's cottage. The hoofbeats diminished in the direction of Bishops Cove, her father's estate. She and Ross could keep moving in the opposite direction.

By the time she reached the point in the hedge where Ross waited on the other side, her lack of sleep the previous night caught up with her like a drenching fog, weighing her down, and she knew she did not have the strength to travel much farther.

At the hedge, she sank onto her knees. "Mr. Trenerry?"

"I'm here."

"Deirdre is there. I heard her say she would stay with the widow all night."

"And your brother?"

"He just rode off."

Ross was silent for several moments—so long Chloe feared he might have run off across the open field.

She listened for the telltale whisper of Ross's footfalls in the dead grass, or the thudding of Kieran's horse returning. Nothing sounded over the bone-chilling wind rustling the branches, and the muted roar of the sea.

"Mr. Trenerry?"

"I'm still here." Ross exhaled like a man carrying a heavy burden. "This means they know I left the cave."

"Yes, and I am with you."

"Go back to the cottage and tell Deirdre you are all right. I will make my own way to Guernsey."

"How? The coast will be watched from here to Land's End and east to Southampton."

"I'll risk it. I can't allow you to ruin yourself for me."

"Let me go tell Deirdre you are here and ask where the boat is."

The hedge rustled as though he grasped the branches. "Do not. Please. I would rather be on my own way to freedom than trust Deirdre."

"But neither she nor Kieran sent someone into the cave to hurt you."

"So you claim." Ross shifted beyond the barricade of foliage. "Once I could have trusted her." He sounded weary, as dragged down as Chloe felt. "But she's married to Kieran now, and rightfully loyal to him."

"But she—" Chloe stopped, remembering Deirdre's harsh words. She didn't believe in Ross anymore. Chloe knew she was all he had to help him, and because she'd chosen to keep the note from her family for his sake, she was all Juliet had as well.

"So we cannot go to Mrs. Alday's," Chloe said. "I will find us somewhere else to hide for the night."

"I told you to leave me, my lady."

"I know I should."

In a flash, she could turn around and retrace her steps to the widow's cottage, to Deirdre. She could confess all and let Deirdre and Kieran manage matters, protecting her reputation. That was the right course of action to take. Yet Ross did not trust Kieran and Deirdre. He might not confide in them everything they needed to know. He was likely to go off on his own and get captured, and then what? Would he tell someone he suspected Kieran could vouch for his innocence because her brother had been Ross's informant? He might to spare his hide or give himself time. And would that sort of accusation, wrong though it was, harm the Ashfords? They would all be ruined—her parents, who deserved none of this; Deirdre and Kieran, whose only crime had been to help Deirdre's crew during the war; and Juliet, who was guilty of nothing but being full of notions of heroes and adventure and perhaps lured by the charm Ross was capable of showing.

In light of those risks, Chloe's reputation meant nothing to her. She could endure life in exile. Society might force her parents to tuck her away or find her a husband, but they would not stop loving her. And her conscience would be clear if she saved Ross.

"I cannot have you going off claiming my brother is a traitor to protect your hide." The truth was her best excuse for staying with him. "I will stay with you until you are no longer a danger to him."

"Your reputation?"

"To perdition with my reputation. My family will do their best to cover up my absence, and getting Juliet safely home is what matters."

"On that, my lady, we agree." As he spoke, the direction of his voice shifted upward, indicating he stood. "All right. I will accept your help for the night. Ashamed as I am to admit it, I don't think I can go much farther tonight."

"Neither can I."

"Do you know a place to hide?"

Relief giving her renewed strength, Chloe rose. "There is a copse of trees about a half mile west of here. I will meet you at the end of this field."

She trudged through the ankle-high grass, breathing deeply of pine hedges, crushed vegetation, and the sea. Ross smelled like the sea, clean and fresh, promising adventure. It was a far cry from the reek of the American sailors racing across the moors from Dartmoor that night. The prison stench had not offended her; it had saddened her. No man should be allowed to live smelling like an animal, especially not a man who tried rescuing dying old men. Now he was living like an animal again, hunted, skulking along a shrub line, starting, if he were anything like her, at every sound. Even if she was taking him to her sister, she would get him free to love whom he liked.

The field ended in a ha-ha Chloe had forgotten about. She teetered on the edge of the grass-covered trench, a cry escaping her lips.

Ross sprinted toward her and caught her around the waist. "Easy."

"I am sorry." She bent to place her hands on his shoulders and leap down. "I forgot about this."

"I stopped when I saw an opening."

She should have done that.

"But I cried out. Someone might have heard."

"You sounded like a screech owl." He released her. "A cold one. You're shivering. Here."

Cloth whispered, then the warmth of her cloak settled around her shoulders. She raised her hands to fasten the frogs, but his fingers were there, deftly hooking the clasp, brushing the hollow of her throat where her pulse raced.

"Better?" He stepped away from her.

"Warmer."

"Then let's get into those trees. We're too exposed here." With his hand on her shoulder, he directed her toward the other side of the ha-ha.

She was glad that the trees gave her handholds so she could climb out of the grass-covered ditch without needing Ross's assistance. She mustn't want his hands on her, even if the hand on her shoulders felt brotherly, especially accompanied by his uncomplimentary comment about some sort of owl.

The trees, wind-bent pines mostly, lent shelter in the event of rain, and a soft carpet of needles cushioned the ground. Best of all, someone would have to walk into the trees to see them, and they could not do that soundlessly. Chloe sat with her back to the largest trunk, and rested her head on her updrawn knees.

Ross crouched beside her and rested his hand on her shoulder. "Once again, I'm going to suggest you go back to the widow's house and trust me to find your sister."

"Once again, I am going to tell you I cannot." Chloe pushed her bundle forward. "My bundle is large enough for both of us to use as a pillow. I mean—" She bowed her head, though she knew he could not see her cheeks heat. "We lie opposite ways."

"Yes, ma'am, that'll work."

Chloe crawled beneath the branches, stretched out on her side, and tucked her warm cloak around her. She heard the rustle of Ross finding his own way under the branches. The scent of crushed pine needles wafted to her nose, making it stink for a moment, then they settled into a pleasant aroma. She felt the pressure of Ross laying his head on the bundle near her, but not touching her. She thought he faced in the other direction. Should she say goodnight? Not saying anything seemed rude. Saying something seemed too intimate.

He shifted, apparently finding his resting place as she had. Except he didn't have a warm cloak.

He'd been a prisoner who had suffered far too much cold. She had piled blankets and then more blankets on him during his wound fever. Had she not feared oversleeping until daylight, she would have crawled beneath those blankets and warmed him with her body. In his fevered state, he had talked about the cold damp of Dartmoor and the warmth of the Carolina Low Country. He had begged for sunshine after being in a place he called the *cacheau*, a cell of dark and damp.

When he slept, he wouldn't notice the chill of night that was worse between midnight and dawn.

Warm enough though she was, Chloe could not sleep. She lay awake, conscious of Ross's less-than-even breathing—breathing that sounded strained, like a man who had been wounded and was trying not to cry out. Needles shifted, whispering in a rhythmic pattern like quick, shallow breaths. Like constant movement.

Chloe reached her hand out from the heat of her cloak and touched his shoulder. Tremors ran through that shoulder like a body with the ague. Or a man who was simply cold.

She couldn't sleep snug and cozy in her fur while Ross shivered not half a foot away. Yet if she gave him the cloak, she wouldn't sleep, and she needed to be alert. They both needed to be alert in the morning. Both of them needed to sleep snug and cozy. Both of them . . .

Chloe sat up. "Mr. Trenerry, there is no help for it. You must share my cloak with me."

"Out of the question." The response was immediate, hard-edged.

"You cannot lie there and shiver all night."

"Nor can I compromise you."

"I am already compromised if anyone in society finds out about my disappearance. Never you mind that. Mama inherited a plantation in Georgia. They will send me there, and I can find a Yankee who wants a titled English lady regardless of reputation."

"You'll detest Savannah."

"I would not hate it. It would be someplace . . . different."

"Then go to Italy. Much better c-climate. And right now, go to s-sleep."

Chloe squeezed his shoulder harder. "Mr. Trenerry, your teeth are rattling like a deathwatch beetle."

"Thank you for your encouragement."

"Stop being noble. You are freezing, and I am warm."

He muttered something that sounded like an expletive. Then he moved from beneath her hand and sat up. "I should be hanged, but, may the good Lord help me . . . All right, Lady Chloe, I'm not too noble to accept your offer."

She was the one trembling now, but not from cold. Her fingers fumbled at the clasp of her cloak. Her mind fumbled at imagining how lying beside a man would feel, how to arrange lying beside a man. She would let him decide. He was far more worldly than she.

Anticipating his nearness, Chloe went rigid. She might inadvertently do something wrong—lie too close and give him the wrong impression of her morals, lie too far away and do him no good.

He touched her arm. She jumped.

"Did I hurt you?" He fingered the lumpy bandage beneath her sleeve.

She swallowed. "I am all right."

"You may rescind your offer, you know. I'll understand why the daughter of a peer of the realm would rather not share her cloak with a near stranger and a man at that." He remained sitting on the ground behind her. "I understand if you change your mind and run off home right now."

"No, I cannot leave you. I told you. I must see to your welfare now that I withheld the letter from my father but showed it to you."

"And you don't trust me to do right by Juliet."

"Should I?"

"Yes."

She let her silence tell him what she thought of his assurance.

"Lady Chloe, I believe I got myself into this mess when I made a bargain with a treacherous Englishman."

"And corresponded with my sister during a war."

"The heart doesn't often make wise decisions."

Chloe had seen that often enough with Kieran and Deirdre, and then Juliet with Ross, to keep her heart clear of entanglements.

Mostly clear of entanglements.

"But if you're certain you won't be offended by my nearness . . ."

"It is quite all right under the circumstances."

He took the cloak from her and stretched out on the ground behind her.

Cold air swept around her for a moment. Then the heavy, fur-lined mantle spread over her, and warmth returned. A great deal of warmth returned. Her body felt as though she suffered a fever. Ross's body, his chest against her back, his thighs skimming the backs of her legs, felt like a cookstove.

"God bless you," he murmured. "Sometimes I fear I will never be warm."

With his breath fanning tendrils loosened from her braided hair against her neck, Chloe needed to create a distance between them that had nothing to do with space, since that was not possible at present. She tried to think of why they were there, of her role in why they were there. She needed more, needed him to tell her how much he had suffered because of her stupidity.

"W-was the hulk colder than Dartmoor?" She stammered like a schoolroom miss at her first assembly ball.

Ross shuddered. "It was more damp. At Dartmoor, we could move around most of the time. If a body was cold, we could run about and, of course, Deirdre provided us with blankets. But the cold on the hulks went straight through a body because of the damp."

"Did you not have blankets?" She pressed for more, for worse details.

"The guards usually took them away as soon as they arrived." His head shifted on their makeshift pillow. "I dreamed of fur like this."

"How did you bear the cold?" Chloe could not keep the anguish from her tone.

"I remembered better places, better times." His voice grew soft, his accent thick. "I remembered the stifling heat of a South Carolina summer, and even the hold of the *Maid of Alexandria* while we were still in the Caribbean. And I thought about Juliet. She is so full of life, she warms a body just being near her."

"She does."

Chloe latched onto the best barricade of all between her and Ross—Juliet.

Neither of them spoke for several minutes. Chloe fixed an image of Juliet in her mind, so effervescent she sometimes annoyed her older siblings, but mostly they loved her and indulged her and spoiled her.

Chloe suspected Ross would treat her the same way. Juliet would love him for it.

Chloe's throat closed on an involuntary sob.

Ross startled. "My lady, what's wrong?"

"I was thinking—will Juliet be harmed?" She had thought of that enough it was not quite a lie.

Ross sighed. "She had better not be."

"Why is he waiting so long to deliver her? I mean, we could be in Guernsey by tomorrow night if we found a boat."

"He wants to make the exchange on Halloween."

"What does All Hallows' Eve have to do with getting my sister back?"

"When my informant and I met has more to do with the ancient pagan calendar than the holy days of the Church of England or Rome. To make matters simple in not having to pass messages back and forth, we met on the eve of one of those celebration days. There are eight in all, counting the equinoxes and solstices."

Chloe shivered. "Something about betraying Britain on ancient British holidays does not sit well with me."

"I didn't think anything of it. We don't even think about such things in America, except for a few who keep their celebrations quiet. But it does seem particularly wrong to abuse a country's history that way."

Another lengthy silence stretched between them. Ross lay too still for sleep.

Then he sighed, pressing his chest hard against her back. "I've never felt guilty about taking from British merchantmen. Englishmen robbed me of my freedom. They robbed me of a great deal of income when the *Phoebe* took the *Maid* and her rich cargo from the China trade. I'd invested heavily in that cargo and lost it all. So I was just taking back my own."

"With interest?"

"Indeed. Like a cent per center taking advantage of a gambler. For months, I was invincible. And I had a goal—get wealthy enough to be worthy of Juliet when the war ended." He laughed. "As if I could ever be worthy of her. Your father made that clear."

"Only because you have a price on your head."

"It's more than that, my lady, and you know it. I'm a homeless vagabond, however much money I have in banks in France and the Netherlands."

"My parents are not snobs. Remember how they welcomed Deirdre into the family?"

Encouraging him to hope for a future with his lady love eased Chloe's guilt, and she managed to smile, though her eyes burned.

Ross, however, tensed behind her. "I don't remember. I wasn't there."

"I am sorry. But they—we all—welcomed her. How could we not love her? Trust me."

"I think," Ross murmured, "I have no choice but to trust you at the moment."

He could. She swore she would die to protect him from capture.

Before she could think what else to say, Ross's long, even breaths told her he slept. For herself, she feared sleep would elude her. But something about the regular breathing and heat from Ross lulled her tension away. Her own breathing slowed. She relaxed her back against Ross's chest, remembered holding him atop that moorland pony as they dodged the Somerset militia from Dartmoor, his back against her chest. He'd been barely conscious, but never once complained of pain. Later, Chloe had listened to him fever ramble about the places he had been, the warm ones. He'd lived a vagabond life since he was sixteen, and Chloe's longing had begun, a yearning to give him a settled, warm home. But she'd made sure he regained his strength, then sent him off to a dangerous vagabond life, the prison with no warmth.

Heart aching, her last thought was that she would like him to wrap his arm around her, a dangerous, treacherous wish.

Ross's first thought upon waking with his arm around Chloe was that he should go. *Now, while dawn was barely breaking.*

He would save them both considerable embarrassment if he slipped away from her and headed across the fields, hid in hedgerows and ditches, and made his way to his friend and distant cousin in Cornwall, where escape from England was more likely. He would save her reputation if she made her own way home.

Except he doubted he could get much farther than the Tamar River. The minute he opened his mouth to request so much as a cup of water, his American accent would give him away. Whomever he asked might not know that he was a wanted man. But most Englishmen disliked Americans on principle, especially in a county like Cornwall, which had given up too many of its men in both wars with their colonial cousins. As much as he disliked it and her reasons for giving it, he needed Chloe's help.

Embarrassment be damned. He couldn't continue holding a female who wasn't his wife.

Interrupting his even breathing as though just waking, Ross rolled onto his back and dragged the cloak off of them. Cold air slammed into him, and he shuddered.

"Sorry," he muttered. "Dashed cold morning."

"Mmmm?" Chloe sounded sleepy. Pretending she slept, too?

Ross sat up and dropped the cloak over her. "Sorry to wake you, but I expect the world will be stirring any moment now, and we'd best be getting on . . . somewhere."

Chloe sat up. She kept her back to him and her head down. "We cannot go to your cousin in Cornwall. Kieran said he is heading west."

Ross shot upright. "Then how the deuce do we get to Guernsey?"

"Kieran will go by land. You remember how bad a sailor he is."

Ross chuckled. "The worst."

"So we will get a boat and go by sea."

"And how, pray tell, do we get a boat?"

Chloe rubbed her arms against the morning chill. "The fishermen will be coming into Plymouth Harbor. We will have to borrow one of their boats."

"Borrow?" Ross snorted. "You mean steal, thus adding to my crimes."

"We will endeavor to get it back to them." Her voice was barely audible in the rising breeze and birdsong around them.

In the smoke-gray light, her skin was ashen, and half-moon shadows lay beneath her eyes. The texture of her face was flawless, and the shadows enhanced the amber of her irises.

If she were that beautiful in the morning after sleeping on the ground, how much more beautiful—

Ross dismissed the thought that was disloyal to Juliet and chose a spiderweb to stare at instead of Chloe. "So how do we get to Plymouth Harbor without getting caught?"

Chloe's long, slim fingers, where an indentation marred the smoothness on her right ring finger, toyed with the gold frogs on her cloak. "I have friends. My family does not know about all of them." She glanced at him, and he thought he caught the hint of a twinkle in her eyes. "What do you think of going straight into Plymouth?"

Ross supposed he should be grateful for all the smuggling that went on in the West Country. Through his cousin, Bryok Trenerry, it had provided boats that carried escaped prisoners to France. With Chloe, it provided farm wagons with false bottoms that could house brandy casks or human beings. He supposed he should be grateful to Chloe for whatever she did that made widows and farmers forget the edicts of the Lord of the Manor and do her bidding.

Feeling crushed beneath ten stone of apples, despite the planks that prevented that from happening, Ross entertained some unpleasant thoughts about what he could do to Lady Chloe Ashford. Except she lay there with him, lay beside him, touching him from shoulder to hip to thigh. Each deep breath he drew to remind himself he had plenty of air, fresh, sweet-smelling air, pushed him closer to her, reminded him of sleeping beside her. He worried Juliet would not understand the need for such intimacy with her sister. He was hopeful it would not be necessary again. If they found their boat, if the wind and tide cooperated, they could be on Guernsey by the end of the day. He could send Chloe home and track down Juliet himself.

If she was on Guernsey yet.

He had been so focused on getting to Guernsey to find Juliet, he hadn't considered that she might not be there until the rendezvous date. Her kidnapper could have taken her anywhere, planning to carry her to the Channel island right before the rendezvous.

If then.

Regardless of how much air flowed between the boards of the wagon bed, Ross thought he would suffocate. What light seeped between slats darkened. Air snagged in his lungs.

Chloe moved just enough to press her hand against his thigh—hard. She dug her knuckles into his muscles. He had to concentrate not to gasp with the pain. He gritted his teeth and drew a deep breath in through his nose. The action calmed his panic. He relaxed. She moved her hand away.

"I'll get even with you for that," he murmured in her ear.

"It worked, did it not?"

He started to respond, but the wagon jolted to a halt. Feet tramped on the ground, what sounded like dozens of them circling the wagon. Men shouted, some in protest, others in command.

The wagons had driven straight into a barricade of soldiers across the road to Plymouth.

This was why Chloe had employed someone with a false-bottomed wagon. They had done this before. No soldier wanted to unload the entire haul of apples to inspect for a false bottom. Surely not. He was safe from discovery. Safe. Safe . . .

"Have you seen a stranger this morning?" an authoritative voice demanded.

"I seen many a stranger this morning." The farmer driving the wagon of apples sounded bewildered. "That against the law now?"

"Do not give me any cheek, sirrah." The soldier sounded young and haughty. "We are looking for one specific stranger to these shores. An enemy of England and his own land."

"That sounds terrible, sir. What do this man be looking like?"

"He is a big man, black hair to his shoulders, dark eyes, bruise here."

Ross's stomach lurched. A description of him, yet none of Chloe. Of course not. The family would keep her disappearance quiet to strangers.

"No, sir," the farmer said, "I ain't seen no strangers answering to that description."

Which was the truth. Chloe had led Ross through meadows and copses of trees where she bade him hide while she arranged transportation. Then they passed through the trees to a wagon waiting for them. They clamored into the bed facedown before the farmer appeared to load barrels of apples overhead and at the foot of the hidden compartment. At no time had the man seen Ross.

The soldier grumbled something not fit for a lady's ears.

"May I go, sir?" The farmer spoke a little too loudly. "The day is awasting."

"You may go."

Someone pounded on the side of the wagon, and it rattled forward. Their progress was slow. Other vehicles trundled alongside and behind them. No doubt more vehicles led the way. Farmers shouted greetings and insults to one another above the rumble of wheels on stone. They cursed the soldiers for delaying their progress to the city markets and seagoing vessels needing their produce.

Dust, along with the stench of dead fish, bad drains, and manure, seeped between the boards. It settled in Ross's nostrils and throat. He had to choke down the urge to cough. And the wagon crawled. Never a swift conveyance, the farm cart took on the speed of a becalmed brig, and the urge to cough became a desire to surge upward, dislodge apples, and run. Run. Run!

The wagon began the descent into Plymouth. Ross braced his hands and feet on the ends of the wagon, and felt Chloe do the same. The wagon turned, and Chloe slid against him, penned him in. *No air. No air!*

Chloe turned her face toward him. "Ross?"

The puff of her breath across his cheek was the breath of life. He inhaled the scent of apples and woman. His lungs relaxed.

Chloe moved her hand to his shoulder. "Soon."

Not soon enough. Not soon enough.

The cry was so loud in his head he didn't realize the wagon had stopped until Chloe removed her hand from his shoulder. A moment later, the farmer let down the wagon's back panel, then slid aside the crates of apples concealing the hiding place, letting in air and light. All Ross could see of him was rough, woolen trousers over legs like tree trunks. "Here's where I deliver my produce. Quick before the brewer comes out to help me unload." The tree-trunk legs vanished.

Chloe crawled out the end of the wagon. Ross followed, then remained crouched, glancing around. They were in a walled courtyard. His breath snagged in his throat, and his hands convulsed on the edge of the wagon.

Chloe took one of his hands in hers. "There is a door around the side of the wagon. It will lead us to the waterfront and the fish market."

"And fishermen have boats." Ross smiled at her, and despite the reek of rotten apples and sour mash tinged with fish offal, breathing came easier. "Let's go."

Still crouched, they skirted around the side of the wagon, then stood far enough to race for the narrow door in the wall. An iron bar locked it from within. He suspected she would have arranged with the farmer to replace the bar when he returned from inside the brewery and cider press.

Sea air met Ross on the other side of the door. Damp, briny, too heavily fouled with rotten seafood and tar to be fresh, it was perfume to his soul. It was also blowing from the south, no good for sailing in that direction.

But they were in the blessed anonymity of a crowd. Innkeepers and housekeepers, flat baskets over their arms, jostled one another for a look at the early morning catch piled in barrels and the nets that had hauled the seafood ashore. Women and men alike bellowed the quality of their wares. Though servants and landlords and a young woman selling oysters looked clean and presentable, Ross decided he and Chloe fit right in with the unkempt souls who had been out fishing all night. If they could find a fisherman willing to haul a catch off instead of in, they could be in Guernsey by the next day, south wind or not.

"How will we know who's trustworthy?" he asked. "Do you have friends here, too?"

"Not here. But I doubt my father's men have talked to them yet, since they are just now coming ashore." She glanced up at him. Then, her cheeks rosy in the dawn light off the harbor, she looked away. "I am going to tell the one with the worst-looking catch that we are eloping."

"That sounds right sensible to me." He touched her arm, felt the bandage through cloak and shirt, and winced. "You'd best approach him alone so he doesn't wonder why I don't speak."

She flashed him a smile, then strode forward.

Ross followed at a discreet distance, watching Chloe, watching the crowd. Baskets and bodies bumped against him. He glanced toward the wharves, where boats ranging in size from bumboats needing only oars to maneuver them to two-masted schooners bobbed on the water. Only painters held them fast.

If necessary, they could indeed borrow one.

"Fresh oysters for your lady, sir?"

Ross glanced at the pretty oyster girl, shook his head, and edged closer to Chloe. She was talking to a man whose face looked cherubic despite its weather-beaten complexion. He was nodding. She gesticulated. He nodded again. The transaction seemed to be going well.

Ross started to smile, but it froze in the making. He halted in midstride. His gaze locked on another pair of eyes, hazel eyes full of outrage.

Henry Vernell stood no more than a dozen feet away.

Chapter 8

Plymouth, Devon, England
Friday, 27 October 1815
8:10 a.m.

*T*renerry!" The shout rang above the tumult of the market like the prison alarm bell.

Chloe spun toward the sound. She caught sight of Vernell, and her stomach plummeted to her lowest innards. Vernell stood not a dozen feet from her.

Where was Ross? Close enough for Vernell to see him. Where? Where?

She spun on one heel, scanning the crowd. There, twenty feet away, but sprinting toward her. She sprinted toward him. *Stop Vernell. Create confusion.*

Swerving, she rammed her hip into a barrel of herrings. Silvery fish and brine slithered across the path. The fishwife shrieked, and a handful of herring pelted Chloe's back. Someone grasped her hand. Ross beside her, running, too. They leaped over the oyster seller's handcart, and Ross kicked the wedges from the two wheels. Cart and contents careened into the throng. The seller shrieked profanity. Oyster shells ricocheted off Chloe's shoulders, Ross's arm. Someone screamed. Her? No, she didn't have the breath. Another woman crying out, lost in the roar of the crowd, the thud of bodies striking against one another, the crunch of shells. Chaos behind them. Only sea ahead of them. No more wharf. Only boats.

Ross slid to a halt before a pinnace. "In."

"Will this get us as far as Guern—"

He grabbed her around the waist and hoisted her over the rail. She landed on her knees, dropped her bundle, glanced back to the wharf—and pursuit.

A mass of bodies topped with red faces and open, shouting mouths surged toward them. No sign of Vernell. He must be lost in the throng of angry fisherfolk.

She scrambled to her feet and raced aft. A single mast would be easy for two people on an ebb tide. But the wind. Wrong. All wrong, coming from the south. The vessel was small for plying a hundred miles of the Channel.

"Take the tiller." Ross leaped aboard and raced for the mainsail. "You do know how to man a tiller, don't you?"

"I do." She sprang onto the quarterdeck and grasped the tiller. It swung in protest. The pinnace spun like an opera dancer twisting away from an unwanted partner. The anchor. They needed to lift anchor. Only twenty feet of water separated them from the mob now. With the anchor down, they were trapped in the harbor. If she had a knife . . .

Ross had an axe off the deck. Its rusty iron head glinted in the light, then bit into the heavy cable. Once. Twice. The line frayed, split. The roar on the wharf grew louder as the pinnace began drifting on the ebb tide, then pitching forward on swells the south wind forced toward shore.

"The tiller," Ross bellowed. He hauled on the mainsail sheet, and the boom swung abeam, blocking the wharf from view.

Without steerage, they were going to cannon into another boat. Too many other boats. A dozen bumboats raced toward them, and Vernell rowed in one of them.

Chloe leaned on the tiller bar. The wound in her arm pulled. She gulped back a cry of pain and willed the pinnace to sail as close to the wind as possible. Five points—ten points off would work. South by southwest. Guernsey lay in that direction. Guernsey. Juliet. Freedom for Ross.

Forward, Ross hauled on the single sail's lines.

Slowly—too slowly—the boom swung nearly fore and aft. The pinnace crawled up a swell, dropped, rolled. Chloe clung to the tiller. She had never been seasick sailing on the Thames, but now she tasted her meager breakfast of apples and bread. No time for illness now. Two score yards lay between them and pursuit. Then a cable. The mouth of the Tamar opened to starboard. So did the naval shipyard. No pursuit from there—yet. When her father learned what she had done . . .

She flung her head back, drank in fresh, damp air, the sensation of her hair flowing loose from its braid. Laughter bubbled up from her chest. Insanity. Exhilaration.

A coast-guard cutter hovered at the mouth of the river. Chloe shoved at the tiller again, willing the rudder to turn the boat away from the coast of Cornwall. She did not have the strength. Ross was busy loosening the lines on the spritsail to give them more speed. He waved to the coast guard. They waved back and shouted something incomprehensible. Then the forward sail dropped from its yard, and Ross raced aft, bounded onto the quarterdeck, and joined her at the tiller.

"We're away now." He grinned at her.

She stared at him, her heart twisting. "We got away."

"For now. But that wind could be lethal for us. If it increases any, we could find ourselves crashing on a lee shore."

"We cannot return a wrecked boat."

"Then we can't wreck it." He rested one hand on the tiller. Opposite hers, his fingers appeared twice as broad, long, their strength effortless. "We'll hold our course along the coast for as long as we can. Maybe the change in the coast will veer the wind enough for us to head south."

"It might. I have never sailed along in this direction."

"I have. But I had more sail and more men to man them."

"Do you need me to haul lines so you can navigate?"

He picked up her hand and turned it over. "You will tear up your palms in a minute without gloves. Hold the course and I'll trim the sail." He returned her hand to the tiller bar and headed forward to make adjustments to the sail lines.

Chloe alternated between watching him work and glancing over her shoulder to look for pursuit. So far, nothing had been able to catch up with them. The wind was acting in their favor as far as anything else leaving harbor. It was acting against them as far as heading straight for Guernsey.

To starboard, the Cornish coast skimmed by, an unyielding landscape broken by inlets, narrow streams, and wider rivers. Perhaps they could sail right around Land's End to the north side of the peninsula, where Ross's cousins lived. Chloe did not know them. Lord Trenerry took his seat in Parliament, but his wife never joined him in London.

Chloe cast her eyes in Ross's direction again. He was twisting the end of a line around a belaying pin slipped through the bow rail. It would hold the mainsail trim on their current course. His movements were quick, efficient, smooth from practice. He returned toward her along the deck with the ease and grace most men did not even achieve on land. Each footfall landed with the roll in precise rhythm so he maintained his balance. Wind whipped through his hair, lifting the heavy strands as though someone ruffled them with their fingers.

Her fingers moved on the tiller, lifting, spreading, remembering the satin texture of his hair.

She must stop thinking that way. For now, too likely forever, he belonged to Juliet.

Beside her once more, he turned his face toward the coastline. "We can't sail south with this wind. I'm afraid it's increasing."

To emphasize his claim, a gust of wind smelling of rain heeled the fishing boat to starboard, flinging Chloe against Ross. He shot out his arm to catch her and held her tight against his side until the little craft righted itself. Then he released her and took the tiller with both hands.

"We should ditch this boat in a tributary and head out on foot."

Chloe frowned. "We cannot sail around to the north and your cousin?"

"Not with a squall coming in."

"But we will be more easily caught on land."

Ross merely stared at the coast without saying anything other than, "I know of a good creek to land in without wrecking this boat. Maybe a half hour away."

"All right, if we must."

"Be prepared when I say so."

"All right."

They remained side by side at the tiller, neither looking at nor speaking to one another. To larboard, the sea rose and fell in ever-increasing swells that were changing from deep blue to a stormy gray-green. Though blue skies still stretched above them, the horizon roiled black in warning of trouble to come for anyone at sea.

"I hope whoever thinks to take Juliet to Guernsey has already done so or knows enough to hold up." Chloe shivered despite the warmth of her cloak. "She is not a good sailor."

"Isn't she?" Ross drummed his fingers on the tiller. "That makes her willingness to sail to Guernsey during the war to meet me even more precious."

"Precious?" Chloe stared at him. "It was the stupidest thing Juliet has ever tried to do. If she had been caught with smugglers, she could have been transported. She could have been captured by an American vessel, or worse, a French one, and who knows what would have happened to her. Those smugglers could have—they could have taken advantage of her a-and—"

"All she was willing to risk for me." His face was soft.

His brain must be soft. Feet braced for balance, Chloe clasped her hands behind her back or she feared she would grab Ross's shoulders and shake him for being nearly as silly as Juliet.

"She hired smugglers to take her to Guernsey to elope with the enemy." Chloe struggled to keep her voice even, though she needed to increase the volume to be heard above the rising wind. "Besides the danger to her, she could have condemned us all if caught. How could you encourage such actions?"

Ross stiffened. "I didn't encourage it. I didn't even know of it until later."

"When you received some of those exchanged notes. Without those, she never would have thought you would welcome her."

"If she had reached Guernsey," Ross said, "I would have welcomed her."

"You—" All the anger of the previous year, how she had come too close to losing her younger sister and perhaps even her own life, boiled inside Chloe. Before she said more than she should, she turned and tried to stalk away.

Ross caught hold of her arm. "Don't. You need to stay here with me for when I spy the creek I want for beaching this boat."

"All right." Chloe allowed him to set her hand on the tiller, but said nothing.

Nothing aboard a boat at sea was silent. Wind howled through the rigging, and the canvas snapped like gunfire. Each wave hissed and slapped against the boat's hull, sending a mist of spray across the deck so the leather soles of their boots slipped and scraped against the planking. Yet the lack of conversation between Chloe and Ross made the cacophony of the sea insignificant in comparison.

Then Ross faced Chloe. "I would not have married her, you know. I would have welcomed her, sheltered her, and gotten her safely back to her family."

"If you could have done so."

"I could have done so. Remember, I had a connection to England."

"With a traitor who could have gotten us all condemned."

"I know. I wrote her and told her to never do anything so foolish again. It was after I delivered that message that I got captured."

Chloe flinched.

More silence flowed between them, thick and heavy like sea spray, before Ross asked, "What is Vernell to the Ashfords?"

"Henry Vernell is—" Chloe hesitated, seeking her words with care. "A friend of the family."

"How good a friend?" Ross looked her in the eye.

"Good enough, I suppose. He—"

"Cut line, Lady Chloe, he's a good enough friend he knows of Juliet's abduction."

"Yes, he is that good a connection."

"Because he is your suitor?" His mouth was grim.

Chloe snorted. "Were I to push him to it, he would probably admit he despises me because I am too outspoken."

"I thought so. He's Juliet's suitor, isn't he?"

Chloe said nothing.

"Or is he more to her than that?"

"He . . ."

"Just be honest with me, my lady." His words snapped like the sail overhead.

Chloe lowered her gaze to the white knuckles of his hand on the tiller. "He was going to propose to Juliet two days ago."

Ross nodded. "No wonder the man wanted to shoot me."

"I am sorry." Her heart burdened, she blinked hard, but a single tear rolled down her cheek.

"Say, what's this?" He traced the path of the tear from the corner of her eye, to her chin, then tilted her head up. His eyes, dark blue-gray like a twilight storm sky, gazed into hers with an intensity that curled her toes inside her boots. "Why does that make you cry?"

For reasons she could never tell him. Yet he waited for an answer.

"I—" She couldn't think with him close enough to feel the heat of his body. "I encouraged her to forget you. I said she could not elope with you, even when you came back."

"Because I'm a traitor?"

"That I am certain you're not."

His eyes widened. "That's right peculiar from an Ashford." He scanned the horizon, the open channel to larboard, and the coast of Cornwall to starboard. "I wonder why you say it with such conviction." He leaned forward and studied the binnacle compass. "We will tack to leeward in just a few minutes."

"It will be a long walk to your cousin's estate."

"I'm happy to leave you in Falmouth."

"Can you find your way overland on your own?"

"I'll have to, won't I?" He rubbed his head where the cudgel had laid him low. "Though I expect your family will have sent people to watch the route between Plymouth and my cousin's house."

"They will have." Chloe could not stop a hint of smugness. "And so have I."

"Of course you have." Ross covered his eyes with one hand. "How do you have so many loyal helpers?"

Chloe shrugged. "One of my people went straight to Trenerry Cove with a message for your cousin to meet us in Truro, in the event we could not reach Guernsey directly."

"And this subject of yours, Queen Chloe, is not going to betray his information to your father or brother or Vernell?"

"I will have him beheaded if he does." Chloe laughed. "Or simply tell his wife tea and silk are not the only articles he smuggles. There is at least one cask of brandy he keeps—"

"Egad, my lady, you blackmail these people into doing your bidding?"

At Ross's look of horror, Chloe laughed harder, but shook her head. "Only the one I sent to Cornwall. He took out a boat and will sail up the Fal to Truro before going overland. That will save him time so he gets there faster than anyone my family sends."

"I see." He thumped the heel of his hand against his brow. "Do you write the novels Juliet loves to read?"

"I do not have the time to write novels." She leaned over the tiller, peering at the coastline. "And we do not have time to land this. There is a mist rising from the shore."

"I see that—and a little creek I know about."

"You have landed on this coast before?"

"Your caves weren't the only places I found to beach British prisoners."

"That was kind of you."

"Not kind. They were deuced inconvenient to have around. Now hold on tight. This has a little deeper draft than a ship's boat, and we may go aground before I intend."

Before Chloe was ready, he twisted the tiller. The sail billowed, then sagged from the yard.

"Hold this steady." Ross grabbed Chloe's hand and pressed it to the tiller before he leaped forward to loosen belaying pins and reset the canvas.

Jolted, Chloe grasped the tiller bar with one hand and rubbed her arms with the other. As she feared, blood seeped through her sleeve. She hadn't noticed it, had experienced only that spasm of pain when she grabbed the tiller. Now the throbbing set in like drumbeats against her arm. She gritted her teeth to hold in a sob.

She did not mask her discomfort well enough. Ross sprinted to her side and grasped her shoulder. "What is it?"

She shook her head. A mistake. Dizziness sent the boat swimming before her eyes. She was going to be sick.

"Chloe." He wrapped his arm around her waist and drew her hard against him. "Sea too rough?"

She shook her head. "It is simply my arm. It got a bit injured the other night."

"The blood on the drainpipe, of course. I forgot." Ross muttered something rude directed at himself. Aloud, he said, "If you crouch down, the impact won't be so great when we go aground."

Whether or not he was right in that Chloe did not care. He had given her a respite from bracing herself on the pitching deck. She sank to her knees, and a moment later, the boat yawed to starboard. The wind buffeted Chloe's back. She rocked against Ross's legs, flung out one arm, and clung to them. Their solidity felt like an anchor, unmoving in a tilting world.

"Hold tight," he shouted above the roar of wind and surf and creaking lines.

She knelt and held on to him with both arms around his rock-hard thighs and her face pressed against his hip. He smelled of aged apples and the fish market, but she drank it in like perfume. She moved with the boat now, felt calmer. The sea was calmer. She turned her head and saw the shoreline slipping close on either side. They had entered a tidal creek, and with the tide running out, they would ground the boat in moments.

Ross dropped to his knees, wrapped one arm around her and the other around the tiller post. "Ready?"

The boat struck bottom with a grinding shudder that ran from the hull and straight into Chloe's joints. Ross swayed no more than the mast, holding her steady.

"The boat will float when the tide turns. Someone will find it and return it." He rose and drew Chloe to her feet after him. "Time to abandon ship. Let me take your bundle. We are going to get a wee bit damp."

By the time they reached a road, Ross was soaked to his waist. Chloe was, too, but he had held her pistol and bundle high enough to keep them dry as they forded the creek and wended their way through trees and underbrush to the lane.

As much as he wished they could hide in the forested hillside, he knew they needed dry clothes, hot food, and an appearance that wouldn't instantly alert anyone at a glance that they were fugitives. In the first four mile markers, they passed farmsteads, a splendid estate, and a few small inns. They skirted all of them, and whenever they heard anyone coming on the road, they hid in the hedges. After the third time a lumbering wagon passed and they slipped into hiding, Chloe staggered on her way back from hedgerow to high road.

Ross stopped walking and looked at her. Her skin was pale, close to the greenish hue he'd noticed on the boat.

He felt as bloodless as she looked, moving through the autumn afternoon with mist blowing in from the sea and darkening the sunlight. He wished he could leave her in a farmhouse along the way, but knew even suggesting it was a waste of breath.

"Take my arm," he offered instead.

She hesitated, then moved to his left side and linked her arm with his. His arm felt warmer as they resumed walking. They trudged in silence to the fifth mile marker. The road was quiet, settling beneath a blanket of fog with only an occasional drip of moisture from the trees or the low of a cow to break the stillness. Even the birds seemed too weighed down with the increasing moisture to sing.

At the sixth mile marker, Chloe paused and looked up at him with troubled eyes. "Where are we going?"

"A church." He smiled. "Churches have their uses. And vicars keep secrets well."

She gave him a narrow-eyed glance, but said nothing.

In the ensuing silence, the rhythmic patter of approaching hoof-beats sounded like an approaching army. He sighed and drew Chloe to the side of the road, thanking the Lord that the English had taken to growing tall hedges to separate fields from roads. He crouched behind the shrubbery with Chloe near and watched the horseman pass. Not that the man meant anything to him. The horse was a nondescript dun, and the rider wore a curly-brimmed beaver hat shielding half his face and shirt points so high they covered the other half, rather like Vernell's had there in Plymouth.

When the man was out of sight around a curve, and Ross and Chloe resumed walking, Ross turned to her with raised brows. "Do all Englishmen wear their shirt-points so high?"

Chloe shook her head. "Only a certain set who consider it the height of fashion." She drew her brows together. "Mr. Vernell does."

Ross winced at the man's name and looked straight ahead, to where farmland was changing to clusters of houses, warning him they neared a sizable village or town. Falmouth? "Is he good enough for her?"

As if he was, even with his prize money.

But he wasn't ready to give up yet.

"How does Juliet feel about this man?" Ross made himself ask.

"Juliet wants to be a wife more than anything."

"She is like my sisters in that."

The thought sent a pang of homesickness through him.

"She held off when she was being courted in London," Chloe continued, "but when she did not hear from you, and Mr. Vernell began to court her in earnest . . ." She trailed off to wipe mist from her face with her sleeve. "He seems to be a good enough prospect. He is wealthy and is soon to gain a knighthood. And he is steady. Juliet needs someone who is . . ."

"Settled." Ross tasted the bitterness of the truth.

Chloe's silence was more anguish to swallow.

"I suppose it's right stupid of me to expect her to want me under these circumstances," Ross said.

Chloe bowed her head. "She was excited about your return. But when she—we—heard the news . . . You cannot truly blame her for being uncertain if she wishes to see you."

"No, I can't blame her." Ross's heart felt as cold and heavy as the atmosphere through which they trod.

He couldn't blame Juliet, so gently bred, for not wanting to associate with a man all but condemned as a traitor.

"Let us get her free and find your informant." She rose, all crisp efficiency. "Once we do that, you can woo Juliet all you like."

He hoped he could. Every step away from her home he took felt like a step away from a future in which she might play an important role.

Which made no sense. He was moving toward her, off to play the knight-errant who rescued her from danger. She would like that.

"I hope we find shelter soon." His lack of sleep over the past two nights weighed him down more than the persistent moisture in the air. "This knight-errant is getting a bit waterlogged."

Chloe laughed. It was a husky chuckle, not at all like Juliet's sparkling giggle, yet the timbre of the mirth was pleasing to the ear, somehow soothing.

He offered Chloe his arm again, and they headed back onto the road. With the horseman—and anyone else—well out of sight, they made good progress from milestone to milestone. The light began to fade, though, hastened by the fog. Ross squinted through the mist for signs of a church tower. They needed warmth, food, rest. Neither of them spoke. Ross wanted to. He wanted to know why Chloe believed he wasn't a traitor when Juliet seemed to doubt his innocence.

In their steady but too slow progress, he had time to let that sink in like someone shoving a spear to his heart by minute degrees. He made excuses for her. He had since learning of how she hadn't wanted to meet in the parkland after all. She was still young, though twenty since May was not all that young for a lady raised to expect marriage as early as seventeen or eighteen. She didn't know him all that well despite her foolish attempt to flee to Guernsey to elope with him during the war.

Chloe knew him even less.

The disloyalty to Juliet at that thought of her sister stopped him as though that spear had been thrust to the shaft through his middle. He wiped his sleeve across his face to clear some of the water, however temporary such an action was, and took a deep breath to steady his mind.

Chloe didn't necessarily believe in him. She might simply be saying so because she wished to stick to him like a barnacle on a hull in order to rescue her sister. In fact, she might even distrust him as much as did her father and his own countrymen and that was her reasoning behind helping him.

Then he would leave her behind. Once they reached shelter for the night, hopefully the sanctuary of a warm vicarage with a kindly woman of the house, Ross would slip away from Chloe and find his own way to Juliet.

If he could. Another thirty miles or so lay between them and Truro, and he didn't know exactly where in that town his cousin was supposed to meet them. And if Bryok Trenerry didn't arrive, getting to Guernsey from there, closer to the north coast of Cornwall than the south, would be far more difficult.

All right then, so he had to keep Chloe with him for a bit longer. Some honesty between them would help—maybe.

"Why do you believe in my innocence?"

"Why should I not?" Chloe shrugged. "You served your country loyally."

"But everyone says I disappeared into English protection because I aided the enemy, the English. Why don't you think that when even Juliet suspects?"

"I do not believe Juliet truly believes it. She simply fears conflict."

"She was willing to go against her family to come meet me during the war."

"You were a hero to her then. Once you were accused of treason, she was no longer certain of that."

"And when I rescue her, will I regain heroism in her eyes?"

"You will, but you must clear your name first. I cannot have my sister allied with a fugitive."

"Nor would I expect you to. Why do you think I risked coming back to England?"

"Is that a church?" Chloe gestured to the southwest, where a spear of darkness soared into the charcoal gray sky.

"Yes, it looks like a spire." He paused and rested his hands on her shoulders. "Why do you believe me, Chloe, when even an old friend like Deirdre doesn't?"

She avoided his eyes. "I am a trusting soul."

He laughed. "Maybe you trust the wrong people."

"If you are referring to my brother, you will never prove it was he. He is too clever to get caught."

"Maybe. I cut the man who attacked me in the cave. On the neck or jaw, I believe. So we trust no one with a cut in either place or a high collar."

Light sparked in her eyes like sunshine breaking through fog. "Will that not make asking help from a vicar difficult?"

Ross laughed.

Chloe stepped past him and headed toward the spire and building to which it must be attached, but paused at a set of iron gates rising from the mist like spectral barricades. "What if he has a large family and has no room?"

"Then we move along, but in my experience, men of the cloth give shelter to any wayfarer."

In the dim yellow glow of light spilling from a window of the vicarage hard by the churchyard, Chloe's face shone pale, her eyes wide with surprise. Her lips parted as though she intended to ask him a question, but she shut her mouth without speaking and tugged on the bell.

It donged deep inside the two-story house, a resonant note suitable for rousing half the village that must be nearby. Despite the cacophony, no one responded.

"Perhaps they will not let us in after all." Chloe stood close to Ross, close enough for him to feel shivers coursing through her.

No, Chloe wasn't shivering—he was. Now they had stopped moving, the cold and damp reminded him of his winter in the hulk, with the dank miasma of the Thames seeping through the badly calked planks and into his soul.

He couldn't help himself. He wrapped his arm around Chloe to share some of her warmth.

"We should move on." As though she understood his need, she unclasped her cloak and lifted the edge to toss around his shoulders.

He inhaled her scent. Violets and lily of the valley. Sweet and springlike clinging to the fur lining of the cloak. He smelled sea air and tar from their journey on the fishing boat, and also caught a whiff of smoke.

"Someone is here." He pounded the knocker this time, making it boom like a ship crashing on rocks. "The smoke wouldn't be strong if they weren't."

"All right. All right." The voice from the other side of the door was deep and melodious and ranged with several notes of impatience. "Give a man time to find his slippers."

"Oh, slippers," Chloe murmured with reverence.

The idea also appealed to Ross—fire-warmed slippers. "I don't remember the last time I donned a pair of slippers."

The door sprang open. "What is—mercy, children, has there been an accident?"

"Something like that," Ross said, forgetting about his American accent.

～⑨

The Reverend Thomas Polhenny set a cup of tea and a crystal decanter of brandy on the kitchen table beside Ross. "I can offer you something to warm you inside."

Ross raised his brows. "That smells like an excellent warmer."

"A bit beyond what a simple country vicar can afford." Polhenny's long, bony face crinkled as he smiled. "But some folk pay their tithe as they can."

"Ah." Ross allowed himself a few drops of the brandy in his night-black tea. "I'll fall asleep again if I take too much."

And he should look in on Chloe, make sure she was warm and still sleeping as peacefully as he had last seen her. That had been five hours ago, after the vicar had provided them with warm food and warmer water. They'd been shown beds with hot bricks beneath the covers. Ross had stayed awake until a peek into Chloe's chamber assured him she slept, curled on her side with her shining, dark hair fanned across the white linens and the bedclothes drawn up to her nose.

"Maybe we should wake my companion and make sure she eats," Ross said.

The vicar drew a stool up to the fire beside Ross. "I looked in on her ladyship while you were dressing."

Ross's hand jerked, and he flashed a glance at the parson.

Polhenny patted his knee. "Settle yourself, lad. I knew who you were the minute you opened your mouth. We have that few Yankees in Cornwall these days. Who else would you be?"

153

"But you know." Afraid he would spill tea onto the worn but warm woolen trousers from Chloe's bundle, Ross set his cup on the table. "The Ashfords have been here already."

"I don't know if t'were an Ashford who came here." Polhenny scratched his balding pate. "Hired man I'd guess. Looked like livery beneath his cloak with those shirt points up to his eyeballs."

Ross wrapped his hands around his teacup. "Was he wearing a beaver hat?"

Polhenny nodded. "But he took it off most respectfully when speaking to me."

"Was he dark-haired?"

"More light brown, I'd say, with light blue eyes."

Not Vernell then. The description meant nothing to Ross.

"Anything else you recall?" Ross asked. "What was his speech like?"

"Gentle."

That could be anyone from an Ashford trusted friend, to some sort of upper servant.

"Odd they'd be asking after Lady Chloe by name," Ross said. "I thought they'd keep her disappearance a secret so as not to ruin her."

"I expect they trusted a vicar as you do."

Ross lifted his cup and took a long swallow of the scalding, bracing tea. "Rightly so?"

"Certainly, my son."

"Still . . ." Ross stood. "I'll look in on Chloe. She's my responsibility."

Polhenny looked at him with shrewd, gray eyes. "She's more than that to you, lad. More like a noose around your neck if you're caught with her."

Ross held the man's gaze. "You said we can trust you."

"I'm that certain the bishop would say I should inform on you. But I'm the Lord's servant on this earth, not a judge."

Expecting a condition, Ross held his sigh of relief.

The vicar gave him a gentle smile. "But you are right about your having a responsibility to her. You have ruined her."

"I haven't—" Ross's chest felt too tight for talk. Too tight for lies. He could have stopped her from coming with him, not gently, not safely for him, but he could have managed it. She'd proved useful, though. With the vicar's honest eyes looking straight into his, he admitted to himself that he liked Chloe's company as he had liked Juliet's in the cave. Resourceful were the Ashfords, yet maintaining their humor, their dignity, their spirit.

"She doesn't seem to care that she's ruined." Ross sounded defensive to his own ears.

Polhenny shook his head. "She will later. For now, she is thinking of you."

"Her sister." Longing to be close to Juliet rushed through him, a need for her sweet warmth to dispel his confusion, and he gripped the back of a chair. "I should rest more. We'll need to be gone sometime in the night."

"See that you honor her," Polhenny said. "She must love you deeply to help you escape like this."

Ross shook his head. "It's her sister. She's doing this for her sister's sake."

"Huh." The vicar smiled.

Ross shifted from foot to foot. "And she knows I'm in love with her sister."

"Huh."

"Truly, sir, I'm not even certain I like such a managing female. She thinks she must run everyone's life, including mine."

"My dearly departed wife was like that. I miss her. A pearl above price indeed, was that good wife."

"Her sister is sweet and gentle, a sunny day in comparison to Lady Chloe's tempest."

"Indeed." Polhenny nodded. "Sunny days are pleasant for fat, lazy cats."

Ross just stared at him, not sure if he truly did not understand the vicar, or if he didn't want to comprehend what the remarks meant.

"You get to your bed, lad." It sounded like a command. "I don't sleep so much these days, so will wake you in plenty of time to be gone before folks around here are stirring."

"Thank you." Ross climbed the narrow staircase to the room adjacent to Chloe's. He was about to remove enough garments to sleep with comfort when he decided to look in on Chloe.

By the glow of a rush light set within a pierced canister upon the commode, he noted she still slept, her face smooth and soft in repose. No tempest of activity now, giving orders, telling him he must do this and could not do that. No sunny day either. She was simply a pretty young woman exhausted by the past two days.

He should leave now, slip away and let her have the comfort of the vicarage and then shelter of her family. He had no business letting her help him, not even help him find Juliet. And yet the idea of traveling without her made him feel hollow inside. That hollowness was the best reason of all to abandon Chloe now.

It was disloyal to his feelings for Juliet, a condition he did not wish to examine.

Chapter 9

Cornwall, England
Friday, 27 October 1815
Near Midnight

*T*he click of the door latch snapped Chloe out of sleep. She lay motionless, eyes half open and peering into the dim glow from the rush light in its pierced canister beside the bed, to see if someone had entered or departed.

Departed. Nothing moved in the shadows inside the chamber, but outside in the corridor, a floorboard creaked. A moment later, the door to the adjacent room snicked shut.

So Ross had looked in on her before going to his own room. Her stupid heart warmed, even thrilled to the idea that he had watched her sleep. He had never watched Juliet sleep.

Only because he had never experienced the occasion to watch Juliet sleep. He wanted a lifetime of watching Juliet sleep. He had merely looked in on Chloe to ensure she was all right, or perhaps that she had not slipped away to betray him after all.

"If only you knew, Ross, my dear." As she rubbed grit from her eyes, Chloe spoke to the empty chamber where no one could hear her.

Ross must never know why she was so dedicated to helping him now—now that he suspected more than freeing Juliet lay behind her reasons. She had seen evidence of his anger with the British when he was imprisoned in Dartmoor. She did not wish to see that anger turned on her or any member of her family. Kieran had redeemed himself with Ross to some extent. Chloe had not seen him captured out of a desire to stop the enemy's merchantmen, or even an enemy privateer. That kind of loyalty to her country Ross would not care for, but would likely understand. But she had seen him imprisoned to protect her family, to keep her sister from following him.

"If only he had been paroled as he should have been." Chloe groaned and flung her arm across her eyes.

Pain shot through the place where she had been cut. Tugging on the tiller while escaping from Plymouth had torn the wound open again. Now it had closed, but did not feel right. Surely it should not hurt so much after nearly three days. Perhaps if she cleaned and bandaged it better, the cut would improve.

She forced herself to rise from bed and don her breeches over the cotton drawers that were so much more comfortable than lacy pantalets. With only a shortened chemise on top, she shivered in the chilled room and hastened to stir up the embers of the fire and shovel on more coal. Somehow, she would get more fuel to the vicar after this night. For now, she needed to be warm.

The water left in the pitcher had grown cold, so she set it on the hearth to warm. Despite eating two meat pies and an apple upon their arrival at the vicarage, she was hungry again after her long nap. She wondered at the time, and as though knowing she would do so, a clock pealed somewhere in the house . . . ten, eleven, twelve times. Midnight.

Heart heavy, Chloe pulled a brush from her bundle and yanked it through the tangle of her hair. Once the tresses lay black and smooth down her back, she tried to form a fresh braid. No good. When she lifted her left arm behind her head, her wound pulled and she gasped aloud with the pain. For now, she satisfied her need to keep her hair out of her face with a simple bow at the nape of her neck. Somehow, though, she must get her hair braided or she would never pass as a male.

For a moment, she envisioned Ross running his fingers through her hair, smoothing it with the brush, then twisting it into a plait. He would be gentle and thorough; his fingers deft with sailor's knots would know how to braid a woman's hair.

But he might find it too heavy and straight rather than Juliet's softer, curlier tresses.

She shook herself to rid her mind of thoughts of Ross in anything but the practical. He wanted Juliet, not her. She would not even try to lure him from her sister. That would be beyond wrong. If he wanted Chloe, he could work that out for himself.

Except he would not want her for long if he worked out how she had betrayed him.

Which was a good lesson in keeping matters as they stood at present: Ross thinking himself—perhaps rightly so—in love with Juliet. Chloe was the helpful, managing elder sister he did not want around, but whom he needed regardless.

She snatched up the pitcher. If the water was still cold, no matter. She would use it anyway and perhaps jolt some sense into her foolish heart. She had talked herself out of caring for Ross in the past. She could do it again.

She splashed water into the basin and dipped in a corner of the toweling left for her earlier. With the aid of the mirror over the washstand, she studied her wounded arm. The slash was red and a little puffy. When she touched it with the wet cloth, pain shot down to her fingertips and into her shoulder. She gasped and dropped her face into her hands, knocking the pitcher onto the floor.

The copper jug clanged against the boards. Cold water splashed across her bare toes, and she squealed.

The door flew open. "Chloe." Ross poised in the opening, his lips parted as though he intended to say more or pose a question, but could not recall what the utterance was supposed to have been.

"I thought I should clean my wound, but I-I—" Chloe met his gaze in the mirror and all thoughts fled.

He looked stunned, as though seeing something that had never occurred to him. A flush crept up his neck, and he turned his face away so fast his hair swung against his cheek. "You need an apothecary. That wound needs to be reopened and stitched."

"We cannot bring one in here. It is too risky." Chloe gave a reflexive response.

"In some matters, one must examine the risks and weigh them against one another."

"An apothecary would expose us in a moment."

"Lady Chloe, I . . . should not give you assistance." He started to back from the room.

"But if not you, who?" Chloe spun to face him, and understood what lay at the root of Ross's discomfort.

For more comfortable sleep, she had removed the bandeau binding her breasts as flat as possible. With only a thin batiste chemise over her chest, her breasts were as good as exposed to his sight.

She snatched up her shirt and tugged it over her head, shoving one arm into a sleeve. With the other arm still bare, the shirt would fall only partway down her torso, but it was enough for the sake of modesty.

"Is this better?" Her tone held impatience she did not bother to disguise.

Ross glanced her way. "A little. But your arm . . ." He turned away from her and stepped into the hallway, making the floorboards creak in two sharp squeals. "I'll fetch the vicar."

She faced his rigid back. "If you tell the vicar my cut is as bad as it is, he will likely change his mind about not betraying us. Or he will make me stay here with him."

"That would be a right fine thing."

"No, it would not, as you are well aware."

"Someone is looking for the two of us," Ross said, "and that concerns me."

Chloe started. "How is that possible? I am more than a little certain that my family will not tell anyone about my disappearance."

"Your brother and Deirdre told that widow friend of yours."

"Yes, because she is a friend and utterly trustworthy not to talk to anyone. That is far different from spreading the news abroad." She hesitated. "Was it Vernell perhaps?"

"The description doesn't sound like it. The vicar says this man had light brown hair and light blue eyes, fashionably dressed and a London—what's amiss?"

"Rutledge." Chloe pressed one hand to her racing heart. "That sounds like Freddie Rutledge."

"Who's he?"

"The man who mangled Kieran's ear in a duel because he thought Kieran debauched his sister."

"Did he?"

"Not a bit of it. But that is why Kieran ended up a privateer."

Ross drew his brows together. "Then I don't like this Rutledge fellow. But you Ashfords do?"

"I would have said he is a sworn enemy of our family, after causing trouble for us, but he showed up at Bishops Cove with Beasley, and he is the one who told Deirdre about the charges against you in America." Chloe pressed her lips into a tight, thin line, thinking. "He has befriended Beasley, apparently, and decided to make amends with us Ashfords."

"Why?"

Chloe shrugged. "Because he has been ruined socially since the truth about his sister and the duel came out. If he can show society that the Ashfords accept him, he can get into everyone's good graces again and find himself a wife with a good dowry."

"Like an Ashford?"

Chloe choked on the idea. "My parents would never condone such a notion."

"Unless word of your ruin got out and he was your only acceptable prospect."

"Surely my parents would never tell a Rutledge I had vanished with you." She covered her face with her hands. "But someone has, which means I am already ruined and nothing can cover it up. Even if I had offers I might want, they would be rescinded now."

Ross returned and retrieved the pitcher from the stand, still without looking directly at her. "I wonder why."

"Because I will be presumed to be compromised."

He did not disguise his look of exasperation any more than she had concealed her impatience with him. "I mean I wonder why you are not yet betrothed."

"Oh, that." Chloe swiped her hand across the air between them. "I seem to appeal to no man."

"You should." He picked up the basin with his other hand and carried it to the window. After pushing up the sash, he poured the cold water into the garden below. "You're quite beautiful."

"Thank you." Chloe allowed herself to taste the sweetness of the compliment for a moment. "Finding a husband is difficult when a lady prefers walking along the sea in Devonshire to walking along Rotten Row in London, or visiting Hookham's Library instead of the Bond Street shops."

"As I said, you should appeal to any number of gentlemen."

"Except for those who believe I should live like I am a fragile flower instead of taking charge of whatever I wish."

"There is that. Deuced annoying."

Chloe's chin set. "Life is otherwise boring, especially in town."

"Juliet says she loves London. How can two sisters be so different?"

"She would rather read about ladies having adventures than be a part of one. She wants marriage and a home."

As soon as the words were out of her mouth, Chloe knew they were not true. Juliet wanted adventure for herself. She simply did not choose the right sort.

"And why has she not married?"

"Because she was waiting for you." The words hurt, but they were the truth, a truth Chloe could speak to Ross.

"I hope her waiting will be done soon." Ross half smiled, then departed the chamber.

Her legs wobbly, Chloe crossed the room to the settle and dropped onto the hard, wooden seat. She was a fool. Worse than a fool. She was a mooncalf, a true knock-in-the-cradle. Ross knew Juliet better than Chloe thought possible, and he still wanted her.

She brushed tears from her eyes and managed to gather her composure around her by the time Ross returned.

He carried a tray on which stood a small sewing box, a knife, and what looked like a glass of brandy.

She eyed the glass. "I trust I am to drink that?"

Ross grinned. "I'm going to use it to cleanse your wound in place of aqua vitae or that witch's brew you used on me."

Her stomach churned. "And the knife?"

She feared she knew the answer, had feared it since he asked about her possessing one.

He sobered. "I need to reopen your wound to cleanse and stitch it." He set the tray on the settle and dipped the blade of the knife into the spirits. "Maybe you'd better lie down."

"I will sit here." Her mouth dry, Chloe perched on the edge of the settle. "I do not want blood on the vicar's linens."

Ross moved behind her and curved his hand around her arm. "If you prefer." His voice sounded too cheerful. "His housekeeper might think he's giving house room to smugglers instead of simply taking their tea and brandy."

"So now you get revenge for me doctoring your wrists—ah!" Fire seared through her flesh, felt as though it reached her bones. She hissed her breath in between her teeth and tried to pull away.

Ross held her fast. "Steady. That's the worst of it."

Chloe swallowed against bile. "Is it . . . septic?"

"A little." His hand was warm and firm on her shoulder. "I'll clean it. Then once it's stitched, you'll be right as rain."

"Except for an unsightly scar." She shrugged her right shoulder. "But it is not the first."

Ross squeezed her shoulder. "No man worth his salt would turn away from you because of a little mark on your arm." He smoothed his fingertips from her shoulder to the inside of her elbow. "You're usually wearing sleeves anyhow. Look what mine are covering." He drew back the cuff of one ivory linen sleeve to reveal the scabbed-over abrasions from the ropes. "There'll be scars."

"No one minds with a man."

"Neither will the man who loves you." He cupped her elbow in his palm. "Why don't you put your head on my shoulder? I'm going to pour the spirits right into the wound, and it'll hurt like the deuce. Bite me if you need to."

She gave out a shaky laugh and rested her head against the smooth brown wool of his coat, inhaled the clean fragrance of sandalwood, Kieran's scent. It was Kieran's old coat, a little snug on Ross's shoulders. Such a nice, broad shoulder to—

Raw heat seared through her arm, and she sank her teeth into the shoulder seam of the coat. A sound like a wounded puppy squeezed from her throat, and she choked against the dryness of the wool.

"Easy, sweetheart." Ross's arms closed around her. "That's just about the worst of it."

"I know. I have been stitched before."

"When was that?" Ross released her, and she heard him rummaging in the sewing box.

Knowing the silence that followed the crackle of Ross pulling a needle from its paper meant he threaded it, Chloe braced herself with her hands gripping her knees and tried to concentrate on carrying on a conversation. "I fell out of the hayloft."

"Hayloft, hmm?" He touched her wound. Her skin throbbed. "Why were you in the hayloft?"

"Jumping into the hay wag—" The needle bit into her skin. She pressed her fist to her mouth and bit down on her knuckles.

The thread seemed to take minutes to draw through the wound. Her stomach heaved.

Concentrate on the hayloft. The fire is the sunshine.

"What cut you?" Ross asked.

The needle nipped again.

She tucked her chin against her chest and willed herself not to cast up her accounts.

"A needle in a haystack?" Ross asked.

She half choked, half laughed.

"Good girl. One more. What made you jump?"

"Flying. I wanted to . . . to . . ." She felt as though she were flying. Well, at least floating. Drifting, then spiraling downward . . .

Pain in her arm shifted to pressure of a hand against the back of her head and her own knees against her face.

"Breathe deep," Ross said in a less-than-steady voice.

She obeyed. The soaring sensation receded.

"You can hear me all right?" Ross asked.

"Yes." Cautiously, Chloe raised her head and opened her eyes.

Ross crouched before her, his eyes full of concern. He smiled. "Thought I'd lost you there."

Chloe straightened. "I was not swooning. I was thinking about flying out of the hayloft and into the wagon." She looked into his eyes. "Have you ever wished you could fly, Mr. Trenerry? Not like this, not running away, but like the birds, like the sails on your ship?"

"Every time I add one more burden to my life." Sadness clouded his eyes, more gray than blue now. "Maybe before I got myself into trouble when I was sixteen."

"Trouble?" She was probing into personal territory, but it kept her mind off the throbbing in her arm. "When you freed those slaves?"

Ross's lips tightened, and he reached for a strip of linen that had been resting on the tray. "I need to bandage your arm."

"Yes, please." Let him avoid the subject if it pained him. Yet she longed to know what he thought of what he had done.

"Forgive me for asking." She smiled at him. "You need not tell me if it pains you to talk of it."

He might be thinking of something other than the story of him freeing slaves and his father disowning him.

"I'm not ashamed of what I did." He slid the strip of linen between her arm and her side. "But it was against the law of South Carolina."

"Oh?" Chloe glanced at him from the corner of her eye. He had his head bent, seeming to concentrate on his task, but his hair hid his face. "Already a lawbreaker at sixteen?"

"According to my fellow Carolinians." He wound the fabric again, and his knuckles ghosted against her breast.

She tensed. "Juliet thought you must be the kindest man on earth."

"I wasn't kind. I was rebellious."

"If you were only rebellious, you would have found something else to overset your father."

He wound the strip once again, and this time did not touch her. "Juliet said she thought breaking the law that way was all right for a youth, but she preferred I stay on the right side of the law now."

"You have."

"She apparently didn't think so." His fingers still in their motion of tying off the bandage. "She believed the rumors about me."

He left her side and stopped to stir the fire. "Would you like some supper?"

"Thank you, not now. I feel a bit unsettled."

"I'm sorry I had to hurt you."

"It was not your fault. I should have been more careful."

"As if you could have been. Those men were fighting to the death, I think. If you hadn't had a pistol with you . . ." He clanged the poker into its holder. "I should have anticipated trouble. There's a price on my head after all."

"But why?" Chloe leaned toward him. "Why are your own country-men so willing to believe the worst of you?"

"The slave smuggling." He picked up the tray that had held the medical supplies. "One gentleman"—he curled his upper lip—"was ruined when most of his slaves disappeared before he could auction them off to pay his debts."

"Barbaric."

"Don't be too sanctimonious, my lady." He managed a smile. "You all still have slaves in the West Indies. And do you all not have a planta-tion on Barbados?"

"We do, but I do not believe it is run by slave labor." She squirmed on the hard wood of the settle. "At least I hope it is not. I should ask Papa. And the same for the plantation in Georgia."

"I don't know the laws in Georgia, but you might not have been able to free the slaves there without transporting them elsewhere. That is common in the South—to free slaves, you have to move them out of the state." He strode to the door. "I'll fetch food, even if you aren't hungry."

"Once my arm stops hurting, I expect I will be starved. I mean—" She pressed her hand to her lips.

He laughed—actually laughed aloud. "A lady never admits to being hungry. It's all right. You don't need to be dainty with me."

"Dainty," Chloe said with a hint of asperity, "is not a word anyone has attached to me probably from my cradle."

But Juliet was dainty. She had the Ashford height, but did not have Chloe's generous proportions in the chest and hips, and her hands and feet were small. Even her hair was not as heavy, but flowed in soft curls and waves like threads of black silk.

But Ross did not mind Chloe's lack of feminine daintiness— because he still preferred Juliet's more elegant stature. She must not forget that, as much as she wished she could.

While he murmured something about fetching food, unless she wished to go downstairs, then departed, Chloe fought an inclination to moon over Ross's compliment. She reminded herself how he said she was annoying with her managing ways. She turned her thoughts to the practical, things they must discuss in this little respite from the struggle with the sea and now the weather on the road. When each step had been an effort, talking was scarcely what she wished to do, and Ross had seemed content with quiet.

When he returned, however, she would bring up the matters they needed to discuss, plans he needed to know in the event something happened to her, and vice versa. Doing so would keep her from having other, sillier ideas. She must, as always when dealing with anything having to do with Juliet, be the one to focus on the practical.

The squeak of the floorboards in the hallway warned her Ross had returned. She knelt to build up the fire, and was on her knees when Ross entered bearing a laden tray.

"The vicar says to eat well and rest some more." He set the tray on the settle.

"Will you join me?" Chloe took her time rising and turning.

The aroma of roast beef and mustard and fresh bread made her mouth water so badly she feared she would stuff everything into her mouth at once.

"I ate earlier, but I wouldn't mind another cup of hot tea. Who knows when I will get a hot beverage again." Ross stood by the settle until Chloe seated herself.

She spread mustard on a slice of bread, layered on thin slices of the pink roast of beef, and lifted the fare to her lips. For several minutes, she simply chewed and swallowed, took a sip of tea, and ate some more. She stared straight ahead at the fire with orange and gold flames, missing the more pleasant scent of wood smoke to the oily stench of the coal, and tried not to peek at Ross from the corner of her eye to see if he was watching her.

When her sandwich was finished, she refilled her teacup and sat cradling the thick earthenware mug between her hands, and finally turned enough to face Ross with her first question.

"Since I know your informant is not my brother, tell me how you will know for certain who he is if he is always disguised in some way."

"Mostly by his voice. He used different accents, but the voice was always the same, and certain words would slip out, especially when he grew excited."

"He is excitable then?"

"He can be made to be." Ross lifted his cup to his lips, but did not drink, and his eyes went out of focus. "He also cannot disguise his build. He is tall and well built. I know men put wadding in coats to enhance their chests."

"And sawdust in their stockings to fill out their calves. Quite ridiculous."

"Like ladies giving themselves smaller waists with stays."

"I do not." The words slipped out before Chloe realized how improper this conversational gambit was. To be fair, she added, "And neither does Juliet."

"Juliet does not need to practice artifice."

Chloe flinched, but did not seek compliments by asking if he was implying she did. She doubted he even considered what she should or should not do to enhance her looks.

"She is beautiful." Chloe spoke only the truth. "But what else about this man do you know, if you are certain he is not applying buckram wadding or sawdust pads to enhance his physique?"

"The way he walks. It's . . . fluid like a dancer."

"Or a fencer?"

"I've never known anyone who fenced, but quite possibly." He set down his cup and lifted the teapot. "More, my lady?"

"Please."

He refilled their cups, then cradled his mug as though wanting to warm his hands more than drink the bracing liquid. "I also followed him after one of our set meetings. In truth, I had one of my crew follow him. A man we call only Blaze for a white streak through his hair. He spent much of his life stalking game in the mountains before he broke some law of his people and fled to the city and then to sea. He knows stealth."

"I know he did. He managed to get in and out of Deirdre's room without any of the watchmen or servants or family the wiser."

"He is amazing that way." Ross flashed his quick, warm smile. "He tracked my informant down to a boat and stowed away until the man returned to Plymouth and a rooming house there."

Chloe jerked upright. "Did he get a name?"

"Unfortunately, he could not stay around to find out. Blaze is hard to hide in an English city, even a port city. And he didn't dare talk to anyone with his American accent."

"Of course not." Chloe leaned into the corner of the settle, one knee drawn up so she more fully faced Ross. "And that is all you know?"

"In St. Peter Port on Guernsey, the inn he chooses knows him as Mr. Vernon Rugby."

"Vernon Rugby?" Chloe wrinkled her nose. "That sounds made up out of whole cloth if ever I heard of such a name."

"I am quite certain it is." Ross drew back his lips as though intending to snarl like a wolf after his enemy. "But I will know him anywhere, whether he has taken Juliet or not."

Chloe shivered, glad she was not Ross's enemy. "But it seems likely he did, considering the meeting time, place, and date?"

"Who else would want to get his hands on me but the person whose life I could ruin?"

Gooseflesh puckered the skin along Chloe's arms as she realized she was Ross's enemy; he simply did not know it.

Striving for a normal tone, she pointed out the obvious answer. "You have a price on your head. That seems like motivation enough to want to capture you."

"But who knows of my relationship with the Ashfords?"

"How does your informant know of your relationship with the Ashfords?"

"An excellent question." Ross met her gaze across the tray of drying bread and beef.

Chloe slammed down her cup. "It is not my brother."

"Then it is someone who is close to you all—close enough he has kept an eye on your comings and goings."

"Such as Juliet's excursions to her secret postbox."

Ross inclined his head. "I figure that's how he knew I was close to the coast enough to betray me to his countrymen, as he had betrayed them to me."

Bile rose in Chloe's throat, and she barely managed to choke out her next question. "What do you mean?"

"I received the message from Juliet telling me of how you stopped her from eloping to Guernsey." He bent his head as though something shamed him in what he was saying—or burdened him. "I would not normally go back so soon because of the risk, but I had to respond to that. I had to tell her not to be so foolish again, that we would meet when the war ended. I was scarcely back to my brig when two English naval vessels swarmed us and took us before we could even think of preparing to fight." He raised a hand to his face, and it trembled ever so slightly. "I never saw my crew again, but learned later they had been paroled out of Dartmoor. Most found their way home as soon as peace was declared. But I was singled out and sent to a prison hulk hundreds of miles away instead of paroled or even exchanged as the captain of a privateer should have been."

"And you believe your informant followed you as you did him and arranged your capture?" Chloe barely managed to speak around the dryness of her throat.

Ross nodded. "I suspect he knew the war would end sooner than later and wanted to ensure he was above reproach. And he is apparently someone with enough influence and power to have me sent to a hulk and then have the records of my capture and imprisonment destroyed."

"But why would he do that?" Even as she asked, Chloe knew the answer, the saving grace that kept Ross from suspecting her. "In the event you survived captivity, you would die at the end of a rope or be so discredited that no one would believe your accusations against him."

"You are a quick study, my lady." Ross's smile failed to cheer Chloe. In truth, she feared she might disgorge her beef and bread, but she had to ask. "So if you are able to catch your informant, how will you get him to help you clear your name?"

"I will take him back to America with me to testify in my favor, then help him start a new life there or wherever he would like. There is a great deal of land in America, and he must have money from our arrangement."

"But what if he does not wish to testify? You have said yourself he has done well discrediting your word."

"Regardless of that, if I capture him, his life here in England is over." Ross's mouth set in a hardness she had not witnessed since he had been in Dartmoor.

"So you have to capture him before he captures you because he will kill you." She felt as though the needle that had sewn stitches into her arm were piercing into her heart. "And my sister is the bait."

"He'll regret that." Ross's voice grated over the words.

Chloe opened her mouth, the words of confession blazing on her tongue. But before she gave them sound, the consequences raced through her head and shoved the confession away.

She was alone with Ross for all intents and purposes. If he decided to make her his prisoner and carry her back to America to testify on his behalf, she could not stop him and doubted the aging vicar could either. Chloe did not believe he would leave Juliet to the hands of her kidnapper, and yet he might have such wrath against the Ashfords, thinking Kieran was his informant and all, that he might no longer wish to ally himself with the family through Juliet. At the least, the public scandal would be so widespread, with news coming out of how Juliet had corresponded, even tried to elope to, the enemy during the war, Australia might be far enough away for them to be able to show their faces in public. Who knew what the consequences to her parents, to Kieran and Deirdre and the children might be. Yet if she did not tell Ross the truth, he might get himself killed trying to capture the informant, who did wish him dead, who had probably seen the prison records altered.

"Could we not simply try to find out who altered the prison records so they show you were never a prisoner the second time?" Chloe tossed out the only lifeline she found.

"For that, I also need my informant," Ross said. "I have been trying to learn who since returning from Charleston in September, but have had no success."

"I see."

She saw indeed. In the end, she likely had no choice but to tell Ross the truth of her involvement with his capture. But not yet. Once Juliet was safe, Chloe would tell Ross the truth for his own safety. Chloe could live with him despising her. Juliet would recover her heart if he rejected her, since she had not been committed in her affections enough to want him after he was accused of treason. But Chloe could not live with knowing she could have spared Ross a lifetime of running for his life, or worse, losing his life.

Shaken, Chloe slipped to her knees before the settle and covered Ross's hand with hers. "Whatever it takes, Mr. Trenerry, I will see to it you end up a free man from all of this."

"Thank you, Lady Chloe. If anyone can help me make that eventuality occur, it is you." Ross swallowed and turned his hand over to clasp Chloe's fingers. "Sometimes I don't think I will ever be free to go about as I choose, or court whomever I please, or live where I wish to live."

"And where is that?" She resisted the urge to lace her fingers with his.

He let out a scoffing laugh. "I would live in a house overlooking the sea, perhaps with a private harbor, where my own merchantmen could anchor. Sometimes I would take a notion to sail one myself, so long as I had a house of my own to return to."

"But would you not miss your wife and children—provided you have them?"

"They could come with me." His voice lightened as he continued to outline his plan. "Deirdre's mother traveled with her husband, and Deirdre continued after her mother died. From all reports, they were happy. And think of the places they all saw together. China and India and South Africa. Brazil and Chile and Russia. This is a vast world, but the ships are getting faster and travel routes safer. Surely a lady like Juliet would love the adventure of that life."

"She might." Chloe pulled her hand free in time to catch a tear slipping down her face.

"Lady Chloe?" He tucked his forefinger beneath her chin and tilted up her head. "Why the tears?"

"Because I want you to have everything you want to make up for what my countrymen have done to you."

Because she doubted Juliet would want that life, and that would break his heart. Because she would love that life and he would break hers since she could never marry a man she had betrayed.

"You risked your safety to bring Englishmen you captured back to their own country," she continued in a halting voice, "while we treated you worse than horses on a transport ship. You sit there shivering by a fire, afraid you will be caught and hanged, and this war cost us nothing." Her throat closed, but she plowed on. "Indeed, we benefited from your first captivity. We have Deirdre in our lives, and Papa bought the *Maid of Alexandria* from the prize court and makes money with it denied you. A-and—I cannot fix it." She blinked, and tears spilled down her face too fast for her to catch.

Ross caught them. He cupped her face in his hands and brushed the waterfall away. "My lady, Chloe, you don't need to weep for me." He knelt on the floor beside her, still cupping her face. "I knew the risks when I became a privateer. No one would have blamed me if I had gone back to America after Dartmoor. With the money I had earned aboard the *Maid* before we were captured, I could have bought land or joined a merchantman's crew. But I wanted revenge."

"On us Ashfords?" With his face so close to hers, his hands warm and strong against her skin, she could scarcely breathe.

"Not after you all helped us escape. I promise." He grinned at her, then bestowed the lightest of kisses upon her lips.

It was so delicate a brush of mouth on mouth she knew he meant it as a brotherly affection and nothing more, yet for a moment, with his face still so close to hers, she considered the merits of luring him from Juliet with what feminine wiles she possessed. She could lean toward him and kiss him in earnest. If he realized his feelings for Juliet were little more substantial than smoke, Juliet's likely rejection of the life he wanted would not hurt him so much.

He was a man who deserved not to be hurt further. He had suffered enough in his twenty-six years.

Which meant she could not confuse him by reminding him he had kissed her on that hillside.

Slowly, she drew away, picked up the serviette that had covered the viands on the tray, and mopped at her face. "I am such a watering pot."

"And I am . . ." He cleared his throat. "I'm sorry for doing that."

"Doing what?" Chloe made herself laugh. "Kissing me? It seems well enough for someone who wishes to be my brother-in-law one day."

"Of course." He rose and crossed the room to the window, his back to her. "I was afraid you would think I was being disloyal to Juliet."

"Not in the least."

Even though Juliet had been disloyal to him with her ballroom flirtations and walks on the secluded paths at Vauxhall, not to mention her lack of belief in his innocence.

He cleared his throat. "The vicar reminded me that I have ruined you. He believes the least I can do is offer you marriage."

"You can offer all you like, but I would not accept." She snapped out the refusal like lashes of a whip to hold him off.

"Your parents may not see it that way." He rested his brow against the glass so she could not see his reflection, and his tone held no expression, but his rigid shoulders told their own tale.

Chloe wanted to riposte with something like "My parents go hang," but could not be so dismissive of their formidable power. If they wanted her to marry Ross because he had ruined her, nothing would stop them, and Ross would become a different kind of fugitive, even if he cleared his name.

"Your heart belongs to Juliet." Her sister seemed like a shield against chivalry at that moment. "I cannot even consider marrying a man who believes himself in love with my sister regardless of her feelings—" She snapped her teeth together too late.

Ross faced her, his face taut. "Even if she doesn't feel the same way?"

"I have no idea how she feels right now, Mr. Trenerry."

"A pity women can't be diplomats or lawyers, Lady Chloe. You would have been good at either." With a faint smile, he crossed the room and gathered up the tray. "We will talk more of this later. For now, try to get some rest. We will leave in the morning right before dawn and the village starts stirring."

"How? We cannot leave his door unlocked."

"We'll leave through one of these upstairs windows. The one out of my room goes out over the kitchen roof, and it's nothing of a drop from there to the ground for a sailor or"—he smiled—"a lady who likes to fly."

Ross carried the tray as far as the bottom of the steps, but did not traverse the corridor leading to the kitchen. The rumble of snores told him the vicar had fallen asleep before the fire. Ross should have stayed there with him or made Chloe join them in the kitchen if she wanted food. He never should have allowed himself to be alone with her in such an intimate setting.

Yet their conversation had been necessary for much of it and necessary, if disturbing, for the closeness they shared in the rest of the time.

He had liked how Chloe encouraged him to talk of the future, as if he had one worth living. For years, other than the letters he managed to exchange with Juliet, no one had been around with whom he could talk of his dreams for the future. Having had Deirdre as a confidant for six years, he missed that feminine camaraderie. He liked women. He had enjoyed far too little of their company since leaving home and losing the interactions with his younger sisters—delightful moppets all of them. He never realized how lonely he had been until Chloe urged him to talk.

The need for human contact had overwhelmed him. When she had covered his hand with hers, he exerted all his will not to seize her hand—both her hands—and hold on as though she were a lifeline. When he had brushed away her tears, he wanted to curve his hands around the back of her neck beneath the glorious shawl of her hair and fit his mouth to hers. Not merely brush his lips across hers, but taste her woman's sweetness.

He needed to go—now. He should set the tray in the kitchen and keep walking out the back door and across the Cornish landscape to Trenerry Cove, or better yet, get to a boat somewhere and sail for Guernsey. Chloe should be left behind. She was so much like Juliet, she tempted him too much.

Or maybe she was a temptation because she was too much like no one else. She was so comfortable with herself and even him, she didn't demur when he suggested they might need to marry. She hadn't gone all giggly girlish over the mention of stays. She hadn't fainted at him seeing her in her undergarment.

He tried to shove that image from his mind, but feared it was forever burned upon his memory like an image on a woodcut. She possessed a magnificent physique, lush and womanly and so proud in her carriage.

Juliet . . . He couldn't even recall what Juliet's proportions were. They didn't matter. He recalled other attributes of hers—her sparkly voice, her unaffected laugh, and the softness of her hand against his brow. He remembered her ever-present optimism, her constant assurance all would be well, as though just her wishing it would make it so.

Maybe it would. He hoped she was keeping up her spirits under her current circumstances, that she had reason to maintain her positive demeanor. If her brother had taken her to lure Ross to him, then Juliet was all right. But if Chloe was right and Kieran would never betray England even for wealth independent of his father's, then Juliet might be in grave danger, and he needed to find her as quickly as he could.

He simply wanted to be the hero of someone's tale instead of the villain. He longed to do right at least once in his life.

And right was not to abandon Chloe, her reputation in tatters. For over two years, he had thought of how he would one day marry Juliet. With each passing day, that dream slipped beyond his grasp. It had gone from his life the instant Juliet did not believe in him. Yet he could not plan to court with the intention of offering for one sister, then turn around and be forced to marry another. Except honor demanded he offer for Chloe now, that he clear his name so he could do so and spare her from the consequences of whatever sense of duty had driven her to set out on this mission with him.

Mind made up, he set the tray in the kitchen, collected another bucket of water, and returned upstairs to Chloe.

She crouched before the fire with a book in her hands. She did not look up at him when he entered, and her hair fell around her face, shielding it from his view. "I thought you were going to sleep."

"I have something to say to you."

"We should not talk more tonight." She held up the book. "This was in the room."

"Voltaire? Seems like an odd book to be in a country vicarage."

"And in French."

Ross arched one brow. "You read French?"

"Better than I speak it. Do you?"

"I speak it better than I read it. When you are a vagabond mer-chantman as we were on the *Maid*, you learn a lot of languages."

"I know. Deirdre is amazing that way." Chloe closed the book and set it on the bench. "What other languages do you speak?"

"Spanish, Italian, some Mandarin and Hindi." He shrugged. "Portuguese, of course."

"Of course." Chloe's voice was dry. "Are you musical as well?"

"I did all right on the harpsichord as a youth, but haven't had any opportunity for music since." He propped one shoulder on the door-frame. "You Ashfords are all musical, are you not?"

"In one way or another, yes, though Juliet cannot sing."

"She can't?" Ross stared at her. "But I thought she sang to me when I was ill. Did I just dream of angels?"

"You most certainly did not dream of angels." Chloe's cheeks grew as rosy as the fire. "That . . . um . . . was me."

"Well, thank you then." His own face felt warm. "It reminded me of my mother."

"I am uncertain as to whether or not that was a compliment." Chloe laughed, then patted the bench on the other side of the book. "Come sit. We need to discuss our route."

"I would rather get a boat here on the south coast, maybe Falmouth."

"We can try that, but I suspect Kieran will have people watching there. Still, we need provisions regardless of our route, and we can be more anonymous in Falmouth than a village."

"I was thinking that as well." Wanting the heat of the fire, Ross crossed the room and perched on the settle.

For several minutes, they discussed what they would do in Falmouth and then what they would do if that proved too dangerous.

Once they finished with plans, Ross said, "Tell me where my cousin is to meet us if we can't leave from Falmouth."

"So you can abandon me?" Chloe shook her head. "I am sticking to you like a winkle."

"I have no intention of abandoning you, Chloe." He took a deep breath. "Ever. I . . . Once I have cleared my name, I will marry you."

"I will not marry my sister's leftovers."

"I let you come with me, knowing it would ruin you. That ended any future with Juliet."

"I came with you against your will for my sister's sake. Even if you manage to rescue her and capture her kidnapper, she cannot be alone with you or she will be ruined."

"Rather you than her? Are you really that selfless?"

She ducked her head. "I kept her from eloping to you last year. Perhaps this is how I can make up for interfering in your life together."

Ross laughed. "You have more excuses than a ship has rats, and they are all about as valuable. If I didn't know the value of a lady's reputation I would think you had deliberately ruined yourself."

"In a way, I did. Juliet needs her reputation as much intact as possible for the future she desires. I—well, I will probably love life on Barbados or in Georgia or Bombay." Chloe rose in one fluid motion. "I think perhaps we should leave now. The fog has lifted, and we might sleep too long."

"We'll draw attention to ourselves if we travel in the middle of the night. Predawn is all right, but an hour past midnight looks suspicious."

"True." Chloe moved up close behind him and rested a hand on his shoulder. "Mr. Trenerry, do you think someone will catch us before we get to Juliet?"

With a sigh, Ross faced her. "I'm afraid so. They got here to this vicarage before us. They were in the fish market in Plymouth. They were at that widow's house on Bishops Cove. My informant knew where to find me after I escaped from here back in 'thirteen. And, of course, there is the person who knew I was close to the coast the night I was captured. Can you see why I thought it was Kieran?"

"I can, but he has been in Hampshire since October of that same year, and he never could have gotten from there to Guernsey to meet you, even if he would consider sailing."

"So he could not have been reading my correspondences with Juliet."

Chloe paled and shook her head.

"What's wrong?"

"The idea of someone reading Juliet's correspondences with you. It is—it is . . . disturbing."

"To say the least. And even if I have been wrongly accusing an Ashford, I can assure you of this." He pounded one fist into his other palm. "If whoever sent me to the hulk is anyone other than my informant, I will see he pays for his night's work."

Chapter 10

Cornwall, England
Saturday, 28 October 1815
Just After Midnight

*H*eat surrounded Chloe, from her coat, from the fire, from the floor beneath her. But Ross's voice was so cold, Chloe felt as though he'd opened the window and allowed the autumn night to sweep through the chamber. Breathing grew difficult, as though someone had laid green wood on the fire and made it smoke.

Needing air and distance from Ross, she paced to the window. The glass was cool against her brow, and her hair fell warmly around her face. She felt sheltered from Ross's scrutiny behind the black curtain of her hair and with the dark night beyond the panes. She wished she could hide from him forever so he would never learn she was the person against whom he sought revenge.

But she could hide from him. She could tell him where to meet his cousin and remain behind and safe and comfortable in Falmouth, ending once and for all his silly notion of thinking he should marry her.

Except he would never get safely to Truro on his own. He would never be able to negotiate the use of a boat in Falmouth on his own. Too many people were seeking an American.

The floorboards creaked behind her, and Ross rested his hands on her shoulders. "I'm sorry if I frightened you."

"You did not."

Not in any way he thought he had.

"But you cannot go taking the law into your own hands," she added.

"I have no intention of killing whoever it is." He sounded defensive.

"How magnanimous of you to say you would not kill my brother." She intended her tone to ring with sarcasm; she succeeded in coming across as bitter.

His face reflected in the window, his mouth tight, the corners of his eyes puckered. He looked like a man in pain. Her own countenance appeared much the same. And beyond their ghostly images, she caught a hint of movement in the garden, movement blacker than the night, the blur of a face.

She shrank back. "Ross. Mr. Tren—"

Ross spun and wrapped his arms around her. They thudded to the floor the instant the window exploded with the crash of smashing glass and the echoing report of a gun. Chloe screamed. Ross rolled her over and over, beneath him, then atop him, then beneath him. They struck the wall with Ross's body wedging her into the corner between wall and floor, cutting off her breath.

"Are you all right?" His lips grazed her ear, his words more breathed than vocalized.

She nodded against his shoulder.

"Good. I'm going to unlatch the door."

She clung to him. "You will have to expose yourself to do that. Whoever it is will shoot you."

"We can't stay in here." He slipped away from her, keeping low. "When the door is open, crawl through."

184

"Wh-where?" Her teeth were chattering, and she choked on sobs of fright, of anger.

"Downstairs. The kitchen. They won't shoot us with the vicar present."

"I did not think they would shoot you with me present." Chloe tried not to wail, but even her murmur sounded shrill. "If you had not acted so quickly, they could have hit me. They could have—" She made herself cease the rise of panic and take a slow breath. "All right. I can do this."

"That's my lady." Ross patted the only part of her within his reach—her ankle—and stretched for the door handle. The latch snicked. The door banged open on a draft of cold air. "Go."

Chloe crawled through the opening, expecting to hear another gunshot, the smack of lead into wood or flesh. Her stomach heaved, and she gulped, then choked on a mouthful of acrid smoke rolling in waves up the stairwell. Above the steps, a window reflected dancing flames. Chloe heard them now, crackling merrily as though they graced a picnic fire. A few more inches forward was far enough for her to see that they could never get down the stairs.

Shaking, she wanted to curl up in a ball and cry like a child. And she did not want to die, roast there in the vicarage. But outside, someone had a gun. He would already have had enough time to reload by now.

Unable to take another deep breath to calm herself, Chloe sat on the floor with her arms pressed to her chest, and twisted her head to see Ross behind her, doing much the same. "Your chamber and the kitchen roof?" She managed the question in a credibly steady voice.

"That's my lady, not a bit of panic." His look of approval gave her genuine strength. "But we'd better not go that way. He'll expect it."

"He who?" Chloe shot Ross a steely glare. "Surely you do not believe any longer that Kieran is behind this. He would never risk my life."

"He would never risk your life. But someone is willing, and we must get outside before this floor catches."

"I know. I know." She glanced around the smoke-filled hall. "That room should face the church. But the drop—"

"Nothing for a sailor, and I can catch you." He crawled past her and entered the room across the corridor.

The room was large with a fire banked on the hearth and top boots set near the fire. The vicar's chamber. "The vicar!"

"I know. I'll make sure he's safe once we're out. The fire's at the opposite end from the kitchen. They went for the stairs—to trap us."

"Oh, Lord, help us!" Chloe didn't know whether she wept or the smoke stung her eyes into tearing. Her throat was growing raw and her chest tight. The crackling grew louder behind her, flames fed by air from the broken window.

Halfway across the room, Ross stood and sprinted for the window. The sash rose without a creak. Instantly, smoke billowed in behind them, and they both coughed.

"Hurry," he said. Then he was gone, swinging over the sill and vanishing from sight.

He had just dropped more than ten feet.

Certain she would find him crumpled and injured on the ground, Chloe scuttled to the window and drew herself up onto the sill. About to turn to lower herself outside, she spotted the bed with its bright patchwork quilt. Her fur-lined cloak was lost back in her chamber, but the quilt would stave off cold. She ran back and dragged it from the bed. It would also help break her fall if Ross failed to catch her. She dropped the coverlet out the window.

Below, Ross grunted. Chloe gazed into the darkness. She saw nothing directly below her. From the corner of her eye, she caught the flash of light—lanterns, not fire—and shouts rang through the night. Help for the vicarage was coming.

"Hurry," Ross said from below her. "I want to be gone before that crowd gets here."

Chloe swung her legs over the sill and hesitated. The last time she had jumped from a height, she got a pitchfork jabbed into her leg and broke her arm. If she broke her arm or so much as sprained her ankle this time, she would be useless to Ross.

But smoke was so thick now, she could no longer make out the coals in the grate, and each breath was a torture to her lungs.

She closed her eyes, then dropped. Ross caught her around the waist, breaking the impact of her fall. She leaned against him, reveling in his strength. Then she caught the flash of firelight through a downstairs window and remembered the vicar, whom Ross had last seen snoring before the kitchen hearth.

"We had best get the vicar."

"I'll fetch him. It's dangerous."

"You will not escape me that way." She grasped his arm and turned toward the kitchen. At that moment, the church bell began to toll. What villagers didn't know about the fire already soon would. She and Ross would be trapped in the crowd if they did not hurry.

"You do not have time to argue with me," Chloe said.

Ross laughed, and started for the kitchen at a jog trot.

Chloe followed, holding his hand. No window faced the end they ran past. At the corner, Ross hesitated. Chloe knew why. Another gun blast might meet them close enough to kill. But they could not leave the vicar asleep inside a burning building. They owed him his life after his kindness and generosity.

Ross looked at her. "Chloe."

A throng burst into the kitchen garden bearing torches, lanterns, and buckets. Chloe peeked around the corner in time to see the back door of the vicarage swing open and the vicar stumble out. Parishioners surrounded him, shouting, exclaiming, faces full of concern beneath nightcaps and wigs donned askew. All but one man looked to have come straight from his bed. That one man, standing well back in the crowd, stood in profile to Chloe, a tall, well-setup man in the powdered wig, knee breeches, and buckled shoes of the previous century, as though he had come from a costume ball.

Chapter 11

Falmouth, Cornwall
Saturday, 28 October 1815
6:45 a.m.

*C*hloe hated to leave the shelter of Ross's arms. Without the warmth of her cloak, she was only warm cuddled with him in the corner of a ruined kitchen wall, where they'd taken refuge after fleeing the burning vicarage. But she heard the rumble of wheels on the road and smelled smoke from cook fires, not just their own clothing. Cornwall was waking. It was Saturday. Market day. Her birthday.

To turn twenty-four and still be unwed was nothing to celebrate. Yet she knew that Mama would doubly grieve to have her girls gone, especially the one celebrating her birthday, missing the receipt of her gifts like the opal ring Chloe wore on a chain now so she could pass as a male with a cursory look, and the earrings she had gotten the year before. She'd hoped for something more practical this year, like a phaeton she could drive around the countryside when she called on the tenants. Now she would not know what her gift was, and if she did return safely, she doubted they'd give her anything less than a tongue-lashing and a month confined to her bedchamber. Exile was more likely, or an arranged marriage, and she would have no phaeton.

She sighed in an effort not to sob in pure self-pity. They did not have time for such indulgences.

Ross tightened his arms around her, drawing her back against his chest. "Should I tell you it was right foolish of you to come with me?"

"No, because it was not, not for Juliet's sake. Just a little more dangerous than I expected."

"Ah, Chloe." He lifted his head, and his lips brushed her ear. "You're one of the bravest, most stubborn ladies I've ever met."

"And most foolish." Aching deep in her marrow, with loneliness, with regret, with something more she understood but wanted to deny, she turned beneath the arm still encircling her waist and gave herself the birthday gift of kissing him full on the lips.

He did not kiss her back. Nor did he shove her away. He did something far worse.

He patted her cheek as though she was a five-year-old and sat up, leaving her chilled where they had lain so close. "I've already ruined you. I won't compromise you further until I am free to offer you marriage. That is, a dalliance with you would make matters worse when I'm not free to offer you marriage."

"You were prepared to dally with Juliet in the parkland."

"I merely intended to tell her of my innocence and ask her to wait for me. But she didn't come, and even if she had, I would not have compromised her."

"But she did not come and spared you temptation, though she is a tempting minx if ever one existed." Chloe regretted the spiteful words the instant she spoke them. Her only excuse for her cattiness was the hurt of that pat on the cheek. All she could do was try to make amends. "I mean because she is so amusing and pretty."

Ross narrowed his eyes. "I think you meant she flirted maybe a little too freely?"

Chloe did not answer.

Ross nodded as though she had. "I shouldn't have expected her to be faithful under the circumstances."

"Why not?" The words lashed from Chloe with more anger toward her sister than she knew possible. "You were faithful to her when surely you were exposed to many temptations, including from me." She scrambled to her feet. "I think we had best get going. We can slip into Falmouth with the market crowd. Surely we can find food there and possibly a boat."

"Practical and beautiful." Ross rose and began brushing down his clothes.

Chloe followed suit, wondering how he could still think her beautiful with her hair a bird's nest and her face likely as smoke-grimed as his. They reeked of smoke, too. Her mouth tasted as though she had been chewing on charcoal. After going into the bushes, she sought and found some mint. The leaves were withering in the cold, but still held their refreshing tang. The juice soothed the pangs of hunger in her stomach.

When she returned to Ross, she handed him a bunch of mint leaves. "Breakfast."

He shuddered, but pinched off several leaves to slip into his mouth. "I feel like a deuced rabbit."

"We smell more like smoked ham."

He emitted a bark of laughter. "Your spirit is refreshing, but Chloe—" He laid his palm against her cheek. His fingers were warmer than her skin, and his eyes held a light that heated her deep inside. "You didn't avoid telling me the truth about Juliet just to spare her reputation, did you?"

"Of course not. I do not wish to sound like a spiteful sister."

"And you didn't want to hurt me."

She moved her head away from his touch. "You have enough hurt in your life. You did not need to know Juliet considers you a hero from a novel, someone to idealize, but probably not live with forever."

"And so you are the one here helping me when you should be in your home delighting a husband's morning. Are Englishmen fools?"

She held his gaze. "Just this English woman."

He dropped his hand. "I see. I thought . . . Juliet said you despised me."

"I tried to." She inclined her head, her heart sinking from the weight of Ross figuring out how she felt about him and responding so . . . so calmly. "I tried to despise you for how you risked Juliet and the family corresponding with her, but these last three days with you . . . They reminded me of talking to you in the Dartmoor prison yard and the escape."

And him kissing her.

"I'm sorry." He began to fold the quilt with precision. "I held you in high regard until—" He stopped on a cough and glanced away from her.

"Until you met Juliet. I know." She swallowed, fearing she might weep and make more a fool of herself than she was already doing. "I never wanted you to know, nor Juliet either. But you need to understand why I cannot marry you. A *mariage de convenable* I could accept to spare my family social embarrassment over my ruined reputation, but not with a man I-I care about who has preferred my sister to me for over two years."

He said nothing, simply refolded the quilt, shook it out, and folded it a third time. As he performed this homey task, he stared into the distance, while the wind ruffled his hair around his face and blended the scents of smoke from their clothes and the sharp sweetness of fallen leaves.

Chloe watched his profile, strong and, at that moment, as hard as a statue's, and pressed her folded arms across her aching belly. "Perhaps now you understand why I am helping you," she said at last.

And in the saying, she realized she spoke the truth. She had told herself it was guilt over hurting him during the war. She told herself

Juliet would need her once they found her. In the end, she had suffered discomfort and danger, would suffer more discomfort and danger, to be with Ross this one last time.

Because she still loved him.

"So you see, I am not selfless at all." She plunged on. "I am doing this for myself."

Ross broke his stillness then. Letting the quilt slide to the ground in a rumpled heap, he faced Chloe, his hands reaching toward her, palms up. "I think you are even more selfless than ever. And I'm sorry I didn't know . . . didn't realize you cared. I would have worked harder to stop you from coming with me. I have worse than ruined you; I have hurt you."

If she was being honest with him, she may as well complete her humiliation. "You hurt me a long time ago, when you chose my sister over me. But I know as well as anyone that one cannot control one's heart, and I am not going to abandon you because my heart is foolish."

"I suspect," Ross drawled, "yours isn't the only foolish heart in this strange duet of ours." He retrieved the quilt and folded it yet again. "In the future, I'll be more careful with the ladies with whom I am in more contact than a brief acquaintance. I've been so focused on getting my freedom from Dartmoor and now this, and giving myself a secure future, I haven't thought of what I've done to those who have helped me along the way—or anyone but myself and my needs."

"You risked your safety to go back to Charleston when you thought your mother was ill." Chloe gave him an encouraging smile. "That was not thinking of yourself."

He shrugged. "Then maybe there's hope for me yet." He glanced toward the road and the increased sounds of traffic. "If I survive this escapade."

"You will. I will see to it, if it is the last thing I do." She slipped her hand into the crook of his elbow, and they clambered over what was left of the abandoned house's wall and pushed through the hedgerow. A parade of two-wheeled carts, lumbering wagons, and men and women with packs on their backs streamed toward Falmouth for market day. That rose and gold brightened the eastern sky promised a good day for merchants. That the wind now blew from the northwest promised a good day for sailing to Guernsey—if they could find a fisherman who wasn't afraid of the Ashfords, or if they could even get to the wharves. If not, they would have most of a day's journey across the moors to Truro for a possible rendezvous with Ross's cousin, Bryok Trenerry. First, though, they needed food.

Another night with Ross holding her. And he would hold her despite what she'd let him know about her feelings. They needed one another for warmth. Of course, if they met his cousin, they would stay in a house or inn with beds and men to guard them. Ross would also have an ally to get her away from him. Well, if that happened, she would go to Guernsey herself.

At that moment, with food vendors streaming around them, Chloe wanted nothing more than to eat. Her stomach cramped with hunger. A pie man strode past them, carrying his fresh-baked wares over his head and calling out claims the delectable smell said were probably true. Chloe raised a hand to stop him, then realized she had no money. Her money, like her cloak and her pistol, were back at whatever was left of the vicarage.

"Many happy returns," she muttered.

Ross stopped, allowing the throng to eddy and flow around them. "What was that?"

Chloe looked away so he could not see the detestable tears of self-pity in her eyes. "I did not have an opportunity to bring my money away."

"I have money for food. But what was that about the returns?"

Composed again, she smiled at him. "I should start wearing caps today, announce that I am on the shelf."

"Don't be absurd. You can't be more than twenty."

"And four—today."

"I'm so sorry I didn't know." He pulled coins from his pocket. "Will a meat pie do for a birthday breakfast?"

"Anything." Trying not to seem too eager, Chloe took the coins and bought two pasties from the man, and bit into the half circle of pastry before even giving the other one to Ross. Gravy burst from the savory pork-and-potato filling, and she licked it from her lower lip and fingers like a child with a strawberry ice. Not until she took a second bite did she realize that Ross was watching her and not eating.

She stopped. Her cheeks heated. "I am eating like I have been starved."

"I think we are starving." He brushed a smear of gravy from her chin with the tip of his finger, then slid it between his lips.

Her body tensed. "I will eat more slowly."

"Don't change anything." He slipped a corner of his own pasty into his mouth. She watched his lips close around the rounded point of the pastry, and remembered those lips on her own the night before, that brotherly kiss that reminded her she had not fully recovered from her feelings for him, remembered her lips on his this morning, her silent announcement that she still loved him desperately, stupidly, hopelessly.

The last three bites of the pasty turned tasteless and dry in Chloe's mouth. Her own smoke stench sickened her, and her toes felt as though every cart horse that passed her had trod on them.

Feeling the effects of two nights sleeping on the ground and only a few hours in a real bed, Chloe trudged toward the town on legs that felt increasingly more like jellied eels than human limbs. Only the thickening crowd and Ross's relentless strides forward kept her going. Houses grew more frequent until they lined up cheek by jowl with one another. The streets narrowed, and, above the smell of coal smoke and the sea, she caught the unpleasant odors of waste and too many people too close together. She longed for the open moors.

The closest she got was an open market square already teeming with shopkeepers, country vendors, and shoppers. Sellers and purchasers alike shouted about the quality of their wares or the inferiority of others' wares respectively. Chickens cackled, somewhere a dog barked, and above it all, Chloe heard the rhythmic pounding of a hammer. Overwhelmed as to which way they should go, she stopped and stared toward the hammering. A man stood on a bale of hay nailing notices to a sign board over the inn door. The notices ranged from rewards for the return of a lost kitten "of special lineage," to directions to the shop of the best milliner in Falmouth, to the already weather-marked announcement of a reward of five hundred pounds for—

Chloe dug her fingers into the hard muscle of Ross's forearm, hard, she realized with a glance, because he stood in rigid posture beside her staring in the same direction. He could not miss the notice. It was larger than most, and the notice of five hundred pounds had been outlined in red paint. Five hundred pounds to the man or woman who apprehended an American of better-than-average height and breadth, with shaggy black hair to his shoulders and blue-gray eyes.

"Someone, Chloe said, "is one step ahead of us."

Ross turned his back to the notice. "Someone is always one step ahead of us."

Chapter 12

Cornwall, England
Saturday, 28 October 1815
8:55 a.m.

For the first time since they began this crazed quest, Ross read panic in Chloe's eyes. She had been frightened a time or two, but this time her eyes darted from side to side, her lips quivered, and her skin had grown so ashen he feared she would faint.

Afraid she would draw too much attention to them, he slipped an arm around her shoulders and began to draw her through the crowd, affecting enough of a British accent to mutter "Excuse me" and "Lad's never seen so many people" until they left the market square for an alley. It wound them past noisome piles of refuse and manure until it disgorged them onto a narrow thoroughfare, to another alley, to a smaller lane.

In the quiet of that lane, Chloe's labored breathing grew audible, rasping as though she were running. When, at last, they emerged onto the primary road still teeming with carts and wagons, Ross stopped and faced her.

"You need to stay here. Go to an inn and send for someone in your family. I can give you coin enough to pay your shot and get food. You will be safe there."

"No." She lifted her chin, and the calm assurance had returned to her eyes. "I will not leave you."

"You were frightened back there. I haven't yet seen you so scared. You can't continue with me if you are that frightened."

"I am not frightened for myself; I am frightened for you."

"Chloe. My lady." He gripped her hands. "Your caring for me is misguided. I have done nothing but cause you Ashfords trouble. This has got to stop."

"Not as much trouble as we have caused you." She touched his face with fingertips as light as sea mist, and turned away.

In a flash, she darted between a wagon bearing a load of flour barrels and a cart packed with wide-eyed children, then ducked beneath the hedgerow on the far side of the road. With her heading into the countryside, away from any way to get back to her family and safety, Ross had no choice but to follow her.

Knowing how she felt about him, whether a simple *tendre* or outright love, felt like a burden, another layer of guilt to add to his life. Once he met up with his cousin, she had no more reason to stay with him, but she still hadn't told him where they were to meet, so he couldn't set out on his own.

He took more care in crossing the lane, not wanting to draw attention to himself, and walked down the road until he found a break in the hedgerow. Chloe waited for him on the other side.

"I thought we should get off the main road." She offered him a wobbly smile.

"A good idea." He scanned their surroundings of rocky hillside too rough to be a field or even a meadow, some pathetic trees battered down by the wind, and nothing resembling so much as a deer track to follow. "Do you know how to get to Truro from here?" he asked.

"As long as the sun shines, I can hazard a guess." She squinted toward the east. "That's not likely this time of year, but we're too exposed on the road, and it takes longer."

"Then I'm game to go cross-country."

He took her hand in his and fell into step beside her. For a while, the terrain, coupled with their lack of sleep and food, was too rough for talking. Then they reached a stile allowing access to a flattened field harvested of its grain, and they sat to catch their breath.

"They call this the spine of Cornwall." Chloe gestured to the rise of land beyond the field. "It is a high ridge that runs down the center of the county."

"It's a harsh land, but good for hiding."

"If you want to feel like a hunted animal." Chloe shoved her fingers into the tangled mass of her hair. "I must look a fright."

"You look—" He stopped.

She looked a little wanton, but he wasn't about to tell her that.

"Charming," he concluded.

She snorted. "You are a starving man seeing gnawed bones and thinking them a feast if you think I look anywhere near charming. My hair is a rat's nest, and I cannot get my left arm up high enough to help make it look even halfway presentable."

"Let me help." He climbed a step up the stile behind her and pulled the weight of her hair from the collar of her coat.

Despite the tangles, her hair was as soft as satin, sliding through his fingers in skeins of so dark a hue it shone with blue lights beneath the cloudy sky. He used his fingers as a comb until they were smooth enough for him to twist into a braid that reached her waist. Absent of anything with which to tie the end, the plait would unravel, but he wouldn't mind making repairs in the least, though the process left him with a hollowness in his middle he didn't wish to examine.

Neither of them spoke throughout the process. Ross concentrated on detangling her soft locks, on reminding himself this was Chloe, an

Ashford meant for men in high places before he had failed to stop her from accompanying him, and ruined her.

He hadn't tried hard enough to stop her from coming with him, selfish beast that he was. For the past year and more, all his journeys had been alone, from the one to the hulks, to the one to France; from the one to South Carolina, to the one back to England. He had needed her assistance. He didn't think he would have gotten as far as Cornwall without her presence. Likely he would have told Deirdre where to find Juliet by now and lost his chance at catching his informant or seeing her again, for Deirdre would not have let him go free once she had his information, of that he was certain. But Chloe had come with him because she loved him, and he could offer her nothing she wanted because he feared, despite her unwillingness to believe in him, he had fixed his dreams on Juliet so long she was all he could see in his future, though he owed Chloe marriage at the least. Convincing her she should marry him would make up for some of the harm he had done to her out of need, out of selfishness, out of fear of one more prison, and the way she calmly reassured him she would see him free and back with Juliet. And yet, he could no longer have Juliet because he had ruined her sister in the name of rescuing her.

Ross speared his fingers through the disorder of his own hair. "What chaos."

"All will become straight and much simpler when we meet with your cousin. Cornwall is his land, his people. He can get done what you need done."

She drew the braid over her shoulder and inspected his handiwork. "How did you know how to do that so well?"

"I have three younger sisters. Once upon a time, I braided their hair after they pulled it loose in one escapade or another. Sarah Jane, the eldest, liked to climb trees, and Mary Louise—" Suddenly, his throat closed and the rest of his explanation refused to emerge.

"Ross." Chloe turned and rested her hand on his knee, her face full of compassion. "I am so sorry you have lost your family. If we can clear your name, will they take you back?"

He shook his head, still not trusting his voice.

"Not even your sisters?" Her smile was encouraging.

He swallowed. "Maybe. They adored me once." He managed a smile. "Probably because I adored them. They were so lively and energetic and refusing to do what was expected of them as fine young ladies. All of them have married city merchants, not men with plantations. Hannah Beth, the youngest, her husband helped me get back on an England-bound ship. So maybe they haven't yet given up on me. My brother and parents have. My crew seems to have. And Juliet . . ." He laughed. "Listen to me sounding like a maudlin poet. Woe is me. Everyone has left me behind."

"I have not. I will not." Her hand was warm on his knee, exerting pressure.

He covered her fingers with his. "I'm afraid you're going to get hurt, my lady."

"I do not expect you to care for me simply because I helped you escape." She smiled. "I am not that besotted."

"And I am not so vain that is what I meant. I'm afraid you will get physically hurt. You have already been stabbed and had to escape from a burning house. What's next?"

"Truro." She rose. "And time is wasting."

They climbed the stile and headed across the fallow field, keeping an eye out for a farmhouse beyond the rises in the ground. They saw no one across the open land. This was indeed a good land in which to hide—and be hunted.

"So if my informant is putting up signs in Falmouth and burning down a vicarage where we were hiding, who is with Juliet?"

"Perhaps she is nearby and not on Guernsey yet at all."

"Or he has accomplices." Ross paused at the fence on the far side of the field. This side boasted no stile for easy crossing. "Let me help you over."

"I can climb myself."

He scowled at her. "Not with that arm of yours. You don't want to undo my doctoring, do you?"

He shouldn't have thought of that. It reminded him of the smoothness of her skin, and worse, the sight of her in just her thin undergarment, so unselfconscious, so beautifully womanly.

Juliet. He cried inside his head.

But Juliet was a will-o'-the-wisp, a mirage belonging to the past. He must teach his heart not to so much think of loving her.

Chloe went up and over the fence, landing on the other side with the grace of a cat. With a sigh that emerged half on a chuckle, he climbed after her. They entered a copse of trees with a path well-worn enough someone had passed through there often and recently.

"We should have a care through here. This is well traveled."

"I know." Ahead of him, Chloe held a branch so it didn't smack him in the face.

He passed her and began to scan the ground for footprints left that morning after the rain. "Why did you help with the Dartmoor escape? You didn't know me then."

"Deirdre was my friend, so I took her there once, and after I saw you all, I had to help."

"And Juliet?" He had to know. "Why didn't she help?"

"We kept our plans from her." Chloe darted past him to lift a tree branch before it smacked him in the head. "She knew nothing until after the escape, and then she followed me into the cave to tend you one night."

"And continued to help nurse me until I left."

"If you call—" Chloe stopped and rested one hand on a sapling, her back to him. "Yes, she insisted on helping after that."

But she hadn't done any true nursing, not cleansing and bandaging his wound or spooning broth into his mouth. Juliet had sat at his side holding his hand and reading to him or telling him tales from the books she read. She had made him laugh. Chloe had made him well.

"She did none of the unpleasant tasks of nursing me, did she," Ross stated more than asked.

Chloe said nothing, but her fist curled against the smooth bark of the young tree.

"Did you resent her for how I came to feel about her?"

"Resent her? Resent her?" Chloe's voice rose. "Of course I resented her. I especially resented her when she risked the safety of the entire family to communicate with you, the enemy, during the war, and worse, when she tried to get to you on Guernsey. I would be a liar if I said I did not. But every action I have ever taken has been to protect her." She faced him, and her amber eyes were bright with tears. "That includes coming with you. Whatever happens, please believe me in this. I want the two of you together if that is what you want at the end of these troubles of yours."

Uneasiness that had nothing to do with their current circumstances coiled through Ross's gut. Chloe was simply too earnest in her declaration to him, too insistent she could not let him make things right despite knowing she was ruined socially.

"What aren't you telling me, Lady Chloe?" he asked softly.

"I . . . that I . . ." She gave her head such a violent shake tears scattered, catching the sunlight like beads of molten gold.

Ross took a step closer to her. "You are helping me because you have misguided feelings for me, but you don't trust me."

"I am so sorry." She wiped her face on her sleeve and started to turn away.

He wrapped his arms around her and held her. "I don't blame you. I have done you no good."

"Nor Juliet." Shaking, she sagged against him, her head on his shoulder. "I am so scared for Juliet and for us. I have never been scared

203

in my life, not even during the escape from Dartmoor. That was an adventure, a lark. This is . . . deadly."

"I know." He pressed his cheek to the top of her head.

She smelled of smoke with a hint of sweet flowers beneath. Her body against his was sturdy and soft, strong and vulnerable. She fit well against him, warming him from the endless chill that had pervaded his bones since the hulk, since Dartmoor.

Around them, the woods were still save for a wind high in the treetops. On the ground, nothing moved except his heart beating too fast and too hard.

The urge to tilt her head back and kiss her tremored through him. He pressed one hand to her shoulder and the other at her waist to stop himself. He was not a roué. He did not take advantage of situations for a few minutes of forgetfulness. He had not done so in the cave with Juliet, though he knew she had wanted him to kiss her good-bye. He would not do so with Chloe in that quiet woodland. He would do so from pure physical hunger, not affection or the better motivation, love. Brave, loyal, kind, managing Chloe deserved better than desire without love behind it. He had already done her enough harm.

Slowly, reluctantly, he let her go. "You didn't expect this to involve attempted murder when you foisted your help upon me?"

"Trying to get you hanged for a crime you did not commit is attempted murder."

"But someone is asking for two people and still tried to burn us in the vicarage."

Ross paused to lean against the trunk of an oak. For a moment, the lyrics of an old song ran through his head.

> *"I leaned my back against an oak*
> *Thinking it was a trusty tree*
> *But first it bent and then it broke*
> *So did my love prove false to me."*

Juliet, the lady he believed his love, had proved false when she didn't believe in his innocence. Yet he had proved false to her every time he found Chloe attractive, that kiss in the vicarage, needing to offer her marriage. He had never kissed Juliet. He had only kissed Chloe on another hillside in another county during another escape.

"I am frightened because whomever we are after must have friends in high places to get your prison records erased." Chloe's words brought him back to the present.

He shook his head to clear it of the fog of too little sleep and less nourishment. "That's why I thought it was your brother. You know I didn't simply believe him guilty because I was angry with him. There is also the notion he was reading my correspondences with Juliet to know my movements like the night I came to the park."

"So since it is not my brother, it could very well be someone else close to the Ashfords, at least close enough to know our movements."

"As in you vanishing with me."

"That sounds like Vernell, but he was not the man at the vicarage."

"He did try to shoot me on the roof when he had no cause to do so."

"But he's a member of Parliament."

"And Benedict Arnold was an officer in the Continental Army."

She gave him a blank look.

Ross smiled. "He was a traitor during the American Revolution."

"Obviously, we have had our share of traitors as well." Chloe's face worked, as though she were trying not to say something.

Ross considered pushing her to talk, to stop holding back whatever thoughts ran through her head, but daylight was short that far north in the autumn, and they needed to be on their way.

"When do we meet my cousin?" he asked.

"Tonight around nine of the clock." She glanced at the sky, then started up the path.

They didn't speak again until they reached the crest of the hill. Below and to the northeast, a hint of smoke drifted in a silvery gray thread.

"Which way is Truro?" he asked.

"Northeast."

"Dare we stop at that farm there and ask for at least some water?"

"I intend to ask for more than water. Or do you think we can strut into an inn looking as we do?"

He gave her a suspicious glance. "More friends?"

"Not here in Cornwall. But I have a thought if you will trust me."

"I do," he said, and meant it.

The way down was often steep and always rough. He held her hand, liking the human contact. She didn't object, but she didn't meet his gaze whenever he glanced at her, and she never returned one of his smiles.

"What's troubling you?" he asked at last.

She shrugged. "Getting to Trenerry without someone catching us. Getting to Guernsey even if your cousin does meet us. Finding Juliet safely. Staying alive."

"Is that all?"

She smiled at him then. "Mostly."

"And the rest?"

"There is—" She paused, worried her lower lip, then rolled her shoulders as though shrugging off a burden. "What if my message never reached your cousin?"

Ross gave her a sharp glance. "Are you concerned your farmer friend isn't trustworthy?"

"Not at all. He helped me get a few men out of Dartmoor a second time. The crew from your privateer in fact."

Ross stopped and stared at her. "That was you, on your own?"

"Not on my own." She glanced toward a field of sheep near the farmhouse. "I had Tom Appelgard, the farmer smuggler."

"And why is that?"

"Because I couldn't do it on my own."

"No, Chloe." He slipped his fingers under her chin and tilted her head up. "Why did he help you get Americans out of Dartmoor?"

"I paid his rent a time or two when his wife was ill and the free trading was bad along with the harvest."

"You paid his rent?" Ross studied her face, all but expressionless, as if what she told him was nothing special. "Do you have an inheritance of your own money?"

That would be odd for a single female, yet not unheard of.

She shook her head. "My father gives me a generous allowance."

"Enough to pay this man's rent, like for a year, if he was willing to commit treason for it. And that widow we were going to stay with? Do you pay hers, too?"

"Always. She's a widow who kept herself sewing, but she has cataracts now, so can only knit a little. That buys her food and things, but she couldn't make enough for the rent."

"Others?" He suddenly needed to know all about her.

She stepped out of reach of his hand. "My family is shockingly rich. I do what I can to help those less fortunate, who have landlords less understanding than my father."

"At the cost of many shopping excursions I presume."

"I make my own gowns instead of wasting money on paying a seamstress. I am a fine needlewoman, and that saves a great deal of my money for better things."

"Then I shouldn't be surprised that you're helping me."

"I have not done enough for you." Tears starred her lashes. "I did not get you out of prison the second time." She brushed past him, and sprinted a hundred yards to where a low stone wall held the sheep in their moorland pasture.

He wanted to call after her, stop and talk with her longer, but feared he would startle the animals, so sidled up beside her. "Chloe, shouldn't we see if anyone's about we'd rather not know we're here?"

"No horses," she said. "We would have seen them from above if anyone were here."

"They could have walked too or hidden the horses."

"Possible, but not likely." She looked at him with intensity. "We have to trust someone or we will starve out here."

She was certainly right about that. One pasty since their supper the night before, a supper of which she had eaten little, was not enough for the journey they had taken or the one still ahead. For practical reasons, if nothing else, they had to stop.

They climbed the first wall and crossed the field. A second low wall held the sheep from coming into the garden, where a few chickens scratched amid the brown remains of the vegetables.

A stout woman with black eyes and the weather-beaten skin of a sailor stood on the back stoop with one hand on her hip and the other clutching an iron skillet. "We don't give nothin' to gypsies."

"We are not gypsies," Chloe said. "We were shipwrecked on our way back from eloping to Guernsey, and now we are trying to get to Redruth."

As Chloe spoke with her precise lady's speech, the woman relaxed, and a twinkle brightened her eyes. "You're no tinker, that's for sure, I'm thinkin'. I suppose you're wantin' some victuals."

"We can pay," Chloe said.

Chloe, Ross learned moments after they'd consumed eggs, ham, and thick slices of hearty bread, intended to pay for more than food. With the persuasion of the tinkers the woman had feared they were, Chloe obtained clean, homespun garments for them to wear and hot water for them to have a wash. The woman's husband, wherever he was, must have been a big man, for the clothes fit Ross tolerably well, though they held a bit more of the sheep's scent than he liked. Chloe, when she'd gone to change, hadn't fared so well. The gown hung from her shoulders like a sack, and the sleeves flopped around her wrists. Due to the breadth, however, the dress hung low enough to cover all but the heels of her boots. Still, the shapelessness and dust from the trail clinging to her hair made her look twenty years older. No, that wasn't dust from the trail, or he'd have noticed it sooner. It was flour. She'd combed flour through her hair.

She held out a dish and a comb to him. "You do the same. We will be an old married couple."

"You have no ring," the farm wife said from the back door. "Wonder even the Guernsey parsons let you wed without one, I'm thinking." She gave Ross a suspicious glance. "If you've been lyin' to me . . ."

Chloe looked stricken, and her hand flew to her throat.

"No, ma'am," Ross said, hoping, not for the first time since their arrival, that she didn't know what an American accent sounded like. "I haven't lied to you." Well, he hadn't.

"No, he has not." Chloe tugged on the chain around her neck. "I have the ring here. I was afraid I would lose it on the boat crossing, and after that crossing, I think I would have." She pulled the chain over her head and unfastened the clasp. When she released it, a ring slid onto her palm, where it lay with gold gleaming and a stone smoldering with hidden fire. "I had best wear it now. And we can be on our way."

Ross laid four crowns and a shilling on the table, reasoning the woman would have an easier time spending the smaller coins than she would have with guineas. The gleam in her eyes assured him he had, if anything, overpaid her.

He smiled at her. "If her father comes looking for us, we weren't here, right?"

She scooped the coins into her apron pocket. "I don't give house-room to strangers."

"Thank you." Ross turned to Chloe. "Shall we be going, my love?"

Chloe slipped the ring onto her finger, then wrapped a mulberry-colored shawl over the black gown, wafting the sweet scent of rose petals over the oily stink of lanolin. "I am ready."

Once they rounded a curve in the lane leading from the farmhouse, Ross stopped and caught hold of Chloe's hand. "Once this is all settled, I'll buy you a true wedding ring. A body doesn't need a special license to wed on Guernsey."

"So Juliet told me." Chloe's tone was dry. "She expected you to wed her there. Perhaps she still does."

"My responsibility is to you, Chloe, not her. You're the one who has believed in me and stayed with me despite the consequences to you. Once this is over—"

"You will not wish to wed me." Chloe's declaration rang through the quiet afternoon with such conviction, Ross knew once and for all she was, if not outright lying to him about something, withholding vital information.

"What are you not telling me, Chloe?" he demanded.

With Ross's eyes intent upon hers, Chloe could not think. She needed to tell him the truth about her role in his capture. Yet it would serve no purpose except to make him an enemy of her family, to disgrace her family worse than she already had in coming with him, should the truth reach the ears of society, and with Vernell and possibly Freddie Rutledge knowing, it quite likely would. And telling him would not change his course. He still needed to find Juliet and her kidnapper. If her abductor and his informant were one and the same, as they believed, the man needed to be caught, stopped before he succeeded in killing Ross.

"A lady need some secrets." She tried to give him a coquettish smile.

He narrowed his eyes. "Why do I think this one isn't the sort a lady needs to keep?"

"Because nearly three days with me on the run makes you think you know me better than you do." She focused her gaze past his left ear, thought they should have cut his hair to enhance his disguise, thought of how soft that hair was and how she would like to bury both her hands in it and draw his head down to hers. And she could only think how the whole truth would send him running.

"Chloe." He brushed his fingertips across her cheek. "What about me frightens you?"

"Nothing." She took a deep breath. "Everything. I do not want to see you hurt. I do not want Juliet hurt."

"And what about you?" His smile was gentle. "Doesn't anything ever hurt you? Or do you think so often of other people's feelings you forget about your own?"

She shook her head. "As far as I knew, I never had a chance to have you care about me."

"You didn't try. You let your sister usurp your place with me."

"It was never like that." She dropped her gaze to the dusty toes of her boots peeking from beneath the hem of the heavy gown. "I thought we would never see you again, so when Juliet wanted to practice her wiles on you in the cave, I saw no true harm in it."

"Until I set up a correspondence with her."

She nodded. "The loyalty of the Ashfords has been questioned in the past because Mama was a spy for America during the last war with your country, and then with Deirdre and all. So Juliet writing to you was dangerous."

"Why didn't she think so?"

"Because she does not know about Mama. Her eloping to you on Guernsey could have seen us all in prison or worse."

"I'm sorry. I didn't know how serious a crime a few messages could be." He laced his fingers with hers. "I feel even more responsible to make things right for you now."

Though she welcomed the warmth of his hand curled around hers, Chloe looked into Ross's eyes and spoke what she knew was the truth. "You can never love me; thus, marrying me will make nothing right."

"Chloe, I—"

She held up a staying hand. "We need to move along."

"If you insist." He released her hand. "How far to Truro?"

"Two or three miles."

They were long, uncomfortable miles, though the track sloped down into a respectable road the closer they grew to the town, where mine owners brought their ore for assessment and stamping. A better road meant more traffic, and they began their routine of the previous day, ducking behind hedgerows and walls to avoid individual travelers. Eventually, traffic grew too heavy for them to avoid every wayfarer. The afternoon drawing on, most of the merchants and farmers headed out of the town, with empty carts for vendors and full ones for those who had done their marketing.

Walking in a dress proved cumbersome after days in breeches. She had to take mincing steps due to the gown's weight, and her feet began to ache.

Her heart ached, too, for Ross said nothing to her other than what was necessary for their next course of action. Each time she glanced at him from the corner of her eye, he looked pensive and remote. Yet he took her hand in his again, and a few people smiled at them. She did not smile back, afraid a show of her still good teeth would show she was neither poor nor middle-aged. But she looked at them, scrutinized each face for sight of someone they should avoid.

At last, they strode into Truro to the market square. They were so close to the inn where she hoped Ross's cousin would meet them that night. They would be safe with Lord Trenerry's help—if he helped. He might think his cousin was too lawless to risk aiding.

"What if Trenerry does not meet us?" She paused to gaze up at Ross. "We have been presuming he will be here, but he might choose otherwise."

"He told me during the war that family always comes first." He grinned. "How did he put it? The English way is to serve family, then country, then God."

"That sounds like my father's philosophy. He left the navy for family." She glanced around. "I have never been here before, so I told your cousin to meet us at the inn Tom Appelgard recommended here—the Red Lion. We may have to ask directions."

She sought for a likely person of whom to make inquiries. A cherubic gentleman in city garb directed them through the streets to the inn. A few vendors remained in front of the establishment, mostly those selling hot food. Smoke rose from a chestnut-roaster's cart, and her mouth watered. An old woman gathered the last of her apples into two baskets beside the inn's taproom door. Beyond her, the notice board carried the usual advertisements for laborers and workmen. Prominent among these hung the same notice they had seen in Falmouth, and directly below that notice, directly in front of the inn's front door, stood Henry Vernell.

Chapter 13

*C*hloe's fingers flexed around Ross's. She started to turn, intending to run. Holding her fast, Ross drew her behind the chestnut-seller's cart. She resisted. The red cart only came as high as her chest, and the smoke was not thick.

"We can't run," Ross murmured. "He hasn't noticed us yet. If we run, he will."

"Where will we go?" A quick glance told her Vernell still lounged beside the inn door. "We cannot leave here, or we will miss Trenerry, and Trenerry Cove is another thirty miles. That is not enough time if we are to get from there to Guernsey by Tuesday night, and—"

"Shh." Ross laid his finger on her lips. "Think. We've got to get Vernell away from the inn."

Chloe took a deep breath. She would not have hysterics and make a fool of herself in front of Ross. She would think. "Or we could simply go to the rear door."

"He may have that watched. And look. There's no way to get back there."

Chloe looked. Ross was right. The stables to the inn ended at a high brick wall on one side and the terraced gardens to some city merchant's house on the other. To get to the rear entrance of the inn, they would have to traverse the market square and walk along the street adjacent to the lane they had taken. Square and street were visible to Vernell. They would be caught where they were if the crowd shifted or something drew Vernell's attention to the chestnut cart.

Drew his attention . . .

Chloe grasped Ross's arm. "May I have some coin?"

He gave her a narrow-eyed glance. "Do I want to know why you want it?"

"Just be prepared to take refuge in the inn if I am successful, or run like the devil if I fail."

He squeezed her hand. "Chloe, I don't think—"

She drew away from him. "If you have to run, the coast is north and Trenerry Cove is west." Before he could respond or catch hold of her again, she spun on her heel and marched around the cart to where the chestnut seller presided over his brazier, heavy iron tongs poised to turn roasting nuts or fill a paper cone for a customer. As she walked, praying her scheme would work, she loosened her shawl so that it dangled from her shoulders.

She faced the chestnut seller. "A smallish cone, good man."

"Right away, ma'am." He swooped down with his tongs and selected a chestnut.

"No," Chloe exclaimed, "that's too brown. Those in the corner." She leaned forward.

"Have a care," the chestnut seller cried. "Your shawl—"

Without the lanolin milled out of it, the shawl caught fire the instant it touched the hot coals. Chloe let out a powerful scream and flung the garment away from her. Shoppers scattered, shouting protests and alarms. The chestnut man waved his tongs bellowing something about not being responsible.

And two strong hands grasped Chloe's shoulders.

"Lady Chloe, what the deuce?" Vernell said behind her.

"Unhand me, sirrah," Chloe shouted.

"My lady, it is—"

"Constable? Where's a constable?" As she had done to Ross on the roof, she lifted her skirts and kicked up and back. She aimed higher on Vernell than she had on Ross. Her boot heel connected with soft flesh. Vernell howled and released her.

Chloe sidled away from him, shaking her finger though he was doubled over. "That man accosted me. I want him taken up," she announced to anyone listening.

A score of people listened. They stared at her, the men with pained faces, the women with smiles half hidden behind their hands.

"Planted him a facer," a child of about six said.

"That weren't no face," a youth twice his age announced.

Afraid Vernell would recover, Chloe glared at the crowd. "Are you people in the habit of allowing ladies to be accosted in your market?"

"No, ma'am." A burly constable pushed through the gawpers. "What occurred here?"

"I was trying to buy chestnuts," Chloe said, "and this man grabbed me after my shawl—"

"She is a runaway daughter," Vernell said in a rather strangled voice. He rose to his knees. "Her father—"

"She addled your wits, man," someone in the crowd shouted, "if we're to believe she's a runaway anything 'cept maybe wife."

"But I tell you—" Vernell staggered to his feet. "She is—"

Chloe backed behind a broad woman with a basket the size of a sheep and skirted the market square in the direction of the inn. With each step, she kept her attention on the ruckus before the chestnut cart. Vernell was surrounded, and no one seemed interested in letting him go anywhere. As she reached the inn door, a last glance told her that the constable was escorting Vernell out of the square. How long he'd be detained, she did not know, and she and Ross had to remain at this inn to meet Bryok Trenerry. Once released, Vernell would come seeking either a woman alone or a woman and a man. So she simply could not be a woman when she walked through the door.

She veered to her right and entered the stable. In the late afternoon, it was a quiet place smelling of horses and hay and not too much manure. The thought of riding instead of walking reminded her that her feet hurt. How she longed to get her boots off! For now, she had to satisfy herself with getting her gown off. She ducked into an empty stall, and yanked the smelly wool over her head. Beneath, she wore her breeches and jacket. She should have worn a vest to hide her breasts, but she had no luggage. The dress did hold ample fabric. She could tear out the sleeves and create a bandeau to flatten her chest and form a bundle from the rest . . .

A simple solution to think up, difficult to execute. The stable was cold, and her fingers proved to be stiff. She tore off the sleeves and tied them together to form the bandeau, then she had to remove jacket and shirt, which made her colder and her wounded arm ache. The tumult in the square had dwindled, and she feared someone would walk into the stable and catch her with her shirt off. Someone like Vernell, freed from the constable. What of Ross? She was taking so long, she feared he would weary of waiting for her. If his cousin were already there, would he simply leave her behind? She could not let that happen. If Ross failed to catch his informant, she needed to be there to confess her knowledge, her role in, his second captivity before he made a fugitive of himself to the lonely, vagabond life he no longer wanted.

Hurrying, she fumbled with knots and buttons. She was all thumbs. Like this, she was doing neither him nor herself any good. She had to slow, think, plan better.

With her movements more deliberate, she finished tying the band of scratchy wool around her breasts and replaced her shirt. Then she fashioned a bundle from the remains of the gown. She was certain she looked odd, but this inn wasn't the best sort in town, the reason why Tom Appelgard had recommended it.

Chloe's fingers froze on the top button of her jacket. How, out of all the inns in Truro, all the inns in Cornwall, had Vernell known where to wait for them? Coincidence, possibly, but she feared it was not. Truro boasted at least half a dozen inns. Vernell must have caught Tom. Vernell, one step ahead of them.

Once again, she considered the possibility that he was whom they sought. Yet he had not been the man at the vicarage. An accomplice, of course. Someone must be looking out for Juliet.

But Vernell was a member of Parliament. Surely she had to be wrong. His appearance on the fishing wharf, his appearance here, were coincidences. Yet, how many others were close enough to the Ashfords to have kept an eye on Juliet's movements over the past two and a half years? On shaky legs, Chloe went to the stable door and peeked out. The square looked rather peaceful, and, she was pleased to see, the chestnut seller was doing a brisk trade.

Assured the coast was as clear as it would get, she started out, then remembered her hair. No one would believe her a youth if her hair looked gray. But she had no comb.

She stood in a stable full of grooming implements. The tired horses munching hay in their stalls had paid no attention to her, so she doubted they'd mind if she borrowed one of their brushes for her own mane.

Smiling at the idea, though she had to wrinkle her nose at the strong horse aroma, she brushed the flour from her hair and tied it into a rough queue with another strip of fabric from the gown. With her hair stuffed down the collar of her jacket, she slipped along the wall to the inn door. Now to see if she could pass herself off as a youth in the dim interior, and then find Ross.

◌

Chloe huddled before the fire with her arms wrapped around her updrawn knees. Her hair lay around her shoulders like a cloak. Still, the dampness of a room only recently warmed by a fire and a deeper cold shivered through her each time she thought of how close they had come to having Vernell catch Ross.

"But he didn't catch me," Ross had assured her once they were safe behind the room's locked door.

Vernell was nowhere in sight when she emerged from the stable and swaggered into the inn. The landlord had looked at her askance until she handed him two crowns on account. He had then led her up to a chamber that overlooked the stable yard. Ross, waiting in the shadows, had followed her into the chamber as soon as the landlord was out of sight, and for the moment, they were secure.

The musty smell of dampness warned her the bed was likely not safe to sleep upon, but the floor and hearthrug were swept, the quilt on the bed bore no stains, and a plentiful supply of coal lay in the scuttle. She also noted that the window was a good twelve feet above the ground, too far for anyone to climb in, and the door possessed a bar rather than a flimsy key lock. They would be safe. As far as the landlord knew, no one of Ross's description had ever entered the inn. Vernell could ask about two strangers taking rooms in the inn, and the answer would be only one had taken a room, a youth. As far as Vernell knew, she was posing as a lady of middle years. The only danger lay in the moment when they needed to leave their room and meet with Bryok Trenerry— provided he arrived. But perhaps Vernell took a room, as well.

Another shiver passed through Chloe. "Ross? Do you believe in coincidences?"

"They happen." He spoke from his seat on the settle behind her, where he finished the rest of the mulled cider she had ordered along with hot water and some sandwiches. "But that beau of Juliet's being here is right too much of a coincidence for me."

"Me, too." Chloe clasped her hands over her arms, felt her bandage, and knew she should have Ross tend her wound for her. But that would mean taking off her shirt, risking him seeing her, touching her . . .

She must not give in. That would hurt them both.

"We must be extremely careful when meeting your cousin," she said.

Ross's hand stilled on her shoulder. "I think you should stay behind here once I'm with my cousin."

"But—" Unless she told him her reason for going with him, she had no more excuses to continue.

"I'll come back for you once my name is clear." Ross stroked one finger along the side of her neck.

She shivered. "You will have to bring Juliet home."

"I will see she gets home safely, but I can't bring her back here until I'm a free man." He rested his hand on her cheek, warm and rough. "I can't be alone with her, too. That really would be a muddle."

"Not if you care about her more. I mean—" Chloe swallowed a lump in her throat. "She won your heart. I did not."

"But you were my friend there in Dartmoor." He tucked his fingers beneath her chin and tilted her face toward him. "And I kissed you during the escape. Do you remember?"

Before she could answer that she had never been able to forget no matter how hard she tried, he kissed her again. No brotherly kiss this time. No kiss of excitement and victory as during the escape. He kissed her like a man long deprived of sustenance takes in his first nourishment—slowly, gently, urging her lips to part beneath his and touching his tongue to hers.

He was tentative at first, lifting his mouth from hers, waiting a heartbeat for her to draw back or protest, then resuming the contact when she did not.

She was not about to protest. She had spent too many aching nights dreaming of him kissing her as he had during the flight from Dartmoor. And this was so much better. That had been rushed, a mere contact of lips. The intensity now seared through her more than fulfilling her imaginings, yet raising the need to be closer to him.

She wrapped one arm around his neck and slid her free hand into his hair. Silly humming rose from her throat, but she could not stop herself. If she tried, all the words she wanted to say and thought she should not might spill from her lips and seal him to her forever when she knew they could enjoy no future, not with her betrayal of him and Juliet lying between them.

The clatter of several horses arriving in the stable yard below broke the moment. Ross released her, then crossed the room to the window. He stood to the side so he could not be seen from below.

"Hard to recognize anyone from this angle." He stepped back, then moved to the other side. "Likely others needing an inn for the night." He returned to Chloe's side. "Do you think my cousin received your message?"

"I do not know." She sighed, and it held a quiver. "Tom may have sent it on before Vernell got to him. Provided he did get to him. And we can hope that if Vernell is not detained very long, my ruse worked."

Ross chuckled. "No one who knows you would mistake you for a youth, Chloe." She felt him lean close, then his fingers brushed along her cheekbone and smoothed her hair back from her face. "You look wholly female to me." He traced one finger along her jaw. "But that landlord seemed more interested in your silver than your gender."

The shiver that ran through her had nothing to do with her chill. Anxiety. Excitement. Anticipation. Nothing that had to do with Vernell or betrayal or apprehension that Bryok Trenerry wouldn't arrive that night to help them. Everything to do with the man behind her, who had kissed her with all the passion she dreamed about until she learned he had been corresponding with Juliet.

Those letters should still be giving her pause. She should tread with care to preserve her heart.

Ross lifted a strand of her hair and stroked it between his fingers. "Did you think of me during the war?"

"How could I not when Juliet talked about you to me nearly every day?"

And her conscience stabbed her too often.

"She showed me your messages when they came, then tucked them away in a box of lavender so I would not read them again."

"Why not?"

"Lavender makes me sneeze."

"Ah. I suppose I should be flattered." He sounded anything but flattered, more subdued and thoughtful.

Chloe sat cross-legged on the hearthrug, watching him pace around the chamber, startling at each new arrival in the stable yard. He looked like a caged animal, his face and every strong line of his body tense.

That tension ran to Chloe, setting her senses humming like harpsichord strings repeatedly brushed by cold fingers. No wonder both of them jumped at every sound. Vernell was somewhere in Truro. Who knew who else was chasing them, or if Ross's cousin had gotten the message to meet them. Beneath all that lay the knowledge that Ross still cared for Juliet despite her not believing in him, and felt responsible for destroying Chloe's reputation.

She simply needed to tell him how she could help him. He would despise her, but she could live with that knowledge. It would raise one more burden from his shoulders. Once his cousin arrived, he would no longer need her help. She would tell him then. In the meantime, she should get him to rest.

"You should sleep, Ross." She wrinkled her nose at the mildew aroma wafting from the mattress. "The coverlet looks clean enough. You can lie by the fire."

"I couldn't sleep. What if I miss my cousin?"

"I will stay awake." She retrieved the coverlet from the bed.

He eyed it with a flash of longing. "You must be worn to a thread yourself, my lady. You had as little sleep last night as I."

"I can sleep later." Chloe spread the coverlet out on the hearthrug. "You are right. Once you leave me, you no longer need me, so I will stay here and send word to my family to fetch me." She swallowed and avoided his gaze. "If you need me further, send word back with Juliet."

He crouched on the edge of the coverlet. "After trying to send you away from me for three days, Chloe, I'm uncertain about leaving you behind. If Vernell is up to no good, I don't see how I can rightfully leave you here on your own."

"He would never dare hurt me."

"Can you be sure of that?"

Chloe gripped the edge of the coverlet and stared at Ross.

"You never would have suspected him of anything but being a gentleman courting your sister three days ago," Ross continued. "But now you suspect he is working against me in some way."

"But that is you, not me. No one is trying to harm—" She stopped, still able to smell the smoke of the vicarage fire on her clothes.

"When and where is my cousin to meet me?" Ross asked.

"He is supposed to come at nine of the clock because that is well after dark and before moonrise. He will come to the stable entrance and wait."

"Good. Plenty of light down there for me to see him by without being seen." Ross stood. "We should both rest before then, but shouldn't I tend your wound for you?"

"No bandages," she said.

"The towel from the washstand will do. It looks clean."

"And I am cold." She sought for another excuse. "I will freeze if I remove my shirt."

He paced toward her. "I'll build up the fire." He stooped and, shoveling more coal into the grate, studied her face from beneath half-lowered lids. He smiled. "We've only the harsh soap the landlord gave you, but clean wounds seem to heal faster."

"Yes. Yes, of course." Her heart thrummed in her chest, and her breath snagged in her throat. She tore her gaze from his and rose so she could turn her back on him. She heard the clink of silverware and the rip of fabric. He must have used the knife from the dinner tray to tear the stout linen of the towel. She needed to remove at least her left arm from the sleeve. But her fingers were clumsy on the buttons, stiff as though she'd been in the October night instead of sitting by a fire.

"Allow me." Ross moved up behind her and nudged her fingers aside. With two deft motions, he had the buttons out of their holes. The tips of his fingers lingered on the base of her throat, and her pulse leaped. "Don't be afraid, my precious lady. I'm not going to hurt you. Just your left arm," he said.

Nodding, she pulled her shirt up enough to remove her left arm from the sleeve.

"Good. Does this hurt?" He pressed his fingers on the wound.

She winced. "Not much."

"It's a little red, but no sign of sepsis." He smoothed his hand along the inside of her elbow. "And this?"

It felt amazing. She'd had her arm, even her bare arm between sleeve and glove, touched by gentlemen a half a hundred times at the least. None of those touches had sent a thrill racing up her arm and into her body. She should not be surprised. If a mere smile from this man made her toes curl, no wonder his touch made her insides melt.

"Let me get this washed," he said, "so you don't have to stand there shivering."

Shivering and speechless like an awkward schoolgirl required to recite without knowing her lines. She should say something witty, coy, admonitory. Words eluded her along with the full understanding of what he was about.

Water splashed into the basin. He intended to clean her wound, nothing else. He was an honorable man. He had offered her marriage, though he did not want her in his future. In a matter of days, he would want even less of her in his life. For herself, her heart ached as it had two years ago when she realized his affections lay with her sister. They still did, and Chloe knew only ways to make him despise her, not love her.

Oblivious of the Judas he tended with such care, he returned to her side. "This'll sting a bit." He sponged her wound. "Sore?"

"Not much." She welcomed the bite of the soap and the discomfort of pressure on her cut.

"I'll wrap it now," he said.

She braced herself for his hand to brush the side of her breast as it had when he'd wrapped her arm the night before. But he touched her arm with only the cloth, assuring her that her notion was madness.

Then he tied the bandage off. She expected him to move away, but he remained close behind her as she pulled her shirt over her head and fumbled with the buttons. Every bone and muscle in her body yearned to lean back against him, feel his strength solid and warm. She longed for his arms around her one more time.

"You should lie down." Her voice sounded strangled, her chest tight with the wish he would ask her to join him. They could not both risk sleeping. At that moment, knowing she would soon lose him forever more profoundly than when she realized he had fallen for Juliet, she did not trust herself to lie beside him, not after that kiss promising more than he could give her.

He touched her shoulder. "You rest, Chloe, I'll keep watch."

With a sigh, she dropped to the makeshift pallet. "I could never sleep."

"Then we'll talk." He drew the free edge of the coverlet over her and remained seated behind her. "We have two hours."

"I have no idea what to talk about. Shall we plan how we will get to Guernsey if Lord Trenerry does not arrive?"

"I expect we will wait until the inn is quiet, then slip out and head to the coast." He lifted a handful of her hair and began to run his finger through it. "I hate taking another boat, but we have no choice if we are to rescue Juliet."

"And you."

"And me." He released her hair.

For several minutes, they sat in silence. Somewhere a church bell tolled three quarters of an hour. Six forty-five by Chloe's reckoning. Two more hours.

"So what was life like growing up an Ashford?" Ross asked.

Chloe turned her head to look up at him. "Do you truly wish to know?"

"I do. I'm concerned about you. Will your father punish you?"

"If you mean will he beat me, never. But I will have made him and Mama terribly unhappy, I know, and that is nearly worse. Papa has always expected us to be obedient, and he was not above making us stay in our rooms or do unpleasant things like muck out the stables for punishment. Once he sent me to his estate in Northumberland where my aunt and cousins live because I rode my horse across the moor after he strictly forbade it. But Mama was overly indulgent. Her father was mean, so she could not bear any sort of unkindness."

"Is Northumberland so bad?" Ross stretched out on the rug with his head propped on his hand, mere inches from her.

Chloe shivered. "In June, it is lovely. In January, it is cold and damp, but the boredom is the worst part. My aunt and cousins do nothing but read sermons and knit shawls."

"You don't like sermons or shawls?"

"I knit quite well, thank you, but I was ready to read one of Juliet's novels after a month of sermons." She hesitated, then admitted, "I prefer poetry to novels."

"I haven't read much of either, I admit, as my classical education was poorly neglected most of the time other than how to run a plantation. But a few books have come my way over the years. Shakespeare. That ridiculous novel by Walpole. William Blake."

Chloe grimaced at mention of the poet Blake, and Ross laughed.

"Too tame for you?"

"I do not make a very good lady. I am supposed to love that sort of thing."

"I think you make a fine lady." He smoothed her hair away from her cheek. "If I come out of this with my neck intact, I will be proud to have a lady as fine as you as my wife."

Chloe rolled onto her belly, her face buried in her folded arms. "You might be proud to have me as your wife as a salve to your conscience, but in your heart, you want Juliet."

Ross was silent for far too long before he said, "What I dreamed of with Juliet is done, and nothing that happens will change that."

Chapter 14

Truro, Cornwall
Saturday, 28 October 1815
7:00 p.m.

*R*oss felt like the worst of rogues. He had kissed Chloe. He had thoroughly enjoyed kissing Chloe, convincing himself marriage to her would have many benefits. Yet too much of his heart still wanted, considered maybe he needed, Juliet's lightness of spirit. Life with Chloe might be interesting, might hold passion aplenty, from arguments over whose way they should go, to the intimacy of the marriage bed. But Juliet's bright spirit gave him peace. Chloe would never bring him peace.

Chloe gave him warmth. Just lying near her reminded him of lying beside her, holding her through those two cold nights on the ground, and heated his skin. Since Dartmoor, he believed he would never know warmth again. He had rarely been cold since Chloe offered him shelter beneath her cloak.

Eventually, he suspected he would love Chloe, not simply feel obligated to marry her, and desire her physically. But for now, he could not shake his heart loose of two and a half years of believing he loved Juliet, and he couldn't blame Chloe for rejecting his wish to mend her reputation. For now, the best he could do for her was rescue her sister, clear his name, and keep Chloe safe. Above all keep Chloe safe.

Resisting the urge to wrap her in his arms, he said, "Go to sleep."

"There is no need for me to." Despite her protest, she snuggled more deeply into the coverlet and yawned.

Ross smiled and laid his hand on her arm.

"Perhaps I could rest a minute or two." She yawned again. In moments, her deep, even breathing said she slept.

He listened to the soft exhalations of her breath mingling with the whisper of the burning coals in the grate. Warmth stole through him until his own eyelids began to droop. To keep himself awake, he concentrated on sounds penetrating the old, wavy glass of the windows—the clatter of hooves in the stable yard, the shout of hostlers, the church bell intoning each quarter hour passage of time. Eight o'clock struck, and Chloe rolled toward him in her sleep. He slipped his hand into hers. Even in repose, she gripped his fingers as though needing them to keep her afloat.

Oh, she tempted him. With her beautiful face mere inches from his, he wanted to kiss her again. He wanted to wrap his arms around her and—

He drew his mind up short. In spite of having offered Chloe marriage to save her reputation, those thoughts seemed disloyal to Juliet.

As though he owed her loyalty. She hadn't waited for him. She had carried on numerous flirtations and had been prepared to accept a marriage proposal from someone else—a scoundrel, apparently, if their suspicions about Vernell proved true—which made matters worse. Not that he was much above the level of scoundrel, writing to a single lady on the enemy side during a war.

The action seemed innocent enough. Apparently, for the Ashfords, it was not. The family had no reason to like him, to accept him as a suitor for either daughter. But they would have to accept him as more than a suitor for Chloe.

Another reason to clear his name—so he could spare Chloe social ruin.

The church bells rang the quarter. Less than an hour before he would learn whether they had help from his cousin, or if Vernell would catch them instead. Maybe he would arrive with reinforcements. Maybe with a new way to kill him.

He might never see Chloe again. The idea disturbed him, and he lay on his back, her head on his shoulder. Comfortable despite the hardness of the floor, he began to drift to sleep.

A shout from outside startled him out of the doze he'd been slipping into. ". . . catch 'im, guv," the declaration rose from the stable yard below.

Ross shot to his feet.

"See that you do," another man called back.

Ross strode to the window and threw back the bolt. The casement swung out, letting cold air smelling of tin ore and coal smoke sweep through the chamber.

"What is it?" Chloe's voice was blurry with sleep.

"That voice."

"He has gone free long enough." Clear with the casement wide, the speaker's intonations rang through Ross like a blow to the skull.

He stepped to the side of the window frame. A man with a pipe stood on the edge of shadows between two torches. He wore no hat now, and smoke further obscured his features. Those were features Ross had never truly seen. But the profile looked all too familiar. Accompanied by the voice, Ross knew his informant had come to him.

"It's him." With the window still open, he made his announcement in an undertone.

Chloe shot upright. "You cannot go out there unarmed."

"Oh, can I not?" Seizing the knife from the washstand, he shoved it into his belt, then he grasped the windowsill, swung his body through, and dropped to the ground. He hit the cobbles—hard. His left foot twisted. Little pain.

His quarry stared at him, a face distorted by the white lead paint and patches of an earlier age. Ross sprinted toward him. The man flung his pipe at Ross. Sparks flew like fireflies. Ross closed his eyes, avoided ash, lost seconds.

Footfalls rattled across the cobbles. Ross followed the sound. Around the corner of the inn, he caught a fleeing shadow melting into the blackness between two houses. Ross charged in pursuit, reached an alley, slammed to a halt, his back to the house wall, the silver dinner knife in hand.

He'd lost the man too soon. No one's footfalls grew instantly silent by chance. The man had grown stealthy, or had stopped altogether.

Fool, of course he did. He recognized Ross, and he'd run away from the inn, away from people, from safety, from Chloe. He'd led Ross into darkness, into a trap.

"Come get me, you coward." Ross spoke into the darkness.

More silence met him.

"I should have guessed a traitor would deal in backstabbing." Ross emphasized the taunt to his tone.

Continuing silence filled the alleyway.

"I can help you, you know. Help you start a new life." He tried reasonableness and calm this time. "After all, you have more to lose than I do."

He, Ross Trenerry, had more to lose if this man managed to kill him, or even elude him forever. If Ross lost this chance at proving his innocence, he may as well be dead.

"The Americans will give you immunity for your work to take merchantmen from the English." He tried to spell out bargain and threat in one speech. "And if you kill me, the Ashfords will hunt you down."

And probably him, too, for ruining their daughter.

"Do you want to spend your life in England looking over your shoulder, wondering if someone can identify you?"

A whisper, a rasp sounded like a shoe scraping against stone.

Ross tensed. "Ready to bargain?"

Another rasp of a footfall, closer. Ross crouched, prepared to fight. Another scuff, a crunch.

Footfalls raced toward Ross. They did not try to mask their approach. They sped from the other end of the alley than the earlier steps.

He had the knife against Chloe's breast before he realized his quarry would have come the opposite way.

"You nodcock," Ross ground out. "I could've stabbed you."

"I know. I know." Chloe spoke between gasps for air. "Had to come out window to find . . . you." She gripped Ross's lapels. "Kieran."

Ross lowered his hand, but kept hold of his knife. "What about your brother?"

"He is here." She dropped her head against his shoulder. "He is at the inn."

Chapter 15

Truro, Cornwall
Saturday, 28 October 1815
8:20 p.m.

*C*hloe grabbed Ross's hand and charged forward. He held her back. She kept moving, forcing him to follow.

Then a shout sounded far too close behind. Sounded from the mouth of the alley. They ducked down a gap between two houses. Mistake. A stone wall rose before them. Not high. Chloe grasped the top, gasped at the bite of sharp edges against her palms, and dug her toes into the crevices between stones. Ross's hand on her seat gave her the last boost she needed. In an instant, she was up and over the wall. He followed. They landed in a cobbled yard—too hard. Her knees buckled. Ross's boot heels reverberated like thunder. A dog began to bark ahead of them.

"Back over the wall?" Chloe asked.

Footfalls charged toward the barricade behind them. The dog bayed and flung himself against the other side of a gate before them.

"This way." Ross grasped Chloe's hand again and ran straight for that gate.

Mad pursuit had cost him his reason.

He raised the latch, then dragged the gate open—with them behind it. The dog raced out, lunged at the man scrambling over the far wall. Ross led Chloe into another yard, across a garden to one more gate, and into a street. Lights flickered along the lane, brighter at the far end, coming to life nearer them. Townsfolk would join the hunt. She and Ross would not have a chance to escape.

Feet pounded behind them. They rumbled like an entire platoon. Ashford men, no doubt. Fit men from the fields, not the lame house servants. Chloe's lungs burned. The rough paving stones cut her bare feet. They needed to hide. No shelter presented itself. Blank house faces, glowing windows. Shouts to stop. Then a shot.

Ross swore and ducked. "Down, Chloe."

"No, keep going." She tugged at his hand. "They cannot mean to hit us. Warning . . . only. I'm—"

A second shot echoed off the house walls, and Chloe heard the bee-buzz whine of the ball swoop overhead. She would have screamed had she any breath to spare. Darkness ahead gave her hope. She pointed and forced her legs into more speed. Ross sprinted on beside her, propelling her toward that darkness of hope. It lay beyond the church. A churchyard offered potential hiding places.

The yard was dark. The vicarage beyond the expanse of tombs and headstones was darker. Leaning gravestones beyond the lych-gate offered a score of hiding places that would not be traps like a building or a yard. Chloe and Ross spared themselves a few moments to catch their breath before anyone knew where they had gone.

Chloe, knowing what she must do, dropped to her knees behind a chipped angel. "That was your informant?"

"Yes. He lured me out." He clasped her hands in his. "To kill me, of course, when we were alone."

"And now Kieran's here, too." Her hands shook in his warm clasp. "You have got to get away. I will run into the street and distract them," Chloe said. "You hide. Perhaps your cousin will find you."

"I'll hide in plain sight." Ross spoke between gritted teeth. "No one will expect me back in the inn yard. But your brother? He won't hurt you?" Ross gripped both her hands, his finger rubbing her ring band. "He will protect you from . . . anyone?"

"Of course he will. He is my brother. Ashfords do not harm one another regardless." She kissed him. "Remember, our motto is family first."

"I hope it is the same motto for my cousin." He did not move.

In the street, the voices grew nearer, louder.

"Go." Chloe wrested her hands from his and blinked against the tears in her eyes.

She might never see him again.

A single tear rolled down her cheek. "You must go now."

Ross stroked her cheek and paused with the pad of his thumb against the drop of moisture. He moved his hand to the back of her neck and kissed her, swift and hard. "I'll find Bryok so we can find Juliet."

"Or go on your own." She could only whisper beyond the lump in her throat. "Stay alive."

"I will." He touched his lips to hers again. "Keep yourself safe."

She rose. "I am not in danger—"

"But those shots—"

The clang of the lych-gate sounded across the churchyard.

"Run." Chloe tossed the word over her shoulder as she leaped across the angel's broken wing and sprinted for the lights at the gate. Tears blurred her vision so badly she could scarcely make out the features of any of the men streaming through the gate. But she heard one of them shout her name and felt the hand close gently on her bandaged arm.

She faced him. "Beaumont, you found me."

"Yes, Lady Chloe," the groomsman said, running one finger around the inside of his high collar. "We've been that overset about your disappearance."

"I'm sorry. As you see, I'm safe."

"Only because I have not gotten my hands on you yet," Kieran said from behind her. "Beaumont, go after—"

"Do not give that order," Chloe said. "I am here in exchange for Ross's freedom. If you go after him, I will—he will—"

What? She must think up a credible threat.

She faced Kieran. "He is prepared to kill the first man who comes near him."

That lie was just one more thing for which Ross needed to forgive her, and probably never would have the chance to do so.

Kieran's eyes narrowed. "The devil he will. Beaumont—"

Chloe kicked Beaumont in the groin. He doubled over, moaning.

"He is not going anywhere," she said. "I will do the same or worse to anyone you send."

Kieran's face whitened beneath his day's growth of beard. "You have lost your wits, you silly chit."

"You have lost yours if you think a man should be hunted down like a hydrophobic dog."

"Chloe, be reasonable." Deirdre, wearing breeches and a sailor's leather jerkin, strode across the churchyard. "We need Ross."

Vernell strode up behind her. Not one of them, Chloe noted with bewilderment, was carrying any form of firearm.

She looked at Deirdre. "You all cannot have him." She didn't realize she was crying until Deirdre moved up beside her and produced a handkerchief.

"This isn't the place for this." Deirdre looked at Kieran. "Send Vernell and your men after him. We'll take Chloe back to the inn."

"Do not." Chloe drew back her foot.

Kieran picked her up and tossed her over his shoulder. "Chloe, let us go back to your room."

She pummeled his back. "Let me down, you bas—"

"Shut up," Kieran said with perfect calm. "Vernell, send the men—"

Chloe rammed her knee into his chest.

"Hellcat." Sounding amused, if somewhat winded, Kieran wrapped his arm around her legs, holding her fast.

She continued to pound her fists on his back, but it did not stop him from carrying her past faces of men she knew from home and others that looked unfamiliar and grotesque from her upside-down position. Light swirled past from torches and lamps in windows. No amount of illumination showed a man or woman with a gun. But someone had fired upon her and Ross.

She thought she was going to be ill. That would give Kieran pause. She tasted bile, but that was as far as that went. She prayed for Ross to find his cousin, and hoped her words made more sense to the Almighty than they did to her.

They reached the inn. The landlord stood in the taproom doorway with a sea of onlookers behind him and his mouth hanging open like a carp. "He had enough coin to pay his shot."

"Stolen, no doubt, the brat." Affection rang in her brother's voice, and tears threatened to spill from her eyes again.

Kieran pushed past the gawpers, stalked through the taproom and up the stairs. Light at the end of the passage told her the door to her room stood open. Impossible. They had set the bar in place.

"Deirdre was a sailor, remember," Kieran answered her unspoken question. "She climbed up to the window since it was open."

"And Ross always thought she was his friend," Chloe said.

"She is my wife now." Kieran set Chloe on the floor. "And your sister by marriage. That makes her loyal to us."

Her legs too weary to hold her upright, her eyelids too fragile to hold her tears back, Chloe sank onto the settle and covered her face with her hands. Tears poured through her fingers, and she breathed in long, ragged gusts that shook her entire body.

"Ah, Chloe." Kieran crouched before her and drew her head against his shoulder. "You poor child. That man has been nothing but trouble since I captured him."

"You do not understand."

"I'm afraid we do." Deirdre strode into the room and slammed the door. "The man has ruined you."

"We did nothing wrong."

"He touched you," Kieran said. "That is enough wrongs for me."

Chloe hugged her arms across her chest. "He was always respectful. And he has offered to marry me to save my reputation."

"And last week he loved Juliet. You little fool." Deirdre slammed her fist into her open palm, and tears shimmered in her eyes. "What's happened to him? Before the war, he never would have allowed himself to compromise a lady, not even me."

"He had no choice. I foisted myself upon him, and he needed my help."

"No, he did not." Kieran fisted his hands against his thighs.

"We were going to help him," Deirdre spoke with rare gentleness.

"By sending someone into the cave to kill him?" Chloe was on her feet now, her hands on her hips.

Her brother and sister-in-law stared at her.

"We did not," Kieran said.

"We just wanted him to tell us what he knew of Juliet's disappearance," Deirdre added.

"And left him in the cave vulnerable to attack." Chloe strutted across the room to lean her back against the window. Perhaps she could hear if Lord Bryok Trenerry arrived. "If I hadn't arrived, he might be dead now."

"A pity," Kieran muttered.

Deirdre shot him a withering glare. "You don't mean that, and we all know it."

"Especially since I nearly died with him," Chloe pointed out.

Grim faces turned her way, so she told them about the fire and the shooting in the street that day. She did not tell them about her suspicions of Vernell. Now that he was with them, she doubted her correctness in thinking him guilty of wrongdoing where Ross was concerned.

"You would not have been in danger if you had not gone with him," Kieran said.

"Nor would you be ruined." Deirdre stood beside her husband, the two of them forming a formidable front against Chloe, against Ross despite his absence.

She pressed her hand to the window as though she could feel through the glass what she could not see with her eyes—Ross's whereabouts and safety. "He didn't ruin me any more than Kieran ruined you."

"Kieran had the decency to marry me first."

"Trenerry has ruined both my sisters." Kieran's amber eyes blazed. "You have spent two nights alone together, and you were in an inn room together for hours—"

"Nothing immoral happened," Chloe began.

"And," Kieran finished, "he used Juliet—"

"He did not—"

"And will only stop at the good Lord knows what to get revenge on the Ashfords." Kieran got in the last word.

"Revenge?" Chloe stared at Kieran. "Ross does not want revenge."

"Oh, does he not?" Kieran spoke between his teeth as he strode to answer a knock on the door.

"Sit down, Chloe," Deirdre said. "We need to talk to you."

Chloe leaned against the settle's high back and prayed for Ross again as she had not prayed for anyone since she had learned all the American prisoners had been released. She had stopped praying for

Ross then, hoping he would be safe in America, safe at home. But he was anything but safe. He was out in a town he did not know, with men chasing him, possibly with orders to kill. She could stop Kieran for a day or two, give Ross better odds. He was a sailor, and the night was clear. He had a million stars to guide him, and she could hope God would see fit to answer her prayer that Ross meet up with his cousin, or someone who would help him for Ross's sake, for Juliet's sake, for the sake of justice, even if she was now ruined.

Did God answer the prayers of wayward daughters?

Behind her, the door shut. Kieran returned carrying a tray with tankards and the makings of hot punch. The scent of oranges and rum made her sick, but she accepted the tankard he handed her a few minutes later because it was warm.

He kicked the coverlet away from the hearthrug and sat cross-legged on the floor. Deirdre sat beside Chloe on the settle. They sipped from their mugs, but did not speak.

Chloe cradled her cup between her knees and went on the attack. "You risked Juliet's safety and Ross's life in intending to keep him in that cave."

"We were trying to save both," Kieran explained.

"Without involving the Ashfords any more than we already had," Deirdre added. "If he had simply told us—"

"You would have turned him over to Beasley." Chloe slammed her tankard onto the floor and rose to pace.

A knock on the door brought her up short.

"That will be Vernell." Kieran rose and crossed to open the door.

"I am sorry, Ripon," Vernell said from the doorway. "We could not find him, and it is too dark out there to search in unfamiliar territory."

"Never you mind." Kieran sounded weary. "We will search tomorrow."

At last Chloe found something to smile about. "You cannot go hunting tomorrow. It is Sunday."

Kieran faced her. "I do not care a fig if the locals look down on me for working or traveling on a Sunday."

"Especially with Lady Juliet missing," Vernell said.

Chloe fixed her gaze on him. If he was Ross's informant, then he knew exactly where Juliet was. And yet, how could he be the one who had taken Juliet and be with Kieran and Deirdre? Then again, the informant and the kidnapper were not necessarily one and the same.

Chloe decided to test the waters. "I have reason to believe that Juliet is safe."

"What?" the others cried in chorus.

"Tell us," Kieran demanded.

"Does Trenerry know who has her?" Vernell asked.

"I do not know." She could not give them more reason to hunt Ross down, and if she mentioned Guernsey, they would know where to catch him.

Kieran opened the door wider. "You had best come in. Have some punch and warm yourself. You should hear what Chloe has to say."

Vernell strode in, looking immaculate in his blue coat and fawn breeches despite the day Chloe had put him through. He bowed to Deirdre and gave Chloe a cold glare.

She smiled at him, then picked up the discarded coverlet and wrapped it around her shoulders. "I will stay here by the fire."

With more punch served and everyone seated on settle and hearthrug, Kieran turned to Chloe. "You had better tell us what you know of Juliet if you care about your sister."

"That is unfair," Chloe cried. "I will not say because I do care about Juliet. About all of you. What I have done for all of you—I can prove Ross is innocent of treason."

"Interesting," Vernell drawled. "I cannot imagine how a . . . er . . . lady like you could do that."

Chloe shook her head, realizing she had said too much. "I can, if necessary. Trust me."

"When you are acting like a—"

"Kieran." Deirdre's rich, low voice broke over Kieran's tirade. "You're not going to force anything out of her."

Kieran curled his upper lip. "Not while that man has her in his thrall convincing her to trust no one because someone is trying to kill him."

"That man needs to swing at the end of a rope." Vernell scowled at Chloe. "And you, my lady, should be locked in a tower for everyone's safety."

Remembering what she had done to him that afternoon, Chloe stared at her bare toes, dirty, bruised, scratched. One nail was cracked deep enough to bleed, and the instant she noticed it, it began to throb. Tears of pain and fear filled her eyes.

She had to swallow twice before she could speak. "Someone tried to kill Ross—Mr. Trenerry—in the cave Wednesday night. Then someone shot at us through the window of a vicarage and set the house on fire." She hesitated. When no one spoke, she finished. "And someone shot at us tonight."

"None of us were armed tonight," Deirdre said in a gentle voice. "We had pistols in our saddle holsters for road safety, but we aren't fool enough to shoot in a public street."

Chloe flashed a glance at her. "But someone did shoot at us. Twice."

"It was not you?" Vernell managed to look at Chloe with more interest than ire.

"We no longer had a weapon."

She regretted the admission at once. If Vernell was their quarry and knew Ross was unarmed, he would know he held an advantage.

"I heard the ball," Chloe said. "It was too close for my comfort."

"I saw no one shooting either." Vernell shrugged. "Probably some townsman trying to scare you all off."

Chloe did not think so, but changed the subject. Fixing Vernell with her fiercest of glares, she asked, "So how did you know to meet us at this particular inn?"

"Tom Appelgard." Kieran smiled. "Everyone knows you have paid his rent more than once."

Chloe's lower lip quivered. "And now you have turned him into a snitch."

"Egad." Kieran flung his hands in the air. "Where did you learn that term?"

"Well?" Chloe prompted.

Kieran sighed. "I threatened to report his false cellar to the excise men."

Chloe sprang to her feet. "How could you? The man has an ill wife and five children and needs that extra income."

"And one of my sisters is in danger, and the other sister was as well, for all we knew."

"Only because someone wants Ross dead so badly you will risk my life, too."

"I wish someone had succeeded in killing him before he tapped my maiden sister—"

"Kieran, don't be so vulgar." Deirdre's voice cracked like a mainsheet against wet canvas.

"He did not . . . do that. He is not a stupid man, and only a stupid man would attempt t-to . . ." Blushing hot, Chloe faltered.

"If he was an intelligent man, he would not have corresponded with Juliet then run off with you." Kieran's face was also flushed, but with anger, not mortification. "Surely he knows he will pay for both regardless of what his countrymen do to him."

"You will do nothing to him. We have done enough to hurt him." Chloe stopped before she began to cry again.

She missed Ross so much at that moment, if he had walked into the room and asked her to marry him, she would have said yes. Part of her wished he had done what Kieran suspected, though she knew that was genuine ruin, not the appearance of ruin society would consider her escapade these past days and nights. A good thing Ross had been gentleman enough not to attempt seduction. She was not altogether certain she would have resisted. Her reaction to his kiss warned her of that.

Suddenly weak-kneed, she sank onto the edge of the musty bed. "Stop maligning Ross. Yes he was wrong to correspond with Juliet. But he needed hope during the war, a war you dragged him into, dear brother."

"And that is the difficulty here." Deirdre rested one hand on her husband's shoulder. "Ever since you captured him, Kieran, and he ended up in Dartmoor, he has dedicated his life to revenge against the Ashfords."

"He is not like that." Chloe squeezed her cup so hard she nearly crushed the thick pewter. "Ross is no longer angry with the Ashfords. He is grateful to us for—" She glanced at Vernell.

He stared toward the window, his face expressionless.

"Do not be a naïve fool, Chloe." Deirdre's glance held pity. "Ross wants revenge on all the Ashfords, and doesn't care whom he hurts to get it."

"But Ross—"

"Be quiet, Chloe. And listen," Kieran said.

Chloe opened her mouth to object to her brother's order.

"Chloe," Kieran began.

"Let it go, Kieran." Deirdre walked to the window, where she stood with her back stiff for several minutes. The only sound in the room was the hiss of coal in the grate and the distant rumble of voices from the taproom. Then she faced Chloe and the others with her hands shoved into the pockets of her breeches. "You all know why we took Ross aboard our merchantman."

"Are you saying something is wrong with freeing slaves?" Chloe demanded.

"Stubble it," Kieran said. "You know she does not."

"We helped him do it," Deirdre said. "But a planter friend of Ross's betrayed him, and he had to get away in a hurry. In 'thirteen, when Ross was collecting a crew for privateering, he took that man aboard because he'd become an excellent sailor himself—or so I thought. But a year later, that man was in prison, and Ross wasn't with him."

"But he—" Chloe snapped her teeth together. She could not admit what she had done, especially not in front of Vernell. But she had to defend Ross. "Ross wouldn't do that to anyone, even for forcing him to lose his inheritance."

Deirdre looked unhappy. "I didn't think so either. He was the kind of man who wouldn't go, um, with the light skirts in port like other sailors because he felt sorry for those women. He said it was a kind of bondage. But he'd give them money anyway. He wouldn't let new crew members get hazed, and he defended my right to be a ship's officer in spite of me being female, when the others wanted me put ashore. So when this man accused Ross of betraying America out of revenge for Charlestonians exiling him, I didn't want to believe it."

"But you did believe it." Chloe rose from the edge of the bed. "You believed it that morning you told us about him."

"That's because we had other information we didn't share that morning."

"I had received a message threatening me," Kieran said. "The handwriting was Ross's."

"No." Chloe's hand flew to her mouth.

"Why do you think we packed up the children and headed to Bishops Cove so quickly?" Deirdre asked.

Chloe wrapped one arm around a bedpost. "What did the note say?"

Kieran grimaced. "That the Ashford responsible for him losing his ship would regret it very soon."

"But—" Even the bedpost wasn't enough to give Chloe's jellyfish knees support, and she sank onto the ancient mattress. The reek of mold and dust rose around her. She sneezed, and was grateful for watering eyes that disguised her tears. "He lost his ship to you three years ago, and you—" She glanced at Vernell.

"I know he helped him escape from Dartmoor," Vernell said. "I had some dealings with the prison governor, and he wrote me of his suspicions. It was not a difficult conclusion to make, but no one in Whitehall was interested in prosecuting an Ashford on mere suspicion. You would have had to have gotten caught red-handed with the enemy to hang."

A likely story that gave strength to Chloe and Ross's suspicions of him.

Chloe made herself be calm, think, prod for more information. "Juliet came close to being caught with him."

Vernell's hands balled into fists on his thighs. "And you Ashfords wonder why you are accused of being treacherous."

Chloe bit her lip. His words meant nothing of whether he understood or not.

Kieran shot to his feet. "Explain yourself, man, or I will—"

"Don't." Deirdre bounded across the floor and grabbed Kieran's arm. "Henry, that was uncalled for, and you know it."

"You are right." He rose and held out his hand. "Please accept my apology." His face worked. "I am distraught over Juliet's abduction. And to learn how this man used her . . ." He swiped his sleeve across his face. "And what Juliet, the sweet child, must be suffering, while he roams free and—" He looked at Chloe.

No matter what Vernell did or did not give away, what he had or had not done, what—who—mattered now was Ross and his behavior toward two Ashford sisters.

Chloe spoke through stiff lips. "So you think that Ross tried to lure Juliet to Guernsey, hoping they would be caught so all of us would be attainted traitors for consorting with the enemy?"

Everyone focused on her.

"But why would he risk his own safety?" she asked.

"It was not much of a risk for him." Still white around his lips with anger, Kieran began to pace about the room. "He was on Guernsey. It

248

is English soil, but no one would brand a Frenchman or American a spy for being on a Channel island, especially because he made no secret of being American. Juliet, on the other hand, being the daughter of an English earl, would have been considered to be consorting with the enemy."

"But Juliet never made it to Guernsey, thanks to you, Chloe," Deirdre continued the explanation, "and soon afterward, Ross was captured."

Thanks to her.

Afraid she was going to be sick, Chloe whispered, "But he was never paroled as he should have been."

"That's because he wasn't imprisoned," Deirdre said. "No record of it."

Vernell curled his upper lip. "He sold out his countrymen, and is now using my lady to hurt the Ashfords."

"He is using both of my sisters," Kieran said.

"He never used me."

But then, she had not been as naïve as Juliet. She never would have continued to put the family at risk, so Juliet was a better pawn. Ross might have initially been attracted to Chloe when she helped his life in Dartmoor be more comfortable, but he would have realized straight away that Juliet was far more gullible. And he resented Kieran for his capture, for all the income he had lost with the capture of the *Maid of Alexandria*, his imprisonment, and the death of his friend. Until Chloe convinced Ross otherwise, he had believed Kieran was his informant.

She stumbled across the room and flung open the casement. Cold air blasted into her face and restored her good sense.

Ross was hurt and angry, but he was not cruel. He'd intended to return to a burning house to make certain the vicar was safe. He had made certain he sailed the boat they stole into a creek where the owners would have a chance of recovering it. He paid the farm wife far more than what her services were worth. And the way he had treated her with kindness and consideration.

"He did not write that note to you, Kieran." Chloe made the declaration with conviction.

She sensed someone close behind her, and Deirdre reached past her to close the casement. "You're freezing. Come back to the fire."

"I do not want to hear more malignant talk against Ross."

"You won't. The men are leaving."

Chloe turned in time to see Kieran and Vernell walking out the door, talking in low voices, their momentary spat apparently forgotten. Relieved, she returned to the fire and crouched before it.

Deirdre crouched beside her. "You know, I've watched a dozen females fall for Ross over the years. He's about the finest looking man I've ever clapped eyes on and more than a little charming when he sets his mind to it."

"He ran back to save that old man," Chloe said in a small voice. "He risked his life for someone others might think does not matter. How could he want to harm any of us?"

"He was loyal to his crewmate. He has no reason to be loyal to us."

"But you were his captain's daughter."

"I married an Ashford, the enemy. That changed everything."

"But he says he loved—perhaps still loves Juliet." Chloe shifted to kneel before the fire, her fingers speared through her unkempt hair.

"He might have been smitten with her," Deirdre admitted. "She is so pretty and lively and unaffected." Deirdre kneeled beside Chloe, an arm around her shoulders. "But she was a convenient way to work on harming the Ashfords."

"And now he knows I care for him." Chloe's face burned with shame that she had humiliated herself by admitting that to Ross when she knew he wanted her sister. "And he offered me marriage to repair my reputation."

"Your parents will find you a suitable husband for that," Deirdre said.

"I would rather be exiled someplace awful. I cannot marry someone when I love someone else any more than I can marry him knowing he cares for someone else." Chloe squeezed her burning eyes closed.

"Or wants to harm your family," Deirdre reminded her.

"I think he did hold some animosity to Kieran when he thought he was his informant, but he does not believe that now."

But he still believed his informant was someone close to the Ashfords because of how he knew of Juliet's movements. Vernell seemed logical to Chloe, yet not now that he was with Deirdre and Kieran. Ross was likely to draw that same conclusion. Vernell could not have Juliet. Either that, or he would realize his informant and the person who had betrayed him to the British right after he was ashore delivering a message to Juliet were two different people.

Or perhaps he already had.

"Deirdre." Chloe rose and leaned her shoulder against the mantelpiece, her arms crossed against her pounding heart. "I offered my help to Ross. He needed it, and I felt responsible for his situation."

Deirdre stood to face Chloe. "How could you possibly be responsible?"

"I am the one who betrayed him and got his privateer captured last year."

Deirdre's eyes widened. "Oh, Chloe, why?"

"To stop him from corresponding with Juliet and luring her to meet him. I thought he would be paroled, or I could get him free, but it all went wrong." Tears ran down Chloe's face. "I told him this morning that I love him because he kept asking me why I would not let him go off on his own. But then I refused to marry him even after he kissed me."

"And ruined you by not stopping you from going with him."

Chloe inclined her head. "But what if he kept me with him because he has come to the conclusion that I betrayed him? After all, who is closer to Juliet than I?"

Chapter 16

Truro, Cornwall
Sunday, 29 October 1815
12:05 p.m.

*C*hloe edged through the crowd in the narthex to the open area in the church porch. A blast of mist-laden wind struck her in the face, and she wrapped her borrowed shawl more tightly around the shoulders of the gown Deirdre had lent her. The inn to which Kieran had moved her and the rest of the Ashford party was far warmer than the church, but she could not bear confinement one more minute—confinement and a lonely bed that smelled so strongly of lavender she sneezed for half the night, and wept for the other half. When church bells had begun to ring in the morning, she asked Deirdre if she would persuade Kieran to let them go to church if they were to obey the unwritten rule that no one traveled on Sunday.

Kieran, hollow-eyed from spending the night trying to find Ross and any compatriots without success, thought church an excellent idea. "We can pray we find him before he destroys both my sisters."

If Juliet was all right despite her abduction, then Ross had not destroyed her. As for Chloe, she was made of stronger stuff than Ross Trenerry could damage. Or so she told herself.

Another burden to lie upon Chloe's shoulders. If she had not interfered and sent Ross to the hulk, he would not feel the need to lash out at the Ashfords. Juliet would be home where she belonged. Kieran and Deirdre would be with their children. Mama and Papa would not be suffering with worry over their unmarried daughters.

And yet part of Chloe's heart rejoiced at her time with Ross, which made her feel more than a little guilty to think about there on the church steps.

She covered her face with a corner of her shawl to wipe away stray tears she didn't want to shed, to hide her face from the good Christian people around her. From the moment she had seen Ross risking his own freedom, even his life, to save that old man during the escape from Dartmoor, she had made a fool of herself over Ross Trenerry.

She could never disentangle herself and everyone else from this coil, not in a thousand hours of good deeds to her neighbors, in a thousand pounds in donated pin money, in a thousand prayers. Every time she tried to make amends, she made matters worse.

And she would have to keep doing something until everything came out right for her family, for Ross, for anyone else hurt in this debacle.

"Come along, Chloe." From close behind her, Kieran gripped her arm as much as possible with her shawl wrapped so close. "I need to see if I can persuade someone to sell a horse on a Sunday. I want you and Deirdre to get an early start home tomorrow morning."

Chloe glanced back at him. "You mean you will not make me ride with Deirdre?"

"Can't," Deirdre said from beside Kieran. "We're both too big." The crowd surged around them, and someone nudged Chloe forward.

"Did you not think to bring another horse?" Chloe asked.

"We left in a hurry," Deirdre said. "When Henry came back to tell us he'd seen the two of you take a boat from Plymouth, we headed for Cornwall at once."

"After hunting down Tom Appelgard," Kieran added.

"Of course," Deirdre said, "we had no idea where you were headed, since Tom said the meeting at the inn was a secondary plan."

"We would have gone to Guernsey immediately." Chloe gazed across the throng rather than look at her brother and his wife, her friend. "The wind was from the south and we could not manage with only the two of us aboard."

The crowd undulated down the steps and around the church garden. Most had walked, some had ridden, and one or two ladies climbed into carriages.

"Vernell told us about the wind," Deirdre said, "so we figured you were likely to go to the north coast."

Chloe looked past Deirdre to Vernell, her brows raised.

He inclined his head, as he still would not offer the courtesy of a bow. Not that she blamed him. "I am not a stranger to sailing, my lady. I have crossed the Atlantic more than once."

"I should have guessed," Chloe muttered. "You are from Devon, after all."

She shivered in another blast of wind and headed for the steps.

"Doubt we will find a horse for sale today," Kieran said. "These Cornishmen seem so devoted to their religion they will not engage in trade on a Sunday."

"I have one you can buy." The announcement emerged from the worshipers in the yard in an accent that was pure Cornish.

Chloe looked toward the speaker. He had a sailor's queue so dull black it might have been tarred and wore clothes so tattered she doubted even their multiple layers kept the man warm. Judging from the way other churchgoers were giving him a wide berth, the garments likely smelled as unwashed as they looked.

"Where," Kieran asked, "would you get a horse?"

The man shrugged, then headed up the steps.

Chloe caught her breath. She didn't want to cover her nose and offend him, but he smelled like a sheep pen.

He did, however, have fine, clear gray eyes and a friendly grin. "It ain't naught but a pony. Farmer gave it me for some work I did. Said I could use it to get myself home."

"Indeed." Kieran sounded skeptical.

Deirdre turned to Kieran. "Give the man a guinea, and let's be gone."

Kieran nodded, then reached for his purse.

"No," the man said. "I won't take no charity."

"Do you have a bill of sale or trade?" Kieran asked.

The man scratched his head. "Don't know. Can't read the paper." He reached inside his garments. "I got this—"

Steel glinted dull gray against the man's hand.

Chloe screamed and leaped back. Deirdre flung up one arm, knocking Kieran sideways. The man lunged forward. Strong hands grabbed Chloe's waist.

She shot back her elbow, struck nothing. She tried to kick. Her heel slipped on wet stone. One foot flew off the edge of the step. Someone screamed. Others. Her. Faces flipped past her—white, wide-eyed, open-mouthed. Her other foot left the steps. She flipped through the air to land across a strong shoulder with her shawl over her face.

"What the deuce!" The wool muffled her voice. She wrenched the cape away, then beat her fists against the solid back beneath her chest and face. She twisted her body and caught a glimpse of Deirdre still on the porch, crouched with her skirts billowing around her, and a knife in hand. She was ready to fight—no one. The laborer was gone. Vernell stood behind Deirdre. From the corner of her eye, she saw Kieran running, then disappear through the gawking parishioners.

The man who held her began to run. Chloe tucked her face against her arm and grabbed his belt. She knew that belt, thick leather over gold coins.

Chloe let herself go limp. With his shoulder pressing into her belly, she could barely breathe, but she managed enough air to demand, "What are you doing with me, Ross Trenerry?"

Chapter 17

Trenerry Cove, Cornwall
Monday, 30 October 1815
5:15 a.m.

*H*alt." The man holding the reins of Chloe's pony followed his command with a tug that brought the animal to a standstill a dozen yards from a looming edifice.

The early morning was still too black for Chloe to see whether the structure was a house or cliff. The air was thick with mist that smelled of the sea, yet she heard no crash of surf.

Chloe grabbed the pony's neck. "Are we dismounting?"

"Yes, miss," the man said.

Around her, Chloe heard the jingle of the other ponies' harnesses and the low murmur of voices too quiet for words to be distinct.

"Do you need my assistance?" her guide asked.

"Thank you, no." She hoped he thought fatigue caused the tremor in her voice, not her entire body shaking.

Fatigue was part of it, the bone-deep trembling. Seventeen hours of riding astride a moorland pony over terrain surely meant only for goats was another cause. Not knowing what was going to happen to her now that they had stopped was the greatest cause of all.

Grasping the pony's reins for support, she swung her leg over the animal's neck and slid to the ground. Her feet sank into sand rather than the rock she expected, and she staggered.

"Steady there." Ross curved his hands on the sides of her waist. "You should have let your guide help you."

"Guide?" Chloe snorted to cover up the quiver that ran through her at his touch. "Do you not mean guard?"

"I said guide." His voice held an edge. "He and his companions have brought us safely across Bodmin Moor and along the north coast to Trenerry Cove."

"Of course." Chloe curled her upper lip. "The haven of North Coast smugglers. You are mad."

"Yes, ma'am. That's the tenth time you've told me that."

"And it is ten times as true." Chloe flung one arm around the neck of her warm pony. "This is the first place they will look for us."

"No, they won't."

"But Kieran and Deirdre know you took me."

"Yes." Ross sounded self-satisfied. "And they've been told not to follow you."

Chloe hugged the pony. Ross had provided her with a woolen jacket and breeches to replace her gown, but they were no protection against the penetrating damp. Nor were they any protection against a shiver of apprehension. Notes. Ross was too good at sending those to her brother, apparently, though she had defended him, sworn Ross would never threaten to harm Kieran.

She swallowed in an effort to find moisture for her dry throat. "You are saying that you abducted me to keep anyone from following you?"

He brushed her cheek with his fingertips. "I'm keeping you safe."

"If you think I will believe that, you are a bigger fool than I already think you are." And she was a fool for even a part of her wishing she could believe him. She squeezed her eyes shut. At least the mist, touched with a salt tang from the sea, confused even her as to whether or not she was giving into tears.

He was not worth her tears.

But of course he was. Her heart squeezed in her chest. She was nothing more to him than a pawn, and pawns were easily discarded once they had served their usefulness. Yet since he had taken her to where his cousin's brother-in-law and men waited, every touch of his hand, every word from his lips wrapped her in longing for what could not be. With every mile of mine-pocked countryside, she realized more profoundly that she loved him despite what he was doing to her. She could not despise him. She could not even blame him. And she despised herself for a love that was probably disloyal to her family.

Ross touched her arm. "Let's be on our way."

Chloe straightened. "I suppose walking is far better than staying here. But I cannot see a foot in front of me."

"We'll walk along the base of the cliff where a light won't be visible from above."

"But the sea? What if a ship thinks it is a signal?"

"It's a smuggler's lantern." Ross tucked his hand into the crook of her elbow. "The sand is smooth. You won't fall."

"Then I do not need you to hold on to me."

He squeezed her arm. "I want to."

"I am scarcely likely to run away."

"That's not why—never you mind that now. He has the lantern ready."

For a moment, Chloe saw nothing; then she caught the narrow beam directed toward the ground straight ahead. Rather than being square with glass panels on the sides, this lantern had a long, metal tube to funnel the light in only one direction.

She shivered. These were no gentlemen of the society variety smuggling for a lark; they were "gentlemen" of the free-trader variety, smuggling for gain. And she and Ross could identify all of them. If one of them was not a Trenerry and the Trenerrys were not assisting them, she and Ross might be murdered for what knowledge they possessed, or she might be held for ransom. Abducted from her abductor.

She felt a bubble of laughter rise in her chest and forced it back. Now was a time to think, to act, not to give in to hysteria.

For now, Ross's hand on her arm as he applied pressure to urge her forward felt gentle enough. Yet she wondered if he would release her if she insisted. His hand might be on her arm to prevent her from running.

No, she must stay. To protect her brother and sister-in-law, to find Juliet, she had to learn what Ross intended next.

Ross sat beside the bed watching Chloe sleep. He'd rested awhile himself, stretched out on the hearthrug, warm in the knowledge that Chloe lay near, cold in the knowledge that she hadn't once met his eyes since he carried her away from the church. She hadn't spoken to him since they had arrived at his cousin's house five hours earlier and ascended to a room in a little-used wing. She'd eagerly welcomed the hot water and night rail Lady Trenerry had thoughtfully provided, then consumed two cups of mulled wine before climbing into the bed and falling asleep without a kind or thoughtful word to him.

Ross didn't need to read her mind to know that while she was with Kieran and Deirdre, she had learned something that turned her against him. Thoughtlessly, he had compounded the situation when he told her of the message he had sent Kieran regarding the risk of following him. Not that he could imagine harming Chloe under any circumstances. On the contrary, he had brought her with him for her own safety.

He had initially believed she would be better off with her brother and sister-in-law. But as he watched her run toward them in the church-yard, he realized none of them were armed, yet someone had shot at them while they ran through the streets. Someone had fired a pistol knowing the ball could as easily strike Chloe as him. That someone didn't simply intend to shoot him; that someone wanted to harm Chloe as well.

If the Ashford party were trying to catch him and retrieve Chloe, they would have been armed for travel at the least. But their weapons had all been discarded.

Someone in the Ashford party wanted to harm Chloe. Because she could identify him from the night of the fire? Either that or in some other way. Regardless, he had wanted to go after Chloe then. Good sense stopped him. He would be in custody in moments the instant he tried to penetrate the crowd around Kieran carrying his sister. He needed to wait for the right moment.

He needed to find his cousin, if he arrived.

He had, locating Ross in the churchyard as though Bryok Trenerry could see in the dark.

"You have made bad enemies there," Bryok had admonished him.

"And I'll make worse. We have to get her away from them. She isn't safe."

For now, he and Chloe were both safe. Even if an Ashford appeared at the gate, even if the king's soldiers arrived at the gate, Ross and Chloe could be gone before anyone unwanted gained admittance.

In eight hours, they would leave Cornwall for Guernsey. The sail could take anywhere from ten to twenty-four hours, depending on the wind. That left precious little time to get to the rendezvous on Guernsey, catch his quarry, and find Juliet before she was harmed. If Ross failed to clear his name, he wouldn't be able to return to England and make things right for Chloe—marry Chloe.

In the hours he'd been separated from her, the notion of marrying her—even if it was from necessity, not because she was the lady he had set his heart on for years—grew less burdensome a notion. Life with Chloe would never be dull. That kiss in the inn assured him they shared passion.

Guilt twinged him for Juliet's sake. She had risked much for him, foolish though those risks had been on both their parts. Yet he had given her a hope of a future with him.

And she had sought a future with others. Even if his message to her asking her to wait had been stolen, she had given up on him at the first sign of trouble. Chloe had not because, she claimed, she loved him. Juliet had declared her love as well. Chloe had believed in him. Juliet had hidden from him and sent her sister to send him away. Could he be blamed for finding an attraction to the one who was loyal, for wanting to convince her she was safer with him now than she was with her own family?

Perched on the edge of the bed, he could not resist the urge to touch her. He cupped her chin in the palm of his hand and brushed his thumb along her lower lip, risking waking her. Her lips felt dry. Moorland winds and a sea fog had that effect on a body's skin.

He stroked the curve of her lower lip again. She made an "Mmmm" sound, and the tip of her tongue slipped between her teeth to make contact with his thumb. The touch was as brief as the caress of a passing breeze. Its impact went straight through him. Despite knowing he should not be so bold with an unmarried lady, he gave in to the temptation of finding a few moments' respite from trouble and strife and still fighting the war nearly a year after treaties were signed.

He leaned forward and covered her mouth with his. He caressed her lower lip with the tip of his tongue, then the upper, moistened the dry but still smooth skin. He went deeper, met her tongue with his. She tasted of cinnamon from the mulled wine. He burned as though he'd bathed in oil of cinnamon.

Fire and sweetness. That was his Chloe.

He rose and stalked across the room. Away from the fire and close to the window overlooking the sea, the air was cold enough to keep milk from spoiling. But his body flushed with longing.

Lord help him, he was falling for—maybe had already fallen for—Lady Chloe Ashford.

Sheets rustled behind him. He faced the bed. "Chloe?"

She lay on her side, propped on one elbow with her hair spilling in a blue-black cascade, and her eyes reflecting the golden flames on the hearth. "Do not take liberties with me, Ross. Fool me once, shame on you. Fool me twice, shame on me."

Ross took a step toward her. "What are you talking about?"

"Do not pretend you care about me or any other Ashford, including Juliet or Deirdre." She closed her eyes, and a sheen on her dark lashes told him the golden flames in her eyes stemmed from tears.

Feeling as though his heart lay squeezed between his stomach and his liver, Ross closed the distance between them. "I do care about you. I care enough to have risked getting you away from your family to where you are safe." He smoothed a lock of her hair across her shoulder.

"I was perfectly safe with Kieran and Deirdre." She shook his hand off and sat up. "May I have some tea by any happenstance?" She sounded as brisk as a matron ordering tea in an inn.

Ross turned away. "There's a kettle of water on the fire." He strode to the hearth to tip steaming water into the waiting teapot. "A few minutes to steep."

More sheets rustled. "You are making the tea here? Are we locked in?"

"Well . . ." Glancing back at her, Ross shoved one hand into his pocket.

Chloe glared at him from beneath arched brows. "I see. You are not, but I am."

"It's to keep servants out, not you in." Ross tossed the key onto the bed beside her hand. "The household thinks I'm here alone, except my cousin and his wife, of course."

"And the smugglers on the beach."

"They won't dare say anything to anyone."

"Hmm." She crossed her arms over her chest. "If that tea is good and hot, I just might not do something violent like gouge your eyes out with this key."

"That's my Chloe."

Her eyes flashed at him. "I am *not* your Chloe." A single tear sparkled on her cheek. "I never was."

Ross set the teapot on the hearth to steep, then gave her his full attention. "You always were from the moment you decided to come with me on this rescue mission—"

"You knew I was a gull, game ready for your snare."

"What are you going on about?"

She swung her lovely long legs off the bed. "You talk of wanting to marry me to spare my reputation, but then you kidnap me in front of a score of witnesses. That does not look like sparing my reputation to me."

"I think your life is far more important than your reputation."

Ross could think of nothing more decisive to say. He turned to busy himself with the tea, pouring dark liquid into two china cups to give himself time to think of words that would soften her heart, or, at the least, her demeanor toward him. "When you visited me in Dartmoor, I thought you the bravest, kindest lady I knew other than Deirdre. Everything else became a blur during my wound fever in the cave. And then I woke up to Juliet. In those hours I spent with her chattering to me and reading some nonsense novel to me, she gave me the kind of brightness, the sort of belief in a bright future I needed to get me through the war and that second imprisonment. I will never forget that. I will do everything I can to rescue her now, even if I don't catch my informant, or whoever abducted her. But these past few days have shown me that my future lies with you—"

"And Juliet believed your future was with her." She stalked toward him as though the blue wool blanket she had pulled from the bed was a queen's coronation robe. "And with me, I took the risk with my reputation by coming with you to help you on this mission, but I might have been able to salvage something if you had not snatched me off the steps of the church. But gulling a starry-eyed innocent like Juliet and then carrying me off like I'm some prize of war in front of everyone has put us both beyond the social pale. Is that good enough for your revenge against my family? Or will you go after Kieran and Deirdre next? What about their children—"

"Stubble it, Chloe," Ross said without emotion, though he felt as though she were tearing him in two. "You're making little sense. Why would I wish to harm either you or Juliet? And your niece and nephews? What sort of a worm do you think I am?"

"One who hates all Ashfords."

"I have told you half a dozen times already. I don't hate any of you." Ross poured tea into the cups. "And, as you said yourself, you came willingly."

"The first time."

His conscience searing as though he had drunk straight from the kettle, Ross faced Chloe with a cup of tea in each hand. "The first time, yes."

She took one cup from him, then sat on the hearthrug with the coverlet wrapped around her shoulders. "And you say this time it is for my own safety. But how can I believe that when I was not safe with you in Truro or the vicarage?"

"Because I'm leaving you here."

She clattered the cup into its saucer. "The deuce you are."

"I won't risk your safety again. You were not safe with Vernell around, if we are right in our suspicions of him, and you will not be safe on Guernsey."

"And I will not let you go after my sister without me. Unless—" Her face paled, and she leaned forward to lay her hand on his arm. "Your cousin's men just delivered a message to him, did they not? They did not hurt him, did they?"

Ross covered her hand with his and started at how cold she was. "Chloe, my precious, I won't hurt your brother or Deirdre. I don't even want to harm my informant. I need him alive. Why don't you believe that?"

She turned her head and drew away. "You say a great deal I no longer believe."

"I haven't lied to you."

"I think you used me as you used Juliet."

He grasped her shoulders. "So you only believe the worst of me now?"

She hugged her arms across her chest. "When there is only the worst to believe."

"Chloe—" Struggling against a sense of defeat, Ross took her hands from where they clasped her arms and held them between his. "Look at me."

She bowed her head and drew his hands to the warm, soft cleavage between her breasts. "Can I persuade you not to hurt my family?"

He snatched his hands free. "Not like that."

"You have already gotten from me what you want. Is that it? I am ruined, so you have achieved victory?" She flung the words at him like darts. "You have no more need to play games with me as your pawn?"

"Chloe." His throat tight, Ross knelt before her and held her face between his hands. "It wasn't a game. I have never desired any woman as much as I desire you."

She looked at him with haunted eyes. "Then desire me now and accept as much revenge as you need."

"Oh, my dear lady." Shaken to his soul, he rested his brow against hers. "If I have to never touch you again, I will do it to show you I did not bring you here out of revenge." He kissed her cheek, then drew away. "Please believe me."

Her face worked. She rose and walked away from him. "It is too late for that."

"Why? Deuce take it, Chloe, what did they say to you to turn you away from me?"

"It was your message to Kieran. I defended you, but now—"

Ross sighed. "I only warned him not to follow us—"

"Not that one." She turned on him, white-lipped and golden-eyed. "They came riding ventre- à-terre to Bishops Cove last week because you wrote Kieran and said the Ashford who betrayed you would pay."

Ross rubbed the still tender bruise on his head, and stared at her. He was certain he must be slack-jawed with bewilderment. "I never sent such a message."

"That is what I told them. I did not think the man who tried to save an old man's life at risk to his own would make such a threat. But then I thought about how you led Juliet along into believing you cared for her, and how you think marrying me will restore my reputation. You have kissed me like you have wanted to . . . to seduce me . . ." Her cheeks flamed like a sunset over the sea. "You cannot harm a lady more than to destroy her good name. And that will harm all of us. Word of Juliet's abduction will be halfway to London by now, and mine not far behind."

"I'm sorry about what I had to do in the churchyard, but your safety is far more important to me than your reputation." He took a step toward her, hands outstretched. "I can mend your reputation. I cannot bring you back to life if someone kills you for knowledge you possess."

"I possess no knowledge—" She stopped talking, but her lips remained parted, her pupils dilated, and all the bright color drained from her face.

"What is it?" Ross clasped her hands between his. "What do you know?"

She shook her head, satiny black hair swinging around her shoulders. "I cannot."

"If it brings an end to all this, or gives us a clue, you must."

"Do not ask me now." She pleaded with her eyes, and her fingers writhed between his. "Take me with you to Guernsey."

"No. It's not safe."

"It is safer than me going on my own."

"You can't go on your own. You would never get out of here."

Chloe just looked at him and smiled, and he sighed. Of course she could get out of there on her own and find her way to Guernsey regardless of risks.

"All right, Chloe, I'll take you with me."

The knock on the door startled Chloe awake. She did not even realize she'd been sleeping, curled in a chair with a book she hadn't read a bit of while she and Ross pretended to read or sleep to avoid speaking to one another in the confines of the room. But the knock broke into the chamber's stillness, and she jumped to her feet, staggered on a numb right foot. "Who is there?"

"It'll be Bryok." Ross rose from his seat in the far corner and went to unlock the door.

Bryok, Lord Trenerry, strode in, bringing the scent of the sea and a draft of cold air with him. "It is full dark, and we will lose the ebb tide soon if we are not on our way." He smiled at Chloe. "My wife says she is happy to entertain you until—"

"I am going with you," Chloe said.

Trenerry flashed Ross a narrow-eyed look. "You did not agree to this, did you?"

Ross looked at Chloe with such tenderness she almost believed he meant the kind things he had said to her off and on all day. "She says she'll go on her own if I don't take her."

"Not if we lock her in here," Trenerry said. "It is a sheer drop to the sea out that window."

Ross gave Chloe that sleepy-eyed glance that curled her toes. "You don't know my Chloe. She'll find a way down."

His Chloe.

She turned away from him, aching because she wished she were. In spite of everything, a day and a half in his company warned her only harsh, hurtful words from her would keep him at arm's length. Harsh words and a clumsy attempt to seduce him.

Could a man who refused hours of pleasure on principle be an unscrupulous man?

"Well then." Trenerry looked nonplussed. "We had best be on our way. I suppose Captain Ashford's daughter knows her way around a boat?"

"Well enough," Chloe said. "Did you know my father?"

"Only by reputation in the last American War for Independence."

Ross snorted. "Last one, my—"

Trenerry chuckled. "Conflict is not over yet, whatever treaties we have signed. Too many of us lost money to you Yankee privateers. Or did you think I smuggled for the thrill of it?"

"I know deuced well you do," Ross said. "It's in the blood."

"Aye." Bryok gave Ross a shrewd glance. "Heard you did a bit of smuggling yourself in your youth."

Chloe's heart skipped a beat at the reminder of just what Ross had smuggled and what it had cost him. Surely he could not be the vindictive man who would use ladies to gain revenge for his own losses. Handwriting could be imitated.

"Ross smuggled for good," Chloe said. "He was not lawless to make money off French goods."

Trenerry inclined his head. "Spoken like a true law-abiding Ashford."

Chloe flinched. "I see you fight with buttons off, my lord."

"The only way to fence, my lady." Lord Trenerry bowed.

Ross held out his hand to Chloe. "Let us be going."

She looked at it for a moment, then accepted its strength, though his fingers felt as chilled as hers.

They crept from the house the same way they had come up earlier that morning. The stairwell was steep, narrow, and stone. Steps cut for feet far smaller than hers twisted around and around until she was certain she would have fallen if not for Trenerry ahead of her and Ross behind. Long after she thought they should have reached the ground floor, they continued down. The scent of the stone grew dank. The pervasive chill cut through her coat and set gooseflesh rising on her skin. Somewhere below them a low rumble vibrated through the stone.

Then Trenerry stopped. Keys jangled, and hinges creaked. The roar rushed in on a blast of misty air smelling of seaweed and fish.

"The boat is in here," he said.

Steel scraped on stone, and light flared. In the narrow beam of a smuggler's lantern, wet rocks and churning water gleamed around the squat, black hull of a lugger.

So they had not come up that way. This was Lord Trenerry's private cove, a miniature harbor within a cave where the excise men dared not search.

She shivered. It was not the sort of place she liked knowing about. One was better off not knowing about smugglers' doings.

She hugged herself.

Ross wrapped his arm around her shoulders. "We're safe."

Chloe continued to quiver.

Ross patted her shoulder. "Let's go."

He released his hold on her, then moved forward. With a leap, he grasped the lugger's taffrail. A surge of strength that bulged the muscles in his arms took him up and over and onto the deck.

Chloe's mouth went dry. Not even when he'd carried her had she realized how strong he was. Not even his abduction of her had warned her how reckless he was. If he had missed that rail, he would have ended up in the water, frozen . . .

"Come aboard, my lady." He leaned over the rail. Even in the lantern's feeble light, his face glowed. His teeth flashed in a grin.

"You are mad," she said.

But a thrill of anticipation fired through her blood. Under other circumstances, she would have enjoyed this adventure. But at the end of this one, she would tell Ross who had truly betrayed him, and see his regard for her dissolve like stone under acid.

Not so sure of herself, she reached up to clasp his hands. Trenerry gave her a knee on which to brace from below, then she too was up and over and onto the deck.

Freedom for Ross—almost! She would ensure he received the whole of it. Then the Ashford debt to him would be paid.

The deck shifted under her. She staggered toward Ross, caught her balance with her hands against his chest, then braced her legs. "I did not expect so much current in a cave."

Ross grinned at her. "One of my ancestors made this hidey-hole. There are other ways out of this cave than that door."

"You will have to marry her now, Cousin Ross." The deck shifted as Trenerry leaped aboard. "That knowledge is only for members of the family."

Chloe beat a hasty retreat to the wheel. "I can manage the tiller. Easier than stealing a pinnace out of Plymouth Harbor."

"Not so easy on the open sea," Trenerry said. "But Cousin Ross and I will have the sails set as soon as we reach open water, and we can help navigate then. Ross, there are two grappling hooks on the main deck. We use those to repel the boat away from the walls of the cave until we are clear enough to step up the mast." He vanished into the darkness forward, beyond the dim glow of the lantern.

Chloe rested her hands on the tiller. The teakwood was smooth and damp beneath her hands. She wiped it with her sleeve, then gripped the dried places.

Ross squeezed her shoulder. "With the wind that's blowing, Trenerry says we'll be in Guernsey in fifteen to twenty hours. More than enough time to meet the deadline on that ransom note you received." He followed his cousin forward. His footfalls sent vibrations through the deck planks as he strode past her and leaped down to the main deck.

"Ready to cast off?" Trenerry called from starboard.

"Ready," Ross responded from the port side.

Chloe swallowed a lump in her throat. "Ready."

The lugger lurched as though a giant's hand yanked it forward. Water gurgled and splashed against the hull, loud above the constant roar of surf pounding rocks. The lantern cast a feeble glow behind her. Ahead, she caught the glimmer of phosphorescent wave crests beneath a mist-streaked sky.

Freedom for Ross—even closer.

Her hands trembled on the wheel. "Which way will I steer when we are in the clear?"

"West by northwest." Ross called out the direction. "When we have the mainsail set. See the compass?"

She narrowed her eyes against the feeble light, and found the compass beneath a glass dome on the binnacle before her. "Well enough."

A grunt and the scrape of metal boat hooks against stone walls drifted aft. The boat lurched. Chloe compressed her lips and held the wheel steady against the pull of the ebb tide. The cave mouth grew nearer. No more than the length of the bowsprit, then the boat itself. Holding the mainsail halyard rather than a boat hook, Ross stood outlined against a backdrop of sea and night sky, tense, poised, graceful despite his size. She felt the shift of his body place pressure on the deck planks.

Except he had not moved yet.

Chloe shook her head. Lord Trenerry must have shifted, though she could not see him beyond the mast and did not know how she could feel his movements from the quarterdeck. No matter. Everything moved on water. She would not feel Ross's footfalls with him on a different deck.

The cave slipped away behind them. Ross pulled the belaying pin from the rail, and the mainsail flapped overhead, dropped between her and Ross, then caught the wind and streamed out to starboard.

"Course," Ross shouted above the rumble of sea and creak of the boom.

Chloe turned the wheel. The deck heeled. Forward, Ross disappeared on the other side of the streaming sail and swinging boom.

Behind her, the deck shifted again. The lantern light died.

"Lord Trenerry?"

He must have gotten behind her without her noticing.

She clutched the wheel as though it were an anchor holding her steady. "My lord?"

Silence. But she felt something—someone—behind her and started to turn.

A hand clamped across her mouth, and cold steel pressed against her throat. "Do not move," an unfamiliar voice commanded.

Chapter 18

Atlantic Ocean
Monday, 30 October 1815
7:15 p.m.

*C*hloe's hands convulsed on the wheel. If she spun it, she would alert Ross and Bryok to danger. She might also slam the boom into someone's head or crash the boat against the cliffs.

She swallowed. The motion pressed the knife into her flesh. Blood trickled down her neck, the only warmth in a world turned arctic cold.

The man pressed his body to hers, trapping her against the wheel. "Keep yourself still." His voice was raspy in its murmur. The intonation was oddly familiar. "And do not make a sound."

As if she could.

But she had to warn the men before one of them returned aft. Surely Trenerry was forward with Ross.

She tightened her grip on the wheel to give herself stability against the sudden roll of the deck.

"We're drifting leeward," Ross called from the other side of the mainsail. "Up helm two points to windward."

"Keep yourself still," her assailant said.

"I—we will wreck on a lee shore," she managed to say in a throat-clenched voice.

"Not if you cooperate."

"H-how?"

For response, he pricked her with the knife again. The message was clear—*keep quiet*. If she did not warn Ross, he or his cousin would come aft to discover why she hadn't changed course. They would walk into a trap.

Then she must simply change their course.

She exerted minute pressure on the right-hand spoke. Sweaty, her palm slipped.

"Do not move," the man repeated.

"My hand—"

The knife pricked again.

"Trenerry? Chloe," Ross shouted. "Change our heading."

She considered kicking the man. But no, that would not work, not with the wheel blocking her in front and his body crowding her from behind. A big man, and strong. Ross's informant with them, not Juliet. Not on Guernsey yet. Or perhaps this was merely an accomplice. They were up against a man with friends willing to take great risks.

"Chloe!" Ross's voice held irritation. "We're sailing around Cornwall, not into it."

How many words could she get out before the man slit her throat? Enough to save Ross and Lord Trenerry.

She ran her tongue along her lips, tasted salt from sea spray, but felt no moisture. She saw it, though, the spray flying off the weather rail to obscure the main deck. Even if the boom swung fore and aft and Ross or Trenerry glanced back, mist and darkness would blend her form into that of the man behind her.

She would not get enough of a warning out.

She must do something—now!

She remained steady with her hands on the wheel, but the assailant held nothing save her for support. If she pushed back . . . She thrust back with her hips. The man didn't move. He had to be standing with legs braced . . . like a sailor. The man knew how to stand motionless on a rolling deck. He was not simply experienced. He had practice recently to have muscles still that powerful.

"Chloe? Trenerry?" Ross's voice held concern now, and she thought she saw him peer around the mast. "Do you need help?"

"Tell him yes," the assailant murmured.

Chloe opened her mouth. She would say a great deal more.

Nothing emerged. Her throat felt as though the man had rammed the hilt of his knife down her gullet.

"Tell him." The man scraped the blade of the knife along her skin.

She swallowed. "Yes, Ross, I—"

"Louder," the man said.

She took a deep breath. Her lungs felt as though she inhaled the blade. "Ross, I need more help than you can im—"

The man struck her in the diaphragm. She choked on a surge of bile.

"Chloe!" Ross sprinted around the mast. "What the—"

"That is close enough, Trenerry," the man said.

Ross staggered to a halt and grabbed for the quarter rail a yard away. "So it's you."

The man said nothing.

"You won't hurt Chloe," Ross said.

"I have already overpowered your cousin," the man said. "His body is against the quarter rail."

Ross turned his head, and Chloe squinted into the darkness. What looked like nothing more significant than a pile of discarded cloth lay crumpled against the bulwark.

Chloe caught her breath. "You killed him."

"Not likely," the stranger said. "He's no doubt as hard-headed as all Trenerrys."

"Let me help him," Chloe said.

"Not now." The man touched the knife blade to Chloe's neck again. "We are returning to England."

"Devil-a-bit," Ross said. "Chloe, can you steer?"

"Yes, I am certain I can."

"But I have a knife," the man said. "I have already scratched her."

"Then I'll kill you," Ross said as though speaking of introducing himself.

"I will kill her first," the man said.

Ross laughed. "You wouldn't dare."

"You cannot be sure of that."

"Right so." Though she couldn't make out Ross's features, she saw him nod. "But I can be if I do what you say. Is that your game?"

"I will not kill you either if you surrender peaceably."

Ross snorted. "To a prison with a noose waiting for me? That's not living." He placed one foot on the bottom step of the ladder. "What do you want from me?"

"No, Ross," Chloe choked out. "Let me—"

"If anything happens to you," Ross said, "I'll have the Ashfords on my head forever. That's a hell I can live without."

"As if it mat—"

Her captor squeezed the air from her lungs again. Her expulsion of breath sounded like a sob. Or perhaps it was. The moisture on her cheeks felt too warm to be sea spray.

"Don't hurt her," Ross said in a tender voice.

"I would rather not," the man said. "Throw your weapons into the sea."

Chloe wanted to tell Ross not to give up the weapons Trenerry had given him for defense. Yet one false move on Ross's part, and she could end up dead. If Ross then had to kill his informant, both his chances at proving his innocence would be gone.

In that moment, Chloe realized Ross was right—his informant wanted her dead. Either he feared she could identify him, or he had learned she was who betrayed Ross and did not wish her to help keep him alive.

Ross tossed his pistol and knife over the rail. Dark metal gleamed in the sea's light, then vanished. The slap of waves against the hull drowned the sound of their fall into the water.

"Any others?" the man asked.

Ross hooked his thumbs in his belt. "I could have an arsenal, and it wouldn't matter so long as you have Lady Chloe."

"Do not," Chloe tried to shout. It was nothing beyond a mumble. She should have stayed behind where she was safe.

"Whatever you plan next," Ross said, "you'd better be quick about it. The tide's turning, and the wind's from the north. That means—"

"I know what that means," the assailant barked. "I will see to it your lawless cousin's boat does not wreck on a lee shore."

"I wouldn't want to buy him a new one." Ross still sounded as calm as though he sailed on the Thames while he drank champagne during a sunny summer day, the kind of day she had been having when she'd seen the prison hulks. "But I'm more concerned about Lady Chloe drowning."

"Do not concern yourself about Lady Chloe."

Because she'd be dead?

Chloe's knees weakened. Her brain went numb with fear.

"Back forward to the main hatchway," the man said.

"You want me in the hold?" For the first time, Ross's voice held the tightness of anxiety. "Deck beams are right low for—"

"Go," the man said. "Now."

Ross stayed where he was. "Who will get Juliet released?"

"Do not concern yourself about Lady Juliet either." The voice held a new, sharper edge. "She does not need your help if I have you."

Ross took a step toward the thing Chloe knew he feared most—confinement. Chloe, feeling as though the sea sent the boat pitching and yawing in a corkscrew fashion instead of rolling the hull from windward to leeward, watched Ross reach the hatchway. Then he was over the coaming. Down one step of the ladder. Down two. With his height, he would not vanish totally from sight unless he ducked.

A breaker slammed against the hull, heeling the lugger to leeward. Chloe's captor staggered. The knife blade stung her neck. She clutched the wheel for balance, then threw all her weight against the right-hand spoke. An eddy tilted the deck in the opposite direction, and her attempt to drive the boat seaward failed. Behind her, her assailant had his balance back and his knife in position right under her chin.

Ahead of her, Ross had disappeared.

"Show yourself, Trenerry," the man commanded in a rough voice.

Ross did not appear.

"Trenerry?"

"H-he could be hurt," Chloe said.

Her maneuver with the wheel could have caused Ross injury. Or Trenerry, unconscious on the deck? She glanced toward Lord Trenerry. He no longer looked so much like a pile of rags. The roll of the ship could have moved him, or he could be regaining consciousness and moving himself.

"Trenerry, you have ten seconds to—what the—"

Chloe caught her breath, then made herself breathe again. Air in through her nose. Smoke. Undeniably smoke.

A light flickered in the hatchway, illuminating Ross's face from below as if he were a demon rising from the pits of perdition. "You have ten seconds to release her before I fire the boat."

"You cannot." The man's voice sounded as tight as his hold on Chloe's waist felt. "You will risk all of us."

Ross shrugged. "What does it matter if you're going to kill us any-how?" He raised his torch toward the mainsail. Wind caught the flame and licked it to within inches of the canvas and tar-coated lines.

"Son-of-a-poxy—you are mad." The man released Chloe and dashed for the main deck.

"Luff," Ross shouted.

He sprinted toward the attacker. Flame and smoke streamed with him, carrying the stench of pitch. Torchlight flashed off the man's steel blade flipping through the air toward Ross. Chloe screamed, and dragged on the wheel, but felt no response from the boat.

"Luff," Ross shouted.

Chloe dropped to her knees, dragging on the right-hand spoke of the wheel to tack the boat windward. Hawsers creaked, and the hull shuddered. The boat felt suspended above the water for a heartbeat, then the bow slammed into the trough of a wave.

To leeward, Ross thrust his torch toward the man. With a cry, he spun toward the rail and jumped. The keel crashed against the surf. Silence followed. Darkness followed. The stench of burned pitch and cloth remained in the air.

"Ross?" Chloe meant to call out. She barely heard her own voice. She tried again, but a sob choked off his name.

"I'm here." His voice rose from the leeward side of the deck. "I'm with my cousin. Are you all right?"

"Yes. Is he?"

Trenerry muttered something.

Ross laughed. "Careful what you say about my ancestry, Cousin. I'd have made certain you didn't drown if I'd set your boat on fire. Here, I'll carry you below."

Trenerry groaned.

"Chloe?" Ross asked. "Are you able to man the tiller a bit longer?"

"Yes." She was shaking but, unlike his lordship, she was not injured.

"That's my lady." Tenderness gentled Ross's voice. "Try for a west-by-northwest heading. I'll be back right quick." He lifted his cousin over his shoulder and vanished below to the tiny cabin.

Her hands trembling on the wheel, Chloe wanted to ask him if they should not perhaps turn and look for the man overboard. The stranger, the man who could create disguises and imitate others. Their handwriting as well?

More confused than ever, Chloe bowed her head and determined to think, not weep. She needed to be strong for Ross, for Juliet, for herself. But she could barely stand upright.

"Chloe?" Ross bounded onto the quarterdeck and laid his hand on her shoulder. He felt wonderful, warm, strong, alive.

"I-is Lord Trenerry all right?"

"A blow to the head only. He'll recover with rest."

"I am glad." Her fingers convulsed on the wheel. "And that man? Do you think he is dead?"

"I doubt it. He went overboard too fast for a man who thinks he'll drown. We were dangerously close to shore for a boat, but the current there would carry him to land. If he can swim, he'll survive."

"If he is not—" Chloe's throat closed, and she had to take a deep breath before she could continue speaking. "We need him alive to lead us to Juliet. And for your sake . . . Oh, Ross, you were mad to use a torch against him."

"I didn't have a weapon any longer." He set his hands on the wheel on either side of hers and adjusted their course. "So I asked myself what lunatic feat you would attempt. I found a strike-a-light and remembered that you'd had one, too, and got us out of the caves because of it. There's no greater weapon aboard ship than a fire."

"I would never dare risk that. Not when so many of my plans—" Chloe's voice broke, and she bowed her head.

"Say now." Ross raised one hand from the wheel and slipped his fingers under her chin. His body stiffened. "He cut you."

"A scratch."

"You're bleeding."

"Not more than a drop or two."

"One drop is too much." Ross took his other hand from the wheel and wrapped his arms around her so tightly she could scarcely breathe. "I'll kill him."

"No." Chloe reached up to stroke his beard-stubbled cheek. "Let us hope you have not already done that. As it is, how can he reach Guernsey by the rendezvous?"

"He cannot unless he has another boat waiting." Ross covered her hand on the wheel. "That is a possibility, since he didn't seem to care if we went aground."

"If we had . . . Poor Juliet. What she must be suffering!"

"As if you haven't gone through too much yourself." Ross tipped his head down and brushed his lips across her temple. "Would you like to rest for a bit? There's another bunk down there if you'd like. Not very proper, but you've had worse quarters this week."

"You must think I am frail to need so much sleep."

"The last thing I'd call you is frail. But you've been through a terrible experience—"

"And what about you?"

"I didn't have a knife at my throat."

"No, you just have a rope hanging over your head ready to drop over your throat." She curled her fingers around his wrist. "I hope he is alive."

And in that moment, when she nearly lost him, the last shred of will she erected around her heart like a shield over the past two and a half years fell away. As had begun the tenth day of December, 1812, when she first met a bitter and angry prisoner of war, an American named Ross Trenerry, she sank back into longing for Ross, wanting a future with him, yearning for a past and a future where he did not care for her sister.

A past and future where she did not have to admit to him that she had sent him to prison the second time.

She faced him so she could hold onto him. "You cannot run the rest of your life."

"Not and have you, too." He slipped both arms around her and drew her against his chest. The boat rolled, and he turned so his back rested against the wheel housing. "When I saw he had a knife to your throat, all I could think about was getting him away from you." He spoke in a hoarse voice. "The idea of him harming you, killing you—" He kissed her instead of finishing his thought.

As much as she longed to give in, she turned her face away. "You need to see to the tiller."

"I wish you weren't right." He returned to the wheel.

She leaned against the taffrail. Ross stood within touching distance, but now a layer of sea mist spread between them, chilling her. Reason returned with an unpleasant kick to her heart. She was clay in his hands, moldable. Usable. He would draw her right into whatever scheme he had, and she had joined him on this voyage, making that easier for him.

Ruthlessly, she dragged her thoughts away from Ross. "Who can it be? I am no longer considering it could be Vernell either. This man seemed too big."

"He did seem bigger than Vernell. And he might not be my informant at all. I've been so sure of the kidnapper and my informant and whoever is trying to kill me being one and the same, I have no idea who my enemy—my enemies are." He leaned toward the compass, then adjusted their heading. Sails snapped in the rising wind. "For all your assurances, I can't help but think an Ashford or someone involved is part of all this."

"No one in my family would harm either Juliet or me."

"Then there's a traitor in their midst. You heard those shots in Truro."

Chloe shuddered. "Far too close to my ear."

"Too close to killing you." Ross held out his arm. "Come stand beside me and keep me warm."

She should stay away from him. Being near him made her lose her reason. But that extended arm and her own chill lured her a step forward.

He curled his arm around her shoulders, tucking her against his side. "Did you notice anything about him when you had that torch in his face?"

"Yes. His neck. His neckcloth had slipped down, and he sported a cut on his jaw, half healed."

Chloe straightened. "So it was him, the man who attacked you in the cave."

"Yes, ma'am, that's what I'm thinking. He was in the cave. He was in the inn yard. He was stowed away on my cousin's lugger." He heaved a sigh nearly gusty enough to billow the sail. "He knows right too much about my whereabouts, as it's always been."

"But if he is following you around Cornwall, even risking he will not reach Guernsey by the rendezvous, what has he done with Juliet?"

Ross did not answer. Chloe did not wish him to. The possibility was too awful to consider, let alone speak aloud and make seem more of a real risk.

That Juliet was dead.

Chapter 19

English Channel
Monday, 30 October 1815
9:20 p.m.

*N*either of them spoke for a minute, five, ten. The sea and sail filled in the silence around them. Nothing could fill in the hole that would be left behind by Juliet.

"She simply cannot be gone forever." The cry burst from Chloe with all the anguish squeezing her heart. "He would not dare do away with an Ashford."

"Except for in the vicarage."

"Why?"

"Because I was with you. Juliet is not."

He tightened his hold on her. "We can take comfort in that. We can take comfort in knowing killing an Ashford is more dangerous than any man should want to risk."

"Except for a man who has committed treason." Chloe allowed herself to lean against his solid warmth. "Or someone who hates us so much he wants to kill us all." She began to shake from chin to toes, cold, sobs, more terror than she had ever known in her life racking her body and limbs.

Ross turned perpendicular to the wheel so he could cradle her against his chest. "Let's be calm and think, sweetheart. He wouldn't kill Juliet, or he would never get me. He needs his ransom."

"Then why has someone tried to kill us?"

"Because I am proving harder to catch than he thought. Because—I wish I knew." He kissed her temple. "We are getting to Guernsey as fast as we can. We will find Juliet there. We will find this man there. We will stop him from harming Ashfords."

"And you?"

"I'm like you, my dear. I am unstoppable."

She gripped his arms. "I want to believe you."

"I want to believe me, too." He ran his hand down her back. "Please be on my side, Chloe. Please do not think I want anything bad to happen to you or your sister or even your brother. Deirdre was my friend once. I don't want her hurt, whatever she thinks of me now."

"I told Deirdre and Kieran you are not a vengeful man, but she said one of your crewmen—" Chloe stopped herself.

Ross's muscles tensed beneath her hand. "What did Deirdre say about one of my crewmen?" His voice sounded as taut as his arm felt.

She had stuck her foot in it now.

"Deirdre said you took aboard a man from Charleston even though he had nearly gotten you jailed or worse for smuggling slaves out of the state."

"So my good deeds have turned against me." Ross removed his arm from around her back, stretched it out as though intending to slip it around her shoulders, then turned to set his hand on the wheel, leaving her feeling cold and alone despite his nearness. "Sander and I attended school together. I thought we were friends, even though we disagreed on the slave issue. It wasn't against the law to import them yet, and his father had an interest in a slave ship."

"How horrible." Chloe rested her hand on the wheel beside Ross's.

"Not profitable either. I learned years after I'd escaped Charleston that Sander's family had lost their plantation to debt. They were going to sell the slaves we helped escape. The last ones we helped."

"You would have still done it even if you had known of their debt, would you not?" The instant the words were out, Chloe wondered how she could have such certainty of his kindness while thinking he had used her in a plot against her family. The two notions did not go together. She needed to choose whom she believed—Ross or family.

Ross covered her hand with his, and a sense of warmth despite the chill of sea spray confused her more than ever. "I probably would have. It was a family, and they would have been split up, and I couldn't see innocent people suffering because Sander's father liked dice too much."

"But Sander did not see it that way."

"No, ma'am. He sent the authorities after me. I hated him then, but when I learned how his family lost everything and he had to go to sea to make a living after being raised to be nothing more than a gentleman—" He shrugged. "What could I do but try to repay him?"

"So you took him aboard your ship."

"I took him aboard. He was my first officer so he would get the maximum percentage of the prize money for a crew member. But it wasn't enough. I thought he'd let the past lie, but someone convinced him I wasn't in prison after we were captured because I'd sold out to the British."

"In spite of all you did for him, he still wanted revenge on you." Chloe turned her hand over so she could lace her fingers with his. "Why?"

"Because I wasn't in prison with him, and he thought maybe I did get away with it, as I got away with ruining his family." He raised their clasped hands to his cheek, brushed her knuckles against the rasp of his beard stubble. "I used to think my actions were what were right, from helping those slaves go free, to saving your brother's life on Bermuda, even to defending my crewmen in Dartmoor. I thought leaving Englishmen in the caves and letting you all know they were there, rather than having them be prisoners, was the right action. "

"Including taking British merchantmen?" Chloe prodded at him like a tongue against a sore tooth.

Ross gave her fingers a squeeze. "That was war, Chloe, of course it was right. I was fighting the best way my country could without a navy like Great Britain's. And I was building a future for the peace that was inevitable sooner than later. Do you understand?"

Chloe nodded. "Often, we have to choose to take an action that may have consequences we do not like, and if the action is still more important than the consequence, we have to decide to take it anyway."

"A wise lady." The approval in his voice warmed her.

The notion that her action in betraying him had consequences far worse than she anticipated, actions just now driving them through a cold autumn night toward a Channel island, left her feeling as though the icy salt spray off the windward quarter had soaked through to her marrow.

Unable to be near him any longer, she drew away and took a step forward. "I need to rest." Not waiting for him to respond, she leaped to the main deck.

"Please come back," Ross said, as she grabbed the rail to the companionway ladder for the tiny cabin.

⟳

She wouldn't be back, Ross knew, as he watched her disappear below. She was running away from him, when so recently she'd run toward him, run with him. She was only on the lugger to ensure all was well with Juliet when—if?—they found her.

Standing at the helm of the single-masted boat, watching the compass move as he set their course around the tip of Cornwall, Ross considered giving up his chase. He could sail his cousin's lugger to France, find another ship, and head for the Far East. He would lose Chloe and his dreams of a life with her, children, a home. But she would stop thinking ill of him, stop believing he wanted to hurt her family. Yet if he didn't appear at the rendezvous, Juliet might suffer worse than what she must have suffered already—if their worst fears were unrealized.

Ross stared into the binnacle lantern as though its glass sides were a crystal ball predicting a bleak future. Either way, the Ashfords would suffer. He was right and truly trapped.

He caught movement from the corner of his eye, and his heart leaped in the hope it was Chloe returning after all. But Trenerry hauled himself up the quarter ladder, looking wan in the yellowish light and with his hair matted with blood above his left ear.

"You should have stayed below," Ross said.

"Lady Chloe needs her rest, and you need someone who knows the Channel to help navigate."

"I know this Channel better than most Englishmen do."

"Perhaps so. But once we are past Land's End, we'll need to reef that jib sail in this wind."

Ross glanced to the east. Like sea-level stars, lights from the west-ernmost tip of England sparkled along the horizon. "We'll lose speed with that sail reefed."

"Better speed than the whole boat." Trenerry joined him at the wheel. "You will be of no good to your lady's sister if we are all dead."

Ross turned the wheel over to his cousin. "I'm right certain Chloe thinks I'm of no good to her alive."

Trenerry shook his head. "She is a confused young lady. And heart-broken. I left her down there alone because she looked like she needed a good cry."

"I wish—" Ross pushed his damp hair out of his face. No use wish-ing for what he couldn't change.

Once the jib sail was furled against the bowsprit, Ross returned to the wheel and sent Trenerry below before his cousin lost consciousness and toppled overboard. The cabin was tiny, so Chloe being down there with Bryok was improper, but the proprieties didn't matter at present. Trenerry would respect her, and Ross hoped she slept. Except that left him with hours to think, dark hours with England slipping into the blackness of the night and only ocean foaming gray-blue against swells marginally darker than the sky.

He had experienced too many hours to think since the war began, with eight months in Dartmoor and nine on the hulk, not to mention the year he'd been a privateer captain. Too often he didn't like what those thoughts revealed about himself—anger, greed, greed driven by anger. He had wanted America to win the war, of course. Despite the way his country had rejected him, he didn't want to see the United States become British colonies again, and he felt the way the British tried ruling the sea was no different than what the Spanish had done two hundred years earlier. No one country owned the seas.

Mostly he had taken British prizes with the satisfaction that he was paying them back for how they had made him suffer. Suffering worse in the hulk than at Dartmoor, he had taken satisfaction in his victories, his caches of British-won gold on Guernsey and in Brittany and Normandy.

Now he paid the consequences for that greed. His informant wanted him dead, and his own countrymen thought him a traitor. Chloe thought him capable of using her for revenge, and he would quite possibly never be welcomed anywhere, even if he proved his innocence. How could he have even considered she would want him, even to repair her reputation?

He tugged the collar of his coat up around his ears for warmth. It eluded him. Only with Chloe had he felt warm.

He stared past the binnacle to the taut belly of the sail. So what in her time spent with Kieran and Deirdre had changed her heart about him so much? The hours he'd spent with her at Trenerry Cove hadn't proved productive. He'd been wrong to think that eight hours confined together in a single room would make her talk to him. Chloe, when she chose, could be as quiet and withdrawn as a Trappist monk, though he knew she'd been aware of him. Every time he had stood, walked around the chamber, sat studying her averted face, she opened her eyes, turned her head, or hugged herself more tightly. Distrustful she might be. Indifferent she was not.

He stared at the binnacle lantern, noting that its flame seemed dimmer, and wondered how aware of him she was at that moment. So aware she had fled to the confinement of the cabin to be away from him? He smiled at the thought, then the smile faded with the realization that the light was dimmer because the sky was lighter. A lighter sky on October thirty-first in that northern region meant around six o'clock. Fourteen hours and another sixty miles of sailing to go. Not impossible, except the wind had backed to the west, carrying with it the heavy scent of approaching rain. That could slow them, drive them off course, make landing impossible.

He squinted to the east. Grayness without a hint of lemon or rose. Clouds, not sunshine. That would make them less visible if the sea remained calm enough for them to land on Guernsey. They could always cruise straight into the harbor—and straight into an ambush.

Ross pounded his fist on the wheel and cursed the weather for holding them back. He wanted to drop a log line to check their speed. He guessed it was no more than five knots with only the mainsail set. Ten hours. That left four until rendezvous. Four hours to find safe landing and reach St. Peter Port without being seen.

He reached forward and snuffed the binnacle light, useless even in the overcast morning. "Not enough time."

"We might not get there on time?"

Ross started at the sound of Chloe's anxious voice. She stood at the ladder, gripping the quarter rail and looking heavy-eyed. He ached to comfort her and knew the truth was better. "We'll have to risk more sail for greater speed."

"Then let me take the wheel." She stepped onto the quarterdeck.

He resisted the urge to draw her against him with the joy of seeing her, the thrill of her immediate response to the situation. But he wanted to make sure she understood. "If the wind kicks up any more from the west, we could turn turtle. Capsize. Or it could drive us onto the shore."

She rested her hand on the wheel. "Or it could ensure we reach Guernsey on time."

Ross's heart swelled with pride in his lady. "One of the things I love about you is your understanding of what needs doing." He kissed her cheek, then bounded forward to release the jib sail.

The instant the canvas caught the wind, the lugger surged forward, rolled to leeward, then pitched its bow into the trough of the next wave like a corkscrew plunging into the stopper of a wine bottle. Concerned for Chloe, Ross ducked beneath the boom and reached the main deck in time to see her turning green. He grabbed the wheel, and she fled to the rail. She didn't return to him. Her face red from cold wind and likely humiliation, she fled down the ladder and crouched in the shelter of the bulwark on the main deck.

"It even happens to seasoned sailors," he called to her.

She didn't look up. He couldn't go to her. With five-to-eight-foot swells, the rudder needed all his attention. So did the sails. They needed to be braced around to catch the wind at the right angle without taking on too much and sending them all to the bottom of the Channel. He was considering calling for Trenerry when Chloe rose and ascended the ladder to the quarterdeck.

"I can help you now." She wouldn't meet his eyes.

He didn't try to force her to. "Hold the course steady." He went forward to adjust the sails, then aft to drop a log line. Eight knots. He could loose the topsails and give them another two or three knots, but decided they shouldn't risk it unless the approaching rain, as sometimes happened, brought a calmer wind.

It didn't. Soon after sunrise, the first drops joined the sea spray in stinging pellets against their faces and hands. Bryok emerged with oilskin capes just as the full lashing force of the gale pounded down upon them. As the power of the wind and rain increased, Ross admitted they had no choice but to take in sail until the worst of the sea's fury relented.

That seemed to take hours. According to Trenerry's hourglass, the storm lasted no more than one hour. Watery sunlight emerged, playing hide-and-go-seek with the clouds that scudded ahead of a ten-knot wind, a wind blowing from the west. Able to take a sighting at noon, they discovered the storm had blown them off course enough that they had to sail directly into the wind to reach Guernsey. That entailed tacking, a zigzag pattern not easy with a full crew, tedious and slow with a full crew, nigh on impossible with only two men. The mainsail was all they could manage, making their progress so slow it felt like sailing in reverse.

They would have no forward momentum at all without Chloe at the wheel, still looking pale from mal de mer. Once, when showing her how to adjust the heading according to the direction of the sail, Ross noticed blisters on her palms. He kissed her hand, tasting salt and her own sweetness, then kissed her. "You are a remarkable lady."

"It is nothing special," she said, looking away. "It has to be done."

"For me or your family?"

She shrugged. "It has to be done."

It did, and they pressed on, sea mile by aggravating sea mile. Bryok set his hourglass in the binnacle cabinet, and Chloe took charge of turning it. Once. Twice . . . High in the rigging, Ross lost count of how many times she turned it. The declining sun told him more than he liked. But at last, when he thought his arms would not haul one more line, and Chloe looked as though she would crumple if she released the wheel, he caught sight of land he recognized.

It was four o'clock, and the sea was too rough around the cliffs of Guernsey for them to land anywhere except for the south coast and the protected harbor of St. Peter Port.

After he and Bryok dropped anchor, they climbed to join Chloe on the quarterdeck. Her face looked pale, though no longer tinged with green, but she leaned against the wheel as though her legs had turned to jellied eels. She offered him a half smile. "Where do we go now?"

Ross looked to the shore two cables off, where the waves pounded the rocks as though wishing to turn them to sand in an afternoon. Arcs of spray created rainbows against the gray cliffs, beauty amid the turmoil of the sea and his own concerns. "Sailing into St. Peter Port means complete exposure to anyone looking for a smuggler's lugger. And someone will be looking." He didn't say who. Chloe and his cousin already knew—Kieran, Deirdre, or a hired informant.

"They will capture you the instant your foot strikes land." Chloe leaned her head against him for a heartbeat. "I can never repay you for all you have lost."

"You have, and then some."

"No, I—"

Trenerry cleared his throat. "Later. Right now we need to consider the safest way to get Ross to his rendezvous without being captured. Since you realize that whoever hit me on the head knows exactly what this boat looks like, in the unlikely event that he got away."

"I had hoped we could land in that private cove," Ross said, "and enter St. Peter Port by way of a private route I know. But now that we cannot reach the cove, we have to risk sailing straight into the main harbor." He didn't look at Chloe, would not even hint with a twitch of a facial muscle what he wanted her to do.

She turned to him and laid her hands on his face. "What must I do to help?"

Chapter 20

St. Peter Port, Guernsey
Tuesday, 31 October 1815
6:27 p.m.

*C*hloe had never been in a tavern in her life. Only once, in Truro, had she walked into an inn without an escort, and then she'd had the thin security of knowing most casual glances would see a youth. Now, she walked alone from taverns, called cabarets on Guernsey—smoky establishments smelling of gin, ale, and cheap wine, offering a few flea-infested beds for travelers—to inns catering to the needs of the wealthy merchants and noble visitors. She was still wearing her woolen coat and breeches, but with her long hair brushed out and flowing around her shoulders and back. For protection, she carried a knife and a pistol, hastily purchased in a city where anything was available for a price, and she did not stay long in any one place. Still, trepidation followed her like propositions from sailors and shopkeepers and catcalls from the doxies.

"Let me see all of those legs," the *cabaretier* himself called from the doorway to Vinings.

Sickened, Chloe ran with her heart thudding louder than her boot heels on the cobbled streets. She longed to duck into one of the respectable inns like the Royal George and hide in an upstairs chamber until she knew everything was all over. But she was their only hope of creating a distraction great enough to allow Ross and Trenerry to slip ashore unnoticed. Anyone watching was supposed to see Chloe first and follow her progress through the city. She, Ross, and Trenerry hoped that whoever watched would think she too sought Ross or at least sought assistance. Not a foolproof plan, but she had learned the hard way that no plans were foolproof. That lack of infallibility in her own schemes to protect her family had brought her to the harbor streets of Guernsey's capital city. To protect them again, or lead them into worse trouble? At the least, she should get Juliet freed, wherever she might be on the island.

A blast of ale-scented air so thick she could taste the sour brew wafted into her face. She slowed her steps. She had to be seen in every public house she could find between now and eight o'clock. A hand clawed at Chloe's arm. She spun to face a tiny Dutch doll of a female with rouged cheeks beneath hostile blue eyes.

"This is my territory," the woman said in a garbled voice. "You keep moving."

"I am looking for someone," Chloe said, dropping her hand to the knife.

The woman laughed, showing she had wax pads in her cheeks to make them appear plump. "We all are, but you won't here."

Chloe backed away, the heat in her cheeks the first warmth she'd felt all day. She left the doorway and kept moving. Names and direction blurred. If not for the bobbing lights of ships and boats in the harbor, she would have had little idea which way she traveled. Obscene remarks stopped embarrassing her. Although her clothes dried into a salt-stiff shell around her, the wind off the water sent shivers through her with each blast.

She marked the passage of time by the ringing of the clock on the parish church. Six thirty. She had seen no one she recognized. Six forty-five. Ross should be safely ashore by now and safe if her walking about had distracted their quarry from looking at activity in the harbor.

Not caring about the stares of a score of male eyes, she stumbled back into the Royal George and pushed her way to the *cabaretier* just as the parish church clock struck the half hour. "Wine, please."

The man backed off, the stiff posture of his rotund form quivering with indignation. "We don't allow your kind in this house."

"You do," an altogether too familiar voice drawled behind her, "but not dressed as she is."

Chloe applied all her training in proper social behavior to keep herself from banging her forehead against the bar, or throwing her head back and howling like a wolf in agony. She had no idea if she had accomplished her mission, and there was Kieran ready to interfere.

"Kieran, why?" She managed to get the two words out of her mouth with credible calm.

He curled his fingers around her arm. "Do not say a word, and I just might not thrash you."

She kept her head down and trudged up the stairs in front of Kieran, allowing him to prod her into a cozy private parlor with a fire blazing on the hearth and Deirdre leaning against the mantel. She wore trousers, jacket, and kerchief.

"So that was you we saw," Deirdre said. "I recognized your walk from the window here, and sent Kieran out looking for you."

Chloe looked at her sister-in-law. Behind Deirdre's glowing hair, a clock registered seven fifteen. "For me, not Ross?"

"Oh, we are looking for him all right." Kieran ground the words between his teeth. "We have had a watch all day for his cousin's lugger."

Chloe's stomach felt as though she were back aboard the corkscrewing boat. "How did you know about the lugger or to come to Guernsey at all? I convinced Ross you were not involved with the treachery, yet here you are when no one told you we were coming here."

"Vernell told us." Neither Kieran, as he gave the explanation, nor Deirdre, still lounging against the mantel, appeared concerned over Chloe's question, nor their answer.

Chloe crossed her arms over her chest to keep herself from flying at her brother and pummeling him into seeing what was wrong. Knowing he would listen to calmness faster than histrionics, she measured each word and tone with care. "How could Vernell know we were coming to Guernsey?"

"You were followed to Trenerry Cove Sunday." Kieran sipped at a glass of wine.

"Before we got Ross's nasty little message."

Chloe spun the chair toward her and dropped onto the seat. "When did you receive his message?"

Kieran and Deirdre stared at her as though she were mad. She felt mad, but nothing they said was making sense, and the clock hands announced seven twenty.

"Around two of the clock." Kieran crossed the room to where a table held glasses and decanters. "Vernell's man returned in the wee hours of the morning on Monday to say you all had sailed."

"But we had not sailed by then." Chloe clung to the arms of her chair. "We did not leave for Guernsey until last evening."

Kieran and Deirdre exchanged glances.

"I am not sure I like the sound of this." Kieran poured a glass of wine and quaffed the whole of it before holding up the decanter. "Wine for either of you ladies?"

Deirdre waved him off. "Not for me."

"No wine." Chloe shook her head at him.

She did not need anything clouding her head now that Kieran and Deirdre had showed up where they did not belong—showed up where Vernell told them to go.

"Where did Vernell go after he gave you this false information?" Chloe asked with credible calm.

"He left for home." Deirdre had paled. "He was going to stop at Bishops Cove to inform Mama Phoebe and Papa Garrett how things stand, then head for his own home. He said association with the Ashfords is not good for his political career after all."

"Because we have associated with Ross Trenerry." Chloe expected her and Ross's suspicions regarding Vernell since they had seen him at the Red Lion were correct, yet not all the pieces fit as neatly as she liked. "And, as I said Saturday night, someone wants Ross dead. We were attacked on the lugger as we left the cove."

Kieran thudded the decanter onto the table. "By whom?"

"I have no idea." Chloe rubbed her temples. "Not Vernell. The man was too big to be Vernell. I was convinced it was not you, but—"

Color drained from Kieran's face. "We were already here last night."

"We sailed down the Fal River and then across the Channel on a naval sloop of war," Deirdre said.

"Then who is after Ross?" The query burst from Chloe on a cry of anguish.

Kieran strode to her side and wrapped an arm around her shoulders. "Are you now ready to sit and tell us what this is all about?"

"We do not have much time. The ransom note said—"

"What ransom note?" Deirdre demanded.

"Never you mind that now." Kieran released Chloe and nudged up her chin with a knuckle. "What is this all about?"

Chloe glanced at the clock. It registered seven thirty.

"Do not interrupt me or we will never have enough time."

Not waiting for them to agree yea or nay to interruptions, Chloe spilled out the entire story from Juliet meeting Ross in the cave, to his informant approaching him, to the ransom note for Juliet. When she confessed her part in his second capture, Kieran opened his mouth as though ready to protest or commend her, but a single look from Deirdre kept him silent.

"Now," Deirdre said at the end, "I understand why you helped Ross so assiduously."

"She helped him more than she should have." Kieran was scowling. "But she did hurt him, and we need to help him find his informant if we do not want her going to America to testify for him."

"That would ruin her beyond even her father's ability to buy her a husband, I expect." Deirdre's gaze upon Chloe was not friendly. "How could you send a man to prison?"

"I thought he would be paroled." Chloe felt moisture on her cheeks and wiped away the tears she had not known she was shedding. "He should have been as captain of his vessel."

"We can worry about all that after we make certain whoever has Juliet does not get Ross in exchange." Kieran stalked to a bench upon which sat a leather bag and removed two horse pistols. He began to load them. "Give one of yours to Chloe, Deirdre."

"But who do we know to shoot if necessary?" Deirdre began to load her own set of pistols.

"Vernell must be involved," Chloe pointed out. "Otherwise, how would he know to send you all to Guernsey?"

"Why would he send us to Guernsey?" Kieran's voice was a growl.

"To implicate us all in some kind of crime?" Chloe suggested.

"But why would he do that?" Deirdre handed Chloe a loaded pistol without looking at her. "He has been friends with the Ashfords for several years and planned to marry Juliet."

"Political ambitions cost a great deal of money," Kieran said.

"But why would he risk it all?" Chloe asked. "That is what does not make sense to me."

"And why would he ruin an alliance with the Ashfords?" Deirdre added.

"Does it matter now? We need to meet the Trenerrys if we are to see Juliet safe." Kieran glanced at the clock. "For what time is the rendezvous set?"

Chloe stared at the hands pointing to the seven and the ten. "In ten minutes."

Chapter 21

St. Peter Port, Guernsey
Tuesday, 31 October 1815
7:58 p.m.

*R*oss eased open the door of the box pew and glanced around the small, aging church. Though never truly closed to anyone wishing to enter, the building appeared as deserted as it always had. That was why he had continued to meet his informant there through the nearly year and a half of his freedom, of phenomenal success at amassing wealth at the expense of the British. Few candles illuminated the sanctuary, so faces would have been nigh on unrecognizable even to a late-night worshiper who might wander in during one of the rendez-vous. The only danger had lain in someone overhearing their whispered exchanges despite the high back and sides of the pew.

With the market outside closed for the night, the church lay so quiet Ross suspected he could have heard a heartbeat across the aisle. As he latched the door closed, he wondered where Trenerry was, and whether his cousin was in any kind of condition to be helpful. Bryok

Trenerry wasn't a young man, and the struggle with the storm coming on the heels of the attack had weakened him.

Ross crouched in the far corner of the pew. He was ready to meet the man who wanted him dead, the man who had ruined his life so far.

He must be ready for the sort of sly attacks the man had perpetrated thus far. Quite possibly, his informant had planned the time between abduction and rendezvous as a way to wear down Ross. He must expect any kind of an assault, whether there in the church or a knife between the ribs in the crowded market after he had spent a sleepless night waiting in vain. He might receive an assassin's ball fired into his head as he stepped onto the church's porch in the morning. Or an assault on Chloe.

He shouldn't have sent Chloe out on her own. Beautiful, passionate, giving Chloe. As capable of taking care of herself as she was, she was vulnerable, a target as much as a lure. But he hadn't wanted her in the church, especially since he was not as convinced of Ashford's innocence as she was since that pistol shot in the Truro street. If Kieran arrived at the church, Ross would know he was a traitor—or Chloe was. Kieran should not know about Guernsey unless Ross had been betrayed or Kieran had perpetrated the rendezvous now and in the past.

He should not have sent Chloe out as a decoy. She was too vulnerable. If the man harmed Chloe in any way, Ross would kill him.

You don't want to kill him, Chloe had pointed out. *He won't be of much use to you dead.*

Loving, selfless, impulsive Chloe, who thought badly of him yet insisted on helping him. He closed his eyes against an onslaught of longing.

The church's front door creaked.

He stopped breathing and held every muscle tense to prevent himself from springing from the pew and confronting the intruder. It might not be his man. It might be a late-night worshiper come to pray.

A foot scraped on the stone floor. A heel struck the aisle as though the arrival cared nothing for stealth. Then the footfalls grew quiet, no more than whispered movements stealing past the rows of pews. One. Two . . .

Ross tightened his grip on his knife. Another three or four strides would bring the man to Ross's pew. Four strides. Four heartbeats. Four breaths . . .

The person drew near, then level. Ross smelled the sea and something hinting of lemon. Then the scent and the impression of nearness passed. The footfalls reached the wooden steps of the altar.

A worshiper then?

They continued to the choir loft. They continued from there to the far side of the sanctuary. Then they stopped. The church went silent.

Did he wait to lure Ross out? He would catch cold at that. Ross wasn't about to move. Part of proving his innocence lay in the man knowing exactly where to meet him. And Ross could wait out any man for a chance to clear his name—at least clear it in America. He would still have to answer to his abduction of Chloe, sparkling-eyed, bright-spirited, warm-hearted—

"Trenerry?" The name drifted across the church, disembodied like the still, soft voice of God.

Ross held his breath.

"It is Ashford." The voice came again, disembodied, but not nameless. Ashford. Kieran Ashford on Guernsey and in the church moments before the appointed hour, just as Ross had expected.

"If you are here," Kieran said, "I am here to catch him, too."

Kieran Ashford on his side? Not likely. But if he was not, why did he talk of catching "him"? If he wasn't the contact, then how did he know to come to the church at eight o'clock on October thirty-first?

Because Chloe had told him. Chloe, thinking Ross only wanted revenge, thinking he had used her, had betrayed him to her brother. Lovely, lying, treacherous—Ross's mind braked on that track of thought. Chloe spoke of her determination to keep him out of prison. She wouldn't betray him even to her brother. So what was Ashford's game?

Ross dared not move and give away his location. The pew felt like a cell, high-walled and stifling despite the damp chill of an unheated stone building. Even with the kneelers removed, the space was cramped. Now, with Ashford there, Ross dared not move so much as a finger. If the man waited much longer to arrive, Ross feared his legs would cramp and his fingers go numb.

The clock began its ponderous way through ringing the hour. Bong. Bong. Bong. Bong. The church door creaked open. A blast of damp air smelling of pitch and wood smoke cruised through the chamber. Bong. Bong. Bong. Bong. The door clicked shut. Silence, thick, heavy, weighed down on Ross like a shroud. Like a hangman's hood.

Not the slightest murmur of a footfall broke the tension. But Ross sensed the man closing in, believed he smelled him, his rank sweat. Fear.

He smelled burning pitch. Light flared above the pews. The man had brought a torch. Fire to light his way. Fire to smoke Ross out of hiding. Fire for a weapon.

Ross tightened his leg muscles, prepared to vault over the front of the pew. He had to wait for the attack, the attempt to harm him. The man had to reveal that he knew the specific point of meeting. The church alone wasn't good enough.

The light grew nearer, near, flared, arced up and over. It struck the pew seat a foot from Ross. Wood smoked.

Ross leaped up, over. Too high. Too vulnerable.

Steel flashed silver-gilt in the lurid light, a knife arcing like the torch. Ross ducked, twisted. Pain scored his left shoulder. His own knife left his right hand, soared. Behind him, metal rang against stone. Before him, metal clunked against wood. One hit. One miss.

Footfalls clattered in the aisle. Run away? Not again.

Ross charged in pursuit. Throbbing shoulder. Lungs seared from the smoking pew. Fire in his blood to catch the man, the traitor—finally.

He couldn't see him. The church was dark. Dark and filled with noise. Pounding feet from him, his quarry, others. Shouts. His own ragged breaths. The squeal of the door, then the wood panel of the door banged against the stone wall mere feet away.

Cold, wet air swept into Ross's face. Light blazed from behind him, and he saw the man spring for the open doorway. Ross dove after him, touched a sleeve. The man cried out, then dropped from sight. Vanished into the darkness.

Ross skidded to a halt an inch from the top step. The suddenly brighter light behind him revealed two figures. One lay prone. The other stood with her foot in the center of his back. Chloe, dear, precious, dangerous Chloe!

Ross jumped to the ground and grasped hold of the man's hair. A wig flew off, and the man heaved upward, dislodging Chloe's foot and throwing Ross off balance. He staggered, dove, caught the man by one foot. Chloe grabbed the man's arm. The three of them slipped on the mist-wet pavement and landed in a tangled heap in the center of the deserted market.

"How did the two of you get to Guernsey alive?" Kieran spoke from above them. "Need a hand?"

"Not from you." Ross rose enough to hold a knee in the center of the man's spine. Across from him, Chloe scrambled to her feet with one foot on the back of the man's neck. "We manage right fine without you."

"Kieran and Deirdre are here to help," Chloe said, not meeting his eyes.

"Because you told them where to find me." No wound received in battle equaled the pain that sliced through Ross with that knowledge. "You betrayed me."

Chloe said nothing, and removed her foot from the man's neck.

"She was concerned for your safety," Deirdre said from behind him.

"Is it Vernell?" Kieran asked.

"His hair's too light." Ross grasped a handful of the man's real and short hair, and yanked his head back. Bryok arrived at that moment with a branch of candles from the church. Flames wavering in the harbor wind revealed painted features. Ross applied the cloth base of the wig to wipe away the stark white maquillage to reveal—

Ross stared. "He's a stranger to me."

"Not to us." Kieran sounded as though someone were strangling him.

"Freddie Rutledge." Chloe choked out the name. "You nearly killed us."

"Nothing less than what you all deserve." Rutledge lashed out with one booted foot.

Chloe jumped between the blow and Ross, and the kick caught her on the thigh. She cried out and dropped to her knees. Ross twisted his hand in Rutledge's neckcloth, and Deirdre and Kieran grasped his arms, twisting them behind his back.

Kieran raised one fist. "You will pay for kicking my sister, man, and taking Juliet. Where is she?"

"Safe." Rutledge spat blood and a piece of tooth in Chloe's direction. "Locked up like that one should be."

Kieran's face contorted. "If you have harmed her—"

"I hope I sent your ballocks into your liver." Chloe smiled as she staggered to her feet. "If you have hurt my sister, I will geld you myself."

"Chloe!" Kieran looked so shocked, Ross wanted to laugh.

But his quarry was before him, as well as Kieran, the Ashford he'd never trusted, and Deirdre, the Ashford he no longer trusted. He needed to know if this Rutledge fellow, this enemy of the Ashfords, had been in the cave and on the boat.

Ross yanked the neckcloth away. A half-healed cut marred the man's clean-shaven jaw.

"So it is you." His hands fisted on the man's neckcloth. "You always did know where to find me, from Dartmoor on. How? I never met you."

Rutledge curled his upper lip. "I am cousin to the governor of Dartmoor. I watched you escape and bided my time until I could use you to bring down the Ashfords."

"You used Trenerry to betray England." Kieran slammed his fist into Rutledge's middle, doubling him over. "I should have killed you in that duel after all."

"Where is Juliet?" Deirdre asked with more reason to her tone.

Rutledge laughed through wheezing breaths. "You will not know as long as Trenerry is free."

"You will be the one on his way to a hangman's noose," Kieran said. "Treason and abduction."

"Not to mention trying to kill Chloe and me," Ross said in a dry tone. He pressed one fist under Rutledge's chin, compelling the man to straighten. "You're as good as a dead man in England, Rutledge, so you may as well come to America and testify for me. Tell them how spying for America got too dangerous, so you turned me in."

"I did not."

Ross jerked his fist up, snapping the man's teeth together. "You're lying. You knew I was in a hulk. You erased the records and started the rumors of my betraying America."

Rutledge smiled, revealing a broken canine. "Thought that would be easier than killing you myself. But I did not send you there."

"But—" Ross lowered his fist and stared, suddenly aware that the Ashfords were silent. Still.

Trenerry's candles wavered, the flames reflecting in the wet paving stones. "And they call Trenerrys lawless."

"Better that than treacherous." Ross faced Kieran. "And you were going to let me hang rather than admit it, you spineless—"

315

Rutledge lunged to one side. Deirdre skidded, flung out her arms for balance, lost hold of Rutledge's arm. He broke free of Kieran and ran into the twisting lanes of the market.

"Juliet," Chloe cried. "He still has Juliet."

Ross plunged after him. Blood oozed from his cut shoulder, and the wound began to throb. Sliding on wet cobbles, he banged his shoulder into the wooden frame of a stall.

Pain brought anger. Anger lent Ross strength. Speed. But he couldn't see Rutledge in the narrow, dark lanes. He couldn't hear him above the Ashfords racing in his wake.

Rutledge stood with his back to the corner of two stalls with Juliet held in front of him. The silver of a knife blade gleamed just below Juliet's pale face. Just as Ross had seen the man holding Chloe on the lugger. But a rag was tied across Juliet's mouth, so she couldn't speak or cry out, and Ross doubted she had the courage or quick wits needed to fight.

"Let her go," Ross said. Behind him, the others slowed, then stopped. "You win nothing by killing her."

"My freedom," Rutledge said. "The continent. Thanks to you, I am plump in the pocket."

Seeing the gleam of Juliet's eyes, shining huge and dark in her ashen face, Ross was tempted to tell Rutledge he'd help him escape if he'd let the poor child go. But Ross needed him, needed his testimony.

Aware of how unnaturally silent the others were fanned out behind him, Ross addressed Rutledge. "You're better off coming to America with me. The English have no power there, and you'll be a hero for how you helped me bring down English shipping."

"Either you go to America for Trenerry's sake," Kieran ground out, "or we Ashfords will hunt you down and destroy you like the mad dog you are for abducting my sister. Now let her go and we will let you live."

"I think Trenerry will keep me alive even if I keep Juliet with me." Rutledge smiled as he stroked a hand down Juliet's tangled dark hair. "A sister for a sister, eh?"

Juliet closed her eyes and whimpered through her gag.

Nausea gripped Ross. Juliet had been under this man's control for nearly a week. Anything could have happened. A man who did not stop at treason was not likely to have stopped at worse.

He knew then that, even if it meant he lost his chance at freedom, he must take whatever action necessary to free Juliet.

"If you keep Juliet, you will be a dead man." Ross made himself sound casual.

Rutledge laughed. "I know where and how to hide. You will never find me."

"The Ashfords have a long reach," Kieran said.

From the corner of his eye, Ross caught a flicker of movement, a figure shorter than Deirdre sliding along the line of market stalls. Chloe, of course, dashing into danger again.

To draw Rutledge's attention from her, Ross moved in the other direction.

"Halt," Rutledge commanded.

"You won't hurt her," Ross said, taking a step forward. "You won't have protection then."

"And you still want her," Chloe said. "Just like . . . *Ross.*"

Ross took his cue and charged. Chloe sprang, caught hold of Rutledge's arm. Ross grabbed Juliet, dragged her away. She screamed inside her gag. Landed on the cobbles. Rutledge leaped across her and fled. Ross hurtled after him, knocked an arm out of his way, a body. Deirdre's arm, Kieran's body. They could help Juliet. He had to catch Rutledge, take him back to America, or pay him every penny he had earned as a privateer to reverse the records about Ross's imprisonment.

But Rutledge knew St. Peter Port well. So did Ross. The winding lanes of the market led toward the town center in one direction, emerged onto the waterfront in the other. Warehouses. Jetties. Boats. Rutledge would head that way. He'd have a boat ready to take him to France.

Whatever Kieran claimed, they would lose Rutledge in the chaos of that war-torn country, with the German states and even Russia beyond.

Rutledge whisked around the corner of a warehouse. Ross sprinted after him, feeling each footfall jar his shoulder, feeling more blood. He tasted blood in his mouth. He'd cut his lip. He didn't remember how. Salt spray stung his face around the warehouse. The harbor opened before him. A wharf jutted into the churning surf. Small boats bobbed beside it. Boats too small for escape to France. One large enough rode at the end, light burning on its deck. Waiting. Crewmen silhouetted in the light. Waiting. If Rutledge reached it, they'd be gone.

Ross sprang, rammed into Rutledge's back. Rutledge twisted, smashed his fist into Ross's chin. Knocked off balance, Ross fell on the wet planks. Rutledge leaped for the pinnace's rail. Ross grabbed his foot. Rutledge tumbled back to the wharf, staggered, fell backward. He kept falling backward, his head off the edge of the jetty, his feet flying up, pedaling air, propelling him farther over. Ross caught the feet. A woman screamed. Men shouted. Then his own purchase gave way. He released his quarry—too late. His momentum carried him headfirst into the harbor.

Water, paralyzing cold, closed over him. He kept diving, reaching out, seeking for Rutledge, his informant, his savior. His hand scraped on the barnacle-encrusted piling of the jetty. His lungs burned for air. He had to surface. He would die in that cold. He had to find Rutledge. He would die without his testimony. No one else could help him. He had to find Rutledge in the icy water. Had to . . .

His head broke the surface. Brighter light blazed in his eyes. Faces swam before it, voices babbled. He gulped air and dove again. But he found only cold, empty water.

The hunt was useless. When he broke surface once more, he grabbed the rope dangling before him and allowed men to haul him on the wharf.

"You idiot." Chloe knelt over him, spreading a cloak across him. "Trying to kill yourself?" Ross choked on foul-tasting water. "Find Rutledge. Got to find him." He started to push himself up.

Chloe and someone else held him down. "You can't," Deirdre said in a gentle voice. "You'll die for nothing."

"I'll die anyway. Drowning is easier than hanging."

"He has not broken the surface at all," Trenerry said. "Not a sight of him."

"God help me." Ross began to shiver with cold worse than any he'd felt on the hulk. "He was my only real hope of vindication."

"No, he was not," Chloe spread another cloak over him and wrapped her arms around him. "Remember, an Ashford sent you to Dartmoor."

"Chloe, no," Kieran said.

Ross gritted his teeth to stop them from chattering. "You would say that. Let me hang rather than t-tarnish your precious—"

"You don't understand," Deirdre said.

"He must." Chloe crouched over him with her arms around his shoulders and her face close to his. He thought he felt a drop of warmth on his cheek, like a tear. "You see, Ross—"

"No." Kieran tried to pull her away. "I will not allow you to ruin yourself."

"She's already ruined," Bryok said.

Ross already knew, realized he should have guessed long ago what was going to come out of the mouth that gave him so much pleasure in what she said, in how she kissed him, in how she issued orders like a little general. He opened his own mouth to stop her. He didn't want to hear it, have her confirm his knowledge, have her shred his heart with the realization that she had come with him because she owed him his freedom, not because she loved him. But he was already speechless with the lump of cold pain in his chest.

"I am the one who sent you to that hulk," Chloe said.

Chapter 22

*R*oss rolled away from Chloe as though her touch repelled him. Still wrapped in the cloaks she had gathered from onlookers, he staggered to his feet and turned his back on all the Ashfords. "Don't expect me to believe an Ashford will do anything that compromises another Ashford."

Chloe rose and touched his arm. "I will—"

"Let's find an inn with hot water and hotter punch." Ross addressed his cousin, ignoring Chloe's presence and protest.

She began to shake—from cold, from reaction to seeing Ross go over the edge of the pier, from sobs so deep and painful, she feared she would howl if she let them emerge. But she had expected nothing less. She deserved nothing less. Her attempts to free Ross had failed—again. At least he had his cousin.

Lord Trenerry, looking concerned, clapped a hand on Ross's shoulder. "Certainly, lad. I like the Royal George."

"We have rooms at the Royal George," Chloe said in a last effort to help him.

"Then we'll find another inn," Ross said, still not looking at her.

"No, you will not go to another inn." Kieran moved to stand between Ross and the landward end of the jetty. "We need to talk."

"I have nothing to say to any of you." Ross looked at Kieran.

Everyone from Trenerry to Rutledge's crew stood silent and staring to where Kieran stood, hand on his pistol, and Deirdre behind him, one hand on her gun and the other holding the hand of a white and shaking Juliet. Chloe closed her eyes, glad that Ross was no longer armed, disliking her brother at that moment for being an arrogant Ashford.

"Do not." Chloe doubted anyone heard her.

Ross took a step toward Kieran. "Will you shoot me to stop me?"

"You have two Trenerrys here to deal with." Bryok rested one hand on Ross's shoulder.

"And I have no doubt Rutledge's men will assist on my side." Kieran glanced toward the pinnace at the end of the wharf. "I am in more of a position to help them out of the trouble they are in right now than you are."

The men who'd left the pinnace shuffled their feet and glanced toward the boat.

"Yes, you can run." Kieran smiled at the men in a way that surely had their blood freezing. "But you are not all strangers to me, so you will have to keep running."

"So will Ross," Chloe said, "if we do not help him."

"I want to go home," Juliet wailed. "Please take me home."

"We will." Deirdre wrapped her arms around the sobbing girl.

"We will get you home." Chloe wished she could weep like her sister, except she did not wish to go home; she wanted to go with Ross.

"We will take Ross Trenerry back to Devonshire and let Father work this out," Kieran said.

"And discover Vernell's role in all this," Chloe added.

"Vernell loved me, at the least." Juliet's voice was muffled against Deirdre's shoulder, but clear enough.

"Vernell is—" Chloe hesitated. "How was he involved?"

"He was not," Juliet declared.

"We will hunt him down and find out," Kieran said, "but not now. Lord Trenerry, Ross, let us be on our way to the inn to get these ladies inside. Once we are all warm, we will discuss how we will help you."

"We do not need your help." Ross stepped forward, one shoulder turned toward Kieran as though he intended to ram right through him.

"Ross, let us." Chloe made one more desperate plea. "We will not turn you over to the Americans now."

"Forgive me if I do not trust a word from your family." Ross's drawling American accent sounded exaggerated, enough for the sarcasm to drip like poison.

Chloe winced so hard a tremor ran through her.

"Chloe," Kieran said as though no one else had spoken, "will you take Juliet back to the George? I will escort the Trenerry men there, and Deirdre can keep guard over these fellows until a constable can be sent for."

"A constable is on his way," Deirdre said. "I sent a linkboy for one when I went back for Juliet. You men can try to escape, but I doubt you'll get far. I only have one shot, but I can make it count on one of you."

"You are taking us nowhere." Ross ducked his head, ready to charge.

Lights bobbed along the side of the warehouse, and the tramp of booted feet echoed against the stone buildings. The crewmen scrambled for the rail of the pinnace. Deirdre, balancing on the edge of the pier to give herself a clear shot, raised her pistol and fired. The men froze long enough to look to see who was injured, long enough for the constable and his men to swarm down the pier and cut off the crew's retreat. In the mêlée, Ross and his cousin headed toward town.

"Lord Ripon," one of the constabulary said, "we will come to you at the Royal George, if you wish to get your ladies safely away from this."

"We will stay there until you are ready for our statements." Kieran grasped Chloe's arm. "Let us catch up with the Trenerrys and get you inside before you catch your death of cold."

"I am not cold." Chloe was shivering so hard she could scarcely speak. "I am furious. Kieran, how could you think to take him back to England?"

"He cannot go back to America as yet," Kieran spoke with reason, "and I am not about to let him disappear into the rest of the world."

"No, of course not." Chloe stumbled on the rough cobblestones.

Kieran's hand on her arm held her from falling. Ahead of them, Ross and his cousin strode stiff-backed and quiet, with no sign of bolting for anywhere. Between Ross and Chloe, Juliet clung to Deirdre like a limpet to a rock and trudged along like an old woman after a hard day of laundry, with her head bowed and her shoulders slumped. She said nothing. Occasionally a sob drifted on the night air.

Poor Juliet had obviously suffered badly at Rutledge's hands. Learning that Vernell was not worthy to be her suitor must have hurt her as well, and when she learned all her scheming to be with Ross during the war had been for naught, her heart full of dreams was likely to break.

Chloe had a broken heart to live with already. Nonetheless, she would travel to Georgia to testify, whether he wanted her to or not. Seeing that Ross went free was the least she could do for him, regardless of how doing so would ruin her good name so badly she could never take part in English society. She had already worked out how to phrase her testimony so that her family would suffer no serious consequences, other than the scandal attached to her. With the war over, Chloe doubted the authorities would care about the actions of a foolish young lady, especially since the Ashfords had exposed a true traitor in Freddie Rutledge, and possibly Henry Vernell, a truth yet to be exposed.

So cold she could not feel her toes, Chloe welcomed the lights of the inn. Their arrival caused a commotion with the landlord and several chambermaids, who hastened to provide hot water, extra blankets, and steaming punch. But in a quarter hour, the Trenerrys were settled in the bedchamber, and the Ashfords in the parlor. Her hands wrapped around a cup of hot punch, Juliet had ceased sobbing, but sat huddled before the fire in unnatural immobility and silence.

Kieran was anything but quiet. "You are not going to America." His voice rang with the authoritative note that commanded no argument.

Chloe faced him down from the center of the private parlor with her hands on her hips and her feet braced apart. "I am. I am his only chance for getting cleared of treason charges."

"You will be ruined worse than you already are." Deirdre spoke up from beside Juliet.

Chloe turned on her. "So you would rather see him hanged for a crime he did not commit?"

Deirdre scowled. "Of course not, but he should not get away with abducting you."

"Nor corresponding with Juliet during the war." Kieran slammed his tankard onto the floor.

From the hearth, Juliet hiccoughed.

"He did not harm either of us," Chloe said.

She had let her own heart get broken, and Juliet had not believed in him.

"He took me from the church because he was protecting me." Chloe folded her arms against her middle. "Going to America is the least I can do after . . . after what I did to him and the consequences of that."

"You cannot go to America," Kieran said. "We will not let you."

"And how do you propose to stop me?" Feeling tears too close to spilling over, Chloe began stomping around the room. "You will have to lock me in Bedlam to have chains strong enough to bind me, and what a scandal that would produce!"

"Chloe, sit down," Deirdre said. "No one is going to lock you up. We just want to reason with you."

Chloe faced her with her back to the inner door. "How can you simply let him take his chances with the American courts? And you are insisting he return to England first because he was thinking of me."

"You seemed to believe Saturday night that he was bent on revenge against the Ashfords," Deirdre reminded her.

Chloe swallowed the lump in her throat. "On Saturday, I thought he knew I had betrayed him. But I saw his face when I told him. He did not know I sent—I sent him to pr-prison." Her voice broke, and she pressed the heels of her hands to her eyes.

"That changes nothing of how he took you from the church in front of a score of people." Kieran suddenly sounded more weary than angry. "If you having spent three days alone with him already was not bad enough, that puts you beyond the pale, and he is responsible. He is far from good enough for you, but Father may expect him to marry you to make things right."

From the hearthrug, Juliet began to weep again.

"He never wants to see me again for what I did to him, let alone— let alone—" The dam burst, and Chloe began to sob.

"Chloe." Deirdre rose and came to slide her arms around her. "Don't cry over him. What he did, writing to Juliet, was wrong, and he could have gotten caught anyway. And he did intend to make whoever sent him to the hulks pay."

Juliet rose and slipped an arm around Chloe's waist. "And you sent him to prison for me because you were concerned for me and the whole family. And you have had a much worse week than I have because you were protecting me."

"I do not regret a minute of it," Chloe said between sobs. "Now I have got to help him."

∽

Chloe's weeping sliced into Ross's gut. Part of him wished to burst through the door and wrap his arms around her, hold her until her weeping passed. The rest of him wanted to smash the window, turn the chairs to kindling, any sort of action as an outlet for the rage burning through him.

"She betrayed me." He meant to shout, or at the least, growl the words. They emerged in wheezing gasps. He pressed his brow and palms against the frigid glass of the window. "She betrayed me."

"To protect her family." Bryok spoke from where he leaned against the door. "You understand protecting your family?"

"I don't. Mine didn't protect me." A hurt still so deep he didn't know how that would ever heal no matter how much he tried to forget it.

"They got you out of Charleston this past summer."

"They did."

If he reminded himself of that enough, some of the pain retreated.

"But Chloe said she loved me. She said she was helping me because she loved me." He faced his cousin. "It was a lie. She helped me because she wanted to get me away from her family before I learned the truth. She believed I wanted revenge on them because she—" He brought his fist down on the windowsill, sending pain shooting up his arm. "She sent me to that godforsaken prison hulk."

"To protect her sister from you," Bryok said.

"Or to get me away from her sister because she's jealous." Ross seized on the notion, an idea to lower his opinion of Lady Chloe Ashford.

Not that he needed to lower his opinion of her. She had destroyed his life. She claimed she loved him, but she had sent him to a prison hulk, and from there, someone had been able to erase the records and make him appear as though he were the treacherous one. He couldn't care a penny for a lady who acted in such an underhanded way.

Yet the ragged gasps of her weeping shredded his guts like grapeshot from a sixteen-pounder. No one wept like that unless they suffered an ache clear to the heart.

"Why is she crying like that?" Ross yanked off the wet woolen cloak he still wore around his shoulders. "She has everything she wants—her sister back, her family safe from me, and the assurance her parents will repair her reputation."

The corners of Bryok's dark eyes crinkled with his smile. "She has lost you."

"She never had me." Ross stalked toward the door, ready to fling it open and tell Chloe to stop mourning what had never been.

Her words brought him up short. "I do not regret a moment of it," she was saying with conviction despite the intermittent sobs. "Now I have got to help him."

"She can't help me." Ross's hands closed into fists. "She's in enough trouble without doing something stupid like running off to Charleston to give some kind of testimony for me."

"Her family will stop her from doing that," Bryok said.

Ross laughed, though nothing was in the least amusing except his cousin's expectation. "I don't think anyone stops Chloe from doing what she wants."

"But not even the Earl of Tyne can save her standing in society after that sort of escapade."

"I'm not altogether sure she cares. If she says she'll do it, she will."

Unless he let her know he would rather be a vagabond the rest of his life than see her utterly destroy her life. He would survive exile. He might even find a good life on the other side of the world. Many a fugitive had secured a future in a place like Australia. Without her, he would probably be dead now. The least he could do to repay her was ensure she had some sort of future with the family she loved so much she had taken too many risks to protect them.

While Kieran tried to talk Chloe out of being "a nodcock," Ross looked at Bryok. "Will that lugger of yours get us to Brest?"

"If we can find a couple crewmen to help me return to Cornwall."

"Let us be on our way, then." Turning on his heel, Ross strode to the window and flung it open. A roof of some outbuilding stood an easy jump below, making for an easy descent to the ground and his future free of the lady who had betrayed his privateer—

And his heart.

Kieran argued with Chloe, repeating the reasons why she could not run off to America for Ross's sake. Chloe repeated all the reasons why she must. Finally, Deirdre flung up her hands and ordered them to be quiet. "Kieran, go down to the taproom for a bit. I need to talk to your sisters in private."

"With those two rascals in the next chamber—" Kieran sighed and rose. "A quarter hour." He left the room.

Deirdre drew Juliet and Chloe closer to the fire. "No sense in continuing to talk about whether or not Chloe will go to America. We need to talk about what happened to you this week, Juliet."

"I would rather not." Juliet stared at her hands clasped in her lap.

Chloe stared at her sister. "You do not wish to talk when your tongue forever runs on wheels?" She meant to sound light, teasing; she feared she came across as spiteful.

Deirdre's glare confirmed her concern.

When Juliet simply shook her head without looking up, Chloe tried a different tack. "But it was the adventure you have always wanted."

"I was wrong to want adventure." Juliet's fingers writhed on the lap of a gown Chloe had never seen. Though torn and soiled now, it had once been a pretty froth of pink frills that suited Juliet.

"What went wrong?" Chloe asked outright.

Juliet shrugged. "I think nothing. It was simply not in the least amusing."

"You were not with Rutledge this whole time, were you," Deirdre said. "He was at Bishops Cove part of the time."

"He was in Cornwall last night," Chloe added.

"He took me from my bed and turned me over to some men who put me on a boat." Juliet gave the explanation in a soft voice lacking all its usual sparkle. "They kept me on that boat, sailing about, until they brought me to Guernsey this morning."

"With Rutledge?" Deirdre pressed.

A shudder ran through Juliet as she nodded.

"And none of them—" Chloe sought for a tactful word. "None of them hurt you?"

"No, no, they were most respectful." Her face flushing, Juliet began to run her fingers through the tangles of her hair. "No one hurt me."

"Rutledge didn't hurt you either?" Deirdre glanced at the beams of the ceiling as though seeking inspiration, then returned her focus to Juliet. "You do know what we mean by 'hurt,' do you not?"

"I do. Of course I do." Juliet's voice rose. "I may have been a fool over men, but I am not stupid. No one raped me." With that pronouncement, she charged into one of the adjacent bedchambers. Moments later, the sound of retching drifted from the open doorway.

"Do you think she is telling the truth?" Chloe whispered to Deirdre.

Deirdre rubbed her red-rimmed eyes. "I hope so. I think having one of their daughters harmed that way might kill your parents." She scowled at Chloe. "You have made them suffer quite enough."

"And I will make them suffer more by testifying on Ross's behalf, I know. But I have to do it now that Rutledge is gone."

"How do you think you will get to America? Your family won't approve enough money to provide you with the means of transportation."

"I will ask Bryok Trenerry, if nothing else. Or Ross himself." She spoke the last with more hope than belief, more braggadocio than bravado. "I will ask them now."

She strode across the room and flung open the adjoining door. Cold air rushed over her though the fire burned on the grate. A glance to the side told her that the window was open and the room was empty.

Ross and his cousin had gone. The only things telling they had ever been there were a discarded cloak and a note penciled on the pillow slip.

You have no obligation to me, Lady Chloe. RT

When the Ashfords reached Devonshire forty-eight hours later, they discovered that Henry Vernell had vanished as well.

Chapter 23

Brest, France
Wednesday, 8 November 1815
2:35 p.m.

Three thousand miles of open sea lay between Ross Trenerry and a hangman's rope. A hundred miles of English sea lanes lay between Ross Trenerry and prison. He sat on the gallery of a Brest inn, absorbing what warmth he could from feeble sunshine, and looked toward the sea. England and America were both closed to him. In that moment of sentimental weakness, he had freed Chloe from any obligations where he was concerned. He had freed her from having to choose between her family and him. In doing so, he had condemned himself to a lifetime of being a fugitive.

A lifetime of loneliness.

He raised the tankard of mulled wine from the gallery floor beside his bench and laughed without humor. He didn't need to be lonely. The world was full of females. Beautiful women. Intelligent, witty, even brave and loyal ladies.

But how many possessed all those qualities? He knew of only one, and he had let her go. As much as he tried to pretend, as many times as he had told Bryok Trenerry before his cousin had sailed back to Cornwall that he had followed a foolish impulse, when he ran from the Royal George, St. Peter Port, Ross knew differently. He left Chloe because part of him feared she did love him enough to risk all to make up for betraying him regardless of the cost. That was a burden he was not ready to bear when his anger burned hotter than the warmest fire. With him gone, she could forget about him and find a man worthy of her, find the husband she needed for the sake of her reputation.

As if she ever truly needed anyone. Left alone on a desert island, Chloe would find water.

In the week since Freddie Rutledge, Ross's informant during the war, had drowned in the frigid waters of St. Peter Port Harbor, his cousin had learned and written that Henry Vernell had also disappeared. Somehow, he had been involved with the treacherous Rutledge. Ross suspected Vernell had been the person who manipulated the records to obliterate signs of Ross's presence as a prisoner. Rutledge would certainly have earned enough during his treachery to pay Vernell well. But they might never know the whole of Vernell's involvement. In the end, it didn't matter. The only person who could clear Ross's name was Chloe, and he could not let her do that to herself. He did not wish to owe his freedom to a treacherous woman.

A beautiful, brave, generous traitor.

The peculiar tightness that had gripped his chest this past week every time he thought of Chloe returned, and he retreated to his chamber, where he built up the fire and crouched before it, trying to warm his hands. At present, the heat of India sounded like a fine idea. Maybe then he'd be warm again. He had to find some way to be warm without Chloe. He wondered if that would be possible when his own guilt chilled him to the core.

Too confined in the inn chamber, Ross collected a cloak and descended to the street. He headed for the harbor. Brest was about the busiest port on the French west coast and, with the war over, teemed with vessels from all over the world. One, he discovered, was headed for the Sandwich Islands, another for the Black Sea. Nestled between them was the newly reinstated *Plymouth Packet*. Ten to fifteen hours, that was all the farther away Chloe was.

He needed to run in the opposite direction. He needed to forget her. Remembering her, her amber eyes shining in the sunlight, her love for her family, her black satin hair spread across a pillow, her passionate kiss . . . All those recollections pierced him with a pain far surpassing any wound dealt him during the war.

Anger. It was all anger and outrage and grief.

No, not grief. It was only grief if he had loved her. He had not. He did not.

Nor had he loved Juliet. He had let himself believe he loved her. She had been so kind to him when he was ill from a gunshot wound. She had made him forget the discomfort of the wound and the darkness of the cave. He carried those memories into the bloody mess of battle, and it felt like love.

Then Chloe walked into his prison of a bedchamber with her stinging tincture to cleanse his abraded wrists, and taken control of his life, of his thoughts, of his physical desire.

"But not my heart." He spoke aloud to the bobbing ships and swooping gulls. "I cannot love a traitor."

"All women are traitors," said an old sailor in guttural French. He perched on a coil of rope mending a sail. "They make you love them, then the minute you cross them, they'd as soon as see you hang as love them back."

"But this one wants to stop me from hanging." Ross stooped to hold the patch in place for the old man.

"Then why are you complaining?" The sailor cackled.

"She sent me to prison."

"What? *Le mariage*?" The man nearly fell off his makeshift seat he laughed so hard at his own joke.

For the first time in a week, Ross smiled. "Not marriage. She refused to marry me."

She said because he loved Juliet, but surely she had realized his affection for Juliet was shallow at best, just as Juliet's was for him. Even if she had not, she should have wanted marriage to spare her parents, her precious family embarrassment over her behavior in running off with him.

But she had known then he would not want her once she told him of her betrayal. And she had intended to tell him. Whenever he pressed her to know what she was keeping from him, she said she would tell him after Juliet was rescued. She had known how he would despise her, yet she had told him. She could have spared him the knowledge, but she had been too honest not to confess.

She had confessed to ease his mind about his future.

Still holding the canvas for the aged sailor, Ross gazed at the vessels in the harbor. New Delhi, or old Devonshire? India tempted him. He could take on a new identity there, build an empire of wealth and perhaps one day buy his freedom.

Yet it felt like running away. It was the easy road, that escape to the seafaring life with which he was comfortable, if not happy. He wouldn't have to worry about prison or consequences for the errors he had made. He would be free.

He would be free of the hazard of truly seeking what he wanted— love, a family, a wife at his side in that house overlooking the sea. In spite of everything, when he conjured that vision in his head, the only face he saw at his side was Chloe's.

"But she betrayed me."

She had betrayed him out of love for her family. She had betrayed her country, had helped Deirdre get him and the crew out of Dartmoor out of love for her sister-in-law. She had betrayed her good name to save him from being sent back to America with no way to prove his innocence.

She was the most loving, caring lady he had ever known, and he would never see her again.

Unless he wanted to.

No, this had far more to do with need than want.

With an apology to the old man, Ross rose and headed for the *Plymouth Packet.*

Chapter 24

Devonshire, England
Thursday, 9 November 1815
8:55 p.m.

*T*he gates to Bishops Cove rose in an impenetrable barricade across the end of the drive. Beyond, the house was so far from the road not a glimmer of light shone through the trees despite their winter-bare branches. Though a gatekeeper's cottage jutted from the inside of the wall, it, too, lay in darkness.

Ross lowered his hand from the bell rope without pulling. If the gatekeeper had orders not to allow him in, he might not be able to make his peace with the Ashfords. If he could manage it, he had a better shot if he reached the house itself.

He skirted the wall until he reached the overhanging oak. This one was a trusty tree. He swung up and over—

And dropped into the arms of two burly watchmen.

"We was warned you might be coming," one of them declared.

Ross groaned. "I should have guessed. Tyne is no more a fool than are his children."

"Many a man wishes he knew that." The other watchman gripped Ross's arm with a hand the size of a ship's wheel and fingers like spokes.

Ross didn't even try to break free. "What did he tell you to do with me? Toss me out on my head?"

"Bring you to him." The other man was just as large as his companion, but gentler.

"You may let me go. I'll go willingly."

"Ain't risking you sneaking up to see Lady Chloe or Juliet, or whichever of them you're wanting," the gentle one said.

So much for keeping the ladies' escapades quiet.

"I intended to go straight to the front door," Ross said.

The men laughed and began marching him up the parkland path.

"You wouldn't've come over the wall if you wasn't up to no good." If possible, the wheel-handed watchman gripped Ross's arm harder.

The bones of his forearm were surely scraping together now. It hurt like the deuce, but he did not let on he was in pain. Nor did he speak. He needed to preserve his words for those to whom they mattered—Chloe, her family, Chloe . . .

The parkland path seemed like a ten-mile trek through an arctic forest. In truth, he didn't think it above a mile. Yet by the time the two men reached a front door nearly twice his height, he was winded and his heart raced.

One of the men rapped on the door. It opened to show a peg-legged man in formal servant garb and a mammoth hall behind him.

"His lordship was right," the gentle watchman said. "This man came over the wall not a quarter hour passed."

The butler bowed. "You are Mr. Trenerry?"

Ross yanked his arms free, nearly losing his hand on the one side. "I am. I wish to see—"

"Ross." With a flurry of blue ruffles and colorful silk shawl, Chloe dashed across the entryway and flung herself against him. "I do not care what Papa thought. I never believed you would come." She wrapped her arms around his neck and pressed her face into his shoulder. "Does this mean you do not hate me?"

"How can I hate a lady who would sacrifice her good name for me?" Ross closed his arms around her and pressed his cheek to the top of her head.

She looked like a princess with her pretty gown and her hair swirled about and pinned with gold. She smelled like a garden in springtime. She felt like half of his being restored to his body.

"What are you doing with my daughter, Trenerry?" Lord Tyne stalked into the hall at the head of a troop of Ashfords and others.

Chloe pulled free of Ross's hold, but kept one hand on his chest. "I hope he has come to take me back to America, Papa."

Tyne shifted his glare from Ross to Chloe, and his features softened. "You are either weary of this family, or you love this man more than is sensible."

"It is good sense to me to love him and ensure he is not punished for a crime he did not commit."

"But he is not innocent, is he?" Tyne looked at Ross, and his gaze sharpened like a well-honed cutlass. "Since you have the mettle to come here, you may as well enter." He glanced at the hovering watchmen. "You may return to your duties."

The men bowed and withdrew. The butler closed the doors.

Ross flinched at the thud of the iron bar dropping into place. It was on the inside, so this was not a prison, and yet the grim faces of everyone present except for Chloe did not bode well for his future among this family.

His own features schooled into impassivity, Ross looked at each person in turn, from the petite lady with Chloe's eyes, to his cousin, Bryok Trenerry, who looked at him as though he had lost his reason. Lady Ashford, Ross presumed, gazed at him with gentle compassion. Deirdre dropped her eyes, and Kieran and Tyne met his scrutiny with stony faces. Juliet was absent. No, she wasn't. She stood behind Deirdre, her hand to her lips, her blue eyes wide. Beside him, Chloe gazed at him as though he had just performed a miracle.

If anything good came of this night, it would be a miracle. Yet something good had already come to him—Chloe wanting to be with him and settling the last piece of understanding into his heart.

Through the silence as oppressive as a prison hulk, Ross made himself speak. "I'm here because I wanted to assure Chloe I . . . I forgive her." He looked into her beautiful amber eyes and smiled. "I forgive you for betraying my privateer, if any forgiveness is necessary. You were protecting your sister, and that kind of love should be rewarded, not vilified."

Across the room, someone let out a hiccough of a sob.

Beside him, Chloe gulped, and tears starred her lashes. "I thought you would be paroled as a ship's captain. I would not have done it otherwise."

"I know." He raised one hand to catch a falling tear. "Will you forgive me for my reprehensible behavior toward you?"

"I know of none," Chloe said.

"He only kidnapped you," Kieran reminded the room at large.

Ross kept his gaze on Chloe. "You have lost your place in society over that, have you not?"

"I expect I have." Chloe shrugged. "But you did it because you thought I was in danger."

"Which reminds me—" Kieran began.

"I need to beg your forgiveness for thinking for a moment you would allow anyone to harm your sister." Ross spoke quickly to get the words out before Kieran could remind everyone of his accusations.

Kieran's lips parted. Deirdre elbowed him, and he flashed her a quick smile before facing Ross. "You might have had reason."

"And do not forget begging Lady Tyne's and my forgiveness for ruining my daughter," Tyne said.

"He did not ruin me on his own. I intended for him—"

"Shh." Ross pressed his fingers to her lips, then cupped her chin and turned her face toward his. "Don't harm yourself by lying for me. You don't always need to be the one sacrificing your integrity for others. Think of yourself."

She smiled, and even in candlelight, her eyes sparkled. "I am. I will do anything I must, leave my family, lie, to have you to love."

"No, Chloe." Ross smiled at her suddenly blurred face. "You deserve better than what I can give you right now—"

"Perhaps not," Tyne said.

Ross jerked away from Chloe and looked at her father. He was exchanging an intimate glance with his wife, and behind Deirdre, Juliet was wiping her eyes. Even Deirdre's green eyes appeared brighter than usual.

Ross tensed. "What do you mean by that, sir?"

"My lord," Bryok prompted.

Ross ignored the reminder he'd addressed Chloe's father improperly. "Sir, your daughter deserves the best."

"You are certainly not that," Kieran said, though his tone lacked its usual asperity.

Tyne drew his brows together. "You are not what we would want for her. But you were, Lord Trenerry tells us, willing to live as a fugitive to keep her from ruining herself and possibly us. And now you are here because you recognize the fetters of flight. And you obviously love my daughter. That matters the most to her mother and me."

"Thank you . . . my lord." Ross murmured, sensing that Garrett Ashford, Earl of Tyne, wasn't finished yet.

"I was not about to do anything to help you," Tyne said, "especially not let my daughter go to America." He frowned at Chloe. "Then you ran off. But you have shown your strength and integrity of character by coming back, and for that, I will use my connections at Whitehall to learn who were the guards on that prison hulk and have them identify you. Beasley has already been notified that there were irregularities regarding your imprisonment. It will take time, and we will see your name cleared."

"Meanwhile," Trenerry said, "you will be safe in Cornwall. No one there will harm a Trenerry."

Ross blinked, embarrassed to find his eyes misty. He swallowed against a lump in his throat. "I . . . don't know how to thank you."

"You don't have to." Phoebe crossed the hall and hugged him. "Just keep showing our daughter you love her."

Ross looked at Chloe with her sparkling eyes and heart-melting smile. "I'm finding that to be easy."

"You have never lived with her," Kieran muttered.

Deirdre laughed. Kieran and Tyne didn't quite smile, and neither did they look at him with hostility any longer, just a little coolness. But they were welcoming him into their family—because Chloe had shown him how to love.

He reached out one arm and drew her against him. With Chloe nestled at his side, he possessed all he needed to banish the cold.

EPILOGUE

Devonshire, England
Thursday, 30 November 1815
10:30 a.m.

*W*hat looked like a mile of Axminster carpet lay between Chloe and Ross. In her cream-and-gold gown, fragile gold slippers, and hair affixed with jeweled combs, not to mention the score of family and neighbors watching her, she could not run to him as she wished. With Mama and Papa on either side of her, she took mincing steps supposed to make her look as though she floated toward the man she was about to marry.

She wanted to run off to the Bishop of Canterbury and get married by special license without delay. Her parents, with Ross supporting them, insisted they wait a decorous three weeks for the banns to be called. Papa had wanted to wait until Ross's name was cleared, but Mama suggested waiting might not be a good idea with Chloe's reputation in tatters. So they compromised with banns and a license permitting them to wed at Bishops Cove instead of the church.

Chloe grinned in anticipation of being Ross's wife, and forgot about mincing, about her pretty dress, about decorum. The last ten feet of drawing room carpet melted away, and she grasped Ross's hands. "I am here at last."

Papa and Kieran sighed. A few older ladies gasped. Most everyone smiled or even chuckled at such an eager bride.

And eager groom. "I thought you would take until Christmas." Ross rested his hand in the center of her back and turned them both to face the vicar. "What are we waiting for?"

"Juliet," someone whispered into a hideous moment of silence.

Juliet was the one cloud in the sunshine of Chloe's happiness. Even if no one had mistreated her during her captivity, Juliet was not the same lively, sparkly young lady in love with heroic novels she had been before her abduction. She had taken to reading poetry and works intended to improve the mind, and she spoke little.

"I am not jealous of Ross loving you," she had assured Chloe perhaps a little too often. "Of course he always loved you. I was wrong to take him from you—or try to. It was inevitable he would remember you were the true heroine." She would shudder then and add, "And it is a good thing I thought myself in love with him, for it stopped me from marrying Mr. Vernell."

Henry Vernell had been captured when he tried to extract funds from Drummond's Bank in London. He now resided in the Tower for a trial by his peers in the House of Commons. No one believed he would fare well after aiding in the abduction of a young lady of quality, and aiding and abetting a traitor.

The Rutledge family had left for the Continent, reviling the Ashfords still. They declared their son was innocent, and they would mourn him away from those who made false accusations against him.

"Just like their precious daughter was innocent of being a lady of easy virtue," Kieran had begun, but did not continue after Deirdre caressed his cheek in gentle reminder that he could afford to be magnanimous where Joanna Rutledge Brown was concerned. Without her lies, Kieran never would have gone to sea and met Deirdre.

And without that same incident with the Rutledge family, Chloe would not have met Ross. So, with the hope that Juliet would recover her bright spirit in the healing weeks of time, perhaps with Christmas coming, Chloe made the easiest vow of her life—to love Ross forever.

"You," he murmured against her ear as he slipped an etched gold band upon her finger, "are glowing brighter than the diamonds in your hair."

She laughed and blushed. The vicar proceeded with the ceremony, and Chloe was Ross's wife.

Guests surrounded them with congratulations for Ross and kisses for Chloe. Most still stared at him as though he were about to sprout horns, and they were too polite to be anything but courteous.

"What will you do now?" several people asked.

Chloe and Ross exchanged warm glances.

"We will stay here for a while," Chloe explained. "But eventually, we wish to build our own home."

"Here in Devonshire?" That was a Trenerry connection who asked.

Ross cast a glance at Papa. "His lordship has offered us land, but I would rather buy my own."

"I am rather glad Father gave us a home in Hampshire," Kieran admitted.

"I know of land for sale in Cornwall," Lord Trenerry pointed out.

"The land is to be your wedding gift," Papa said. "Perhaps Cornwall won't be so bad, but we will not take well to you keeping Chloe away from us for too long a time."

"Not at all." Mama wiped tears from her face. "I will miss my elder daughter terribly."

"Do not worry, Mama," Chloe said. "We will not keep you from your grandchildren."

The guests turned and stared at Chloe's middle.

She laughed and blushed. "I guess that is impolite of me to say in public."

"Will you return to America to meet Mr. Trenerry's family?" asked Mrs. Trilling, Mama's dearest friend.

Chloe gulped and glanced to Ross.

He tucked her against his side with an arm around her waist. "We hope to eventually."

But both of them knew that was a weak hope.

"The wedding breakfast is served," Addison called from the doorway.

The guests crowded into the dining room for the breakfast that was more like a feast. Chloe could scarcely eat for excitement over the short journey before her. They were to spend the next two weeks in Kieran and Deirdre's house in Hampshire, while Deirdre and Kieran remained in Devonshire until Christmas. Chloe and Ross would return for the holiday.

"For once," Ross said as though he read her thoughts, "we will be traveling together without any more than the normal discomforts of travel or fear of being caught."

"I would take those journeys all over again if they are what is needed to keep you in my life." Not caring who looked on, Chloe leaned over and kissed him.

He kissed her back, holding her to him as though he would never let her go.

A few guests hooted. Most merely smiled and glanced away. Then a tumult in the entry hall had everyone turning in that direction and Ross surging to his feet, drawing Chloe after him. She glanced up to see what he knew she did not. His pupils had dilated so far his eyes were nearly black, and his face had grown as white as the linens on the table.

The hand on Chloe's waist shook as though his old difficulty with cold had returned.

"What is amiss?" Papa demanded of Addison, who stood in the doorway nearly as pale as Ross.

"A dozen people have arrived," Addison said in his quavery old man's voice. "They claim they are Trenerrys, but they aren't Cornish."

"We're Americans." A beautiful young woman probably Chloe's age, with Ross's dark brown hair and blue-gray eyes, slipped past the butler and flung herself against Ross. "We have all come to see you because we knew you would never come to us again."

"You're all here?" He raised his head and stared over the heads of the other newcomers to a man who was an older version of himself. "Father?" Clasping Chloe's hand as though she were an anchor, he stood motionless, staring and silent after that last declaration.

She gazed at the man, with a woman beside him who must be Ross's mother, and her body grew as tense as Ross's. These people had rejected their son. How dare they invade her father's house on the day of her marriage to their son?

"When you came home last summer because you thought your mother was ill," the man spoke in an accent as slow and thick as cold treacle, "we realized rejecting you had gone on far too long."

Mrs. Trenerry smiled, though tears coursed down her cheeks. "We didn't know we would invade your wedding. Do, please, forgive us, and introduce us to your bride."

"Yes, my bride." Ross raised their clasped hands. "Lady Chloe Trenerry, this is my mother and father, Francis and Elizabeth Trenerry."

Chloe released Ross's hand long enough to curtsy to her new in-laws. "Pleased to make your acquaintance."

Mr. and Mrs. Trenerry stood as still as their eldest son, other children and their spouses, and a handful of grandchildren. If someone walked into the room at that moment, they would think everyone posed for a tableau at the end of a drama so still and quiet did the room appear.

Then someone did walk—or rather charge—into the chamber. Juliet burst from the kitchen, her hair tumbling around the shoulders of her pink silk gown. "What is wrong with everyone? This is my sister's wedding, not her funeral." She parted the crowd with the force of her presence and embraced Chloe. "I am so sorry I have been a jealous cat and would not come down for your nuptials. But if these people can come across the ocean to make things right with Ross, I think I can come downstairs and make things right with you."

Her action broke the paralysis of family and guests. A cacophony of introductions and explanations rose to the gilt paint on the ceiling. Ross's family surrounded him, hugging, kissing, weeping. And through it all, he held Chloe's hand, steadfast and strong beside her, as she knew he would remain throughout their lives.

ACKNOWLEDGMENTS

When I was a graduate student at the Seton Hill University Writing Popular Fiction program, so many people helped me get through my thesis novel in our critique sessions I have probably forgotten too many of them to name anyone and thus leave out someone important. Please let me say I am grateful to every one of you and the program that taught me to take an idea and turn it into a novel.

I am also grateful to the usual suspects in my life, like my husband for his patience and my cats for their companionship while I work. Last, but hardly least, I am grateful to my agent, Natasha Kern, for seeing the potential in this early work of mine, and having the confidence in my ability to turn it into something better.

ABOUT THE AUTHOR

Photo © 2015 Marti Corn Photography

Laurie Alice Eakes lay in bed as a child telling herself stories and dreaming of becoming a published writer. She is now a bestselling, award-winning author with nearly two dozen books in print. *Romantic Times* writes: "Eakes has a charming way of making her novels come to life without being over the top."

Laurie Alice has a degree in English and French from Asbury University and a master's degree in fiction writing from Seton Hill University. She lives in Chicago with her husband and sundry pets. She loves watching old movies with her husband in the winter and going for long walks on the beach in the summer. When she isn't writing, she's doing housework, which she considers time to work out plot points, and visiting museums as a recreational activity. For more information about Laurie Alice and her books, visit www.lauriealiceeakes.com.

WITHDRAWN